AER

TRACY KORN

AER | Book Three

Cover Design Copyright © 2018 by James Korn
Photography by J.Korn Photographics
www.jkornphoto.com

ISBN 978-1-946202-72-7
www.TheElementsSeries.com

Library of Congress Control Number: 2017906877

Edited by Ryan Bachtel, Deb Commons, Rachel Carpenter, and Michelle Phillips

Summary: They wanted a chance; they were given a choice: follow the scripted path at Gaia Sur, or face the unknown to find their families. In AQUA and TERRA, Jazz and her friends took the risk and battled through the seven biomes of the "Rush." Now, from high above the earth in Admin City, it's clear their fight has only just begun. Told from two perspectives, the third book in The Elements series sends part of the crew to a topside world that is not the way they left it as the others enter the virtuo-cine network where truth is blurred, and time is running out.

For those above, survival means going beyond.

Second Trade Paperback Edition
Printed in the United States of America

Snowy Wings
PUBLISHING
Turner, OR

For James,
the eye of the storm.

"Reality is merely an illusion, albeit a very persistent one."
~ Albert Einstein

"We, the people of The American Preserve, hereby organize under the articles of the Global Civic Council as agents for public health and commercial responsibility. Herein, we shall investigate and hold accountable by legal due process any organization, regardless of affiliation, which interferes with ecological sustainability."

Mission Statement for The Society for Environmental Accountability and Management
(The S.E.A.M.)

CHAPTER 1
Phase Two
Liddick

I stumble into the port-carnate room at the Phase Two facility, but after all the mind games and illusions in the biomes, I don't believe my eyes.

Riptide? I think when I see Jazz standing in the clear transfer cube at the bottom of the stairs, which seem to multiply as soon as I start down them.

Liddick, come on! I hear her think…it's really her, not some whisper-echo on the breeze like in those trees I just left. *Liddick, tell my dad to unlock the door so you can all get in! Liam said no one would be able to follow us!*

I go halfway back up the stairs to where Jazz is pointing and find Jack struggling to hold up Azeris, who is doubled over.

"Is he OK? What's wrong with him?" I ask, trying to look for some obvious injury.

"He's stunned from the neural baton, just like all these clones. Our transfer to Admin City was…interrupted."

"We need to get him in the hub now then. Jazz said the doors are locked?" I step under Azeris's other arm, then nearly shout when Jack doesn't even move. "Come on, let's go!" I shoot a glance at the downed clone guards on the floor, who are now starting to wake up. "More of them will be coming!"

Jack looks at me blankly and presses his lips into a hard line. "We can't go yet," he says reluctantly, pushing the dark hair out of his eyes like we have all the time in the world. He braces Azeris against a nearby console station, then clears his throat. "The transfer hub doors can't be reopened. I programmed the launch for Admin City to initiate as soon as they closed."

"*Why* would you do that!?" I ask, feeling the blood drain from my face.

"Because I didn't want to take the chance that anyone could interfere with us reaching The Seam," Jack says, then nods to the glowing hubs. "They'll be safe now. Calyx is waiting at the bridge in Admin City."

"*Who?*"

"Calyx, our contact at The Seam—your brother connected us. She'll keep everyone safe until we figure out what to do next," Jack starts to explain, but stops abruptly when a few of the nearby guards try to stand. They fall back down, and he moves quickly behind a console nodding to me. "We'll get there too, don't worry."

I push my hands through my hair and try not to yell at the top of my lungs.

Liddick! What's happening!? Jazz shouts in my mind. A heavy weight crashes into my chest, and I want to crash straight through the floor when I look at her again. I take a deep breath as the light from the transfer hub surges and the ground starts to vibrate. Their transfer to Admin City is starting.

I scramble to tell her we'll find a way to follow them— that *I'll* find a way to her...she just needs to get to the bridge connection and not worry about me—but even in my head, I can't seem to say the words fast enough. She pounds against the clear door of the cube enclosure, and my throat tightens. I press my teeth together as the light surges again, blowing out everything in the lower level of this white room, then nearly fall over as Dez's arms suddenly lasso my neck. I grip her shoulders to move her out of my way, but it's too late. The transfer light swallows the hubs, and my blood goes cold.

"What are you doing? Come on, we need to go!" Tieg says, storming up the stairs after Dez.

"You made it! I knew you'd make it!" she says too loudly next to my ear as she hugs me again. I move back and hold her directly in front of me.

"They're transferring! What are you *doing*?" I say, fighting to keep from screaming in her face. I scan the room behind her for my brothers, but can't see anything in the blinding light that reaches halfway up the steps.

"We've got company," Zoe says, walking toward us along the back wall. She pulls her machete from its sheath on her back, then blows out three sharp whistles. A second later, Cal runs up the stairs toward us while shoving something metallic into his shirt. He draws his machete, too, just as a flood of guards in white uniforms push through the doorway next to me. They're all wearing helmets except for one, whose red hair appears like a gash in the saturated white room.

Rheen…I think, then turn to Jazz's dad. "Jack! She's going for the hubs!"

"I'm almost done!" he says, already typing furiously at the console. Azeris stands next to him pressing a big hand against the back wall to steady himself as Rheen's red hair moves down the stairs, then disappears into the shock of white light. Several of the guards follow while Zoe and Cal fend off the few others who try to engage us.

"Get off me!" Dell shouts from somewhere below in the white haze, and I start down the stairs again as fast as I can.

"It's set! Stand clear!" Jack yells, and immediately, all the clone guards collapse, then lie motionless on the floor.

The white light finally dissipates, Rheen's red hair slicing through it first. There must be twenty unconscious guards littering the ground at her feet when Dell suddenly lunges at her. He tackles her, but she just *laughs* at him, her image flickering several times before it ultimately disappears. Dell slams his fists into the floor and swears, then screams like something wild…like something in pain.

"It was just a port-call image," Jack says, shaking his head. "That means she's still at Gaia Sur. That's good. It buys us time."

"Then let's go!" I shout up the stairs to him as I get into the transfer hub cube enclosure, the energy field of the last transfer still buzzing in the walls. "Come on, they're not that far ahead of us!"

Jack smiles weakly at me from behind the pillar console at the back of the room. "We can't transfer from here with the neural freeze I just launched. Everything is locked down."

"What are you talking about? You said we would follow them!" I yell.

"We will—we just have to go another way, and we have to go now, come on!" Jazz's dad waves Dell and me toward the doorway, then he and Zoe both take one of Azeris's arms to help him off the wall. I take a deep breath, and it feels like my teeth will shatter any second with as hard as I'm clenching them together.

"What other way? Another hub?" I shout up to them as Dell and I take the stairs two and three at a time.

"Yes…eventually," Jazz's dad says.

"Eventually? What does *that* mean?" I catch up to him but he doesn't answer me as we move quickly through the white, sterile corridor. "Jack! What does that mean?"

"Can you stand?" he asks Azeris, who nods weakly.

"I've got him," Zoe says, under his arm.

"We need to find the panel hatch. It should be in this corridor somewhere, but with the neural freeze, the coordinates will be scrambled, and the hatch will jump," Jack adds. "Just feel for a pocket of warm air…a disturbance in the energy field. When you find it, push. That will be the hatch."

"Where are we *going*? There's no hub outside; there's only the Rush—the Woods biome!" I say, confused. Jack steadies Azeris with Zoe, then starts feeling around in mid air like some kind of mime.

"I know, son," he says. "I'll explain after we find the hatch. Help us."

"No, explain now!" Tieg fires at him. "Why are we going back out there?"

"Crite, we have to get to my port-carnate hub. It's our Plan B," Azeris says, coughing as he holds up a hand and starts feeling the air in front of him for the panel. He nods to Zoe, who releases his other arm and does the same.

"*Your* hub? In the *Badlands*?" I ask, narrowing my eyes at him.

Azeris laughs, then coughs again. "Well, it ain't like I got a fleet of hubs."

"But that's topside? How are we supposed to get topside from here?" I ask, but then the answer hits me from nowhere, seeping into my head after a minute like cold, heavy rain. "We're going back through *the Rush*?" I barely whisper, hoping that if I don't say it too loudly, it won't come true.

"No, please," Dez begs. "Don't make us go back through that. Please!" She grips the shoulder of Jack's white jumpsuit, and he stops feeling for the hatch. He turns to her, meeting her eyes.

"I'm sorry, it's the only way. We'll explain the details after we get out of here, all right? It won't be like when you came through the first time," Jack assures, but Dez just shakes her head in disbelief, her face now paler than ever.

"No…no…" she says over and over again until Zoe spins her around and shakes her.

"Listen, the man just said we ain't got a lot of time, so you need to bottle cap all this, wise?"

"Did you *forget* what's out there? Did you forget the *voices*?"

"I heard 'em the same as you, but we can't stay here. Those rubber necks are gonna wake up any minute and be on us like flies on a pile. You just gonna sit here like a pile and wait for 'em, or are you gonna run?" Dez stares at her blankly, and Zoe gives her shoulders a jerk. "*Well*?"

she asks again, her freckled forehead wrinkling when her copper eyebrows fly up, demanding Dez's answer.

"No. I'll run…we'll run…" Dez finally says, nodding. Zoe makes a clicking sound in the corner of her mouth and lets go of Dez's shoulders.

"Damn right. Now help us find the hatch."

CHAPTER 2
Transferring
Jazz

In the dark, I hear something heavy land on something soft. The muted *thud* echoes from below until each impact falls into a pattern…a heartbeat, which just as quickly slips into the background of deep breathing. Of *my* breathing.

Dark haze blurs patches of movement when I open my eyes, but I can see that there's a woman in the distance.

"Try to be still for another few minutes," she says, but her words sound muffled. "Then, we'll open the doors."

The tips of my fingers are tingling and burning, which makes me realize how cold every other part of my body is. My arms and legs are stiff, and I can't turn my head.

"Just take slow, deep breaths. You won't be able to move anything yet," a man says next. I struggle to clear the fog from my mind…to remember something. *What am I supposed to remember?* I think just before the transparent doors in front of me open, and freezing air rushes in.

"Welcome to Admin City," the woman says again. Patches of blue, mottled light give way to the blurred outlines of two people in long, white coats with hoods, and the woman steps through the door toward me into this…cube? The walls are clear, connected by some kind of steel frame, but that's all I can tell when I look around to see if others are in here with me. The woman extends a hand to help me up, her long lapel blowing toward me with the sudden gust of chilled air, but I can't make my arm reach for her. "Take another minute," she says, and I can hear the smile in her voice even though I can't see her face clearly yet. "I'm Calyx Fromme."

I blink hard to focus my eyes, then see that she's probably in her late twenties. Her hair is almost white with thick, erratic streaks of dark brown shooting in different directions, and she has a silver cuff piercing through the center of her bottom lip. "We're going to take you somewhere warmer, don't worry," she smiles, which makes the lip cuff glint as it catches the light from somewhere behind me. Her eyes slant upward in the corners, and are the same shade of icy blue as the Vishan's—

—*The Vishan!* I think, feeling a rush of adrenaline as the fog in my mind finally starts to clear. In a deluge of information, I see flashes of my father, Azeris, and Liddick being locked out of cube enclosures—*the port-carnate transfer hubs…I'm in a transfer hub.* We transferred, and they're still back at the Phase Two Gaia facility…at the bottom of a *volcano* under the ocean floor!

Coming through the Rush, making it to the transport hubs…everything that has just happened reconnects in my separated memory.

"My…dad…" I manage to say as my thoughts gel, but my voice comes out in a cracked whisper, then seizes in my throat and nearly chokes me. The room starts spinning, and my head falls back against someone behind me. I turn as much as I can and see Arco's sharp profile. It's still and backlit, casting shadows over his angled features. His eyes are closed and he's not moving beyond the rise and fall of his chest, but his arm is still tight around my shoulders.

"This must be your first transport?" Calyx asks, raising her dark eyebrows when I look back at her. "Reconfiguring vocal cords always scrambles equilibrium —it will pass as you get used to hearing your own voice again. The more you transfer, the more your body will remember where all its pieces go," she chuckles. "Next time, it won't take so long to feel like a human being again."

"I have Liam," the man says from the other cube enclosure, which is huge—about ten feet tall and wide. "Are Liddick and Jack with you?"

"No. We're missing Azeris and his daughter too. Check the feed," Calyx says, then reaches down again to help me up. I manage to lift my arm this time, but it feels like it's filled with sand. My reaction must show on my face because Calyx abruptly smiles at me. "I know, the lag is terrible up here, especially after a first time transfer, but it will pass once you warm up," she says, pressing her lips into a line as she nods. "Eco, throw me a wrap." She catches a long, white coat like hers a second later and drapes it over me, then pulls me to my feet. "Just stand for a second before you try to walk, all right?" she nods again, which is good because I couldn't take a step now if I tried. I turn around and see the others starting to rouse as Calyx makes her way to Arco, who is now awake and trying to push to his feet without much success.

Watching him sway makes me brace against the door frame to keep the nausea at bay.

The room beyond the transport hub is dimly lit, but otherwise looks exactly like the one we just left at the Phase Two facility. Three rows of metal console stations arc upward toward the back of the room like amphitheater seating, and the wide steps spill down toward me

from the white doorway.

My stomach lurches as I remember everything now… the thought of my father standing near that doorway, then holding out his hand to me as the transfer light engulfed us. I let my eyes fall on the exact place Liddick stumbled into the room—where he stood helpless to stop us from transferring…where he shouted in my mind that he'd find us once we got to Admin City.

Before I intend to, I skim over the smooth stretches of seated metal console stations that descend toward where I saw Dell in the final seconds of light: the console just a few feet in front of me where the guards in white grabbed him, and where I saw Ms. Rheen's—what *had* to be Ms. Rheen's—red hair before the light washed everything away. I squeeze my eyes shut for a second to clear the images, then turn my attention back to Calyx and take a deep breath.

"What's happening back at the other Gaia? The one at the bottom of the volcan—" I start to say, but the words are suddenly ripped from my throat and replaced with violent coughing.

"Easy, little sister…your atoms were just scattered to the wind and then smashed back together," the man says, now standing behind one of the console stations closest to me. The details of his face are still hard to make out in the dim light, but I can see a line of white flashes surging and fading over his skin. They start at his temples and curve along the edge of each cheekbone. I stumble backward into Arco, and the man with the light-up face laughs. "Oh, my neural filter," he says, absently gesturing to the lights. "I'm an Alpha Channel tester," he adds, but I just shake my head at him, confused. "You know, the test pilots…the people who jump off the cliffs and wrestle aliens to set the virtuo-cine adrenaline thresholds for everyone?"

"Did you capture the feed?" Calyx asks before he can explain anything else.

"Yeah, they didn't scan in. Jack loaded a chaser scramble, though, so they won't be following in the same hub. We'll have to give it a few more minutes," the man answers, then picks up several more white coats from the console next to him and crosses to us. He looks like he's in his mid-twenties too, like Lyden and Arwyn, when he's finally close enough for me to see what he actually looks like in the soft, blue-gray light. His dark brown hair rifles out of the white knit hat pulled down tightly over his ears, and the now bluish light from the relays pulsing over his cheekbones reflect in his dark eyes. His smile shows the same solid bar of bioengineered teeth as Tieg and Dez…*ugh, Dez.* My stomach twists when I remember her running out of the cube enclosure and Tieg's carelessness in going after her, knocking the door closed before the others could get in with us. "You all look like shivering puppies," the man laughs again, then drapes a coat over Arco's shoulders before moving behind us to help Vox, Avis, and Ellis, the last of us to step out of our transfer hub. I try to tell the man about the guards … about seeing what *had* to be Ms. Rheen, but I can't get the words to come out through my chattering teeth.

"Why… is it so…cold?" Vox asks, then coughs.

"Alpha channel platforms—everything outside of the cines is cold like this. It's a little warmer once we get away from those cubes, though—can you walk by yourself yet?" the man asks.

"Eco is a friend," Lyden says, walking toward us from the blue, hazy shadows of the room with his arm around Arwyn, who clutches at her white coat against the cold. She sees Arco almost immediately and closes the distance between them in a few strides, then throws her long arms around his neck.

"You used to be the one standing on your tip-toes," Arwyn laughs. He bends down, but then buries his face in her hair.

"I'm sorry…I knew something wasn't right when you stopped port-calling us…" he coughs. "I just didn't know how to—"

"It's OK. There's nothing you could have done," she says through a sob, and I have to look away before I start crying too. I take another deep breath and turn around to scan the other clear cube enclosure for my brother. Liam is just helping him to his feet before he does the same for Fraya and Myra, then passes each of them a coat from the rest of the pile thrown over one of the console tables. Calyx looks at the coats that remain.

"What happened?" she asks, turning back to me, and I will my teeth to stop chattering so I can tell her about how the cube enclosures back at Phase Two locked and how Ms. Rheen and more guards must have come into the room as we were transferring. I close my eyes against the image of her red dragon lady nails tapping on the console table again and the fiery flash of hair I saw just before guards grabbed Dell, then shake my head and open my eyes, wishing it were a terrible dream I could wake up from just that easily. Calyx nods, then looks back over her shoulder at Eco as I make my way to Jax. "Did they scan into another hub?" she asks. "Or are they…somewhere else?"

"I don't see any new Omniclass logs, so Jack isn't locked down again—at least not yet," Eco says. "But he didn't scan out either. I can pull a digital feed at home… we should get out of here. The ping is reporting an active neural freeze under his credential, so there's a good chance they went to plan B."

"All right, shut this down; we'll reconnect there," Calyx answers.

"Wait!" I say as loudly as I can without making myself cough again. "They have to come—they have to follow us!"

"They can't yet—it's not safe," Liam says, pushing his hands into the pockets of his coat as he crosses out of the cube, passing Jax and me to stand next to Lyden at the foot of the amphitheater stairs. "Even if your dad hacks his chaser code, they can't follow us here. It's a failsafe… he'll have to reenter the coordinates from a different hub," he adds, then closes his eyes and presses his lips together against his chattering teeth.

"But there were guards everywhere; they grabbed Dell," I press, trying to keep the panic out of my voice.

"The neural freeze is under your dad's key; they're probably safe, but we really need to go now," Calyx says, looking up the stairs at the doorway.

"And they weren't alone—your friends emptied out the labs from what I saw before we transferred. We'll make contact when the dust settles," Liam says.

"We'll help you, but we can't risk staying here any longer. Come on," Calyx says, motioning us all up the stairs and toward the back door of the room. I start to protest, but then hear Lyden in my thoughts.

Keep your channel open…keep Liddick in your mind, he thinks, then pushes the dark, shaggy hair from his eyes. I nod up at him, and he presses his lips into a thin smile before nodding back to me. *That's how you'll find him, Jazwyn. It's OK. This isn't over,* he adds in a final thought, then turns to walk beside his other brother, Liam. Jax wraps his arm around my shoulder, and we follow Calyx and Eco up the rest of the stairs to the door.

CHAPTER 3
Interra
Liddick

"You're split if you think we're going all the way back through those biomes," Tieg says through his teeth, and I'm about four seconds from putting separations in that solid wedge of enamel once and for all.

"If you want to go back into that transfer room and let them carve gills into you, by all means, man, make my day. You're the reason we're still here!"

He takes a few steps toward me, but Azeris jerks him back by his collar.

"Both of you stow it and keep feeling for the panel," Jack says, closing his hand over my shoulder. I yank out of his grip and go back to focusing on the *nothing* in front of me for some disturbance in the energy field.

"It should be right here," Dell says, his panic sitting heavy on the back of my neck. Jack checks the small panel on his wrist.

"Remember, the coordinates are jumping because of the neural freeze I launched into the system, so it could be anywhere along this corridor now," he answers. "The freeze won't last long, though—not with that many clone systems pulling at it. We need to get to the tree line."

"OK, here. It's here," I say, pushing forward when I feel the shallow pocket of warm air in front of me. Jazz's dad nods.

"All right, let's go. Like I said, we need to get past the tree line."

Daylight falls through the opening made by the panel as we push through, but then I remember that it's not daylight. I still can't seem to get it into my head that nothing here is normal—not the trees, not the grass. It's all been created by the Gaia scientists just like the insects and the mutant animals. *Did my brothers help create them? Did they do it because they were trying to protect me?* We move quickly through the dense evergreens, but I still can't focus. Jack said the transfer to Admin City worked, and if Jazz's own father isn't worried, I shouldn't be either. *She made it…that's all that matters.*

"We won't have to go all the way back through the biomes—just as far back as the Sand. We can get to the Badlands from there," Cal says.

"Did he say the *Badlands*?" Dez grips my arm, and I try not to flinch. If it weren't for her and her mollusk brother, we'd all be in Admin City right now too. I nod in her general direction, but I can't bring myself to look at her.

"It will be all right," Jack says.

"The only other port-carnate hubs within a fifty-mile radius are either at Gaia Sur or right behind us, and everything there us is scrambled by the neural freeze. The only way to catch up with the others in Admin City is to go through my hub. That's in the Badlands," Azeris says, seemingly fully recovered as he holds a heavy evergreen bough out of the way so we can all walk along the narrow path. "We've got a few other things to juggle between here and there, though."

"What's left? Didn't we just freeze everything?" Tieg says, rolling his eyes.

"Temporarily. We still need to get through the Ice biome, deal with the antlions in the Sand biome, and then navigate straight up the main vein of the tunnel shark system to the Badlands," Jack says as he walks under the evergreen bough that Azeris is still holding up. "It's the only feasible way topside from where we are now."

"We're going back to that desert?" I ask, hoping I've missed something.

"It's the only way back up to the surface. We'll just have to stay close to each other," Jack says.

"There are enough of us—tunnel sharks attack solo. We'll be able to take one of them if we have to," Cal adds, thumbing the tooth necklace over his chest.

"Do we have to cross over that ravine? I don't want to hear those voices...not again," Dez says, still holding onto my arm.

"That program isn't running anymore—none of the safeguards for Phase Two are in place. No more head games, but all the abnormally large insects and animals are still here...those, unfortunately, are real," Jack answers, and a chill runs down my back when I remember that idiotically huge ant crawling on Jazz when we first started crossing the Rush.

"We're clear..." Jack says, facing the chasm in front of us. It isn't nearly as deep as it looked when we were crossing over before, and the fog is also gone.

"What happened to it? It's not bottomless anymore, and the path is wider," Dez says.

"Like I said, no more mind games. What you saw before was your worst case scenario come to life—the program was designed to read your fears and then put them between you and where you were trying to go," Jack says as we walk along the dirt path between the evergreens.

"But...*why*?"

"Because no one is supposed to know about Phase Two—the first team designed the Rush in the first place to swallow up the original group of test subjects when they escaped. Figured they'd just leave it in place if any one ever escaped again," Jack says. I resist making eye contact with Dell, and especially with Cal. Dell was right, the whole Vishan origin story was nothing but the result of the Phase Two science experiments.

"We need to go back for the others still in there—the people those sharks pulled from the Badlands. We can't leave them," Dell says.

"We won't," Cal answers. "We won't leave anyone, but we're going to need help."

Dell nods. His hollowing guilt hits me in the chest as he moves past me to start on the stone path that crosses the ravine, which must be almost ten feet wide rather than the two feet it was when we crossed before.

"Like Jack said, we're going to have to go through the Freeze before we'll be able to get to the tunnels—that's not going to be comfortable, especially now that your treatments are neutralized," Azeris says, looking back over his shoulder at Tieg, Dez, and me. "You should all stay close."

"Wait, how did *that* happen to our nanites? When?" Tieg balks.

"When Liam coded the transport hubs—it removed the Vishan splice and the tunnel shark nanites, if you still had any," Jack says.

"But you didn't get in the hub until after the others transferred..." Zoe says to me, then bites her lip, obviously wishing she hadn't said anything.

"There is still enough of a DNA neutralizer charge in those hubs as they're cycling down." Jack's voice is careful, no doubt remembering me screaming at him to get in the hub just after he launched the neural freeze. He takes a deep breath to change the subject. "*So,* only your baseline regulator nanites are still active—the ones that are adjusting your blood levels for pressurization at this depth—but those will only work while we're in range of the Phase Two platform...the Sand biome is on the cusp; it may get uncomfortable there unless we can find a tunnel shark."

"*Unless* we can find a tunnel shark?" Tieg's eyebrows shoot up, and I want to punch him all over again.

"So we can dose with their nanites again, *crite* haven't you been here for the last 24 hours?" I nearly choke on the words as my throat closes in frustration.

"Liddick..." Dez says, tightening her arm around mine, but I'm done with them both.

"*What*?" I snap, then sigh when I see her unnaturally blue eyes widen. I take a deep breath. It's not her fault... she ran out of that hub because of me. She was happy to see *me.* This is my fault. "I'm sorry," I finally say, crossing onto the grass at the end of the wide stone path. "We just need to get to Admin City."

CHAPTER 4
Admin City
Jazz

The port-carnate room we just transferred into was similar to the one from the underground Phase Two facility, but the rest of this place looks nothing like it. The walls in the corridor just outside the transport room are white, but only the bottom half—the whole top half is a window that opens to the endless black sea of space sitting just above a glowing, milky haze. It reminds me of how the cloud blanket over the Rush spread out below the Vishan's Lookout Pier, and then it seems to hit me for the first time…that is *actually* space out there.

"There's a better view from my hab. Come *on*," Eco insists as most of us slow down, trying not to trip over ourselves or each other when we see the huge satellites emerging like giant white, leafless trees from this opaque blanket of air below, which must be the port-cloud.

His hab? Vox thinks, and I actually hear her snort in my mind. I roll my eyes at her, but she just shakes her head at me like *I'm* the one being overly critical.

"I know we've seen this view a million times in school feeds, but it's surreal to actually stand here," Arco says, shaking his head in amazement as he looks out the window, the light bouncing off the port-cloud and illuminating the angles of his face with a soft glow.

"Earth is really under there somewhere," Myra says, nearly pressing her face to the window in an effort to see what is below us.

"We *really* need to get out of here before the storyboard crew comes in," Eco says, raising his eyebrows at Calyx. She nods quickly and wedges her lip ring between her teeth as she waves us forward.

"Let's go. We'll get clothes and ID chips for you tomorrow when we go to the Boneyard to run another sweep for the rest of your crew."

"The Boneyard?" Arco asks, jerking his attention from the window to Calyx.

"It's just what we call The Seam building," Eco says as we follow him and Calyx down the corridor. "Everything is built from scrap tech, so our code signature doesn't draw a lot of attention on the Grid. The Boneyard isn't pretty, but it's powerful," he adds.

We eventually turn, then move down a short flight of steps. Eco opens another door to a frigid breeze that hits us from across an open lot with an illuminated floor. Several evenly spaced white pillars run from the ground to the ceiling with digitized words hovering in the air next to them.

"Fever Plank?" I read one of the floating, shimmering words. "Garden Plank?" I read another sign next to a different pillar. "What are Planks?" I ask as we make our way to a column to the right that, from here, looks like it's made of light.

"Planks are just different levels—we're at Fever Plank. The bridge transport we just left is in the Orion Complex —it's a virtuo-cine compilation studio," Eco explains without slowing his pace toward the column of light, which must be about five feet wide and ten feet tall.

"A what?" Jax asks. Eco stops for a second to look over his shoulder, astonished until he blinks it away.

"A virtuo-cine compilation studio…it's where they put the components together that go into a cine plot. You've *been* in a virtuo-cine, right?" he asks.

Jax huffs a laugh and narrows his eyes. "Well, yeah. Of course," he says with an exaggerated shrug, and now it's Eco's turn to narrow his eyes. He nods as we cross the illuminated lot.

"*Right.* Well, it's where the storyboarders thread the plot sequences. There can be any number of them—it just depends on your neural ranges."

"Our *ranges*? Does that mean how many realities we can tolerate?" Myra asks, and Eco raises an inky eyebrow at her.

"*Imagine* is a better word than *tolerate*. You could be flying a twenty-first century commercial plane, but if you've learned how to push it to become a dragon, suddenly you're riding a dragon," he says, and lets his dark eyes go wide.

"I'm totally riding a dragon." Vox turns to me.

"Good for you," I say, giving her a sideways look. "When can we find out where my dad and Liddick and the others are? How soon can we—?" I start to ask, but stop when we all walk straight into the column of light, and a gust of air pushes us toward the curved wall at our backs. "What's hap—" I gasp, cut off when the light encloses us, and I feel everyone's anxiety push in on me.

"Take a deep breath and touch your head to the wall behind you, quick," Eco says.

Before I can ask anything else, a whoosh of air passes over my ears, and Myra's head and torso elongate like stretching elastic. I try to yell, but nothing comes out. *What's happening!?*

It's OK, don't try to talk. Lyden says in my mind. *These are just shifts…like the shuttles back home in Seaboard. We're not really stretching out, it just looks that way because of how fast we're going.* I try to blink, but my eyes won't even close until Myra's head, neck and torso start reforming, and the whooshing air finally stops.

"What was *that!?*" Avis shouts when we're all still again.

"Outer ring, yeah?" Eco laughs. "They're shifts. It's how we get around here in Admin City. The distortion you saw was because of the speed…it's just warped light."

I don't even know what to say in response to that when we step out of the bright column of light and onto another wide, illuminated platform. It turns into an illuminated sidewalk that runs along the base of several tall, rounded buildings with vertical windows that I can't see into. The people walking toward us are all wearing the same long, hooded white coats as we are. Some of them seem to be talking to someone who isn't there, and others just stare straight ahead with eye colors I've never seen on anyone before…bright purple…orange.

"Admin City really *is* a city," Fraya says, her arm threaded with Jax's. "All these people make virtuocines?"

"That's the official story," Calyx says, leading us toward one of the cylindrical white buildings to our right. We stop at it, but there doesn't seem to be a door anywhere.

"How are we supposed to get in there?" Ellis asks just as Eco flattens his palm on the building, which fades into an archway, then disappears.

"Coming?" The lights over Eco's cheekbones flicker as he smiles to one side, then moves through the arched doorway. Arco nods to me, then slides his hand over my shoulder.

"They're going to help us," he says. "They'll help us find your dad again."

I nod back at him, then follow Eco and Calyx down the narrow white corridor—is *everything* in Admin City white?—which opens to a blank wall. Eco flattens his palm against it, and another archway appears, then fades into an opening.

"You'll all stay here at my hab tonight. Tomorrow, we'll go to the Boneyard. Are you hungry yet?" Eco asks, walking through the opening to a brushed metal countertop that reminds me of the kitchen area of the relay sub we boarded for Gaia Sur. *Is that a—*

"You have a matter board?" Avis finishes my thought, then looks directly at Vox. "Don't even think about it."

Vox smirks. "Want some ice cream, Jax?" she asks with a wink. Jax rolls his eyes.

"That's not even funny," I say, remembering the parson fish she called up that almost disintegrated my legs. *If it weren't for Joss*—I start to think of how he speared the fish with that icepick, and then remember the zephyrs from the edge of the Rush….how they pulled him up into the air and devoured him. I close my eyes to block the thought.

"You OK?" Arco whispers behind my ear, startling me.

Don't worry, sand dollar. I'm not in the mood for seafood, Vox says in my mind. I narrow my eyes at her.

"When can we scan for the others?" I ask again, then clench my teeth to keep from screaming at *everyone*. How can they be making jokes right now? *We left our people down there…*

It wasn't your fault, Lyden thinks, but I don't want to hear his consolation thoughts. I want someone to *do* something!

"I can only tap the hub scan from the Orion Complex to see if any signatures have registered since we left. We'll have to wait until we go to the Boneyard to widen the reach of the scan," Eco says, which I only halfway understand, but I think he's trying to say he can only *partially* scan for the rest of our group. That's not going to be enough. He pulls off his white knit hat and tosses it on the counter. "So, anyone hungry?" he asks again, then closes his eyes and holds his hand over the matter board, which looks like a small slab of white marble. After a few seconds, a pot of noodles appears. "Plates are in the cupboard," he adds, gesturing off his shoulder to the cabinet that suddenly pushes out from the wall.

"Whoa," Avis says, walking toward it.

"Just hold your hand up there."

Avis complies, and the door disappears just enough to see where the plates are inside. He pulls his hand back in surprise, and the door solidifies.

"Whoa!" he says again, and both Calyx and Eco chuckle.

"It senses the heat from your hand—it's OK," Eco says. Avis reaches up again and disappears part of the cabinet a few more times before he finally pulls out a stack of plates. Eco puts a handful of forks on the counter from somewhere, then starts serving the noodles.

"Are those meatballs?" Jax's brows shoot up. I shake my head and close my eyes in a long blink. How can he even care about stupid meatballs when our father is *still* stuck at the bottom of a volcano under the ocean floor!?

"You should eat something," Arco says, putting his hand on my back. *Eat*? Is anyone listening to me? There's no way I can eat right now. I take a step forward and push my hand through my hair.

"I'm not hungry," I say, trying to keep my voice level. "Can we *please* just scan now?" I try to stare a hole through Eco, and he finally stops forking noodles onto the plates. I feel a hand move to my shoulder and look up to find Calyx looking down at me like she has bad news.

"There are some things you need to understand first, Jazwyn."

CHAPTER 5
The Storm
Liddick

Crossing the ravine is easy this time, considering the mind-jack it was before with the voices…with Jazz's voice in my head telling me I was unstable, that I wanted too much from her. I shake my head to clear the thoughts. They weren't real then, they're not real now. I saw the look on her face when she figured out how to use the Vishan's NET device to find me out there in the Woods biome. I saw the relief on her face when I finally made it back to the Phase Two facility under that volcano, and then again the panic that took over when she screamed and pounded at the transfer hub door, realizing I was locked out. You don't fight like that unless you love someone.

"Liddick? What planet are you on?" Dez asks me, startling me back into the here and now.

"Wh—? Nothing. I mean, I'm not. I'm fine. Just focusing on getting out of here." I stumble through the words as we approach the end of the ravine and cross back into the tall pine trees on the outskirts of the ice caves.

"Crite, it's at least thirty degrees colder on this side," Zoe says, hugging herself against the wind. Dez curls herself under my arm. I clench my teeth and take shallow breaths to keep my irritation about her proximity in check. *It's not her fault we're stuck here...It's **mine.***

"The clouds are gathering into ribbons..." Jack says, craning his neck back. "That's not good."

"Those aren't the zephyr things again, are they? Like over the Bale field?" Dez asks.

"No. Those don't come this far out," he answers, then shakes his head at the ground. "They shouldn't even exist at all. None of these creations should exist at all." He pushes a hand through his hair, temporarily straightening the thick, black curls.

"Let's keep moving," Cal says.

"Isn't this the same mineral rain that fell back in the Sand biome?" Dez asks, tightening her grip on my arm.

"Best not to find out, wise?" Dell answers, clicking the side of his mouth and winking.

"Those clouds really are starting to twist and fold like the ones over the Bale field," Dez whispers to me, but all I can bring myself to do is nod at her. I need to channel my focus.

"How far away are the caves? When we came out before, the ravine was almost directly in front of us...we barely walked at all," I say, scanning everyone until I see Azeris off to my side. I fix my eyes on his and wait for him to say something that makes this all seem *less* impossible.

"They should be just beyond that evergreen line, but that's based on the map I made before all the neural hooey got turned off."

Azeris's last word is swallowed by a blinding flash of light and a crackle that feels like crumpling paper behind my eyes. The crashing sound that comes next is so loud I feel it ricocheting in my chest. floating black dots distort my vision. The wind picks up with a high-pitched gust, and I try rubbing my eyes to clear the spots.

"Let's move!" Jack yells, but he sounds like he's underwater as he ushers everyone toward the evergreen tree line.

"Look!" Tieg shouts, pointing to a smoking, charred patch of earth not far in the distance. *That must be where the lightning hit...*

"Move! Move!" Azeris waves everyone on, and for a second all I can think about is Joss being jerked up into the air just a few inches from me as we all tried to outrun the zephyr tornado creatures. One second he was right there, and the next he was yards in the air being tossed and peeled until he was just...*gone*. I shake the image out of my head. *We need to get out of here.*

We make it to the trees just in time for the second impossibly bright flash of lightning and thunder crash, but this time, it's muted a little by the cast of trees behind us now. The few raindrops that start to fall are heavy and cold, and it isn't long before the smell of sulphur fills the air.

"Don't let any of those drops get into your eyes or mouth—they're acidic...like lemon juice, but even more concentrated," Jack shouts above the roll of thunder that is still rumbling in the distance.

"Where are the caves?" Tieg shouts, looking from Jack to Dell, then finally to me. I squint at him, then shake my head. *Mollusk...how would I know where anything is down in this hell hole?* I think.

"Not too far from here, we just need to keep moving," Jack answers over his shoulder, but doesn't slow down. His white jumpsuit stands out against the trees with the clouds darkening everything around us, so I try to keep my eyes on him.

"In there! In there!" Dell shouts, pointing to the cave opening just ahead. It has to be where we came out the first time.

Heavy drops of rain fall like tiny bags of sand from the sky, pelting my shoulders and back. Some of the water gets into my eyes and makes them burn. I wipe the drops away with the back of my hand, but there are too many, so I try to shield my eyes instead..the threshold of the cave is *right* there.

"I can't see!!" Dez yells from somewhere next to me. I stop running and find her a few feet back, lying on the ground with her hands over her eyes.

"Bring her! We need to get out of this!" Azeris yells at me, which snaps something in my head and makes everything around me louder. I cross to Dez and lift her shoulders.

"Hey! We have to get out of this, come on!" I say, but she just keeps screaming.

"Liddick! I can't—I can't see! It burns!"

"I know! It's the rain! That's why you have to come with me now! Let's go!" I pull her to her feet only for her to fall to her knees. "Dez!" I shout, trying to keep the rain out of my eyes, but I can't, and it's almost impossible to keep them open. I grab her around the waist and lift her back to her feet, then pull her toward the cave opening.

"We're almost there!" I yell again, a message to myself just as much as it is for her.

I don't hear her sobs again until we finally cross the threshold of the cave, and the roaring rain moves to the background.

"Here, sit her down here! Give her some room!" Jack says, taking Dez's arms and guiding her to the floor of the blue ice crystal wall.

"What's wrong with her!?" Tieg yells, pushing past Azeris and grabbing my collar. "She was with you—what's wrong with her? She insisted on being with you!"

"The rain got in her eyes—it got in mine too. You see it out there, don't you!?" I shout back, barely able to see, then shove him away from me. I can't keep the anger out of my voice any more than I could keep the rain out of my own eyes, let alone out of Dez's.

"Stow it! It's no one's fault. It just started coming down," Azeris says, exasperated.

"He's right. That's how it works down here, there's no big build up or taper—everything just starts and stops. We can't see it coming," Jack adds as he tilts Dez's chin up. "All right, kiddo, I need to look. You need to let me see your eyes. Let's move these hands, OK?"

Dez sobs again and rocks her head from side to side.

"No…no, it burns. They burn too much."

"Dezzie, listen to him. He has to see. Come on," Tieg says, kneeling next to her. He takes her hands in his and tries to pry them away from her face. She cries louder, but finally lets them fall. Before I realize it, I'm covering my mouth to keep the gasp in. I look at Azeris, who blows out a breath.

"It's all right," Jack says, pushing the wet blonde hair from Dez's face.

"What happened? Why are they black!?" The panic in Tieg's voice shoots straight down my spine.

"*What's* black!? What's wrong?" Dez tries to scramble to her feet, but Jack braces her shoulders.

"You need to be still for a minute. It's just a chemical reaction—you're from Skyboard North, right?" he asks, and Dez manages to nod erratically. "OK, are your eyes genetically engineered?"

She doesn't nod; she just keeps crying.

"Of course they're GE. No one naturally has eyes that light blue. Why does that matter? Why are they totally *black* now?" Tieg almost yells again.

"My eyes are black!?"

"Listen, just sit here and get some breathing done," Zoe says, elbowing past Tieg to kneel next to Dez. She pulls her close just like she did for Myra in the hollow tree after…after Joss was killed by the zephyrs.

"It's just a side effect of the encoding. DNA takes millions of years to develop. When we poke around in that code and start reprogramming it, there can be a ripple effect," Jack sighs.

"So what does that mean? She's blind now? Both of her eyes and the sockets are black!" Tieg shouts *again* and takes a step toward Jack. Azeris puts a forearm in his chest and pushes him to the wall.

"How much *exactly* do you think you're helping your sister right now?" he says under his breath just beyond Tieg's ear.

"Look, it may just be temporary. I can't do anything about it here. I need a lab, a molecular reader…the only thing we can do about it now is keep the area cool to slow down the spread," Jack says. "I need some cloth."

"The *spread*?" Dell asks quietly, tearing the bottom lining out of his satchel and handing it to Jazz's dad, who picks up a fallen ice shard and begins scraping shavings from the blue wall into it. I feel my blood freeze in my veins and move my hand to my own face.

"Your eyes aren't modified, don't worry," Jack says, shaking his head to me to address my unspoken fear. My chest falls in relief.

"Mine are—I got rain in my eyes in the Sand biome when we were fighting the tunnel shark. So did Dez—why didn't this happen then?" Tieg asks, glaring at Jack.

"Listen, every interruptor is off now because of the freeze I launched. Every piece of code that kept things controllable down here, just like those neural echoes—those voices I'm sure you heard crossing the ravine the first time—every piece of that code is connected. To shut down control of one part meant shutting down control of all parts. Things are in their natural state down here for the time being…well, as natural as they can be. The good news is this rain will do the same thing to the tunnel sharks now." Jack presses the cloth with the ice shavings over one of Dez's eyes and ties it under her ear, then around the back of her head. "I need another cloth."

CHAPTER 6
Debriefing
Jazz

Calyx moves in front of me too slowly, like she's trying to postpone saying whatever it is she has to say. I'm about to crawl out of my skin if I don't start getting some answers right now.

"Jazwyn, there could be a reason we didn't see your father on the first scan back at the transfer hub bridge. He had a back up plan if something happened with your transfer. If we don't pick up the others on the feed, it doesn't mean they're not out there, all right? I just need you to know that." Calyx nods several times, making her white, darkly streaked hair fall into her eyes. She flips it back.

"So where would they be then? What was the plan?"

Calyx glances over at Eco, who raises dark eyebrows at her. He returns a long shrug as he forks a meatball into his mouth.

"If something happened with the transfer, your father planned to launch a neural freeze into the Phase Two system. That would drop the guards and give you time to make your way back to the tunnels that lead to the Badlands. Your friend, Azeris, has a port-carnate hub there."

"Wait, they went back into *the Rush*!?" I lose control of my voice and take a step back from Calyx. Arco is already behind me and catches my elbow. "We barely made it out of there the first time!"

"Jazwyn, it's all right," Liam says from across the room. "The neural programs that made everything down there so much worse would be off—no voices. No mind games."

"But the monsters? Those zephyrs and the enormous bugs? What about those, Liam?" I ask, searching his face, which is too much like Liddick's, for an answer. When he doesn't give me one, I turn to Eco, and finally to Lyden.

"One of those giant pincer bugs ripped my entire sleeve off," Vox says around a mouthful of meatball. She sucks a strand of spaghetti into her mouth too quickly, and it whips her across the face, splashing her with sauce. I pinch the bridge of my nose.

"All right, we need to scan right now. I need to know what happened to the rest of our group," I say, stepping out from Arco's arm.

"We can only see if Jack is still on the Grid—the others were never on it, so we won't be able to see them," Calyx answers.

"Unless..." Vox speaks up, and everyone turns to her. "I gave Cal back the NET. He knows how to use it. I mean, Jazz and I had no idea how to make it work, but *we* did."

"Maybe he'll use it to let us know where they are," Myra nods.

"How do we start a scan for them?" Arco asks, lifting his chin to Eco. "I don't see a console in here."

I scan the room again only to realize there is just this kitchen...*where's the hallway? The living room?*

Eco smiles. "It's through there." He nods toward the solid white wall off to our right.

"It's like the volcano Gaia, isn't it? We just walk through?" Myra's laugh laces her voice as she takes a step toward the wall with her hands already in the air trying to push through it. Ellis follows.

"Are the consoles the same here too?" he asks, approaching the wall. Myra gets close enough that it starts to fade. She jumps, and it rematerializes.

"I knew it!" she says, then walks straight through the wall. It surges with a low, brief, hum, and then solidifies again after Ellis makes his way through too. Eco sighs as he forks the last three bites of his spaghetti into his mouth all at the same time and then heads for the wall.

Lyden walks through the wall next, followed by Arwyn and Liam. I turn to Jax, who is still forking up spaghetti, and narrow my eyes at him.

"Are you kidding?"

"I'm sure the thing has to heat up or something, right? Besides, they're OK. You heard Calyx."

"*Jax*! This is our—"

"OK!" he cuts me off and puts down his plate. "I'm coming. Put your skin back on."

He looks at me for a second too long, all the levity draining away, and I know we're suddenly both thinking about Joss, about how we'll never use that phrase again because like so much else now, it's more than just a phrase.

The rest of us walk through the white wall, which is just as surreal as when we did it at the Phase Two Gaia compound. On the other side, a small, white couch sits in the middle of the room. A round, white coffee table sits in front of it with an empty glass bowl in the center.

"Where do you sleep?" Vox asks, looking around as she wipes her hands on the sides of her black jumpsuit, or, what's left of it. The sleeve is torn to the shoulder, and her winding, twisting map tattoos look like fraying threads from this distance.

"There's another cell through there," Eco says, nodding to our left. "The walls wouldn't dematerialize at all if the hab didn't register my bioprint when we came in. Security, you know..." he says with a shrug. "Anyway. Rosie?"

"Good evening, Eco. Welcome home," a woman's light, crisp voice says from...everywhere.

"Thanks, Rosie. Console, please," Eco says, then takes a seat on the white couch, and we all follow him. He taps something into the coffee table, and after a second, a wide, wall-sized web of green lines fills the air.

"Whoa..." Fraya whispers to Jax just off my shoulder. "It's like when Mr. Tark was briefing us before going out in the Leviathan."

"Populate, encrypted...ready, Rosie?" Eco asks. After a second, the green lines snap to red all at once.

"Ready," the computer voice says. Eco starts typing onto the floating holographic keyboard that has appeared in front of him. Several pieces of code start scrolling at different places on the network of red grid lines. Frustration swells in my stomach, and I clench my jaw to hold back my impatience until I can't anymore.

"Eco! What is—" I start, but then hear Lyden in my mind.

Can you...look through it, Jazwyn? Lyden asks in my head. I snap my eyes to his, ready to fire something back, but then I suddenly understand.

Look through it...like on the Leviathan when the self-destruct sequence launched...when the scrolling code turned into ants, I think. They looked and felt like *actual* ants, but they weren't. Liddick said they were neural codes, designed to fight back if you tried to modify them. I turn back to the huge red Grid and try to focus on the scripts, to do what I did before, only instead of pushing them away, I try to pull something out of them. I imagine every breath I take is a vacuum, that every exhale is blowing the numbers and symbols away like it's sand covering something buried. After a second, I see people moving... playing a piano—no, typing. *That's not my father,* I think, and move my eyes to another stretch of projected code where someone else is yawning, then another person. And another that is *not* my father.

"Where are they!?" I shout. Calyx jerks her attention from the Grid to me. "They're not there. They're not *there*..." I say, hearing my voice waiver, and I swallow hard to keep my throat from cutting off my words.

"What's happening?" Arco asks, then waves his hand at the codes jumping across the grid in front of them. "These don't look like location signatures."

"That's because they're not," Liam answers when Eco doesn't. "They're activity logs of everyone who has accessed the Grid in the last 24 hours—anything from reading newsfeeds to joining a virtuo-cine." He shakes his head, then looks at Calyx. "I don't see Jack."

"Keep looking," I say, trying to focus again on the codes, but all I see are the same various people typing, eating, laughing, pantomiming movements like climbing and swimming…it's like watching everyone through tiny windows.

"Did you enter the filter? There are too many entries to extract otherwise. Try just looking for an Omniclass log," Lyden says, and Eco nods.

"Ohhhh, yeah. Forgot about that," he answers, then taps a few more keys on the floating red keyboard in front of him. After a few more seconds, a blue image comes into focus near the bottom of the Grid. It's blurry at first, but then I see him. I see my father.

"He's there!" I shout, pushing past Arco and nearly running into the back of the couch. "What's happening? What's he doing?" I ask, turning to Liam. "Can you see him?"

Eco narrows his eyes at me. "What are *you* seeing?" he asks, confused.

"I see him," Vox says from behind me with her arms crossed over her chest.

"You see his *code*?"

"That too," Vox answers. "He's typing. Fast—wait, it just smeared out. Where did he go?"

I look back at Vox, straight into her yellow eyes, which suddenly light like matches when they meet mine.

"How do you see him? See his actual self in all those numbers and letters?" Ellis asks, gripping the back of the couch.

"I saw him too, and others for a second..." Myra says in a quiet voice. "Just flashes, and then the code came back."

"So did I. I thought it was just my eyes playing tricks on me," Fraya says.

"That's what I thought too," Arco adds. "It was only for a few seconds...the different people. I thought it was some residual effect of our transfer."

"Oh no..." Calyx says, sitting next to Eco in front of the Grid screen and taking over his keyboard.

"You're all Empaths, at least Hybrids, aren't you?" Lyden asks. We look at each other. "That's why you could see the images and not just the code. It's a kind of mental syncing that happens when one Empath is exposed to a neural thread," he adds. "You must have picked up the neural thread from Liddick. It just wasn't supposed to work for any of you until we triggered it."

"How?" Arco asks, shaking his head.

"Heightened awareness and DNA integration is all it takes, even a handshake—any exposure to Empath DNA that has the neural thread embedded in it will result in a transfer to another Empath," Lyden says. "I suspected this is what happened for Jazwyn, but now with the rest of you, I'm sure of it," Lyden adds.

"So now *all* stressed out Empaths can pick up this neural thread just by being around other Empaths who already have it in their neural channels? Is that what he's saying?" Eco asks Liam, all the blood draining from his face when he doesn't get an answer. He turns to Lyden. "How is this even *possible*? You planned for this?"

"No…I mean, yes, that's what the neural thread was *supposed* to do, but not until we triggered it. Until then, it was only supposed to reveal for Liddick," Lyden answers, trying to make eye contact with Calyx, but she doesn't look up from her typing.

"How long have you been able to see things Jazwyn?" Arwyn asks, and something about the gentleness in her voice makes my throat start to close up again. I swallow hard.

"I don't know, since the port-festival I guess."

"Since the *marlin*," Vox says over my shoulder.

"You did see it that night. You *did* hear it," I ask all at once. "I knew it. That's why you were in my face everywhere after that. Why didn't you just ask me about it? You *broke* my nose!"

Vox fights the smile pulling at the sides of her mouth, then lets it spring free with a chuckle.

"You couldn't even manage your love life. Tell me how you were supposed to help me figure out why a dead fish was talking to us?"

I open my mouth to argue with her, but nothing comes out. My voice is strangled somewhere at the base of my throat, and all I'm able to get out is the beginning of a choking scream.

"All right," Arco says, putting his hand on my shoulder, then stepping between Vox and me. "So the Gaia bracelets they cuffed on us must have made us more aware or whatever…we already knew that."

"That must have been the catalyst," Liam says, glancing up at Lyden and Arwyn. They both nod.

"So, what's the problem with some of us seeing pictures in code now?" Arco adds.

"The virtuo-cines they originally coded for Liddick are still in circulation. Some of them are archived, but the latest ones like *Xenotrope 6*, those are out there," Lyden says, turning to us. "If those of you with Empath tendencies can see the neural thread here on the Grid, that means it's probably accessible now to any Nascent Empath going into those virtuo-cines."

"*Nascent* Empaths?" Fraya asks.

"Any untrained Empath, no matter the prominence… Readers, even just a latency," Lyden answers.

Liam sighs, then shakes his head and moves his hands to his hips as he turns his back to everyone. "But how could their bracelets have triggered *this*? We never opened the door for The Seam's transmission."

"It's a bleed…" Arwyn says to the floor. "The neural thread is evolving."

CHAPTER 7
Damage Control
Liddick

Jack chips more ice from the blue glacier wall into the cloth I hand him, then ties it over Dez's other eye.

"The cold will slow the cellular breakdown from the mineral rain. That's the best I can do without any equipment, but once we get to Azeris's hub, I'm sure I'll be able to do more.

"And in the meantime? What happens to her?" Tieg says, shifting his weight from one foot to the other like a racehorse just waiting for the gate to open. Jack looks at him for a second too long, then sighs.

"The cellular damage will try to spread to any other genetically engineered material in her body—it doesn't have to be external. Once the minerals from the rain are in her system, it's just…" he takes a breath.

"What?" Dez says through a sob after another second.

"We're going to fix everything—we just need to get to the hub as soon as possible. Can you walk?" Jack asks. Dez nods, and Zoe helps her to her feet.

"There might be another way," Cal says, thumbing the point of his tunnel shark tooth necklace. "We could re-treat her."

"Are you split? It took us days to recover the last time," Tieg says through his teeth.

"Hang on—re-treat her with what?" Jack asks.

"With Vishan DNA." Cal pulls up a small flame in his hand, then smothers it in a clenched fist as he punches the glacier wall hard enough that it leaves a hole. He pulls his hand out and opens it, then shows Jack his unmarked knuckles.

"Fire and strength…" Jack whispers.

"You all right?" Azeris asks him, raising an eyebrow.

"Fine…I'm fine. *That's* the treatment…" Jack shakes his head, then clears his throat. "But how can you infuse DNA? There are no plasma converters out here…no grafting lasers."

"We just need vein rock and the three fires. Well, and a few long reeds," Cal answers.

"*Vein* rock?"

"There's some at the edge of the ravine—I saw it when we crossed," Zoe adds. "We have to burn it in the three fires with some of Dez's blood and some of Cal's mixed together. That will bind the DNA, and then it will replicate once it's injected back into Dez."

"Wait, do you have any idea how dangerous that is?" Jack narrows his eyes.

"They've done this before—to all of us," Dell says, squaring his stance on the threshold of the glacier opening. He starts to step outside just as a flash of lightning turns everything white. He and Zoe exchange glances.

"I'll get the reeds and the vein rock if you get the yellow fire," Zoe says. Dell nods, then turns again toward the trees just beyond the glacier threshold.

"No way; we're not doing that again," Tieg says. "How much farther is the hub?"

"How long do you think she's going to make it if we get attacked again by a tunnel shark out there? She's blind, you mollusk!" I try to control my voice, but can't rein in the frustration with his constant whining. He tries to advance, but Jack puts a hand in his chest.

"No, he has a point. We have a long way to go, and the ice won't last much longer," Jack adds. "If this will fortify her DNA, it may be the only thing that can save her at this point. We're almost out of range from the Phase Two facility, and the baseline nanites in your blood will be offline soon."

"And if we don't run into a tunnel shark this time, there will be no temporary nanite infusion to cover the ground between here and the hub," Azeris says.

"No. There has to be another way." Tieg shakes his head and crosses his arms over his chest like he's bracing for a shuttle bus to run into him.

"Well, please enlighten us with your better idea, or shut your vent already," I say, flicking a shard of ice at him.

"That's it—"

"Stop! Just stop fighting. I'll do the treatment," Dez says after another bolt of lightning flashes, and a crash of thunder rattles the frozen walls. She brings her hands over the cloths of ice on her eyes and almost starts to cry. "I don't want to be blind. I don't want this to spread."

Tieg sighs and scrubs his hands over his face, then looks at Cal.

"Fine," he says just as Zoe returns with a bundle of reeds. She empties a handful of black stones from her pocket, and another handful of white rock chips with dark lines running through them.

"Hematite and Boron?" Jack asks, raising his eyebrows at the rocks Zoe has put in front of Cal.

"Bloodstone and vein rock," she answers. "They're for the treatments."

Jack shakes his head and takes a deep breath. "You just plan to heat blood over these rocks?"

"No, we need the fires," Dell says, uncovering a stack of smoldering sticks. "Just managed to pull these from the lightning strike…it's the last of what's dry out there."

"Put them here," Cal says, fashioning the last of the reeds into makeshift syringes just like Vita did back in the Vishan tunnels. "It's burning fast; we need to hurry—give me the cup from her satchel."

Cal puts the metal cup over the yellow fire, then pulls up a red flame from the palm of his hand and catches one end of the kindling. The vein rock sparks, then ignites a green flame on the other side. Red, yellowish-orange, and green flames dance around the metal cup as he tosses in a few black stones, then jabs his arm with the reed and puts the extracted blood over them. The stones hiss.

"OK, grip my hand if you want to—this is going to smart again," Zoe says, pushing Dez's hair back from her neck.

"Wait, why her neck?" Jack asks, holding up a hand.

"Can't roll up the sleeves on these things," Zoe answers, flicking the sleeve of Dez's black dive suit. "Jugular is the next closest to the heart—gotta be the freshest blood for this to work right."

Jack's narrowed eyes relax, but not in relief. He's... *exasperated*?

"Here," Zoe says, taking a deep breath and pointing to Dez's neck. "We'll put the needle right here."

Dez pulls in a quick, short breath when the point of a reed breaks her skin, then another when Cal extracts the reed. She presses her palm against her throat as he adds the blood to the stones, which hiss again.

"It's OK...just one more stick and you'll have all your superpowers back," Cal says, kneeling back down next to Dez. She smiles.

"That's *hot*—you can't inject it now," Jack protests, taking a step toward Cal.

"It has to be hot to bind," Zoe says. "It's all right. We really have done this before."

"Be still," Cal says, bringing the reed full of mixed blood back to Dez's throat.

She moves her hand, and tries to strangle the scream as he injects the blood.

"Hang on, Dezzie...just hang on..." Tieg says, pinning his bottom lip down with his teeth.

"Rinse the bowl so we can do the next one," Cal says, carefully reaching into the fire for the metal cup.

"*Wait!*"

"They can't feel it, Jack. And it only marks them if they touch all three of those fires at the same time," I say.

Jack shakes his head. "How is this possible? That DNA strand was corrupted—they abandoned it..." he says to himself, and Cal shoots him an icy glare.

"What are you talking about?"

"Your DNA..." Jack says, taking a breath. "Son, the reason you can bind your DNA with others just by mixing your blood—the reason this *treatment* works to make others like you...it's because your DNA can only be the first strand Gaia created for genetic testing," he adds after a second, then looks apologetically at Cal. "The first twelve subjects they bonded it to escaped the Phase Two labs. They're the whole reason these biomes are predatory, but they must have survived...your people aren't just a Badlander subculture, are they? They're *from* the biomes?"

Cal's face blanches as his eyes dart to Dell's.

"It's like I was telling you. I'm sorry," Dell says. "They were science experiments...*the twelve who became six families, who became five,* and all that. It's exactly what will happen to the rest of those people still stuck in that facility if we don't stop Gaia. You can show Veece and Jove everything now."

"So it really is...*a lie*, then...our whole culture," Cal says, looking into the flames. "When there was no Motherland in that volcano like the Origin Wall said, I knew it then...but part of me still hoped," he adds in a quiet voice.

"I'm sorry, son," Jack says, surrounded by swirling smoke that makes the air feel thick and suffocating. After a second, Cal blows out a breath, then looks up from the fire. He jabs his original reed into his arm again and adds the blood to the cleaned cup. "Who's next?"

CHAPTER 8
Evolving
Jazz

The room is silent for a long time as we all look at Arwyn, waiting for her to elaborate. Eco turns to her as Calyx continues typing on the couch in front of the red Grid lines.

"What do you mean the neural thread is evolving?" Eco asks. Arwyn brushes her long, light brown hair from her face as she looks at Liam, then at Lyden before getting to her feet.

"It's...complicated," she sighs.

"We'll listen slow." Eco cocks his head to one side. Blue and white lights blip on and off along the wire network running from his temples into his cheekbones, just under the sharp edge of his dark hair. *Does that mean he's registering an emotional response right now like he would if he were inside an alpha channel?* I think. *Does he ever get to turn that off?*

"OK, I tried. Been trying. Done trying now. I can't figure it out...what's a neural thread?" Vox asks.

"You're kidding me?" Eco blanches.

"Well, I'm sorry very much, Sparkles, but not all of us are half computer."

I fight to keep the smile off my face, and Jax thins his lips into a hard line to keep his expression neutral too.

"A neural thread is programmable organic matter made from DNA…it helps people have more realistic virtuo-cine experiences," Arwyn answers.

"How did *you* get mixed up in this? Is that why they put you in biodesign in the first place?" Arco asks his sister.

"Sort of. Lyden and I found out what Gaia was doing our last year there…we didn't even get to graduate with our class before they sent us to Phase Two…the underground volcano facility. We thought we were getting promoted, until we realized that's not what was happening—they just wanted us to help with the experiments on people. They threatened to hurt you and Lyden's brothers if we didn't cooperate, so we tried to build the neural thread to weave into the virtuo-cine network…that way, we could get a message to Liam before he went to Gaia, but we couldn't get it to work. When Ms. Rheen and Mr. Styx brought Jack Ripley on board, we asked him if he would help us."

"That's when they faked the plant explosion and told us he died," Jax says to no one in particular. Arwyn nods.

"But by then, Ms. Rheen and Mr. Styx had already tried to promote Liam—to bring him into the fold and have him help advance their genetic engineering cause. He wouldn't do it, so they moved him to Phase Two against his will with us and sent a long term clone to be the biodesigner on the Skyboard Hill that everyone was expecting."

Liam blows out a breath. "Phase Two is where I saw Jack, but I thought he was dead," he says. "The newsfeeds told everyone he was killed in the plant explosion. I knew Gaia was dirty then. No way I was going to let Liddick get pulled in too, so, we went to work. Jack figured out the only reason the neural thread fell apart under coding was because the original sample of Lyden's DNA chain wasn't strong enough—nobody's would be strong enough to carry the whole message we were trying to program—so we accessed one that had been enhanced from the Gaia mainframe archives and laced it into Lyden's sample. It worked like a backbone, but because of the splice, Liddick could only see parts of the warning messages in different virtuo-cines. It must have made him think he was going crazy," Liam says, lowering his eyes to the ground and shaking his head. I feel the wave of guilt start to drag him down.

"He didn't go crazy. He just became obsessed...shut everyone out to find the answers. He knew you were trying to tell him something. He knew your clone wasn't you," I say, trying to lift the heaviness settling in my own chest from Liam's reaction to his memories. He absently rubs the scar in his left eyebrow...the same scar Liddick has from the night he fell down the dune as a kid, and Liam tried to stop him from panicking by cutting his own eyebrow with a rock.

"Yeah, well, a lot of good it did. He wound up there anyway, and now he's stuck somewhere six miles deep into the planet," Liam adds, crossing his arms over his chest and turning to the wall, which becomes a window as he approaches it.

"That's not your fault. It's no one's fault," Arwyn says.

"All right!" Eco scrubs his hands over his face, then takes a deep breath. "Enough with the history lesson...

someone tell me what any of this has to do with the neural thread *evolving*? You know, the problem at hand here?" Eco raises his dark eyebrows and scans the room for answers.

"It must be evolving because of the archived DNA we used as the base," Arwyn starts to explain. "We didn't think anything of it at the time because all we needed it to do was stabilize Lyden's DNA sample so we could code the message onto it, then thread it into the virtuo-cine mainframe and get it into the storyboards for Liddick."

"And? Get on with it," Eco says through his teeth.

Arco glares at him. "She's *saying* that now people with even a secondary Empath classification can *hear and see* the neural thread that was used as a foundation for the code they embedded for Liddick…right?" he asks, looking back at Arwyn.

"Right. It must be extra sensitive to stimulus, and when you got your Gaia bracelets, the heightened awareness all at once must have been enough to trigger the viral component of the message we wrote—I mean…" she says, glancing again at Calyx as she trails off.

"The other Empaths out there will begin to see and hear the message, it will just take longer like it did for Arco and the other Empath Receivers and Projectors," Liam finishes.

Eco leans toward them and pinches the air with one hand.

"I will *literally* kill you if you don't stop tap dancing right now—get to the point," he says in a quiet voice.

"*Why* does it matter that the code is evolving to the point that all Empaths can see images in the scripts?"

"It's human instinct to want to communicate—this neural thread is trying to do exactly that, with as many people as it can. It could even evolve to the point that it tries to reach people who only have *recessive* Empath traits," Arwyn adds. "And maybe by then, it won't need the Empath platform at all anymore. It could eventually learn how to talk to *anyone*, regardless of their neural structure."

"Should I stab you or just liquify you? Never mind, too much white furniture...where's my neural rod... Rosie! Where's my neural rod?" Eco says, rifling through the drawers near him.

"Locating..." the computer voice says. "Bedroom, side table shelf." Eco raises his eyebrows and nods at us, then starts to head for the wall behind the red Grid lines.

"Eco, listen..." Arwyn says, glancing desperately at Calyx again, who is still focused on searching for something on the Grid. She doesn't look up, and Arwyn turns to Lyden.

"Wait..." I say, putting the pieces together. "The message you coded for Liddick is still fragmented, right? Like when the marlin talked to us, and then we heard some random phrases when we were under stress in the Stingray vessels?" I ask, feeling my pulse jump with the implications.

"Yes, but that's not exactly why this evolution is so dangerous..." Lyden says, looking over to Calyx, who is *still* engrossed in the Grid. "Cally..." he starts.

"Finally...here it is..." Calyx says, blowing out a breath as she taps another holographic key, but then covers her mouth with her hand. "Crite...we really do need to stop the replication. Right now," she adds, then pushes the floating red keyboard toward Eco. "Tell your gatekeeper to get me an open line to Skull. It locked me out, and I don't have time to hack it again."

"Why did you—never mind," Eco closes his eyes and shakes his head. "He's not going to be there at this hour," he adds.

"Just get the line open."

Eco moves back to the couch and starts typing, but then stops after a second and narrows his eyes at Liam.

"Wait a minute...how did you even get access to those archives? You're not a hacker, and Lyden was in a tank the whole time you were anywhere near those databases. Not to mention, those DNA samples were archived for a reason. They're volatile—self-destructive if they're hit with infrared light. You thought using them as baseline organics would be a good idea? More than that, how did you *even know* about them in the first place? And how did you—"

"Enough," Calyx sighs, pushing her hands through her hair. "It wasn't him."

CHAPTER 9
Eyes Wide Open
Liddick

I expect searing pain the second I try to move, and I'm surprised I didn't wake up sooner without that root Vita gave us the first time we had the Vishan treatments. *How long have I been out*? I think, trying to brace myself to blink.

I open my eyes fast, wide, but the pain never comes. I should feel it shooting down my temples and drilling into my teeth like it did back in the Vishan tunnels the first time they treated us, but there's nothing. I push my luck and take a deep breath, expecting my ribs to feel like ten thousand needles pushing into my skin from the inside, but that feeling never comes either. *Why doesn't this hurt*? I think, finally taking notice of the milky blue ice crystal walls that bend and warm in an arc high over my head. I don't know where the leaves I'm lying on top of came from, but they crack and break into pieces when I roll onto my side.

We're still next to the ice cave opening, but the light outside has turned to a smoky, dark haze—it must be night, or what passes for night six miles into the earth. There's just enough light to see Dez sleeping next to Zoe across from me, with Tieg not too far away. He's snoring with his mouth wide open so I can see his solid wedge of polished white teeth reflecting the hazy glow from the cave opening. Dez looks like a marble statue in this light; that's what I thought when I first saw her too, standing there in line for a tray at lunch that first day at Gaia Sur. She didn't move even to breathe. I'd never seen anyone be so calm and still, especially not in the middle of all the foreign happenings that first day--strange food, strange clothes, strange people, not enough information…and I thought I'd seen it all. I think the only time Dez could ever be still like this again is when she's asleep. She's not the cool, ethereal thing I thought she was then, and maybe that's my fault for giving her mixed signals… maybe Jazz was right about me all along. Maybe I am reckless.

I push these thoughts out of my head for what must be the tenth time, if not the hundredth. I can't get sucked into thinking like this again; it just slows me down. Cal, Del, Jack, and Azeris are all asleep about ten feet deeper into the cave, and I start to push up to see if I can go take a leak without waking up everyone in here.

"Liddick?" Dez whispers from the shadows across from me. "I think the treatment worked…I can see, but it's blurry."

I nearly hit my head on one of the ice crystals in the sudden startle of her voice breaking through the silence. I blow out a breath, mainly in thanks for not bashing my skull, but it sounds like exasperation, and I feel the twinge in my gut when it registers for her too.

"Give it a little while," I say, trying to sound consoling to make up for the misunderstood frustration that I don't have the energy to explain. "I don't think we've been out that long. Not like before."

"And it doesn't hurt like before," she says after a second...always so quick to forgive me. "Do you think we can still make fire?"

I hold out my palm and try to focus on making it itch. I didn't have to do that the first time I pulled up fire after the Vishan treatment...it was automatic. Nothing happens, and my heart starts pounding with the initial panic.

"I can't do it," I say, then narrow my eyes to focus harder.

"Maybe that takes time too," Dez says, a smile in her voice as Zoe starts to stir.

"You're awake already?" Zoe says, slurring all the words together as she stretches her arms beyond her head and yawns. "Can't have been more than a handful of hours."

"Did it work? Can you see?" Tieg asks, suddenly sitting up like something jabbed him.

"I think so. Everything is still blurry, but I couldn't even see that before."

"Come into the light here," Cal says, now awake behind me and holding a small red flame in the center of his palm. *Show off.*

"I tried that—it didn't work. Not even the itch," I say to Cal.

"I don't know why that would be. We've never had to re-treat anyone, so there's no telling what may still work and what won't...or what may be new," he says without looking at me. Dez moves into the light. Her eyes are still dark, shadowed like she hasn't slept in weeks, but also dark inside…marbled navy blue and a charred gray around the iris.

"They're clearing. The treatment worked, but it's slower. Maybe that's what's happening with the fire too. We'll just have to keep watching it," Cal adds, then turns to Jack for confirmation.

"That would be my guess as well. Since the first treatment and then the reversal at the Phase Two port-carnate hub, you've probably developed a bit of resistance to the DNA fuse. We'll know more with a little time," Jack says. "We should get moving again."

Cal takes a square of bread from his satchel and throws it into his mouth. The Vishan packed some rations for us too when we set out into the Rush, but I suddenly can't eat. The pain of the treatment didn't register this time, and I'm wondering if it just made the nausea worse…more abrupt. I try to take a deep breath to push down the swimming feeling, and when that doesn't work, I just try to think about getting into the Sand biome tunnels.

"Once we get into the tunnels, how long is the hike to your hub?" I ask Azeris, leaning my head back against the cold wall.

"No idea—we'll have to scope it when we get there. I can't get a read on anything in this ice," he answers, tapping the mapping unit on his arm as he swings it through the strap of his satchel.

"It will take at least a complete cycle stone spectrum to climb to the surface once we get clear of the ice, and that's if we don't have to scrap with tunnel sharks," Cal answers. "Don't count on that."

"A spectrum?" Jack asks, cocking an eyebrow. Cal takes his cycle stone from his satchel and hands it to Jack. It's oval and smooth with bright, thin bands of yellow streaking the length of it.

"It keeps track of the days…when the red is gone, it should be light again," Cal says with a quick nod. Jack rubs the stone between his fingers and holds it up to the flame in Cal's other hand.

"Fascinating…is it connected to your ability to produce fire?" Jack says, gesturing to Cal's flame as he moves closer. "May I see your hand?"

Cal extends his arm. "I don't know if they're connected to the fire. The stones have always been with us—they don't come from the tunnels, or anywhere else we've seen. And the fire is just one of our gifts," he rolls his eyes. "Crite, I'm starting to sound like Veece."

"You're starting to sound like a topsider," Dell says, clicking his teeth as a grin tacks to one side of his face. "Only took a year to convert you."

Jack studies Cal's still burning palm, turning it sideways and looking at it from the underside knuckles facing the dirt mottled ice on the ground.

"Fascinating…truly fascinating. It can only be the parent gene that was used to experiment on Arwyn. You can summon these flames?" Jack asks, looking from Cal to Del and Zoe. "And you can as well?" They all nod.

"So can everyone who was just treated…well, they're supposed to be able to do it, anyhow," Zoe says, glancing at me.

"Let's just get moving. Obviously, we're not going back to sleep. All the head games are turned off out there, right? Is there anything we need to worry about in the dark?" I ask, impatiently because it's freezing in here, and I need to be in motion.

"Nothing programmable should be functioning so long as the neural freeze is still holding at the Phase Two facility. Unfortunately, we won't know if it is or not until it's obvious that it's not. Listen for a low grade buzz—it will seem like it's not really there. If you hear that, the neural freeze has been hacked and terminated. Phase Two will be back online…along with the head games," Jack explains, pressing his lips into a flat line.

"There's enough light to get by," Azeris says, nodding to the corridor behind us. If we're lucky, by the time we make it to the Sand, there will be more."

"And you can fix us when we get to your hub? You can reverse these treatments?" Tieg asks, slinging his satchel strap over his shoulder.

"Not exactly…" Azeris answers.

"*What*?" I hear myself almost shout, my attention ripped back to the present moment from wherever I'd let this fog in my head carry it. "What do you mean you can't reverse it? We can't port with these mutations, and we can't get to Phase Three without port-carnate transferring. We can't—"

"*Relax*, chief…" Azeris says, holding up a hand and shaking his head at me like I'm some kind of tweaking child. "I don't have the parent gene for the Vishan DNA at my hub, so I can't reverse anything made from it. We're gonna have to hack the Gaia mainframe to get the genetic components for the program. *Then*, I can fix you up," Azeris says, looking from me to Zoe. She gives him a small smile as she shifts her weight and adjusts the satchel on her shoulder.

"It shouldn't take long once we get there. We missed the first transfer; Calyx will know something went wrong. She'll look for my signature on the Grid, and will find me launching the neural freeze code. That will tell her we're on the run and will have to find another hub… she'll be waiting to hear something from us. We'll make contact, and she'll help us get the archive for the DNA. We just need time," Jack says, drawing his absurdly thick dark eyebrows together and nodding like he's trying to convince himself too.

"We don't have time! Aren't these treatments permanent after so long? What was it, a week?" Tieg nearly shouts. "Is that how long we've got!?" he actually does shout this time as he grips Cal's shirt. Cal grabs the base of Tieg's thumb and pulls it back and down, which makes Tieg drop to his knees before Cal finally lets him go.

"I don't know. Like I said, we've never re-treated anyone!"

"Tieg!" Dez rushes to her brother, stumbling into him.

"I'm fine!" he says, pushing to his feet and glaring down at Cal.

"If you're all done, maybe we should just go and find out what can and can't be done. Ain't a thing that's gonna be accomplished scrapping in here," Zoe says, shoving impatiently past Tieg and down the tunnel, where she suddenly stops and then comes back just to hook Dez's arm and glare at me.

"What did *I* do!?" I shout after her, but she doesn't turn around.

CHAPTER 10
The Beginning
Jazz

"What do you mean it *wasn't* him?" Eco asks, narrowing his eyes at Calyx.

"I gave Liam and Jack the DNA archives and the access ports to the virtuo-cine network in exchange for them building a code that *we* could eventually use to get our message out," Calyx says, frantically typing something onto the floating red keyboard that Eco has returned to her. She sighs in frustration and starts all over again when the screen suddenly refreshes.

"Are you *split*? Do you know what you put at risk by opening that door to non-Seam members?" Eco says, getting to his feet, clasping his hands behind his head in amazement.

"Do you actually think this was my decision alone? *Damn it!* Answer your page, Skull!" Calyx says through her teeth as she starts typing again.

"I'm the one who told Jack how to get in touch with Skull, then he dragged Calyx into this," Lyden says. "There was no choice. It's like Arwyn said…we had to keep our brothers out of Gaia, and we knew Jack would want to keep Jax and Jazwyn out too."

"So you jeopardize nearly a decade's worth of work for your own short term goals? How is it possible that

Skull agreed to that?" Eco says, the now red and white lights on each side of his face pulsing faster.

"Because it *wasn't* just for their selfish goals," Calyx says. "Like I said, in *exchange* for the access ports to the virtuo-cine network and the DNA strands that they knew would get their code to graft, Jack and Liam built something that The Seam could repurpose."

"No one else is going to stop Gaia from experimenting on people, especially not when it's funded by Biotech Global and Carboderm funneling people to an overpriced port-call system," Liam says.

"Which could all be *reversed* by making port-carnate tech mainstream—that's been The Seam's goal all along, hasn't it? That's why you leaked the port-carnate tech in the first place?" Ellis asks, and I remember Liddick talking about this in the Rush.

"*Yes*, and it would have organically caught on if enough people had access, it was just a matter of—"

"You know that would never happen because the port-cloud industry makes too much money for Biotech Global and Carboderm. You've seen the public service announcements they've put out to make everyone afraid of port-carnate transfer," Liam says, holding out a hand to his side like he's waiting to physically throw more proof at Eco. I can feel his conviction tightening in my veins and pounding in my chest.

"When did they get Gaia involved? How long has this been going on?" I ask Calyx, but now she's too busy furiously typing to register my question.

"It's the other way around, Jazwyn," Arwyn says. "Gaia approached Biotech Global and Carboderm—they both had the same vested interest...money. It started when The State put out the first topside stability reports about fifteen years ago...that's when Gaia started working on their genetic engineering initiative so that anyone who was willing to pay for the procedure could *transcend their environments*—they could spend the summers in space, the winter on the ocean floor; they could take random weekends straight into the center of the earth thanks to genetic transmutations."

"And in the meantime, Biotech Global and Carboderm had the promise of a constant source of income in the port-cloud because Gaia would singlehandedly make port-carnate transfer seem unsafe for those who couldn't afford the secret genetic surgeries. What better authority than the center for recruiting and placing the top minds in diplomacy, science, and technology to lead that charge?" Lyden adds, trying to sound compassionate rather than alarmist.

"But the port-cloud is *killing* people...it's killing the topside environment and everyone in it. Didn't the last report say there are only something like five more generations it will support?" Jax says.

"They don't care," Arco adds. "They're not going to be around to suffer it, and neither are any of their families. They can transcend everything with the genetic mutation surgeries. They can go anywhere...it's the ultimate Skyboard North fashion trend, only it's not just iridescent eyes and bar-wedge teeth anymore," he continues, looking from Jax to me. "This is survival of the richest now."

"This is all beside the point," Eco says, the lights from his temples flickering red and white again. "We've been building evidence against these people for over ten years. You can't bring down the most respected educational facility and the two biggest corporations in the entire American Preserve without having all your pieces in place. We don't have that yet!" Eco starts to yell, then closes his eyes and takes a deep breath before resetting. "Our contacts at The State and within Gaia are still in harm's way. If this news breaks now, they'll be compromised. That's just one of the problems here."

"No one is arguing with you," Liam says. "We just have to—"

"Skull! Finally…something has happened. We need to meet," Calyx cuts Liam off, pushing the holographic keyboard away from her knees. It disappears, and she gets to her feet. I can't make out the face on the screen because it's rippling like water after a rock…no, after five rocks have been thrown in.

"I'm not in range until tomorrow. Do you have the packages?" the man says. His voice is hard, even though it's muffled like it, too, is underwater.

"No, that's why we need to meet. Boneyard?"

"Tomorrow. Two p.m."

"Thank you," Calyx says, then reaches out for the keyboard that reappears in front of her. She pushes a series of buttons, then it and the wall-sized screen in front of her both disappear.

"What's this going to accomplish?" Eco asks, crossing his arms over his chest.

"This is beyond what we can do on our own now. I just tried to pull up the message we encrypted on the back end of the neural thread you used," Calyx answers. "It's incomplete too. Whatever put holes in the message to Liddick also put holes in our message. If this neural thread code is evolving like Arwyn said, Jack is the only one who can stop it from the outside. We need to patch the holes in The Seam's message, and we're running out of time." Calyx looks over her shoulder at Arwyn, who reluctantly nods.

"I can try something if you can get me access to the virtuo-cine entry port. Maybe I can slow it down," Liam says, coming out from behind the couch to stand next to Lyden.

"Oh, I think you've done more than enough. Whatever you programmed onto that neural thread in the first place just figured out how to work its way into the neural channels of any half-empathic person out there. Do you realize that you and Jack are responsible for the impending insanity of thousands of people once they see these flashes of the real world nightmares going on under their noses right now? Not to mention, you've created a time bomb that will obliterate our undercover connections with the insiders we have at Gaia and The State? You've put the *whole world* at risk!" Eco nearly shouts, the lights on either side of his face a steady stream of red and white now instead of a pulse.

"Don't you think I *know* that!?" Liam yells back, taking a step toward Eco. "Let me try to *fix* it!"

"Stop, we can't fix anything tonight," Calyx says over them both. "It's not his fault, either. The materials are volatile to begin with—it's *engineered* human DNA, Eco."

"Who else knows from The Seam? And were you ever going to tell me?"

"Besides the people in this room, only Skull and me. I didn't tell you because it was a need-to-know basis. We couldn't risk the plan leaking," Calyx answers, then pushes her hands through her white, erratic hair. "We have a bigger problem now. If The Seam's incomplete warning message gets out, not only will some people lose their minds, several *won't*. Several will be subliminally convinced that our top scientists are trying to *save* everyone through gene splicing, and that the port-cloud is actually helping to fund that research for *everyone*.

"That's the opposite of what's happening..." Arco says.

"Exactly. The holes in the message couldn't be more precise or damaging than if someone put them there on purpose."

"Then this is the beginning," Eco says, quietly now and withdrawn. "We're not ready, Cally."

"I know. That's why we need to talk with Skull," she answers, then looks to Liam. "We can't stop the message on our own, and if we can't find Jack in time, we'll have to patch it manually."

"What does that mean?" Arco asks.

"Get some sleep," Liam says. "We may need to send you into the Grid."

CHAPTER 11
Cracks
Liddick

Zoe is several feet ahead of me, her arm still hooked in Dez's. Azeris and Jack are going back and forth about something just in front of me, but I can't focus enough to make out what they're saying. *What's happening to me...I* think, then close my eyes hard until I see little flecks of white. It helps to push down this...what is it, panic? Fear? Guilt? Maybe a little of all three. *I* was supposed to be the one going to deal with Phase Three, not Jazz, at least not without me. None of this is going the way we planned...is it getting colder in here?

"How much longer does this stupid thing go on?" Tieg asks too loudly, and I accidentally bite my tongue when my teeth start to chatter.

"Still no readout, so the ice must still be pretty thick," Azeris says.

"Do you see the lines of brown in the ice now, though?" Cal says, pointing to one of the milky blue walls. "Those are dust layers. It means we're getting close to the outside."

"Finally," Tieg says.

"I didn't say we'd be out soon. Being close will still take awhile."

"So this lets out where we came through the first time? The desert with the scrub everywhere?" I ask, then remember the branch that punctured Jazz's lung when we were fighting the tunnel shark. The memory squeezes my chest until it feels like I can't even get a breath.

"Close enough," Dell says. "We'll need to be ready to fight as soon as we cross the perimeter. That's no place to rest."

"Because of the tunnel sharks?" Dez asks over her shoulder in a small voice. Dell nods, and I know in that second *she* cracks—the memory of the tunnel shark attacking her, of it almost taking her leg off—and the ice pours into her too. I press my teeth together to keep her feelings out, but it doesn't work.

"Hey…" Azeris says, suddenly at my side. I jump and bite my tongue again.

"Damn it!" I yell. Azeris's eyes go wide, and I blow out a breath. "Bit my tongue. Again. Where the *hell* does this thing end?"

"What's going on with you?"

I glare at him, then realize my expression and stop. I feel his confusion and concern, and I don't care about any of it.

"You mean aside from being stuck in an *iceberg* that's six miles deep inside the *planet*?" I ask, trying to modulate my voice by forcing a laugh.

"Nothing you haven't seen in the virtuo-cines. You're starting to spin."

"Get out of my face, Azeris. You don't know anything about me."

"I don't? I'm the only person who probably *does*. Except maybe your girl," he says quietly.

"She's not my girl. Just do something to your mapping unit and get us the hell out of here," I say just as Jack slows enough to walk at my other side.

"Is your throat dry?" he asks. I narrow my eyes at him.

"*What*?"

"Do you feel like it's closing up?"

"No. Why?"

"If you're dehydrated, your chances of pressurization problems in the blood increases. Are you shaky? Feeling like you're going to crawl out of your skin?"

"I'm fine; I just need some space. Can you both just give me some *space*?" I say, holding out my hands as if I could push them both away. Jack nods to Azeris, and something inside me lights. "What was that? I *said* I'm fine!"

"All right, let's stop and rest here for a bit," Jack says. "Just have a little water."

"We need to keep moving—we need to get out of this ice and contact Calyx."

"We have time, and we won't get there at all if you lose your head down here; you need to hydrate. It won't correct the pressurization in your blood if it's off, but it will help slow down the symptoms."

Azeris, nods at me, decided, and I know that even if I were to press on, I'd be going alone. We need to stay together down here. I sigh in resignation and pull the water jar out of my satchel, then throw the bag to the ground and sit on it.

"There, happy?" I say, holding up the water before taking a long swig. Everyone follows my lead. Zoe still won't look at me. Anger starts rising up from my stomach, but I'm too exhausted. I roll my eyes and drink more water.

"Everyone who has just been treated needs to take a little personal inventory right now. You all received blood stabilizing nanites at Gaia Sur, which went out of range after you left. They reinitiated when you got in range of Phase Two, but we may be getting far enough away now that they are starting to glitch. The treatments, we've seen, aren't as predictable as they apparently were your first time, so you may be experiencing symptoms of Decompression Sickness with the varying level changes down here," Jack explains. Now he has my attention.

"Symptoms like what?" Tieg asks, quietly for once.

"Pain in the chest, headache, disorientation, paranoia and anger…some of you have been getting a little edgy, which is understandable, so this is just a precaution. Over exertion also increases the chances of an imbalance, and we can't take the chance if you're nanites are glitching," Jack adds. "Is anyone feeling any sharp pains?"

I look around at everyone, but they're all just shaking their heads. I don't know if the sharpness in my chest is physical or just the backlash of everyone's fear and frustration, so I keep my mouth shut.

"All right, well that's good news then," Azeris says, nodding.

"But if the nanites stop working…" Dez starts. "I mean, if they stop entirely…we'll die?"

"We're not going to let that happen. That's why we're resting, staying hydrated. The Vishan DNA will also help...but if my guess is correct, it will just take time for it to reach its potential. Until then, you're at risk for a pressurization gap. We need to play it safe," Jack answers.

I take another swig of water and try to imagine staring a line of fire through the ice wall—something to channel my focus to anything other than this new fever of anxiety Jack just dropped on everyone, making them all doubt and question now. If feels like I'm going to drown in it.

"What are they doing up there, do you think? What were we supposed to do when we transferred with them?" I ask, not looking at Jack or Azeris at all.

"Calyx would have met us at the hub bridge, and probably taken us back to a safe house," Jack starts to answer. "We would brief her on what happened those last few hours in Phase Two, and she'd likely take us to the Boneyard to meet with her superior—he's the one your brother, Lyden, connected me to back when we were trying to keep you and your group out of Gaia," Jack answers.

"So The Seam has a plan to stop Gaia's experimentation? They have something in place to bring down the port-cloud?" I press, but now look directly at Jack, daring him to keep something from me.

"Not exactly," he says, to my surprise. "At least not yet. In exchange for the DNA samples I needed to get the bio-code to work—the code that facilitated the messages you received in the virtuo-cines, at least in part—I promised to build in a sleeper system for the code to evolve, to reach everyone who went into a virtuo-cine, not just nascent—untrained—Empaths like you and Jazz were. When everything was in place, The Seam was going to activate that sleeper code, and then the world would know what Gaia, Biotech Global, and the Carboderm Corporation were really doing. I imagine that is still the intention."

"So our job is done? Jazz and the others are at a safe house just waiting for The Seam to pull the trigger on that sleeper code?" I ask.

"That would be my guess, but they wouldn't pull the trigger until *we* get there too."

"And how do you know that?" I ask.

"Because I'm the one with the gun."

CHAPTER 12
The Boneyard
Jazz

It seems like only ten minutes have passed when I open my eyes to the sound of someone rustling. I blink, then see the white walls, the brushed metal cabinet and counter space in the kitchen just a few feet away. Eco is pulling down square, white cups from the open cabinet just over his head and putting them on the counter next to the matter board. Arco is still asleep just behind me on the couch, his long arms crossed over his chest, and I notice the long, ragged cut on his shoulder through the tear in his dive suit. *That must have happened when we were fighting the tunnel shark,* I think, and my stomach sinks at the memory of falling on something sharp, then slipping out of consciousness…of slipping into the strange, bent reality of Vox's consciousness through the Vishan's neural connection tool…The NET, or whatever it was called. I look to my left out of some instinctual pull, and Vox's yellow eyes are already staring at me.

So, it looks like it wasn't all a bad dream, unfortunately, she thinks. The corner of her mouth twitches as I shake my head.

They're going to take us to that Boneyard place today… they said we might have to go onto the Grid. What do you think that means? Do you think my dad and Liddick will be there somewhere? I think in answer. She shrugs, but I feel a bubble of panic well up in my chest, then blow out like a candle. It must be her feeling. Arco suddenly takes in a quick, sharp breath. I turn to face him, and his eyes are wide and scanning.

"Whoa…you OK?" I ask. He swallows a few times and then closes his eyes in a long blink before opening them again.

"I'm fine," he says, scrubbing his hands over his face. He stands up all at once, leaving a blanket of cold in his wake. Vox pulls her knees to her chest to get out of his way as we both watch him cross to the kitchen to talk with Eco. She turns to me and raises a burgundy eyebrow.

Brrr, she thinks. *What did you do?*

I didn't do anything, I answer, but I know this cold, hard edge feeling in the bottom of my chest. It's the same thing I felt from him when I ran to Liddick after I finally got free of that giant bullet ant in the Rainforest biome back in the Rush. He thought that because Liddick and I could talk telepathically, because Liddick is the one who helped me stay calm then, that I wanted Liddick instead of him.

*Leave it to that tree trunk to be jealous when we've just escaped a mad scientist school six miles underwater, discovered a new, tornado-monster fighting culture under the ocean floor, **and** crossed seven biomes of random nightmare beasts only to get launched into the stratosphere where we wake up on a couch owned by a guy with sparkly lights in his face,* Vox thinks without even pausing. I gape at her, but she just stares at me blankly like I owe *her* an explanation.

Stop…eavesdropping in my head. I hadn't even thought any of that yet, is all I can manage to answer. She rolls her eyes and pushes off her knees to join Arco in the kitchen. He hands her one of the square, white cups.

"Ugh. Is this supposed to be coffee?" Vox asks, wrinkling her nose in the steam rising from the cup and encircling her face. "Did the matter board make it?"

"Yes, and yes," Eco says. "It's infused."

"With what? Burned hair?" She takes a sip, then sticks out her tongue.

"That's disgusting," Myra says through a giggle, stretching her arms over her head in the corner of the couch across from me as she watches Vox. Her reddish blonde hair is everywhere before she pulls it into a bunch behind her head and stands.

"As long as it's hot, I don't care what it tastes like," Ellis says, rubbing his eyes. He pushes Avis's shoulder, which almost knocks him out of the chair he's sleeping in, but this just moves him enough to shift his wing of blue-edged bangs over his face. Fraya laughs next to me, Jax's enormous arm draped over her collarbones. She carefully slips out from under it, which makes Jax snore abruptly in surprise. Fraya covers her mouth with both hands to keep from laughing out loud.

"Where's Calyx?" Arco asks, then takes a long swig of his coffee.

"She's meeting us at the Boneyard," Eco answers. "You can change clothes and clean up there. Tell the matter board whatever you want to eat, and let's get going. There might be some tests we need to run before you meet Skull."

"What kind of tests?" Arco narrows his eyes.

"Threshold scans. Not all of you will be able to go into the virtuo-cine network, if that's what Skull decides to do with you."

"Threshold scans for what?" Fraya asks, then sips her coffee. Eco sighs.

"Too much to explain here, and we're going to be late. Wake up the rest of your group."

***

There aren't many people on the street when we leave Eco's habitat. In the distance, the sky, for lack of a better term, is a charcoal black, and I remember that this isn't night, it's *space*. The light from the sidewalk, which fades into the darker road at our left, stretches out to a horizon with intermittent, tall, cylindrical buildings stretching so high I can't see the tops of them as they disappear into a gray haze.

"Is that the port-cloud?" Myra asks, craning her neck upward at where the buildings disappear.

"No, the port-cloud is below us. That's just light pollution," Eco says, pulling the collar of his long white coat around his neck.

"If this environment is sealed somehow, which it has to be or we would all choke to death, why can't they climate control it to be warmer? Hello, maybe program summer? Why is this hard?" Avis says, rubbing his arms as we walk.

"Has to be cold—this whole place is built on top of a moon-sized server cooling system," Ellis says, nodding at Eco for confirmation that he doesn't get.

"This way," Eco says, leading us back to the column of light that we came out of on the way here yesterday.

"Where is the Boneyard?" I ask, trying to push the nausea down in anticipation of the G-force waiting for us in that tube.

"A few hops from here—it will be a shorter trip than the shift we took from the transfer hubs last night."

"Are we going to feel like we're being turned inside out again?" Myra asks, already turning a little green.

"Probably," Eco says without even the slightest smile.

"What's his problem?" Jax whispers down to me.

"I think he's upset that he was left out of the loop about the Vishan DNA code that Calyx gave dad. He doesn't seem mad, just…offended," I answer,

*Fever Plank…River Plank…Solis Plank…*I read the floating, glowing signs that sit just in front of different light columns—*shifts*, as Eco called them—to the different destination hops here in Admin City.

"Where is the Boneyard? Which Plank?" I ask, trying to decide how close we are to our column of light.

"Tide Plank—right here," Eco answers, pointing to the glowing, shimmering letters suddenly above our heads. "Remember the drill; try not to move once you feel the air rushing in, and make sure you touch your head to the back of the light column. Seeing your own face stretch out in front of you is disturbing—trust me," Eco says, managing a small smile.

In seconds, another whoosh of air washes over us. I touch my head to the back of the column and shut my eyes tightly.

You all right? I hear Lyden in my mind and nod, unable to form words. I try to catch up to my stomach, which feels like it has dropped about a hundred feet. The memory of Myra's elongated neck stretching out what seemed like several feet from her body with the light distortion jumps into my head, and I almost scream out loud. Almost, because I can't seem to open my mouth.

Another whoosh of air passes over us before the feeling subsides.

"Let's go," Eco suddenly says, ushering everyone out of the tube.

"So…did we go up or down? Or sideways?" Avis asks, holding his palms to his temples without having yet opened his eyes.

"Up," Lyden answers when Eco doesn't. He seems to be even tenser now. "The Boneyard isn't far from here."

This Plank looks almost exactly like the one where Eco lives—tall, white, simple buildings that all seem to be the same height, none of them with any windows to one side with a stretch of light-to-dark fading road to the other. The haze in the sky seems a lot closer to us now too.

Eco suddenly stops, then holds up his hand over a door, which then disappears.

Inside, music that sounds like someone is playing a set of wine glasses suddenly fills the air, and a man about my father's age nods to us from behind a brushed metal countertop like at Eco's hab. He's typing on a floating blue, holographic keyboard also like the one back in Eco's hab, but I can't see a screen. The walls in here are made up of a series of criss-crossing lines of differently colored light, which appears and disappears like shooting stars. They move so quickly it's almost like tiny fireworks explosions filling the walls.

"New graduates?" the man says, looking up quickly from his invisible screen to scan us. He forces a smile comprised of exactly one spaceless bar, just like Tieg and Dez have.

Eco nods. "Cally make it in yet?"

The man returns his nod without looking away from the screen this time. "You know the way," he adds.

"Come on," Eco says, walking behind the counter. He raises his hand to a spot on the flashing fireworks wall, which disappears after a second. We follow him down a corridor, and the wall closes behind us.

"Whoa…" Avis says. "What was that back there?"

"That was Nev. He runs the Plank shifts."

"Is that what all those lights were? Trajectories?" Ellis asks.

"Something like that," Eco says without turning back to us.

"Like the old air traffic control grids," Ellis adds, elbowing Arco in the arm, which only earns him a scowl.

"What?" Arco says.

"The walls back there. What planet are you on?"

"Right, yeah. Sorry. I guess I didn't notice."

"How could you have missed that!?" Avis says, scurrying past us like a monkey. This is the most excited I've seen him in awhile.

"Keep up!" Eco shouts back to us, and we all break into a jog.

We come to a fork in the corridor and follow Eco to the left. He places both palms flat on the wall in line with his shoulders, making this wall fade away too. Behind it, people either slow down or stop walking entirely to stare at us. Several different port-call stations like the ones at Gaia Sur line the walls, but these are mismatched with some of the cylindrical bases being the normal, polished white while others are metal. The screens sitting on top of the bases are also erratically shaped—some rectangular, some round, and some that are just hovering in the air like the ones in the port-carnate hub of Phase Two.

In the center of the room a large, roped off pad sits on the floor. It's white in places, metal in others, and a row of differently shaped screens arc behind it. People are sitting at each of the stations, and everyone seems to be wearing the same style, but differently colored jumpsuits like the teachers at Gaia Sur.

"Are they from Gaia?" Arco asks, seeming to pull the thought right out of my head.

"No," Calyx says, walking up behind us. "These are all Admin City employees. It will clear out when their shifts start wherever they're supposed to be normally."

"What do you do normally?" Arco asks with an edge in his voice. Calyx just smiles at him for a second, then meets my eyes.

"Ready?" she asks, and my heart starts pounding in surprise.

"F-for *what*?" I stumble.

"Skull is waiting for you."

CHAPTER 13
Breaking the Ice
Liddick

"We should get moving," I say, tossing my water bottle into my satchel and slinging it over my shoulder. "We're going to freeze down here."

"Aren't you getting any warmer since the treatment?" Dell asks, then darts a glance from me to Tieg.

"We'll warm up by walking; let's go," I say, pushing past him. I've had it with this tunnel, with everyone's lack of urgency.

"Liddick, wait..." Dez calls after me, but I don't slow down. She's at my side in a few seconds, hooking her arm in mine; I let it fall through, and the whip of pain she feels lashes into my chest.

"I just need some space, all right?" I say, too harshly, but I don't care. She doesn't deserve it, but I just don't care.

"It's Jazz, isn't it? You blame me, don't you?" she finally asks. I blow out a breath as an answer. "When did you get so selfish? Have you always been like this and just pretended to be interested in me at Gaia?" she keeps pushing. I don't know what to tell her—more accurately, I don't want to put the work into figuring out how to tell her anything in a way that would spare her feelings. I wasn't thinking at all when I let her believe we were a thing back at Gaia, if she wants to know the truth. But she doesn't...not really, so I don't say anything at all. "Liddick! Are you at least going to answer me? You blame me for getting locked out of the transfer hub? Getting locked away from Jazz and being *stuck* down here with me?" That's the last of this pushing I can take.

"Yes! All right!? Is that better?" I round on her. "You and I are over, Dez. It's been over since before we left Gaia. I don't want you, OK? Is that what you need to hear?" I say through my teeth and watch the tears pool in her sooty eyes. My stomach instantly falls, and whatever heart I might have drying up in my chest somewhere breaks under the weight of these feelings that aren't even mine. I'm just a mirror. That's all I've ever been.

The thought is knocked out of my head when I realize I'm going to hit the ice floor, and it's too late even to get my hands out to break the fall. My cheekbone and jaw hit at the same time, the instant cold cancelled out by the burn of the scraping. I look up as fast as I can only to see Tieg hovering over me, then reaching down, and the ice underneath us both starts to crack.

"Stay back!" I hear Cal's voice raise above everyone's shouting in the growing distance. Tieg's eyes are wide until he takes a deep breath and then closes them tightly. A second later, we must hit another level of ground below us because everything in me feels like it's on fire, and I can't get my breath. But we don't hit the ground. We keep falling—floating, and the fire over every inch of me gives way to a prickly, stabbing pain before it goes numb. I open my eyes, not realizing that I had closed them, but see nothing except distorted colors as I gasp for a breath. Freezing water pours into my nose and mouth, then reaches down my throat. I choke, but everything is in slow motion. *Water…no more water…*I hear in my head again—the same fragment of virtuo-cine script that has been playing in my head for years. *Swim…*I think. Or do I just hear this word too? *Riptide? Jazz, is that you?*

I squeeze my eyes closed to keep the freezing water from burning them, and will my arms over my head. I can't feel the water, but I know it's there. I push my arms down to my sides, then force them up again. *Am I moving? Is this up?* I break the surface of the water and choke again, but I feel nothing. *This is how it should be. This is what I deserve. This is what they all deserve.*

"Liddick!" Jack calls. "Hold on! We're coming!"

I can't see him, but he's somewhere above me. My shoulder hits something hard behind me, but I only feel it dully until I'm yanked violently upward by the collar and then dropped onto another hard surface. I cough, which feels like daggers in my chest. I blink hard to clear my vision and see Tieg sitting against the ice wall stuffing white, shimmering fabric into the toes of his boots.

"Mollusk—you blew your impact gear when you jumped off that waterfall in the tunnels before," Tieg says, pushing an already packed boot into my ribs.

"No," I cough. "It didn't…blow…"

"Then you didn't reel it in right last time because it didn't deploy this time," he laughs. "Saved me the trouble of having to beat you through the ice, though."

"Can you hear me? Tieg, is he conscious?" Jack yells again.

"He's fine! Head's bleeding, but it's nothing I wasn't already going to do to him," Tieg shouts.

"We're scaling down—stay on that ledge until I can get down there!" Jack's voice sounds closer, but like reverberation inside a bowl, and then I realize that the bowl is the inside of my head.

"There's…sand in here…" Tieg says to himself, and then shouts it: "Hey! There's sand in here!" He pushes up to his feet and starts walking toward the ice wall, which starts to blur.

"Stop! That ledge could give way any second!" Cal yells down to us. "About seven feet above you is a crevice! Wait for us to scale down to it, and we'll pull you up! It runs parallel to the water—just be still!" he adds, but the rush of the water and the pounding that has started in my head make him sound muffled. I close my eyes, and after a second, everything is quiet and still again.

***

I can't see when I open my eyes because the light is blinding. My head feels like it's filled with sand, and when I try to sit up, that's exactly what I feel between my fingers.

"What?" I hear myself say.

"Welcome back," Dell says from somewhere. I squint in the general direction of his voice and start to see his outline through the enormous red campfire between us.

"We're out of the glacier? How?" I ask.

"You two mollusks made yourselves useful for once and found us a shortcut," Zoe says, flicking a small, red flame to life in the palm of her hand, then studies it. "Sand was already in the ice wall where you landed—we just scaled down and burned through it." Her reddish hair looks like it's just an extension of the fire in this light, but when she turns to look at me, her dark eyes are cold.

"You hit your head pretty good, so be still—the Vishan DNA from the treatment isn't doing anything more than making sure you don't implode," Azeris says around a mouthful of something. I look around for Tieg, remembering that he must have hit me, and we must have fallen through the ice floor. *The water…we fell into some kind of pool in the glacier,* I think.

"That's all we need it to do for now. We're definitely too far from the Phase Two hub for your Gaia nanites to function—your dive suit is damaged enough now that your baselines could start to glitch at any time. We're lucky we got as far as we did without that happening," Jack says.

"Where's Tieg?" I ask. "And Dez?"

"Asleep." Cal jerks his chin over his shoulder. I look past him and see them both a few feet behind him.

"And the dead tanglebushes? Where's all the brush?" I ask, looking around and seeing nothing but sand and more sand.

"Not there yet—with any luck, we won't have to go that far," Cal says, poking at the fire with a long stick he must have picked up before we left all the trees.

"Then why are we stopped? How close are the tunnels to the Badlands?"

"Well, up until about 19 seconds ago, you were out cold, and nobody was trying to carry your sack of self through any tunnels, wise?" Dell laughs. "Besides, can't see the antlion funnels so well in the dark," he adds, poking at the fire. I raise my eyebrows.

"Vox squared off with one of them," Cal says, looking at the fire with a laugh. "She was rabid about her dive suit sleeve getting chewed off—*her sleeve*...can you believe that?" he asks, looking up at everyone and shaking his head. Dell and Zoe exchange glances and smile. *So, he has a thing for Vox? Is that it now?* I wonder, then roll my eyes, which sends a bolt of pain straight through the center of my head.

"How long until the Cycle stone is green again? When is the light coming back so we can get to the tunnels and get the hell out of here?" I ask. Dell pulls out his stone, which is completely red except for a few threads of yellow. Nowhere close to green. I catch myself before I roll my eyes again and then scrub my hands over my face. "We can't just sit here," I say too loudly, which wakes up Tieg and Dez.

"*What* are you constipated about already?" Zoe says, needling me with her dark eyes. I fire back at her.

"What part of my motivation is confusing for you, red? Were you not in the port-carnate transport room when we got locked out of the hubs? Are you somehow oblivious to the fact that we're surrounded by subterranean bio-nightmares that want to eat us, or that are just programmed to stab us with tentacle tusks and drag us *right* back to Phase Two where Styx and Rheen will, without a doubt, kill us this time?" I answer, trying to stare a hole through the center of her head. She doesn't even blink.

"I was there, *Cred-Fed*—you may remember me saving your ass right after the others transferred and Styx tried lighting you up with one of those baton things," Zoe says, then turns to Dell and shoves him. "Zapped that dragon lady and saved you, too!"

"There can be only one dragon lady, eh?" Dell laughs, then holds up his arms to brace for the punch he knows is coming.

"Stow it," Zoe says, trying not to laugh, which is easy enough when she looks back to me. "Anyway, something crawled in your ear and died back there, wise? But ain't nothing we can do that we ain't doing already to get caught up with the rest of your group, so why don't you just unclench a little from here on out."

I start to answer her, but Dez cuts me off.

"It's Jazz. He's wound up like this because he's not with her—he can't talk with her in his head anymore, and he can't get in between her and Arco now," she says with a cold edge in her voice I never would have expected from her. She narrows her eyes and presses her lips into a satisfied, half grin line when I look at her, but I'm so shocked I can't think of anything to say in response before Jack steps in.

"That's enough," he says. "I'll take the first watch— everyone get some sleep. We still have a hike in front of us before we get to the tunnels that lead to the Badlands."

"And we only have about six hours until light. The sharks will be running again by then, so rest up…just in case," Azeris adds, nodding to me. I nod back, remembering again the tunnel shark fight coming through the Rush the first time…when I severed its head and didn't even realize it after I thought it killed Jazz. I can't lose my grip again like that. I can't lose control again, or we're never going to make it to Admin City.

CHAPTER 14
The Grid
Jazz

Arco has dark circles under his eyes, and the cut on his cheekbone is starting to bruise. He pushes a hand through the light brown curls falling into his face and raises both eyebrows.

"Why me?" I ask him. "Why do you think Skull is waiting for me?"

Arco shrugs, uninterested. I know he's still bothered about thinking I want Liddick, and I'm half tempted to shake him. Doesn't he realize we have bigger issues right now?

"Only one way to find out," he finally says. I turn to face Calyx, who tries to smile at me, but then just starts chewing at the metal cuff in her lip.

Why is she anxious? Who is this Skull person, and how does anyone ever get the name Skull anyway? I wonder.

"This way," she says, waving at us to follow her. She walks us past the roped off white square patch that looks like a little landing pad on the floor to our left. Some people in differently colored jumpsuits are typing into floating holographic keyboards while others swipe and throw holographic screens like they're looking for something they can't find on the ones in front of them.

"What are they doing?" Fraya asks from behind Arco and me. Calyx turns to answer over her shoulder.

"Trying to slow the code evolution."

"The code our dad helped Liam and Lyden make? It's really happening that fast?" Jax asks.

"Exponentially."

We turn around a bend in the white corridor and walk straight into a dead end. Calyx flattens her palm against the wall, and a doorway appears. *I'm never going to get used to that,* I think.

Yes, you will, Lyden answers in my mind. I grin without turning around to look at him, forgetting that he can read my thoughts just like Liddick. *Liddick…* I think, and my stomach drops. *Where are you?*

The room we enter is also white, but the entire back wall isn't a wall at all—it's a beach that stretches out to crashing surf and a wide, blue sky. I stop dead in my tracks, like everyone else in our group.

"That's the barbarian beach!" Myra says. "The one from Tark's class at Gaia!"

"Whoa…" Avis echoes her surprise.

"It's just a virtuo-cine program—we're in Admin City, people. Where do you think the programs come from?" Ellis snorts.

"But why th—"

"Why *that* one?" A deep voice interrupts me. I spin around to find the source.

"*Mr. Tark!?*" Avis's voice shoots up nearly an octave.

"In the flesh," Mr. Tark says, holding out his arms at his sides, but he doesn't smile. His dark skin isn't flickering in and out like it was when we were six miles underwater watching him deliver our dive instructions, either. He's here. He's really here.

"Or maybe you're just a clone..." Arco says abruptly as he takes a step forward.

"Never. I don't trust those things to speak my mind," Tark replies, letting his mouth peel back into the same brilliant white smile he gave me just after our virtuo-cine test, his gold eyes blazing again like he's trying to figure out which one of us to eat, just like before.

"We call him *Skull* here," Eco says, weaving his way through our group and surprising everyone. He's barely said a word since we left his hab.

"You work for The Seam?" I say, still not quite sure I believe he's really here. Tark's eyes dart to me, and he lets his huge smile peel back again.

"Good to see you again, Ms. Ripley," he says with a nod, then scans the rest of our group as his face falls. "You seem to be missing a few?" he asks, then raises an eyebrow at Calyx.

"Styx got to the Phase Two facility before everyone could transfer—Jack, Liddick, Tieg and Dez Spaulding, as well as Azeris and his daughter are still there," she answers.

"What about the other Skyboarder? And Joss Tether? They both escaped Gaia with you," Tark scans us again, but no one answers.

"They're both...gone," Arco says after several eternal seconds. "Pitt was infected by the spores before the Leviathan imploded—he died in the tunnels not long after we docked. Joss was attacked by some...tornado animal in this...*other* place under the seafloor," he continues, seemingly not believing his own voice. He sighs, then grips the back of his neck.

"A zephyr?" Tark asks, his eyes drilling into Arco.

"You *know* about those?" Arco's hazel eyes flash, then narrow, and I can see the muscles in his jaw tighten as he clenches his teeth.

"Of course we know about those. And the sand sharks, and the antlions, and the oversized everything else down there—this isn't a club we've just started up here in Admin City, Mr. Hart," Tark answers.

"OK…so, *how* are you here again? Are you the only teacher from Gaia who works for The Seam? What's *happening*?" I ask in a louder voice.

"I'm not the only one, no," Tark says, turning abruptly back to me. "There are a few others."

"And you just go on everyday down there, teaching class like people *aren't* being dragged six miles through the ground by sharks with tentacles and legs?" Avis barks.

"We have counterparts in place—someone has to be on the inside to inform those counterparts. It's more complicated than you think," Tark looks straight through Avis, who can only scowl in reply. "Lucky for you, too, or you never would have made it to those tunnels in the first place. There are records imprinted every time you make a clone with that replicator; if I hadn't gone in an erased the files you created when you made copies of yourselves, you never would have had the three week's head start you did before your clones expired," Tark says, sliding his glare back to Arco. He raises an eyebrow. "Should have stayed another few days, Mr. Hart. We would have covered that in class." He steps toward us, and the beach virtuo-cine behind him disappears.

Arco doesn't smile. "We had a job to do. We did it," he answers coolly. "What's yours? Since it's obviously not being the Adaptabilities professor.

"Oh, it's that too. Why do you think I'm able to pull off working both sides of the fence?" he asks without looking back as he crosses to Lyden, Liam, and Arwyn. "It's good to see you three again. I'm sorry it took this long."

None of them answer, but Lyden nods subtly. "Couldn't be helped," he says, clearing his throat after a long pause.

"Were you able to reset their DNA with the portcarnate programs?" Tark asks, turning to Liam, who lowers his eyes and shakes his head.

"I tried, but the mutations were too far gone—cellular modification was irreversible with the equipment and time I had down there."

Tark nods, then nods again to Lyden and Arwyn.

"One of the cines in the cue takes place on the sea—might go easier on your psyche if you already have gills," Tark tries to loosen the tension in the air. He winks at Lyden, whose mouth tacks in the corner. "And who needs a neural baton when you've got your own personal blowtorch in the palm of your hand?" he adds, putting a long arm around Arwyn. She tries to smile, too, but it quickly withers into a thin, pressed line.

"We will reverse what they did to you both," Liam says, pushing every word through his teeth.

"It's all right," Lyden says, nodding to his brother. "That's not the priority right now...we need to stop the code from evolving."

Tark shoots a hard yellow glare at Calyx.

"I didn't have to say a thing," she says, holding up her hands in protest. "Liddick wasn't the only one who received the last message Jack and Liam programmed—Jazwyn heard it too," Calyx answers.

"And Arco..." I add. "He started to hear it repeating when we were in the Stingrays, just after we left the cave where Vox and Fraya disappeared."

Arco nods, but doesn't meet my eyes.

"That was months ago...which means it's been evolving since then...crite," Tark says. "All right, this way," he says flatly, then walks past us back through the doorway we've just come through.

"Where are we going?" I ask Eco, who is suddenly next to me.

"If he's thinking what I think he's thinking...to the Grid."

***

We walk back through the corridor until we return to the white, roped off platform area we passed on the way in.

"Queue it up," Tark says to a few people in green jumpsuits.

"What's happening? Queue what up?" Fraya asks in a thin voice. Jax puts his arm around her and pulls her closer to him.

"The Grid," Calyx answers as several reclining, curved chairs emerge from the floor to encircle the platform, which begins to glow blue.

"Those are virtuo-cine interfaces..." Ellis says.

Behind the reclining chairs, an unbroken circle of holographic keyboards and consoles surround the platform with silver stools every few feet from each other. People in differently colored jumpsuits gravitate toward the consoles from every direction, then immediately start typing. The blue glow of the platform in the center rises about twenty feet in the air. Just below it, several other layers appear: one white, one yellow, one green, blue, purple, and finally, black, each layer fading into a lighter one, a gradient of colors hovering over the darkest one closest to the floor. After a second, the colors and textures shift and change until I see dirt roads and… *wagons*?

"That's a flat-cine on the bottom?" Avis asks the question we all must be thinking. "Some ancient wild West adventure?"

"Not a flat-cine—it's still a virtuo-cine. Give it a second," Eco says as another exact copy of the animation appears just above the flat layer, but this one is more transparent with shifting colors. "*That* is the alpha channel. The rest of the colored layers are alternate scripts," he explains as all of the colored layers begin to take on similar scenes with horses and wagons and people. They multiply so quickly that they bleed into each other, and all we can see is the twenty-foot tall cylindrical color gradient spinning over the miniature 3-D virtuo-cine at the bottom, the transparent, color shifting copy of it playing just above.

"These are the guts of a virtuo-cine? Is that what you're telling us?" Jax asks, his dark eyes beaming with excitement.

"More or less," Eco answers. "Kira, what cine is this?"

"*Dustbowl*," a women at the console closest to us answers. "It released two days ago."

"And you're generating this?" Vox asks, narrowing her snake-green eyes at Eco.

"Yes, and no. We hacked the Grid, so now we have access to all the virtuo-cine raw files—all the layers, all the scripts."

"Why hack into that?" Ellis asks.

"As an instrument," Tark speaks up. "Newsfeeds are on a delay—anything we tried to tell the public would be wiped before it ever got to them using that avenue. In the cines, we can bring the message straight to their neural feeds, buried within the stories."

"So how long will it take to stop the code from evolving?" Arco asks.

"We can't stop the spread, and we can't rewrite anything without Jack," Tark says. "Without him, at this point we can only patch the holes so people get the right message."

"Why haven't you done that already? Launch the patches with automators, no?" Arco raises an eyebrow.

"It doesn't work like that. Patches need to be manually applied to the Glyphs."

"To the *huh*?" Avis asks, raising both feathered eyebrows until they disappear under his blue-edged bangs.

"Glyphs. You know, the programed characters in the cines," Eco says, rolling his eyes. "You'll need to swallow the bio-code chips and then touch the Glyphs to launch the patches. That's the only way to be sure the code will incorporate since we can't directly modify it like *Jack* could." Eco narrows his eyes for just a second as his lights flicker red, then return to white.

"Writing himself as the only one who could launch the sleeper was a security precaution, for us and for The Seam." Liam glares at Eco. "A precaution that should have prevented this whole situation."

"None of that really matters now," Calyx says. "We just need to do damage control."

"And who will swallow the biochips? What has to happen?" I ask, but none of them answer, so I ask another question. "Are the biochips like the automators? Like when Liddick launched them back at Gaia so we could connect the port-call hubs?"

"Yes, it's like that," Tark finally responds, then looks around at all of us. "I know that none of you signed up for this, but we need the Empaths to go into the Grid."

CHAPTER 15
Funnels
Liddick

It's almost light when I wake up this time. The fire is out, except for some smoldering embers. Tieg kicks sand over them, which also hits me in the face.

"Watch it, mollusk!" I growl at him. He just laughs. Heat fills my chest, but there's nothing I can do to retaliate when I'm blinded. I spit and try to blink the sand out of my eyes.

"Cycle stone is yellow—should be green within the hour, so it's safe enough to set out," Cal says from somewhere behind me, then suddenly, next to me. "What happened to him?"

"The skod just got a little too close to the fire," Tieg laughs again. I can hear the smirk in his voice and have to press my teeth together to keep from lunging in his general direction.

"You'd think with a bar of soap wedged in your face, you'd have a cleaner mouth," I say, rubbing my eyes. I'm pretty proud of that one until the rage in my gut settles back in.

"So that's what you think of our teeth after all. I knew it," Dez says, which puts a ball of ice in my chest, smothering the anger.

"You all are making me old," Azeris adds just before I feel a slap on my back. "Come on, we need to get moving before the sand heats up."

I spit more sand and blink several more times until finally, I can see again.

"We need to head toward the dark part of the sky," Dell says, pointing directly ahead of us. "Tanglebush and whatnot are that way, but we won't need to go that far."

"How are we supposed to find the tunnels in all this sand?" I ask, scanning the ground for some kind of opening.

"Funnels are tunnels. Usually, anyway," Cal says, then laughs.

"This is funny?" I narrow my eyes at him.

"You really are constipated, aren't you? Have you been eating the Bale-meal in your pack, or—"

"Don't you have the tuning fork? The NET? Can't you do something useful with that, or are you just comic relief while we hike up sand dunes and wait for the whole world to turn into fish and fire starters?" I ask, stopping in my tracks. Cal turns to face me, and his smile slips off the corners of his mouth. He reaches into his shirt and pulls out the silver, connected parallel bars that fork out from the metal handle. He strikes it against his walking stick, then holds it close to his chest and closes his eyes for several seconds before he speaks up again.

"There's still nothing—I've been trying to reach Vox with this since she vanished in the hubs with the others. They're either too far away now, or..." he trails off, then shoves the NET back into his shirt. "We need to keep moving."

"Could I see that for a second?" Jack asks, holding out his hand to Cal, who looks at him suspiciously. "I think I've seen it before." Cal pulls the NET back out of his shirt and hands it to Jack. "You call this the *NET*?" Jack asks again.

Cal nods. "Neural Enhancement Tuner."

"Where did it come from? How did you get this?"

"The Vishan have always had it. It's one of the artifacts left to us by the ancestors who went to the stars. Or, that's what the artifact records say at least."

"It *is* called a Neural Enhancement Tuner...a very, very old one, but it may still do the trick," Jack answers, examining the slim, silver tool in his hand that looks like a compacted divining rod. "This is a receiving unit, but I may be able to reverse its polarity for transmission. We may be able to send a message to Calyx...to the others, with this."

"Vox and Jazz were able to connect with that when we were in the Vishan tunnels. It knocked Jazz out cold before we got the DNA treatments," I say, scanning Jack and Cal for answers to questions I don't even know I have yet.

"We've also used this as a beacon. I took it with me when I made my way to the Motherland after we pulled Dell from the Rush. My people were able to keep track of me as long as I had this...it works with the rocks on our Lookout Pier," Cal adds.

"So it's already been modified...but how did you...I mean, you say you've just always had this?" Jack asks, raising both his eyebrows at Cal in disbelief.

"It goes back to the beginning of our people—the story is written on our Origin Wall," Cal answers.

"Fascinating…"

"You said this is a receiver unit?" Azeris asks.

"Yes. But if it's been modified, it could potentially project and receive neural wavelengths, which travel parallel to magnetic waves. When people have neural channels installed, they're able to receive newsfeeds, participate in virtuo-cines, all that." Jack shakes his head. "This NET is designed to work with those channels…but if your people have been down here as long as this thing has been around, how could you have ever had a neural channel installed? And you must have, or I don't see how it's possible that the NET could work for you," he explains, studying Cal.

"I've never had anything *installed*," Cal answers, his nearly white eyebrows drawing together, wrinkling the diamond and arrow scars on his forehead. He takes a step back from Jack. "So this comes from your people at the facility we just left too?" he asks, but the tight look on his face suggests he already knows the answer.

"Truly fascinating," is all Jack says in reply, not even looking up from the NET for a few more seconds until he seems to remember himself. "And yes…this was designed as a precursor to port-call technology. I haven't seen one in years, though. They're obsolete."

Cal nods, pressing his lips into a line.

"Not to us right now," I say to Jack before Cal can respond to his oblivious, blunt answer. "Does this mean you can contact Jazz? Can we find out if they made it to

Admin City?" I add in a rush. Has *everyone* except me forgotten what we're supposed to be doing here?

"Theoretically. I just need to see if I can open a channel. But we can't do that now. There isn't enough coverage out here."

"This is exactly where Vox opened a channel to Jazz. She'd just lost her sleeve to one of those funnel trap spider things and managed just fine," I say.

"I mean it's too dangerous, exactly because of those funnel spiders. They're actually called antlions—at least, that's what we've categorized them as in the Phase Two database. They are not genetically modified implants, though, like the tunnel sharks; those creatures have naturally evolved here," Jack says, then holds the NET out in front of him before pulling it into his chest. He turns to me again. "You said *Vox* used the NET to contact *Jazz*? But she couldn't have known what she was doing, or how she was doing it," he says, confused. Cal nods in agreement.

"We never showed her how it worked. Her natural instinct as a Vishan descendent and by accident are the only ways she could have gotten the NET to transmit anything."

"Jazz didn't have any counterpart tool, though. When we use this, she won't need one wherever she is either, right?" I ask.

"It will depend on if who sends the message has the same kind of neural framework," Jack answers.

"Then it will have to be me—we're both Reader Empaths. No one else here is a Reader, unless..." I trail off, looking at Jack because I'm not sure what his classification from Gaia is beyond being an Omnicoder like Jax.

"No, I'm not a Reader," Jack answers, seeming to read my mind despite not technically being able to. "I am a Receiver, but it is a latency."

Receiver latency. Just like Arco Hart, I think, realizing I must have pushed the question about Jack's classification into his head.

"Then I'll be the one to use the NET. How do you do it?" I ask, looking from Jack to Cal.

"We'll need to wait until we're on more stable ground. It's not safe here," Azeris says, nodding to me.

"The ground is stable enough to see if this will work for five minutes. Just tell me what to—" I start, but then Zoe starts shouting.

"Hey! My foot!"

"Zoe, don't move!" Jack says.

"Crite..." Dell blows out a breath. "This whole entire place is a giant sandbox, and you manage to find a sinkhole. Stop thrashing or you're gonna open up a mouth under there that will swallow us all."

"*What!?*" Zoe whisper-shouts.

"Be still—they're right," Cal says. "It's like the fast floors back home. The ones behind the Bale field after the rain, remember?"

"Quicksand? How can there be quicksand in a giant desert?" Zoe asks in a high, thin voice.

"Underwater springs—they tend to run the perimeters of each biome because the ground is softer there. Transitions are vulnerable places," Jack sighs. I can feel his anxiety squeezing my chest as he tries to figure out how to free Zoe.

"Take this!" Cal holds out the end of his walking stick to Zoe. "Nobody get close, or it will only spread the sinkhole under us."

"He's right...it's like stepping on a bag of pudding with a hole in it; any surface pressure will just force the spread under us," Jack adds.

"A whole biome full of sand..." Dell shakes his head.

"Just stow it and get me out of here!" Zoe says through her teeth as Dez tries to offer her hand.

"Get back!" I shout to her. She shoots me an icy glare, and the backlash of my own harsh, loud voice hits me. I push it out of my head—is she *trying* to get us all killed? "Didn't you just hear him? The whole ground could turn into that mush and swallow everyone—don't get so close," I try to explain, but she just turns away in a huff. *I don't have time for this.*

Zoe grabs the end of the walking stick, but then starts sinking into the sand, which doesn't even look wet.

"I'm stuck! It's pulling both my boots!"

"Just be still!" Dell says, all the teasing out of his voice now.

"Zoe, look at me," Azeris says. "You just watch me, wise? We're gonna get you out."

Zoe nods to her dad, but then suddenly sinks all the way to her hips and yells out in pain.

"What happened!? What was that?" Dez's voice is shrill.

Cal starts to say something low and steady in his Vishan language to Zoe, but Dell cuts him off.

"No! Just pull her out! Make some room and I'll help you!" he yells.

"I'll only let go *just in case.* Keep back..." Cal says.

"*What's going on?*" Dez starts crying, and Jack grabs the back of his neck as all the blood drains from his face when he answers her.

"There's an antlion under there."

CHAPTER 16
Login
Jazz

"Wait, what?" Arco turns to Calyx. "You're going to put us in a virtuo-cine?"

"Well, several, actually," she answers, then pulls her erratically streaked hair into a tiny ponytail and rolls the ring in her bottom lip with her top teeth.

"Going into the Grid *here* means you'll be on the *Platform* layer—the one there at the bottom of the cylindrical color gradient," she says, spinning the ring between breaths. "Once your neural channels are connected, the story feeds will play. The difference here is when participants jack into a virtuo-cine topside, they interact with the flattened storyboard. All these layers you see there aren't flattened yet; that's why we can still go in and patch the code on the Platform level. If we had a storyboarder credential, we could even change the baseline plot around. This is the raw layer, does that make sense?"

Arco nods at Calyx, processing. Myra shakes her head and presses her fingers into her temples.

"So if these virtuo-cines aren't finished, why do we even have to worry about the message being released? The cines aren't available to the public yet," Arco says.

"Oh, they're released, some of them just yesterday," Calyx says. "The network updates and flattens the cines hundreds of thousands of times an hour with the latest changes too...the plots are adaptive, so whenever someone blows up an enemy ship, the narrative takes that possibility into account so someone can't leave the virtuo-cine and tell a friend exactly what he did to blow up that ship. Nothing can ever happen twice in the same way in a virtuo-cine."

"So the *whole thing* runs on algorithms," Arco says to himself in confirmation.

"Right," Eco answers. "This version of *Dustbowl* has probably been updated at least a thousand times in the five minutes we've been explaining this to you."

"So, you're somehow going to send us into the original layers of this virtuo-cine? The Platform master file or whatever?" Avis asks, then nearly *floats* toward to the huge cylinder of gradient colors in the center of the chair circle. He stops over the shoulder of one of the people in a white jumpsuit who is typing on her console. "So all these colors are different storylines *already*? How many right now?"

The girl turns around and looks at Tark.

"It's all right," he nods.

"The different colors represent alternate scripts. These are for *Transcendence*. If participants don't trip the explosives in the beginning of this cine, there are currently..." she pauses, checking her screen, "4,977 other scenarios in which they will still be trapped on the planet with combatants."

"Whoa..." Avis says, his default reaction to everything. Ellis joins him behind the girl's other shoulder as the huge cylinder of colored layers starts spinning faster.

"How many layers are actually there?" I ask, still trying to process the idea that each one of these thousands of color variations is an alternate script.

"It's impossible to say—they multiply every second depending on the participants' choices," Calyx answers.

"So how are we supposed to find these *Glyphs* and deliver the code patches if there are countless alternate scripts? The Glyphs could be in any one of them at any given time," Arco says, narrowing his eyes and shaking his head. "This is impossible."

"No," Tark answers. "All the Glyphs will originate in the background layer—the Platform—that's why you're going in there. Only copies of the Glyphs will move to alternate script layers. That's actually what we're counting on. You patch them in their original form at the Platform level, and any alternate scripts that are created when people interact with them will already have the patch. Patch all the Glyphs, and The Seam's *complete* message about Gaia's genetic engineering funnel, the port-cloud, and the corporations involved, will get out to the public."

"This is giving me a headache..." Myra says, squeezing her eyes closed.

"I think I understand it," Avis says, turning abruptly to face us. He blows his blue-edged bangs out of his eyes and holds up his hands like he's about to catch a ball. "So, it's like, you meet a gunslinger in there, and you know there's no way you're going to be able to outdraw him, and you don't really want to die, so you have to be smarter, right? So you say, 'hey, gunslinger guy, what's that up there?' and you point over his head. BAM! You draw your gun and win! But then you finish the virtuo-cine and go back to tell your friends how you beat the boss bad guy…only now the gunslinger is wise to that trick you pulled, so your buddy is probably going to get one right between the eyes," Avis explains without taking a breath, then looks around the room for marveled approval at his performance. "That's a new colored layer then, right?" he asks Calyx.

She pushes out her bottom lip and nods. "That's about it, yep."

Avis beams and folds his arms over his chest.

"All right, then," Jax says, chuckling. Ellis shoves Avis, causing him to stumble forward. They both laugh, but Arco's expression hasn't changed.

"So, why us? Why don't you send some of these jumpsuits into the Grid? They obviously have more experience with this kind of thing, no?" he protests.

"Because the code was originally written for Liddick, and your Empath compatibilities are almost as strong according to your threshold scans," she adds, looking at me. "You must have grown new neural branches because of the telepathy…like mirror neurons."

"How did you know about our telepathy, and when did you scan us?" I ask, hearing the edge in my voice.

"We finally pulled your readings from your port-carnate transfer," Calyx answers. "It's fascinating, actually. Jazz, it's like your mind could map Liddick's mind—yours built new roads…the same roads he had so that you could understand him better. That's how

Empaths work, and it's why your dad needed to code The Seam's message on Empathic neural thread. It's the only kind with the ability to replicate like that and eventually reach everyone."

"So that means Vox must be able to adapt like this, too, right? She heard the marlin that night before we left for Gaia just like I did. And Arco..." I add, turning around to face him. He meets my eyes, and for one second I see him again—thoughtful and unselfish, brave and kind—but then his eyes cool. "Arco heard the message when we were in the Stingrays on that first exploratory mission," I add.

"His records say he has an Empathic latency, so it makes sense that he would also be able to adapt," Lyden says, but the muscles under Arco's cheekbones just flex as he presses his lips together like he's trying to keep himself from saying anything.

"Well! That's why we're the ones who have to go in," Vox says, clapping her hands once in front of her. "How do we get in there?"

Calyx fights a smile. "We can keep track of you, and we're able to track the Glyphs as well, but your natural abilities will probably root them out before we will. Just like you heard the marlin message—the code the Glyphs are carrying has been activated, and is already trying to reach anyone with Empathic tendencies."

"What about if we never heard any of the messages? What if we never saw anything strange happening because of that code?" Myra asks.

"Because your Empath trait is secondary, it's just taken you longer to hone in. You all saw the images of

Jazz's father in place of the code on the Grid yesterday, so you're definitely wired for this by now," Calyx explains.

"And that leaves us out," Ellis says, angling his head at Avis. "We don't even have a secondary Empath trait."

"And me too," Jax adds as his heavy, dark eyebrows draw together. "I came back as an Omnicoder."

"I'm an Empath Receiver," Myra says. "That's what they said at Gaia. Fraya is an Empath Projector and a Coder…a Hybrid. Hybrids count too, right?"

"Any Empath variation, yes," Tark says, pushing his big hands into his dark green jumpsuit pockets. "Who else has Empath classification?"

"Lyden," I add.

"Then you six are the ones going into the Grid. We'll put the rest of you to work out here, don't worry," Tark adds.

"Wait, so we can't do anything in there? I'm an Omnicoder. I can help do *something*," Jax says, his arm tightening around Fraya.

"You would help the most on the outside if we need to modify the patches that we're going to embed on the biochips. If the Empaths need to ingest updates, it's critical we get those right," Tark explains.

"So, I don't know if anyone has noticed how terribly well behaved I've been over here just minding my own business without comment, but can we stop jawing now and just go in already?" Vox says just before a long, obnoxious sigh. She looks at Mr. Tark like he's holding up the cafeteria line.

"Not yet, Ms. Dyer," he answers, trying to keep his hard face, but his gold eyes twinkle just like they did when Vox and I came out of his barbarian virtuo-cine back at Gaia. "The dive suits you're wearing have been damaged to the point that they're likely inoperable by now," he adds, gesturing to Vox's completely shredded sleeve. "We have channel tester suits you'll need to wear—these will allow us to keep track of your vitals when you're in the Grid," he says, waving us to follow him.

Tark leads us to a small room just on the other side of the huge cylinder of colored layers and its surrounding reclining chairs. We pass the people at the consoles wrapping around behind the chairs, and everyone looks at us like we're heading for death row or something.

Don't worry about them, Lyden says in my mind.

Stop doing that. Does jumping into people's thoughts out of nowhere run in your family or what?

Lyden tries to stifle laughter as we enter the little room with white jumpsuits hanging along the walls.

"Goes by height—they'll adjust to fit you. Mr. Hart, you'll likely find something suitable here," Tark says, pointing to the beginning of the suits on our left. "Ladies, to your right," he adds. "Leave what's left of your black Gaia dive suits in a pile in the middle here; we'll have them recycled.

Vox and I exchange glances, then she shrugs. I pull the release cord at my shoulder, and the back panel of my dive suit falls open. I haven't taken this off since we were training with our fire back in the Vishan tunnels after our treatments. I almost feel naked without it on, the blue fabric of my Gaia school jumpsuit seeming so thin in comparison.

"Whoo!!" Myra almost giggles as she puts her arms into her new, white jumpsuit, which then fastens up the back all by itself with a quick *whoosh* sound. Mine does the same, and even though I just saw it happen with Myra, I didn't expect it.

"Mr. Hart, let's get that treated before you suit up. Like your dive suits, these will take care of hygiene, but not flesh wounds," Tark says, examining the long, ragged gash on the outside of Arco's shoulder."

"It's just a cut," Arco says.

"A cut that you know is there, and that you know is not yet treated. If you know, the Glyphs may also know. Never let them see you bleed, son," Tark says in a quieter voice. "Not in there."

CHAPTER 17
Sinking Feelings
Liddick

No one moves or even seems to breathe for the first few seconds after Jack's announcement about the antlion in the sand. Zoe's face is white with fear, and I feel useless just standing here like an idiot.

"So, pull her out!" I shout.

"Can't—those things are drawn to the struggle. See the funnel forming around her waist? If she moves at all, it will just pull her down," Dell says, gripping the back of his neck and scanning the area. Cal starts talking to Zoe in Vishan again, and this time, she nods in reply. The color starts to come back to her face.

"On my count, though, wise?" she answers.

"What are you doing?" Dell asks, his eyes flashing back to Zoe, then to Cal, who lets go of the walking stick he's extended to Zoe. "What are you *doing*!?" Dell shouts.

"Zoe!" Azeris takes two huge steps forward, but Jack grips his arm.

"Wait! Let her do it…this will work."

"Your blade…get ready to—" Cal starts, but Zoe interrupts him, already pulling her machete from its sheath on her back.

"I got this," Zoe answers, making the diamond pattern scarring between Cal's eyes wrinkle with worry.

She takes the sharp end of the walking stick and pushes it into the sand until only about a foot of it is still visible.

"Tell me when you're ready," Cal says, pulling a short line of rope from his satchel and tying a small loop at each end, then securing one of them around his wrist.

"Almost…all right." Zoe extends her hand to catch the other side of the looped rope, then slides it over her wrist and grips the lead. She lets go of the stick, but doesn't take her eyes off it.

"Grab hold of my waist—make a line. Everyone pull when she says pull," Cal announces.

Pull…just like they did in the Bale field with the zephyrs, I think out of nowhere, and realize this must be what the rest of us who were there are thinking too. I line up behind Dell and get ready to pull Zoe out whenever she gives the word. The stick starts to move, and we get the signal.

"Now! Pull!" Zoe shouts and grips the rope with her free hand. All of us pull back as hard as we can, and after a few seconds, Zoe scrambles to her feet.

"Run! Let's go!" Cal yells as the small funnel that surrounded Zoe's waist starts to spread out, expanding in a perfect circle like liquid dripped onto a napkin. "*Go! Go!*" Cal yells again. Over my shoulder, the funnel races for our heels.

We can't outrun that, I think. *I'm not dying out here—not like this. Not eaten by some monster bug. What if this were a virtuo-cine…if it weren't real…if dying just meant I'd wake up?*

I stop running and pull the machete from the sheath on my back as I turn to face the approaching spread of sinking sand. I yell at the top of my lungs like I have some kind of magical, funnel freezing voice powers, then I yell again.

"Liddick!" Dez calls from somewhere behind me, but I barely register her voice above my own. The funnel gets closer and closer, rushing at my feet, but crite, if I'm going to die, I'd rather die fighting than running. I shout again, and to my amazement, the funnel stops spreading. It just…stops. I cough and laugh at the same time in disbelief. *That shouldn't have worked. Why did that work?*

"Did you just *yell* at that antlion under there? You *yelled* at it?" Dell calls out behind me. He starts to laugh with the others, which starts in a scatter, then everyone is laughing hard all at the same time.

My heart is about to jump through my ribs and straight out of my chest. I swallow a few times, then notice I'm holding the machete so tightly that my hand is shaking. Or maybe it's just shaking because I'm about to roarf like the known universe has never seen a person roarf before.

"Liddick! Are you OK?" Dez says, crashing into me from behind. I stumble forward, then get my feet under me.

"I'm all right," I say, but my voice sounds a thousand miles away. I find Azeris, who looks at me wide-eyed with his mouth open like I'm the stupidest person with godlike powers he's ever seen in his life.

"You're split. You're the splittest person in the world," he says, then shakes his head and laughs until he starts coughing.

"That was brass," Dell says, sticking out his bottom lip, impressed. "Stupid, but brass." He slaps me on the back.

My heart is pounding even harder now as the adrenaline hits, and I sheathe my machete so I can shove my shaking hands into my pockets. I glance over at Tieg, who looks at me like I could catch fire and explode any second, and then I see the flames in the corner of my eye.

"Take a breath, antlion tamer," Zoe laughs. "Before you burn through your britches."

The Vishan fire works...it's back, I think. "It works. It works again!" I shout, watching the fire running down my arms slowly receding until it disappears all together with a *pop*. I stand there a second more, then, like it's in slow motion, I watch Tieg lose his footing and slide down the funnel wall just a few feet in front of us.

***

I don't believe it at first—not until I hear Tieg screaming for help as the sand spits from the funnel in cloud bursts with every snap of the antlion's pincers, stinging my face like a million tiny needles.

"Tieg!" Dez falls to her knees at the side of the funnel.

"Back up! Get back!" I shout. Suddenly everything is loud. I pull her up and walk her several feet back from the funnel. "Stay here!" I move back to the edge and look again for Tieg, but he's...gone. "Spaulding! Can you hear me!?" I shout, but don't hear anything. The sand is rippling in the center of the funnel, though...*Crite...it pulled him down*!

"Where is he?" Cal says, stopping next to me.

"I think he got pulled under. It happened just now, a few seconds ago when he slipped," I say. Cal's diamond scarred forehead wrinkles again, and we both nod, knowing there's only one thing to do now. We both reach for our machetes.

"One...two...three!" Cal says, and on three, we both jump into the funnel, sliding quickly to the middle. The sand undulates, hitting the bottom of our feet like someone with a broom handle below. "Start digging!"

"Spaulding! We're coming!" I shout again. In front of us, Dell slides down the funnel wall, followed by Zoe. With all of us digging, we manage to displace enough sand that we deepen the funnel, but there's still no sign of Tieg. "It just keeps getting deeper! We're not getting anywhere!" I shout.

"There must be a tunnel underneath—it's pulling him into the tunnel—keep digging!" Cal answers. We move sand for several more minutes before Jack shouts down to us.

"It will keep refilling until you hit the bend! You'll have to crawl in! We're coming!" he says, then turns and puts his hands on Dez's shoulders, lowering his eyes to meet hers as he talks.

"The bend is close. Come on!" Cal says to me as he sheaths his machete, then wraps a cloth from his satchel around his nose and mouth like a mask. He takes a deep breath before pushing his arms and head into the center of the funnel, where it looks like he starts *swimming*. Dell and Zoe do the same, and I look up at Azeris in disbelief.

"Everyone is going to suffocate!" I yell.

"The sand is loose here, and it's not backfilling anymore; that means there's give below. The bend can't be far. No one will be in there long," Jack answers, then looks at Dez. "Are you all right? Close your eyes as tightly as you can. Here, tie this over your nose and mouth," he says, pulling one of the cloths he used to ice her eyes from his satchel, then ties the other one around his face too. He nods at me, then at Azeris before pushing through the sand, head first, like the others.

"I'll get your back," Azeris says, looking at me as he ties his cloth over his nose and mouth, then turns to Dez. "Follow Liddick, all right?"

*Crite…*I think, the blood pounding in my ears. I blow out several short breaths before fixing the cloth over my face, then suck in the deepest one I can until it feels like my lungs will explode. I squeeze my eyes shut and feel the sand swallow my arms, then pack in all around me. It pours into my ears, and the world disappears. No light. No sound. Just the distant rumbling of movement ahead, which at least tells me that I'm going in the right direction. I try to take a breath, but can only get a fraction of one before the air stops in my throat, hard, like I'm suddenly trying to breathe liquid. *Keep moving…*I hear in my head, and I know it's her. *Jazz? Jazz!* I think in reply, but I don't hear anything else.

In that instant, I realize it's moving forward that causes the small bubble of air I can breathe, so I keep pushing through the sand until hands grip my wrists and pull me hard. I start coughing, but the only thing I can make out is red light.

"Take small breaths! Lots of small breaths! Clear the dust!" Cal says loudly, close to my ear. I pull down the cloth from my nose and mouth and suck in the biggest breath I can, then start coughing so hard I fall to the ground.

"I got her!" Zoe says. "Help me!"

I push to my hands and knees, then to my feet. The walls are packed earth, dry and cracked with gouges everywhere. It smells damp and the air sits heavy in my lungs, like any minute they'll fill with water.

"This only goes one way, so it must have taken him down there!" Dell yells from somewhere ahead of me. I can't see him in the shadow of Cal's hand flames, which cast wicked dark shapes over the arrow scars down the bridge of his nose. Azeris coughs behind me and falls to his hands and knees.

"Dad!" Zoe says, rushing to his side. "Just take small breaths…small breaths or the dust will choke you!"

Her advice is useless, though. How do you fight the instinct to breathe when there's suddenly air, and a minute ago, there was none?

"I'm…all right. Where's the boy?" Azeris asks, wrenching to his feet.

"He had to go this way; there's nowhere else. Can you walk?" Zoe asks, and Azeris nods.

"Get your blade ready. That thing could be anywhere," Azeris says, then coughs again.

"Is that everyone? Is this everyone?" Jack says, scanning us all in the dim light of Cal's fire.

"Where's my brother!? Tieg!" Dez shouts.

"No, shhh!" Cal hisses. "You'll draw more antlions to us. These tunnels are interconnected."

"Then let's go! We need to find him!" Dez starts to cry, then presses the heels of her hands into her eyes and shrieks. "It's burning! Why is it burning!?"

"We're going to need more light," Jack says. "A lot more."

CHAPTER 18
The Platform
Jazz

There are no pockets in these white jumpsuits. No secret compartments like our dive suits…nothing except a line of small white lights at the shoulders like the ones wired into Eco's cheekbones.

"How are these supposed to monitor anything? They're just like our blue Gaia jumpsuits," I say, examining the sleeves for buttons or…*something*.

"They sync to your neural patterns with those lights across your shoulders," Calyx says, then nods to Eco.

"Hardwire," he adds, then makes a clicking sound with his mouth as he winks at me.

"Great, so they tell you how we're feeling. How are we supposed to find the first Glyph and what happens when we do?" Arco asks, still edgy.

"The code will be self-loading as long as you make physical contact with the Glyphs. Skin to skin—at least five seconds. It seems like a blink of an eye, but it's longer than you think," Calyx says. "Each of you will need to patch your own specific Glyph. It will reach out to you, don't worry."

"And how are we supposed to know what—*who* they are?" Arco follows, the impatience in his voice growing.

"We'll try our best on this end to steer you toward them, but like we said, they're designed to find you just like those messages from Jack and Liam were. Listen for anything out of place—anything that doesn't seem to fit the storyline, or that seems to speak to you particularly," Calyx answers. "You just have to be sure before you make the code transfer. If you upload your patch to the wrong Glyph, it's lost, and you'll have a harder time finding the next Glyph. We need to patch at least four to initiate the repaired code replication," Tark says, looking at me and holding up a small, metallic box.

"Wait…" Myra says, startling me before I can react. "What happens if it doesn't replicate? What if we don't get all the patches loaded?"

"The code will just keep evolving," Arwyn says after a pause.

"And it won't stop until it figures out how to reach everyone. Until it tells everyone that Carboderm and Biotech Global are the *heroes* helping Gaia's genetic manipulation project," Eco adds. Liam starts to say something, but it just disintegrates into a growl.

"What? What's the problem?" Tark asks, turning to face Liam.

"He thinks this is his fault," Lyden says under his breath.

"It *is* his fault!" Eco says too loudly. "And yours, and Calyx's, and Jack's!" he adds, turning back to Liam. "You put everything at risk to keep your own people out of Gaia."

Calyx starts to reply, but Tark beats her to it. "That's enough. I'm the one who authorized this, so if you're looking for someone to blame, you just aim those ice cubes right here."

Eco glares at Tark, and the lights that run along the edge of his cheekbones flash red.

"Without the ability to get the message out on a mass scale, it wouldn't matter that we knew what was really happening behind closed doors. The bio-code Jack and Liam adjusted is doing exactly what we wanted it to do—it's just incomplete," Calyx says, obviously trying to calm everyone down since the people at the consoles are starting to take quick glances in our direction. Eco rolls his eyes, and the lights in his cheekbones change from red to an erratic stream of white and blue.

"So, this seems like a *you* problem…can you pick it up after you jack us in? I'd rather be turning my horse into a dragon right now," Vox says, blinking a few times as everyone stops dead and stares at her. "What? This griping is more fun than a dragon? How are you baffled?"

"Just come on," I say, walking toward the multiple colored layers that form wide, gradient bands over the miniaturized scene of horses and wagons playing out on the bottom level. I stop behind all the people seated at the encircling, brushed metal console stations, then turn to Calyx. "How are we supposed to get in there?" I ask, gesturing to the Platform level scene.

"You'll each need to ingest one of these," Tark says, holding up the small, metallic box again. He crosses to us and takes off the lid. "Take one."

The chips inside are no bigger than the nail on my pinky finger. They're square and silver with flashing white lights just like the ones on the shoulders of our new white jumpsuits.

"They're blinking!" Myra almost squeals.

"That's the bio-matter—it's how we know the chips are viable," Arwyn says, beaming proudly.

"Did you…make these?" Arco asks, unsure for some reason. *He really has no idea what his sister can do,* I think, and a small ache starts in my chest.

"Not those particular chips…I designed the prototypes for them, though," Arwyn answers. Arco starts to reply, but the words stop just short of coming out. He half laughs instead.

"Guess your coding proclivity runs in the family," I say, leaning my shoulder into his. He glances at me and smiles for a second, but then remembers himself, and the wall of ice goes back up. *This can't just be about Liddick…I* think, then close my eyes in a long blink so I don't say it out loud.

"You should have made them flavored—like that candy in Ms. Plume's fake office. The one we went to in our brains at Gaia, remember?" Vox asks, nudging me too hard in the arm as she tries not to choke. "Is there a pooler around here?" she asks, raising an eyebrow when Calyx and the others send her confused looks. "You know, some kind of water shooter? So you can get a… drink?" she coughs. "Crite, why did you even put corners on these?"

Arwyn fights the smile pulling at her lips. "Did you swallow it whole?" she asks around a giggle.

"I mean, we weren't supposed to snort them, right? Tark said swallow it."

"You were supposed to bite down on it…then it would—"

"Dissolve!" Myra almost shouts, the white lights across her shoulders now flickering blue, red, green, white, all different colors until they return to a steady stream of white again.

I can't help but laugh as Vox gags and coughs every few seconds like she has a hairball, her giant yellow-green cat eyes only making the image that much funnier.

I put the biochip in my mouth and almost immediately, it starts to fizz. It doesn't taste like anything, except maybe slightly metallic, and I notice the lights encircling my shoulders starting to flash like Myra's just did. Calyx must read whatever my face betrays because she holds up her hands like she's trying to keep me from jumping off a ledge.

"That's normal; don't worry. The code is just fusing to your DNA. After a minute, it will lace every cell in your body."

"So how do we get rid of it once we upload it to the Glyphs?" Myra asks, studying the backs of her hands, then flipping them around to study her palms.

"It will expel itself from your DNA when the transfer to the Glyph is complete. The patch will be able to sense when it's been plugged into the whole algorithm, so it won't stay in two places," Arwyn explains. "It will just self-destruct…should take about a month, but it won't hurt you in the meantime."

"So what happens to those Glyphs if they get the patch code, but don't need it?" Ellis asks. "Will it just self-destruct in there, too?"

"Probably nothing, but The Glyphs don't shed cells like people do, so it's hard to say what might happen," Liam says after a second. "Just don't pick the wrong one."

I swallow hard and find Lyden. He tries to smile at me, but I can see the worry behind his eyes. He touches the side of his long, sharp nose in a kind of salute, then nods at me.

No one is going in alone, he thinks, and I feel a sudden warmth fill my chest…one that shouldn't be this strong just because of one sentence of encouragement, given the enormity of what they're asking us to do. He must be pushing this feeling on me.

"Is there an order to this? Does one of us have to upload the code to a Glyph first?" Fraya asks. Tark shakes his head.

"The Glyphs will decide that—it could choose any of you in each cine. Just get in and get out as fast as you can. Stick together so you know who has transferred their patch for the virtuo-cine you're in. There's only one per cine, so as soon as the delivery is made, we'll pull you out and reset the Platform. Once you've unloaded your patch, you will just be eyes and ears for the others in the rest of the cines."

"Crite, can we *gooooooo* now?" Vox asks. "We'll figure it out. You act like you haven't basically been living on a different planet for the past few months. We've just got horses, wagons, and old men who walk funny to deal with now. That's it. No shark people, no bugs as big as us with pincer claws, no mineral rain, so relax," she adds, cocking a burgundy eyebrow, then tucking a few stray hairs back into one of her multiple lines of braids.

Calyx walks around to each one of us and squares our shoulders. "Oriah, are you connected to all six?" she asks, letting her eyes wander to Fraya, Myra, Arco, Vox, and Lyden before she returns them to me.

"Yes, they're synced. Everyone looks good. The interface seats are online now too," the girl on the other side of the console circle says, but I can't see her.

"Good," Calyx answers, then returns her attention to us. "All right, take one of the seats in front of the console stations. You may feel some initial heat or gravitational pull from the virtuo-cine layers building that color column in the middle, but just focus your eyes on the Platform level scene, all right? It will keep the nausea at bay when the lock sequence starts," she says, then walks with us to the slim, reclining seats that remind me of the ones in the med-bay back at Gaia Sur. I climb into one of the dark chairs, and it immediately forms to me as two rounded, metal wands appear at my temples. The chair props me up just enough to look into the bottom layer of the enormous column of rotating light and color in front of me, but I can't make out what's actually happening beyond the small movements of cattle moving behind wagons. Farther out from these, several small buildings take shape at the base of mountains in the terrain. *There's no water anywhere...*I think randomly, then feel my heart start to pound.

CHAPTER 19
The Tunnels
Liddick

"Here," Cal says, rushing over to Azeris and Dez with a larger flame now in the palm of his hand. Dell pulls up another, and so does Zoe.

"Try to stay calm. Just breathe, you're going to be all right," Jack says, aligning his eyes with Dez's. "Just keep blinking until the tears stop. Keep breathing."

Dez takes a deep breath, then another before she calms down. "What's wrong with me? It didn't rain anymore…the treatments were supposed to help reverse whatever damage it did, right? What's happening?" she sputters.

"It's hard to tell…can you still see?"

"Yes, that keeps getting better. It just burns now."

"Might just be the healing process. The black discoloration is still receding, and as long as you can see, I'm not terribly worried. We'll take a closer look when we get to Azeris's hab, all right? Just try to stay calm," Jack says, then nods to Dez.

"We have to find my brother," she says in a small, cracking voice.

"We will. We're going to find him right now.

The tunnels are dry, and the red light bouncing off the hard-packed earth makes me feel like we're walking through the intestines of some enormous animal out here. *Don't tweak…*I think, trying not to imagine the walls flexing like whatever swallowed us is breathing on the outside. *Stop, damn it!* I tell myself, then spit out more of the sand in between my teeth. I blow out a breath just as Azeris falls back to walk next to me.

"How are you holding up?" he asks, studying me from the shadows of the light in front of us. "Can you pull up your fire at will yet?"

I hold out my hand and try to concentrate on making it itch, but only a few puffed sparks ignite before they disappear into the blackness pushing in on us.

"Why didn't you need a treatment?" I ask.

"Omniclass nanites—Jack dosed me at the Phase Two station right after we broke him out."

"So, those are what? Adaptable to whatever?"

Azeris laughs. "They're not going to let me breathe like a fish or anything. Don't get antsy."

I start to bark something back at him, but it's suddenly too much effort. The air is heavy and too warm.

"What do you think happened to him—to Tieg?" I ask before I realize it's out loud. "That thing…took him."

Azeris grips my shoulder as we push through the earth intestines. "We just keep moving forward. That's all we can do. Jack says it's not far to the surface once we're in these tunnels. Keep it together," he says. I think of my brother, Liam. *Keep it together until we get home…holding our cut eyebrows together while the blood ran down my cheek. He was laughing like it was the stupidest thing in the world.*

I pull out of my distraction when the walls, the ceiling, the ground under my feet starts to rumble with a low, guttural sound that rattles my teeth.

"What the hell is that?" I ask Azeris once the rumbling subsides. His hard face is dirty, but his normally relaxed dark eyes are wide and afraid now.

"Tunnel Shark!" Dell calls back to us. "Get up here with us!"

"No, no, no…" Dez starts to cry again, then shrieks as the pain of whatever her tears are doing now registers.

"Calm down—you're gonna be fine. We're all gonna be fine," Zoe says, but I feel her fear pushing out too just as she's trying to seem so together.

*Just watch the Platform…keep watching the Platform…*I hear in my head.

What? The platform of what? The ground? Jazz? But she doesn't reply. *It's not her…I'm losing my mind down here.*

The ground rumbles again, and for a second I feel the rain pouring down. For a second, Jazz is bleeding in my arms in the sand, the tunnel shark is growling low and loud, and the thick sound of it fills my chest and suffocates me. *Little breaths, Rip! Just take little breaths!*

"Hey! Let's move!" Azeris yells, grabbing my arm and pulling me forward. I stumble, but at least I pull out of the flashback.

Get it together. Stop tweaking, I think. Over and over again.

"It's not in this tunnel—maybe one or two over, it's all right. Just try not to make noise and we'll skirt it," Cal says quietly as we close the distance between us. Dez covers her mouth with her hands and nods. Zoe's red fire light reflects in her icy blue eyes and makes them almost seem to glow. I nod at her when she looks up at me.

"It's not going to be like before. We're not going through that again. We're going to get out, OK? We're going to get out of here," I tell *myself* just as much as I'm telling her.

"Just be still a second," Dell whispers as a low rumble shakes everything around us again, but it's not as violent as before. "It's pushing on. Feel it?"

We all nod, and Dez closes her eyes for a long time. Tears fall over her cheeks and shine in the firelight. My stomach drops in relief. Hers, mine…everyone's.

"All right, let's move now. We need to find a way up," Cal says. We start moving forward again, and I feel every pebble of earth move under my feet. I hear every exhale, every choked-back sob. I hear the hiss of the fire in Cal's palm, and the heavy, damp air pours into my lungs. Our shadows bounce off the walls around us in erratic, sharp angles so that it looks like there are more of us than there actually are, and suddenly, it's hard to breathe.

Just watch the Platform…keep watching the Platform…I hear in my head. Again. *It's her. It has to be her. What platform? Jazz?* She doesn't answer, but a platform is something on the ground, so I watch the ground. One step, then another, and after a few more, the suffocating feeling recedes. I take a shallow breath, then another until I put myself entirely back in my skin. *One step, then another. Just watch the ground.*

"Here!" Zoe whisper-yells to us. "This one goes up!" She points to a split in the tunnels, one going up at our left, and one turning right that leads down.

"How do we know where he went? How do we know where it took Tieg?" Dez asks. Her eyes are wide and panicked again, and the shine on her face makes it clear that she hasn't stopped crying. Her fear hits me hard and square in the center of my chest, then just sits there like a boulder. Being a Reader Empath *rots* sometimes.

No one answers her, but that doesn't mean no one knows the answer. Jack and Azeris exchange glances.

"He's strong. He could have wrestled loose and pushed on toward the Badlands. That's up…" Zoe says, slipping an arm around Dez's shoulders. "He was on-fire mad last I saw him too, so I don't think that antlion had much of a chance."

"But what if that rumbling just now was…" Dez starts, but can't bring herself to finish the thought. I swallow hard, not wanting to think about it either, no matter that Tieg is a chutz.

"We can't leave him," Zoe says. "You of all people know that," she adds, angling her head at Dell. He pulls in a deep breath.

"We won't," he says after a second. "I'll go that way and circle back to the Phase Two building—if a shark took him, that's where it's heading. I need to get the rest of the captives out of there anyway. We can lead them back to the Vishan for now, until we get word," he says, then turns to Jack.

"I can only reach you if you have the NET…unless they have other equipment in their tunnels?"

"Just the NET," Cal answers, then nods. "I'll go with him." He and Dell turn to Zoe, but Dez grips her arm like she'll fall a thousand feet if she lets go.

"I'm coming with you…"

"Dez, minnow, you have to stay with us. We need to get you out of here," Jack says. "It's what your brother would want."

"No! I'm not leaving him in here! I'm not losing him too!" she shouts, and tears stream down her cheeks again. She presses the heels of her hands into her eyes. If Tieg is gone, she'll have lost both her brothers to Gaia and this nightmare.

"We need to take care of your eyes…I don't know if the damage will be permanent until we get topside and I can take a look with the proper equipment."

Dez slumps against the hard, red wall, pieces of dry rubble earth spilling to the ground at her back. Zoe stoops next to her and grips her arms.

"Listen…I'm gonna stay with you, all right? Your brother is a big growling thing down here all on his own, and these two frogs are gonna be just fine without me bossing them up and down these tunnels, wise? But we gotta make some moves now, and so do they."

Dez looks up at Zoe and blinks back her tears. In the small fire Zoe holds at her chest, I can see that the black under and around Dez's eyes is almost completely gone. She nods quickly, then starts crying heavy, silent sobs. Her head falls against Zoe's shoulder as she helps her get to her feet. Zoe smooths Dez's long blonde hair. The ache in my chest turns hot and sinks into my stomach. We need to get out of here.

Zoe walks Dez over to Jack, who puts his arm around her and starts telling her something while Zoe turns back to Dell and Cal.

"I'll tell Veece..." Cal starts, then trails off. Zoe's eyes fill with tears, but she violently blinks them back and sucks in a hard breath, then clears her throat.

"Don't tell him a thing except he better keep Calliope out of my belongings," she answers with a hard look. "Which includes *him* in that allotment."

Cal smiles and nods, then takes off his tunnel shark tooth necklace and puts it over Zoe's head.

"I want this *back*."

Zoe wipes the tears the instant they touch her cheeks and blinks like she's trying to gain altitude with her eyelashes. She hugs him, slapping his back like they're old military buddies...and I suppose they are.

"That'll be just fine. Gonna get me one of my own anyway," she says through a sniffle. "Go on then."

"Zo...when you get topside..." Dell stops and clears his throat. "If there's time, let my Ma know what happened. Let her know I'm coming back—that we're bringing the others back."

Zoe nods and presses her lips into a line to stop them from quivering as Dell picks her up in a hug, but doesn't let go for a few seconds more after he puts her down. Once he does, she slaps his shoulder, too, and nods again.

"I'll see ya'll soon." She nods adamantly to Cal and Dell, her hands squarely on her hips. "Well, get on! It's a long way back."

They half smile at her, hesitantly disappearing down the bend of the tunnel to our right. Dez throws her arms around Zoe as her composure cracks, and she buries her face in Dez's hair.

CHAPTER 20
Dustbowl
Jazz

Everything is heavy at first. I let my head fall back against the chair that has moulded to me and remember that this is exactly how I felt in the med-bay after my first port-call with Ms. Plume back at Gaia Sur...when I saw the glitches in my neural channel, the flashing pictures of my dad and Liam trying to help Lyden and Arwyn in the Phase Two labs. I had to tell Arco everything, but there was just no time. I feel like there's no time now, too, but I don't know why.

"It will feel like you're about to fall asleep. Don't worry, that's normal," Calyx says.

"Virtuo-cines don't...do this..." Myra protests, slurring her words.

"They're diluted in a way...flattened, remember? You don't get the potency of the background—er, Platform layer because everything else is added on top of it. It's like you're looking into a bright light through lots of filters," Eco explains.

"So...no filters...?" Fraya asks, nearly asleep. I don't think I can keep my eyes open anymore either.

"No filters," Tark says from somewhere far away. "You'll be wide awake in..."

And that's the last I hear of him. That's the last I hear of any of them back in the Boneyard. I open my eyes, but the sun—*the sun?*—is too bright, so I have to squint. I hold my hand up to shadow them and try to look around.

It's warm, and the air is dusty on my lips and tongue. I close my mouth the second I realize it's open. Old, wooden buildings line a wide, dirt street to my left, and horses are hitched to long wooden beams that are driven into the ground in front of almost every building. Three women in long dresses walk past me and go into a building just ahead. The door has gold lettering painted in an arc near the top when they open it. It says, *Mitchell Textiles*, and underneath, *Est. 1871*.

I look down at my feet, but I can't see them under the long folds of light blue, draping *fabric*, which spills over the beams of the wooden porch that wraps around the length of the building. *I'm wearing a dress?* To my left, a wagon moves past, led by two horses, and music is coming from another building across the street. I spin around, but I don't see anyone from my group. I turn forward again in a hurry and run right into someone.

"I'm sorry, sorry.. I just..." I start, trying to look up to see who it is, but the sun is too bright. All I can see is a big, brown hat and a glare of white until the person steps to the side and blocks the sun. "Arco..." I breathe. He loosens his grip on my arms, which I didn't even notice until now.

"Are you OK?" he asks, and I squint again for a second when the sun glints off the metal corner pieces of his collar in a blinding, momentary flash. His white shirt is pulled tight under a linen vest with two small, black buttons holding it closed in the front. An old-time gun hangs around his hips in a leather holster, which looks to be cut from the same piece as the leather coverings over his brown pants. I'm blinded *again* when he takes a step toward me and catches the sun on the metal tips of his old West boots, which are otherwise dark brown and dusty.

"Crite, you're a giant fish lure!" I say, which makes him laugh.

"Jazz! It's a Western like before the floods. Look at my umbrella!" Myra says, opening and twirling a delicate yellow umbrella that wouldn't stop even one drop of rain. It matches her long yellow dress, which seems to be cut like mine. I grip either side of the fabric around my hips and notice that my hands are covered in lacy white gloves. The sleeves of this dress are the same light blue as the rest of it, and the sudden itching under my chin tells me there must be a lace collar too.

"You look beautiful," Arco says quietly, which startles me enough that I look up at him. The sun shoots out in beams behind his head like he's some kind of holy person, and I can't help but laugh a little. "That's funny?" he asks through a spreading smile.

"No..." I laugh. "I mean, you look like a cowboy Jesus...because, um, with the sun just there, and the..." I trail off and blow out a breath. When I look up at him again, I notice the ragged cut on his cheek is gone, and so is the cut through his bottom lip. His hazel eyes are green and gold just like they were next to the moon pool the first time he kissed me, and I can see one of his light brown curls peeking out under the brim of his wide-billed hat.

"Cowboy Jesus, huh?" he says, raising his eyebrows, then looks to the side with a nod. "Not exactly what I was going for, but all right." He smiles—really smiles like before everything turned into a terrible nightmare.

"What in the actual hell is this pink scourge?" Vox says, the urgency in her voice making me spin around again. She's gripping her dress and making a face like she's just stumbled over a dead seal.

"Is that...a *bonnet*!?" I say before I can stop myself, then cover my mouth with my hands before I flood this entire walkway with laughter. Vox's normally hardline, diamond and arrow tattoos that run down the bridge of her nose seem lighter somehow, and I take a step closer. "And powder. *Stop. The. World.* You look like a girl, Vox Dyer."

"Stow it, sand dollar. I can still gut you like a fish even in...aw crite—" she says, lifting her skirts above her knees to reveal several more layers of white, crinkling fabric.

"Petticoats!" Fraya gasps, and Myra almost explodes with excitement. Vox rolls her eyes and rips the bonnet off her head, but her cornrow burgundy braids are gone, replaced with waves and curls that fall loose and wrap delicately under her ears.

"Wow...you, um, clean up OK," Arco says, raising an eyebrow.

"Yeah. Well you missed your chance, cowboy Jesus," Vox says, not missing a beat. We all laugh.

"Everyone all right? Lyden says, dressed much like Arco, only he doesn't have the same leather coverings over his legs, and his hat is black, like his vest. He's leading a horse behind him. An actual *horse*.

"When can I—" Vox starts, but Lyden holds up a hand.

"We'll have to acquire a wagon…ladies here don't ride horses cross saddle in lovely pink dresses, I'm afraid. Much less dragons."

Vox rolls her eyes and scratches at the lace under her chin.

"I wish Jax could see this," Fraya says, almost to herself as she holds out the front of her long, light green dress. Hers buttons up the front instead of in the back like I assume mine does, then immediately wonder how anyone gets these things on or off. Fraya's hair is pulled to the side in a long braid that spills down her back from under her matching bonnet. My hand flies to my head wondering if I'm wearing one too, and something *bites* me. I pull my hand back and see a drop of blood pooling on the side of my finger.

"Whoa…" Arco says. "Careful. You almost knocked yourself out," he laughs, then straightens what must be a hat on my head. "Pin," he adds, pulling out a long needle with a butterfly on the end of it and showing it to me. I feel my hair fall out of the back of the hat and hit my shoulder blades.

"Thanks," I say, taking the long pin from Arco, though I have absolutely no idea how to put everything back together. "Uh…" I say, looking around, my eyes landing on Vox.

"Like I have the first idea..." she says with absolutely no expression on her face at all. Laughter bubbles in my chest again, and I can't help but let it out.

"You don't need it," Arco says, brushing a loose hair from my face and tucking it behind my ear when I look up. I smile at him, but then he blinks and clears his throat before pulling his hand back and turning to Lyden. "So, we just walk around, or what?" he asks.

"Is anyone hungry?" Lyden points to an old-time inn across the street. "They usually have food at places like that in the Westerns."

None of us have eaten since this morning, but it doesn't seem like it will be real if we eat anything here.

"Wait, if this is all happening in our heads, are we really eating?" Fraya asks, as if on cue.

"If we're under long, they'll give us a protein drip. Don't worry," Lyden says. "Arwyn will be all over that," he adds with a laugh at the ground, but I suddenly get the feeling that something is wrong.

*Don't tweak in here...don't tweak. One step at a time...*I hear in my head, but it's not Vox or Lyden, and these aren't my thoughts. I look back at Myra and Fraya, but neither of them are paying attention to anything except the wrist frills on each other's dresses, not that they could talk to me in my head anyway. Arco is walking with Lyden a few steps ahead of me, so even if he could, which he can't, it wouldn't be him either. Can I hear *their* thoughts now, even though they're not Readers? Is this part of the code evolving?

I look around at the people—the...programs?—that are walking up and down the wooden paths in front of

the shops. No one looks back at me. *Who is this*? I think…
but I don't hear a response. It can't be him. It doesn't
sound like him…*Liddick*?

***

The wooden doors of the inn squeak as they swing open
when we walk through. Men are playing cards and arm
wrestling at tables as Lyden ties the horse he had to one
of the posts outside. *Where are we supposed to get a wagon*?
I wonder. A woman with tightly curled black hair in a
low-cut blouse is behind the counter pushing a towel into
a glass. She sees Lyden, and a wide smile moves over her
face.

"*Hi*, lover," she says, then winks. "What can I get
you?"

"What's the special of the day? Lyden asks, pulling up
a stool to the counter like he does this all the time. The
rest of us do the same.

"Got some fresh duck, red potatoes. I'll even cut you a
slice of my famous peach pie," she adds, leaning in on a
whisper.

"Well, how could I pass that up…" he answers, then
angles his head at the rest of us. The woman's face falls,
and she looks back at Lyden from under a cocked, inky
brow.

"She an injun? In pink there?"

"What about in pink there?" Vox says, getting to her
feet.

Are you split? *Sit down*! I think as hard and as loudly as
I can.

"Looks like an injun to me, Faye," a man from across the room says, slamming the arm of his opponent to the table. Men at the next table lay down their cards and get to their feet.

"She's just powdered up," the first man says. His large belly testing the limits of the buttons on his dark shirt.

"Doesn't look like the rest of the injuns, though, does she?" a short, skinny man says from the end of the counter on the other side of us. My heart starts pounding. We've been in here twelve seconds, and already the whole place is up in arms about us.

"Boys, boys, boys…" Vox says, turning to face the men approaching us from their abandoned card game. They stop and hook their thumbs into their gun holsters. The fat man who was arm wrestling pats his stomach and belches.

"She speaks English too!" he says. "Fellas, we got ourselves an *edgi-micated* injun here! She ain't half bad on the eyes, neither, save that warpaint 'tween her eyes. What kind of injun has eyes like that anyhow?" the fat man laughs. "You some kind of exotic injun, Lily pad? They got names like that don't they, Sam…*Lily pad* and *Running Deer,* or some such?"

"My name is Vox. It means…*Stronger Than Fat Old Men,* in my language," Vox says, unbuttoning the cuff of her silky pink sleeve and holding up her hand at a right angle like she wants to arm wrestle the air right there in front of her. The men *explode* in laughter. Everyone else starts whispering and exchanging money.

"You…heh…lemme…lemme get this straight…" the fat man says, wiping his round, sweaty face, then pulling out a comb to tidy his dark mustache. "You can't weigh more than a wet hen in a bucket, and you think you can pin *me*, injun girl?"

"I said my name is Vox, and it looks like you're the only chicken here."

The entire inn is swallowed in low whistles and voices of shock and awe.

"Vox...we should really..." Fraya starts, but Vox just curls her lip at her.

"Look, we don't want any trouble, all right?" Arco says, stepping in front of Vox.

"Well, son, looks like you found it all the same," the fat man with the dark mustache says, then rolls up his sleeves.

CHAPTER 21
The Air Up There
Liddick

We've been hiking up this stupid slab for hours, and the red-wall tunnel seems to get narrower the higher we climb. Dez can't walk alongside Zoe anymore, so she walks in front of her. I'm glad because at least I can't feel the stabbing of her grief as much with some distance between us. The edge of Zoe's short, red ponytail keeps putting out the licks of red fire that shoot up from the inside of her collar, and I know she's barely holding it together. She might never see the Vishan again…Vita… Veece…none of them who helped raise her after she was pulled under by the tunnel shark like Dell and the others. I try to push this out of my head too. There's no sense trading one girl's pain for another. I have my own problems.

"Are we getting anywhere?" I call up to Jack, who is in front of Dez, Zoe, Azeris and me.

"The air up there should be cooler—it's already lighter here, can you feel it? That means we're getting close."

"And if the sun is up…what's the plan then?" Zoe asks after a minute. "We can't hit daylight."

"I know…I've been thinking about that," Jack says over his shoulder to us again. "If we surface in daylight, we'll just have to wait out the sun at the top of the tunnel. It won't be comfortable, and not exactly safe, but it's the only option until we can strip the Vishan splice from your DNA. I need equipment for that."

"But will that mean we can't go back?" Zoe asks quickly. "I mean, ever?"

"I don't know. That's something we'll have to work out when I have access to equipment again."

"We'll figure something out, Zo. Don't worry," Azeris says.

"You can probably kill the flames now," Jack adds, then rubs his fingers together. "Do you feel that? Dew…"

The air is still heavy, but it actually is cooler now. I feel it chilling the sweat on my upper lip.

"We're almost to the top? We're almost home?" Dez asks.

"Not quite your home…but a lot closer," Zoe says. "A whole lot closer."

We hike another several yards before any of us pull back our fire. I expect everything to go pitch black, but there's actually enough light to make out the general surroundings. I lower my palm, finally, and my shoulder and forearm ache in relief.

"It's daytime. We won't be able to surface yet," Jack sighs, his voice seeming to bounce off the earthen walls now that we have a little more room. He takes a seat, then racks his forearms over his knees and leans toward us. "Listen…we're sitting in a *sack hole*. The tunnel sharks dig these out and lie in wait, then snatch anyone walking by. See those vents?" he says, pointing to a few slits several feet away, which are actually the source of the filtered, dim light.

"Is that…the *sun*?" Zoe asks.

"That's the sun, Zo," Azeris answers, then sucks in a long breath and wraps his arm around her shoulder.

"You said the tunnel sharks lie in wait. So, this hole belongs to one of them. Is that what you're trying to tell us?" I ask. My stomach feels like I swallowed a box of lit matches again at the idea of a tunnel shark racing up from under us, forcing us into the sun where we'll be fried alive, thanks to the Vishan treatments.

Jack nods. "We'll need to keep watch. I'll take the first rotation—we're going to be here the whole day. From the looks of that light, it can't be much past sunrise up there. As soon as the sun goes down, we'll move."

Dez leans into Zoe, and Zoe leans into Azeris. They all close their eyes after a minute, but there's no way I'm going to be able to sleep. Not while we're this close, and this far.

"I can take the first watch. You've been on point this whole time," I say, looking across this hollowed out dirt cave at Jack. He pushes out his bottom lip and subtly shakes his head, just like Jazz does.

"I don't mind. It's my fault you're even here at all. I should have done a better job with the code splicing so you got clearer messages."

My stomach sinks a little remembering all the virtuo-cines where I thought I was losing my mind...the characters that just seemed to be saying things they could only know if they were in my head even when I *wasn't* in a virtuo-cine.

"It's no one's fault except my own. I didn't put the messages from you and Liam together fast enough. If I had, Jax and Jazz never would—" I start, but Jack interrupts me.

"That's not your fault…we're in the home stretch now. We'll catch up to them."

I stare at him for a long time, wondering what it must be like for him to sit there, perfectly capable of popping through the hardened earth hatch just above his head and going home to see his wife and Nann, Jazz's little sister. He's been gone longer than any of us have, except for Zoe.

"You should go back—you should go to the greenbed and find your wife. Tell her you're home," I say before thinking it through, and I know instantly what he'll say. It doesn't change the fact that if it were me…if that were Jazz thinking I was dead, I'd have a hard time sitting here waiting to be dragged miles back through the earth by some freak show tunnel shark, or baked alive on the other side of a five-inch thick dirt hatch.

He looks at me like he knows I just needed the extra ten seconds to come to my senses. It's more complicated than what he wants—than what any of us *want* anymore.

"I can't leave them again, you know…" he finally answers. "I can't put them through thinking I might not come back."

"I know. I'm going to find Jazz. I promise," I say. Jack just offers a half smile and nods at me, then we both watch the sliver of light flicker across the hatch.

***

Before I know what's happening, I'm coughing and flinging forward, choking. I force up whatever flew down my throat and spit. Sand covers my tongue and gets in between my teeth...dirt. *How did I get*—I start to think, and another shower of crumbled earth falls onto my head.

"What happened? I fell asleep...what—are you all right?" Jack asks in a panic. His eyes are wide as he scans everyone.

"It was...just dirt," I croak. "Fell in...my mouth."

"OK...all right..." he says, then takes a deep breath. "All right."

The slit of light in the hatch is dimmer now, but not dark yet. It must be evening.

"Is it dark enough? The sun has to be almost down by now if that's all the light there is," I say, pushing closer to the hatch. I startle when long, spindly roots I hadn't noticed before brush my cheeks.

"No, it has to be completely dark. We can't risk anything less after coming this far," Jack answers. "It shouldn't be much longer."

"How are your eyes?" Zoe asks Dez. She pulls up a low red flame in the palm of her hand and holds it in front of Dez's face. "The black is gone except for some streaks here, but that might just be dirt," Zoe says, wiping the dirt away.

Dez smiles, and in the dim light, her solid bar-wedge of teeth almost looks normal.

"They don't sting anymore, but I'm also not crying," she says, trying to force a smile. A lead weight drops into the pit of my stomach, remembering the antlion...

remembering all of it. "Do you think Cal and Dell found my brother yet?" she adds after a second.

"They've only been looking a little while," Zoe answers. "But if anyone can find him, it's those two."

Dez actually smiles now, and the pressure in my stomach lets up.

"Can you tell where we are?" I ask, trying to squint enough to see through the crevice in the hatch.

"It's been awhile for me, I'm afraid," Jack answers. Azeris makes his way toward us.

"Make a hole," he says, lumbering past me like a dog with no concept of how big he is.

"Crite…I'm right here, man," I say when his shoulder knocks more dirt into my face.

"That's why I said make a hole." Everyone laughs at this, but nothing is funny to me anymore. Azeris peers through the slat just over our head. "Sand here, mostly, but some scrub too. Looks like the marketplace warehouse in the distance—could be the Tinkerer shops, though. It's hard to tell from here."

"Either way, we're close to buildings," Dez says. "We're close to people."

Azeris turns to her abruptly. "Listen, we can't let anyone know you're back, understand. None of us. Bigger things are in the works—Gaia is probably looking for you and Liddick, and definitely Jack. We can't trust anyone in the street."

"How exactly are we supposed to get past anyone looking like this?" I ask, looking down at my torn dive suit, which exactly no one else topside would have seen before. "We're gonna stand out just a little."

Azeris and Jack exchange glances.

"Here," Zoe says, taking off her jacket and cutting the remaining arm of it free with her belt knife. She cuts a clean edge on what's left of the burned off sleeve from when she lost her focus over the ravine the first time we crossed. She hands the leather vest to Dez. "Put this on."

"Good idea," Azeris says, taking off his vest and giving it to me.

"No, you better take this," I say, handing it to Jack, whose white jumpsuit, even though it's dirty, is a lot more conspicuous than my torn black dive suit. Can I borrow that tunnel shark tooth? I ask Zoe when my machete won't cut through the fabric that's already ripped at my shoulders.

I perforate the rest of the way around, then do it again since I still can't rip the sleeve free. I do the same to the other side, and finally, I get them both off and hand them to Jack.

"What are these for?"

"Pull them on over your arms. Then just try to rub some of this dirt into your pants—they're too white," I say.

Jack nods. "Good idea."

All of us help scrape dirt from the walls to cover Jack's pants, but stop after a few minutes when everything around us starts shaking just a little again.

"Tieg!" Dez shouts, but doesn't wait for a reply before she drops the dirt in her hands and starts trying to crawl back down the tunnel.

"Whoa, *whoa*..." Azeris says, catching her arm. "Can't go back down there, sorry."

"Let me go! It's Tieg!" Dez's voice is loud and unhinged as another rumble starts all around us—this one stronger.

"That's not your brother down there," Zoe says, unsheathing her machete. A low, almost inaudible buzzing comes out of the dark, and my blood goes cold. "That's a tunnel shark."

CHAPTER 22
Dustbowl: Part Two
Jazz

Arco and Lyden exchange glances as the fat man finishes rolling up his sleeves and takes a step toward us. The short, skinny man pulls out a table and drags a chair to each side, and people start to gather around it. The fat man keeps walking toward us until Vox stops him in his tracks.

"That pile of money there at your seat should do just fine," she says, looking over at the card table just before she nods and meets the man's small, dark eyes again.

"Come again?" he asks, cocking his greasy head.

"Oh, when I win—I'll just take that pile of money off your hands. You can consider it a down payment for me not spreading the word about how the only thing strong about you is the way you smell," she adds with a small grin. I don't realize I've been holding my breath this whole time until I try to gasp and can't. The tavern explodes in laughter again, and a wash of red splotches the mans thick neck and round face. He starts toward us again, this time with purpose. Lyden and Arco both move at the same time, but Lyden is the one who speaks first.

"Whoa, hey…and if she doesn't win—how about you take that horse out there. Right there; take a look," he says, holding his hands out in front of him and nodding to the doorway where we can see the long neck and head of the huge brown horse at the post. "Saddle and bags and all. All right then?"

"Don't worry horsey; that fat man isn't going to break your back," Vox shouts over everyone toward the door as she takes a seat at the table and plants her elbow in the middle of it. "Well come on," she says, then clucks her tongue at him like a chicken. The man flushes red again, his small, dark eyes flashing like the last coals in a fire. He shoves Lyden out of his way and seethes at Vox as he pulls the chair back so hard he completely lifts it off the ground before he takes a seat.

Is he the Glyph? Her Glyph? Is it saying something to her that we can't hear? What if it's not him? I think toward Lyden.

She's not taking off her glove...I think it will be all right. She can't upload the patch without skin-to-skin contact for at least five seconds, he answers.

"He's going to break her arm!" A woman's voice cries out from somewhere in the back of the room, and after a few seconds, everyone is whispering.

"Injuns don't have regular bones. She'll turn 'em to water or something, don't fret," another man from nearby says in a comforting voice.

She can't get hurt in here, can she? He—I mean, it can't really hurt her, can it? I think again toward Lyden.

This is the Platform layer—there aren't any baselines in place for pain or fear or anything, so there's no off switch. Whatever happens in here will feel just like it's happening in reality.

So, you're saying yes? We have to stop this! She thinks this is all pretend like a regular virtuo-cine!

"We need an official over here! Faye!" the short, skinny man calls to the bartender, who glares at him like she's trying to burn a whole through his long, pock-marked forehead. The woman rolls her eyes and whips the white towel she was using to dry glasses over her shoulder, then lifts the hinged bar and walks toward Vox's table.

"Injun's got marks all up and down her arms too, Danvers. Like maps," the skinny man says, noticing the skin exposed between the cuff of Vox's sleeve and the edge of her glove. "But don't look like them's powdered none," he adds. "Got you some wolf-eyes too, don'cha, injun girl? You turn into a wolf at night, don'cha?"

Vox narrows her eyes and almost whispers.

"You can find out by drooling one more word...then I'll have a reason to come rip your throat out tonight while you sleep," she answers, then growls low in her throat, curling her lip again like she did at Fraya a few minutes ago, and like she did at Sarin when we were in line to get inoculations at the Gaia medical bay. The man flinches, then laughs, but he doesn't say another word. She turns her attention back to the round, ham-handed man across from her.

The man folds his thick fingers around Vox's small, gloved hand, which nearly disappears in his grip. She doesn't show any pain, but I can feel the anxiousness radiating from her.

He's hurting her—he's crushing her hand, I think toward Lyden.

"Look, how about you just keep the horse and we walk out of here…just pretend none of this ever happened?" I say, moving toward the table. Vox glares at me, then lets her eyes soften.

Nice to know you care, sand dollar. Now go take some bets, she thinks. I catch my mouth before it falls open.

The bartender next to the table now takes the white towel from her shoulder and lays it over the man's hand and the tips of Vox's fingers, which are all I can see of hers.

"All righty then, on the count of…*Carboderm's safe ongoing port-cloud resources,*" the woman says.

"What? What did you just say?" I almost shout.

"I *said,* on the count of three, I'll pull the towel back," the bartender says, sneering at me. "Stalling ain't gonna help you, honey," she adds, I turn around and grip Arco's shirt.

"That's not what she said. She said 'Carboderm's safe, ongoing port-cloud resources.' That has to be part of the coded message. She's the Glyph—*my* Glyph!" I whisper.

"One!" the bartender says. Arco nods, then scans the room and swears under his breath as she keeps counting. "Two!"

"OK, listen. I'm going to move behind her and get in her way. With any luck, she'll trip over me and then you can hold onto her arm for five seconds as you help her up. If that doesn't work, you need to be in the wings to try again. Bump into her," Arco says, then nods at me before pushing his way through the now dense crowd.

"Three!" the bartender says, then whips the white towel into the air. Cheers and whistles start in every direction, and it's hard to see what's happening with everyone now on their feet. I weave through the people pushing in around the table, and am not sure if the tightening in my chest is because of everyone closing in, or if it's really coming from Vox.

Are you OK? Vox! I think, but she doesn't reply. Her lips are pressed together, and her arm is bent back so far it's nearly parallel to the floor. My stomach jumps into my throat. *Vox!*

I stop cold in my steps when I see this, and for a split second, Vox's lip curls again. She tilts her head, cracking her neck, and all of a sudden her arm starts to straighten. The fat man doesn't say anything at first, but then he starts pushing air through his teeth.

"Danvers!"

"She's winning!"

"Get'cher hands out—bets are placed!"

The fat man makes a fist with his other hand and holds it in the air like he's going to punch an invisible enemy at his side. His face and neck turn red again like he's slowly coming to a boil, and I suppose in a way, that's exactly what's happening.

"Vox! Crite! She's beating him!" I hear Fraya from somewhere behind me.

"Jazz!" Arco calls, and I remember what I'm supposed to be doing. *The bartender!*

I tear my eyes away from the arm wrestling match and scan for Arco. He's along the back wall about five feet behind the bartender, who is still close enough to the table that trying to approach her now would be too obvious. Arco nods at me and starts moving to the front of the gathered crowd. I nod back and make my way to him, the whole time trying to figure out how to get my hand on the bartender if Arco misses. He said I could try to help her up? But what if she doesn't fall? I could just walk straight over to her and grab her, couldn't I? *This doesn't have to be pretty,* I think.

"Injun…witch!!" the man arm wrestling Vox says, spraying spittle through his teeth with the last word.

"She beat him! Pay up! Pay up!

"Let's go! We need to get out of here," Lyden says, grabbing Vox's arm, but she snakes out of his grip. "Vox!" he yells as she disappears into the crowd. I see flashes of her pink dress just long enough for them to disappear again.

"Jazz!" Arco calls, ripping my attention back to him and the bartender. He's pinned against the wall, his eyes wide. "I can't get there!" he says, pushing forward just to be pinned again by the chaos of people swarming, and now starting to throw punches.

I run toward the bartender, who is heading back toward the bar.

"She witched my hand! I can't move my hand!" the fat man yells.

"Get her!"

"Jazz! Now!" Arco calls, just before someone punches him in the stomach.

"Arco!" I can't see him anymore after he falls, but I stop scanning for him when someone grabs my arms and starts pulling me toward the bar. It's the skinny man with the long, pock-marked face and the greasy dark hair. His breath smells like onions, and his teeth—what's left of them—are yellow and broken. He laughs in my face through a twisted grin, and I don't think. I just raise my knee as hard as I can and hit him in the groin. When he doubles over, I do it again, this time, connecting with his nose. He falls to the ground and is immediately swept away in the flood of people. *The bartender…*I think, then turn frantically back to where I saw her last. My heart sinks into my stomach when I don't see her, but then her thick arm reaches for the neck of a bottle behind the bar. I pull off my gloves and gather up these stupid skirts, then jump over the counter, rushing toward her. I grab her wrist and hold on as tightly as I can, shutting my eyes and counting to five. She starts struggling, but I refuse to loosen my grip. *One…Two…*

Jazwyn! Look out! I hear in my head, and open my eyes just in time to see the bartender raising the bottle she'd grabbed now in her other hand. I catch her other wrist.

"Three! Four! Five!" I shout out loud. She stops struggling and stares at me blankly, like I've just unplugged her. A second later, everyone in the saloon stops fighting. They freeze in place, and I let go of the bartender's wrists.

"What happened?" Fraya calls out from across the room, her arms folded around Myra.

"She found the Glyph. It was the bartender," Lyden says, then blows out a breath.

"Is everyone all right?" Myra says, looking around, but no one else is talking or moving.

*Arco…*I think, then turn to the wall where I saw him last. He looks a little green, but he stands upright and meets my eyes, then nods. I look around for Vox, but don't see her before I hear a whistle from outside.

We rush through the door to find her untying Lyden's horse from the post and tossing a pouch of what sounds like money into one of the saddle bags.

"What happened? How did you do that in there?" I ask, out of breath as the adrenaline hits my veins and makes my whole body shake. She raises a gloved hand and wiggles her fingers.

"Pressure. Took me a while to find the exact point on his meat paw since he was a bloated walrus, but..."

"So you pinched him? That's what took him down?"

"I have a talent for finding the nerve in people, sand dollar," she says with a smirk as she bats her yellow-green snake eyes at me, then turns to Lyden and jerks a thumb at the horse behind her. "So...will the saddle change sizes too if I turn this horse into a dragon right now?"

CHAPTER 23
Higher Ground
Liddick

The rumbling isn't as strong or as violent as it was the last time we faced a tunnel shark, so it must be far away, or it must be something else all together.

"Stay quiet," Zoe whispers, pulling Dez's arm to move away from the black hole tunnel behind us. She points toward the slits of light near the top of the hole we're in. "Get as close as you can to the wall there."

I grip the handle of my machete and nod to Dez like I think the look on my face will actually keep her in place instead of laughing out loud at me, but to my surprise, she nods quickly in compliance. Azeris moves in closely behind me.

"You sure it's a shark?" he whispers to Zoe. "That pincer bug is still roaming around down there somewhere, no?"

"Could be that, but the rumble is sudden, then stops, just like it did a minute ago. Antlions tend to skitter more."

"The antlion is what took Tieg. *Tieg!!*" Dez yells down the tunnel. She starts to yell again, but Jack manages to close his hand over her mouth in time to muffle her.

"Stop...*stop!*" Jack says firmly close to her ear as her screams are muted against his hand, but it's too late. The rumbling gets stronger, louder. More loose dirt falls from the ceiling, and a cloud of dust fills the small hole we're in. I try to swallow several times to keep from coughing, but I can't hold out more than a few seconds. Neither can anyone else.

"We may have to do this blind—just keep your blades up; we have the high ground, and as long as we hold it, we won't need to back up none, wise?" Zoe says all at once.

"Just be still. Everyone just be still. Both the tunnel sharks and the antlions are drawn mostly to movement," Jack says, still holding a hand over Dez's mouth. Her unnatural blue eyes are wide and nearly translucent again as she grips his dirt smeared wrist, her knuckles already white.

The sun must be low now since the light coming through the shaft pushes several feet into the tunnel, making the dust float and dance in the air.

"Ten minutes...we just need to hold up here maybe ten more minutes," Azeris says, apparently noticing the same thing I just did with the light. The tunnel rumbles again, this time louder and more violently, but it doesn't stop like it did before. The pulse in my fingers pounds against my machete handle, but I can't loosen my grip even a little.

"Be still...be still..." Zoe chants under her breath, and based on the flames jumping from the back of her collar again, she's telling herself just as much as she's telling us.

"It's not stopping," I say, looking at Azeris. *One... two...* I hear in my head, but it can't be coming from him. Then suddenly, *Three! Four! Five!* Instinctively, I slash my machete into the dark in front of me, and fall backward when I make contact with something dense. A high-pitched whine like air leaking from a balloon keens just a few feet in front of me.

"No!!" Dez shouts clearly just before light floods our hole, and in it, just for an instant, dozens of round black eyes on an angular field of mud gray flash in front of me. One huge pincer snaps closed inches from my face, and I fall backward just as Zoe lowers her machete faster than I've ever seen her or any of the other Badlanders do it in training. It's suddenly dark again, and all I can hear is more high-pitched squealing in the struggle. Something hot passes over my leg, but all I can think to do is kick and kick and kick until finally, the struggling stops. The burning gets worse, but I can't see anything through the dust, which is red in the backlight of our flames. I cough, displacing some of the dust in front of me.

"Where is she?" Zoe says in a panic.

"She pushed up through the hatch; I tried to catch her leg, but she slipped through...she's topside," Jack says, coughing.

"What?" I ask, squinting hard until I see an antlion body in the distance.

"Dez!" Zoe shouts, and then everything registers.

"No...no..." Jack says, scurrying over to peer through the slit just below the ceiling hatch. "She's not there. I don't see her, but the sun is down. It's just the haze now...she must have run for the trees," he says, scrambling for words.

"We can go...we can go in the haze..." Zoe states more than asks.

"Look out," I say, making my way to the hatch. I take a shallow breath, then push my hand into the air on the other side and wait for the scalding pain to start. It doesn't come. "I'm all right…it doesn't burn," I nod to Jack.

"OK…" he says, then pushes the hatch up, slowly at first to let the light pours in again. I let it hit my arm, then blow out a breath when it still doesn't melt my skin off.

"It's safe. Come on," I say, then climb out of the hole and scan the horizon for Dez.

***

We head for the tree line to our left, the rolling sand going in every other direction until it disappears into the flickering lights of the Fringe quadrant in the distance. I see the Skyboard North mountain wedged far out on the horizon, which means Seaboard North is about halfway between here and there. Intermittent flickers of light arc in a line just about where Seaboard should be, and I know they must be the beach fires of the Fisher clan. *I'm home…*I think, letting myself think it for one second, and then just one more before I turn away from the thought, crumpling up the vision and the feeling like a wad of paper and shoving it down into my stomach.

"This way!" Azeris's calls, snatching my attention back. Branches scrape my face in the soft light, and I don't even know how I got over the rest of the sand to the tree line so fast.

"Where is she? She's not right—she can't be alone up here," Jack says, looking around in every direction.

When we push through the other side of the tree line, a few men with spare part appendages circle a barrel fire on the corner closest to us. The light glints off their metal hand bones and wrist tendons. One of them wears a tool belt that sags at his hips, pulling down his dirty long sleeved shirt, just like the one the Badlanders in the Vishan tunnels wore. *These are their people. I could walk up to anyone here and ask them if they knew Dell…Calliope…*

The cracked pavement gives way to huge dirt potholes, some filled with mud puddles skinned with the rainbow effect of spilled oil. No one looks at us so much as they look through us, and I remember everything about this place now. I could disappear, be invisible, because everyone is a ghost anyway.

"What happened?" Zoe says, but just barely. She's stopped in her steps, her eyes glinting in the firelight with tears.

"It's been six years, Zo. But not everything has changed," Azeris says, and suddenly Zoe blinks several times, then shakes her head.

"We need to find Dez. She won't last a second here."

"Would she really have known to run to the tree line? Has she ever been to the Badlands?"

"No, she's never left the Skyboard mountain," I say, then look hard at Azeris. "Wait…that's where she's heading."

He takes a slow breath and lowers his chin. "We don't have a lot of time." And I know what he's trying to say. What he's trying to make me consider and decide. Like this whole thing is up to me? I'm supposed to choose to go after Dez or push on to his hab to find Jazz? I narrow my eyes at him, but can't think of anything to say. It is my choice…and the rage that rises up like lava in my chest at how *stupid* and irresponsible Dez is almost burns me down from the inside.

"She's not right," Jack says in a quiet voice, as if reading my mind, and I wonder for a second if he actually *can* or if I'm just radiating that much hate. "She's been through a lot, Liddick…she's afraid, and her mind isn't working right."

I blow out a breath, then startle as an old woman cackles so hard she works herself into a coughing fit several feet away. I look straight at her as she adjusts the eyepatch over her dirty face, then pulls the remains of a dark patchwork shawl over her hunched shoulders. She glares at me with her good eye and goes back through the door of her dilapidated brick apartment building.

"I'll find her. I'll meet you back at Azeris's hab before daylight—as long as we're inside, we're all right? As long as we're out of the sun?" I ask. Jack nods.

"Good, then I'll go with you," Zoe says, taking a step toward me, but I hold up a hand.

"No, go home," I say before I realize the impact it probably has on her. She swallows hard a few times before she nods.

"You have about twelve hours before sunrise," Azeris says, gripping my shoulder. "Still know the way to my hab? Got your bearings?"

A fight breaks out across the alley just as I'm about to answer, then ends as quickly as it starts.

"Enough of them," I say. "I'll find the rest."

CHAPTER 24
One Down
Jazz

We all stare for a second, fully expecting Lyden's horse to transform into a dragon right there. Vox rolls her snake eyes at us and snorts.

"I mean, I was just trying to involve you in the process here," she says. "I don't *need* a saddle for a dragon."

I start laughing, but not because anything is particularly funny. I feel hysterical, and my hands won't stop shaking…*is this adrenaline? Shock from the saloon fight, or something else?* I think.

Are you all right? I hear Lyden in my mind and turn to him.

"Now what, then?" I say entirely too loud and entirely too fast.

"OK…right *now*, you get moving before you redline," Lyden answers, scanning my face. "Remember, there are no established thresholds in here. It's like the alpha channels, except instead of just setting the baselines for fear or anger at one time, we have all the emotions at once on the Platform level. No filter—hey…" he says again, this time waving his hand in front of my face.

"I'm all right, just…jumpy, like I had too much caffeine or something," I answer, but I can't keep my eyes fixed on him for more than a few seconds. I turn to Arco, whose eyebrows are drawn together as he looks right back at me—studying me.

"What's happening? What's redlining?" he asks Lyden without looking away.

"She transferred the patch. It can wreck your nervous system for a few minutes because layers of code are stripped from your DNA and loaded onto the Glyph. She's just adjusting," Lyden answers. Myra shakes her head.

"No one said that would happen…no one said our nervous systems would get wrecked," she says.

"It's not permanently wrecked, and it might not even happen, but if it does, it's just like a caffeine buzz, see?" Lyden answers, nodding to me, but Myra's fear has already bloomed, and I can feel it spreading to everyone like water spilled on the floor.

"I'm *fine*," I say, trying hard to keep my voice calm and evenly paced, but it's starting to feel like there are ants crawling under my skin.

"It's normal, and it will pass soon enough. It helps to keep moving," Lyden says, looking over his shoulder, then out at the wide, desert horizon.

"Where are we supposed to go now? Don't we need to reset or some—" I start, but then everything and everyone freezes. The words stop in my throat. I can't move. I can't even *blink*. In a few seconds, everything starts to fade to white until it's blinding, just like when we port-carnate transferred. I try to close my eyes against the glare, but they won't shut. Needle fine pain drills into my eyes and pushes through the back of my skull until I don't think I can take it anymore, and then finally, I close my eyes.

When I open them again, Calyx comes into view—first her almost white hair with dark, erratic streaks, then the sliver cuff ring through the center of her bottom lip, and finally her huge, water blue eyes and cat-like, angular face.

"You did it, Jazwyn," she says, but she sounds miles away. "The first Glyph is patched. Three more to go," she adds, and my stomach churns.

"You can…see us…in there?" Myra asks, mumbling her words.

"Only if we access your channels to read your baselines," Arwyn answers. "Then we can see what you see and measure your emotional thresholds against it."

Like when you were dying, Vox thinks, abruptly, and I feel a jolt of panic as the memory of the tunnel shark attack in the Rush comes flooding back.

"Whoa. Check her cortisol," Liam says to someone, then crosses behind me in a whir. "Never mind, I'll do it."

"A little reckless," Tark says as he walks over to Vox, then turns to face the rest of us. "But you got it done." His giant white smile is bright in contrast against his dark skin.

"Ready to go back in?" Eco asks from somewhere, and I try again to sit up so I can see him. My head pounds with the sudden shift, so I quickly lie back in the chair.

"Jazz should stay here," Arco says from the seat next to mine, and now I force myself to sit up.

"I'm not staying here. I'm *fine*," I say, willing the ants under my skin to stop crawling. To my surprise, they do. A little.

"You're wrecked, and you know it. We can handle the next Glyph. Get your bearings back, and then—" Arco starts, but I cut him off before I realize I'm even talking.

"I have enough of them. I'll find the rest," I say, but the words feel foreign. *What does that even mean? I'll find the rest of my...bearings?* Frustration and anger pulse just under my skin and chase off the ants, but at least the world starts to slow down again. Whatever just happened to me must be wearing off.

"Cortisol is back in range—she's fine," Liam says. I see him just over my shoulder, his sharp profile and blond hair with dark roots making my mind register him as Liddick for a second, and my whole body floods with relief until reality crashes in.

"What's the next cine?" I ask, turning from Arco to Eco.

"Wait, this one?" Eco asks after a second, shoving his clear tablet at Calyx. She glances at it and nods without changing her neutral expression.

"What's the problem?" Ellis crosses to Eco and looks at the tablet. His face falls as he meets my eyes.

"*What?*" I ask impatiently, and the knots in my stomach start to tighten.

"*Blackwater,*" Ellis says in a low, quiet voice. Myra immediately sucks in a sharp breath.

"Pirates..."

***

"Do I *look* like I care about pirates? Crite, if giant mosquitoes, pincer lion whatever bugs, and the bloated whale I just arm wrestled didn't—" Vox starts, but Tark holds up a big hand and stops her words in the air.

"That's fine, Ms. Dyer. This is just for precaution. Now, *please* sit back and close your eyes."

Vox blows out a big breath and lies back on the table in the med bay they've escorted us to, but it's more like a concrete bunker with happened upon medical equipment than an actual med bay. The gurney looks like it's made of iron. The rounded edges of the gurney have a green patina, and there is no padding—just a moulded, semi-formed iron chair that looks like someone took both ends and stretched it into a makeshift bed.

"You feel OK?" Jax whispers through a mouthful of the protein bar they gave us.

"I'm *fine*. None of this is necessary," I answer, but even as I do I can feel the anxiety tightening the back of my throat. *I just don't feel totally…here.*

Maybe you're not, Lyden says in my mind. I close my eyes, still not used to the random trespass through my thoughts, just like Liddick used to do. Now, my chest constricts, too, at the memory.

What are you talking about? I think.

I've been picking up the irregularity too…it's like a sound on the wind that you can't quite make out, but can still hear.

What is it? I ask. *Where is it coming from*?

I think it could be Liddick, Lyden answers, and immediately, I know it's the right answer.

I've been having these random thoughts, saying these things that aren't really my words. Vox used to push me to feel and say things, but it's not quite like that, I say. Lyden nods from across the room, but can't say anything else before Tark startles us both.

"Ms. Ripley!" he calls out too loudly. I turn quickly to him as he extends a hand to the table Vox has vacated at his side, the green patina shimmering. "If you don't mind?"

"Sorry," I say, then clear my throat as I climb onto the iron table and lie back. It's actually very comfortable, which I didn't expect.

"Please close your eyes—this won't take long. We just need to make sure all your wires are still attached," Tark says. I look straight at him, and he quirks a heavy black eyebrow. "Figuratively, Ms. Ripley. Figuratively."

I immediately feel stupid, but push this feeling out with a long exhale. I close my eyes and try to pretend I'm hitting a giant pause button on my life—like for the next five minutes, the whole world is going to stop and wait for me.

A low grade buzz starts in the back of my head, just like the buzz I started hearing when Vox was trying to contact me after she found her way to the Vishan tunnels…just like the buzz I heard the closer we got to her in the Rush.

*Been awhile, man. Thought you forgot about us here in the skids…*the voice in my head trails off, but not before I see a flash of a man in a dirty white, knit shirt. His hair is dark and pulled into a ponytail, and there's a white scar line peeking out from the bottom of an eyepatch. He's older than I am, but not as old as my father...maybe around 25. I gasp, opening my eyes and pulling myself up by gripping the arms of the gurney table.

"What happened?" Arco asks, moving quickly to my side, then turning back to Tark, Calyx, and Eco. Liam holds up a floating screen with green lines and scrolling data columns.

"Her channel...there's a bridge in it for some reason—I can't close it," Liam answers, squinting as he scans the scrolling text.

"Did you see anything just now, Jazwyn? Hear anything?" Arwyn asks, reading the same text next to Liam.

"Um...I heard a man saying *it's been awhile*, and he thought I *forgot about them*. I don't know who *them* is, though," I say as the blood starts pounding behind my ears. I'm suddenly dizzy, so I lie back on the iron gurney.

"Do you know who it was?" Arco asks, moving his hand to my shoulder. I shake my head, which is starting to feel like it's full of water.

"Did you see something too, Jazz? What was it?" Arwyn asks in a voice that seems very far away.

"A man with an eyepatch. He had a dark ponytail...it was night," I say, closing my eyes again. "He had a scar on his face under the patch. I felt like he knew me...like I knew *him*."

"Time stamp on the bridge?" Tark asks.

"It's new," Liam answers. "Within the last 36 hours."

"What bridge? Someone needs to start talking," Arco says, the edge in his voice making me open my eyes again.

"It's all right," Lyden says, his calm voice bringing the tension down a level. "It's nothing that will hurt her—she's just open to more input. Channels are like rooms in our brains, right? Hers just has more doors now than some of the rest of ours."

"What put them there?" Jax asks, narrowing his eyes at Lyden.

No one answers at first, but then Calyx exchanges a glance with Tark, who eventually shrugs.

"Tell them," he says, gesturing to us.

"There was only a small chance this would happen, so we decided not to say anything unless we had to," Calyx starts. "There's no physical danger, first of all…"

"But?" Arco presses.

"*But*…there's the chance of blurring boundaries and getting lost—of not being able to tell the difference between what's actual, and what's happening in the neural channel…so, in the cines, or if you're connected to someone else's channel via a bridge like you just experienced, Jazz."

"So you're saying there's a chance she could lose touch with her own *reality*?" Avis asks, his eyes wide.

"It wouldn't be permanent. We'd never let it go that far," Eco says.

"Whoa, wait…" I say, shaking my head. "So someone is linked into my brain…my *channel* or whatever? Like when Vox and I connected when she had the Vishan NET device? Cal has that now…is it Cal who is linked in?"

"A NET device? A Neural Enhancement Tuner?" Calyx asks. "Did it look like this?" She pulls up a picture of a long, slim, brushed metal bar that forks out into two parallel bars on one end. The picture looks like a letter Y that has been smashed.

"That's it exactly," I say, nodding.

"We haven't used that model in decades…they're micro now and built into the biochips, just like the ones you all just swallowed."

"If they have biochips, and one of their friends at Phase Two has a NET…" Eco starts, and Liam nods.

"That would be both ends of the bridge."

"So Cal tapped into my channel? I didn't have a biochip, or another NET with Vox, though, and I got into her channel somehow," I say, the heaviness in my head finally clearing.

"Because you were already connected to her," Arco says after a beat. "Just like you're connected to *Liddick*."

CHAPTER 25
The Badlands
Liddick

It feels like I've been gone years instead of months, and I don't remember people looking this old—even the people my age look ten, fifteen years older…tired, like they've been carrying around something heavy for too long. And I guess they have.

I hear chatter and the sound of machinery from Tinkerer Square, which is around the corner. The dirty brick buildings seem to groan in the hard gust of air, which whips between them, cold and irritated, like it's in a hurry to get somewhere. In the distance, patches of sand bleed through the crumbling pavement, which is waiting to grab your foot and send you face first into the broken ground. I shove my hands into my pockets and raise my shoulders against the wind, but I won't look down. You can't take your eyes off the world here.

"Well….look who's back from the dead," a man's voice says to me as I round the corner. I stop in my tracks and turn to him.

"Eddie…" I force a casual laugh, surprised to see literally the *last* person in the Badlands I'd want to see. "How have you been?" I ask, though I don't really care. He scratches the white scar line underneath his eyepatch and nods, making his greasy black ponytail sway behind his head.

"I can always complain," he answers, smacking his teeth against his lips, making that suction sound he knows I can't stand. I try to keep the disgust off my face.

"Listen, have you seen a blonde girl around here in the last hour? GE eyes—wild ice blue?" I ask, but he just looks at me like I'm stupid, then laughs.

"Now why would anyone with wild ice blue GE eyes wander down here all the way from the hill?" he asks, narrowing his good eye at me and raising his chin.

"I didn't say she was from the hill."

"Didn't have to. Guess it's been awhile, man. Thought you forgot about us here in the skids."

"Yeah, I've been…away. So you haven't seen her then?"

"Naw, man. But I'll keep an eye out." Eddie points to his one good eye and smirks, then claps his teeth together like Azeris did when he wanted to put Tieg in his place back at the Gaia Sur port-call hub. "You in the market for …anything?"

"Not tonight, Eddie. But I know where to go if I am," I answer, nodding to him.

"Bet you do. Bet you do…"

"If you see my friend—and she is *my friend*—cover her up, her hair, all right? Keep her out of traffic."

"You know I've got you," Eddie says, offering me a dirty hand, which is shaking more than ever. I take it and hold it in place.

"Thought you were quitting Extract," I say, lowering my voice.

"I did!" I give him a deadpan look. "All right, all right..." he tries to laugh. "I'm in a ten-step program; maybe I'm just on step one," he laughs again and sniffs.

"Grisham still running things?"

Eddie nods and sniffs again, then wipes his nose with the back of his hand.

"Naw. Grisham...stepped down. It's Tariff's neighborhood now."

"*Tarriff*? Who let *that* happen?" I almost yell, but catch my voice just in time.

"Business, you know? He had the credits, the pull with the State. Riot drones are even programed to cruise right by him now. He's a ghost."

I press my lips together as words come flying up and crash into the back of my teeth. At least Grisham wasn't just in the tech racket for himself. At least he took care of people here.

"Where's Grisham now?" I ask.

"Around..."

"*Where* is he? I don't have a lot of time."

"Zone, Cred-Fed..."

"Call me that again."

Eddie makes a low whistle and laughs, slaps me on the arm a few times, then nearly falls into me, the nauseatingly sweet smell of rotten oranges closing down my lungs.

"Zone...zone..."

"Man, you *reek* of Extract. Patrol droids are going to smell you any minute," I say, unhinging his fingers from what's left of my dive suit. He just laughs. "Remember what I said about the blonde girl. Cover her up, then take her to Azeris. He'll keep her safe until I get back," I add, then start to walk away.

"Hey!" Eddie calls after me. "You want to catch up with Grisham...go to the Southside. Circuit Street—look for the hole in the sky."

"The wh—?" I start, but Eddie has already been swept up in a group of laughing people coming out of the alley behind him. I take a deep breath and swallow my question, but I have to force it down. This place has gone to hell, and it was *already* hell.

Tinkerer Square smells like dirt and oil mixed with the normal sulphur smell of the air, which is concentrated here. At least in Seaboard North, the breeze coming off the ocean diluted it a little. My chest starts to tighten like it always does when I come to the Badlands, and I can't help but feel like this place is trying to get inside me. I need to find Grisham—Azeris's old partner—and get him to scan the blocks to find Dez. There's no way I can cover them all before dawn. I need to tell him what's happening with Gaia Sur too...that everything we suspected was true.

Tinkerer Square isn't as busy as it is during the day, but it's never deserted. People work around the clock in the Badlands. I keep my chin up and narrow my eyes, scanning for faces I recognize. A sweaty older man fires a blowtorch to life as I pass, and it's all I can do not to jump at the sudden flash of light and heat just a few feet away from me. How did I get this soft in just a few months, and after everything we've been through? The Badlands are nothing compared to the biomes.

"Liddick Wright...can it even be?" a female voice says from somewhere in the swath of Tinkerer bays. I look around for a face to match it. Then I see her. *Hell...*

"Hi, Farah," I say, trying to keep my voice neutral. "Listen, I..."

"I don't care where you've been," she says, dropping the wrench she's gripping into her pants pocket, then pulling her long, dark hair off her neck and tying it in a knot behind her head. Her denim shirt is tied around her ribs, and it makes me think of Calliope back in the Vishan Tunnels. I bet Farah knew her. "What brings you back?"

"A friend of mine wandered in—probably lost. It's no place for her," I say, and wait for the icepick stare to hit me between the eyes.

"*Her?*" Farah smiles to one side and raises an inky black eyebrow at me. She takes the wrench from her pocket. *Here we go.*

"It's not like that," I say. "She's got some problems...in her head, you know? I'm just looking out for her."

Farah nods and blinks her huge brown eyes at me. They're the same color as Jazz's, and I feel a stab through the center of my chest at the thought of it. She pulls at the collar of my wrecked dive suit.

"*What* are you wearing?"

"Long story," I answer. "Is your brother around?"

Farah snorts. "That lazy skod? He's been asleep for hours. What'cha want with him? He owe you some credits?"

"No," I say, scanning the rest of the bays for anyone else who would know how to find Grisham. "I just need to find a mutual friend of ours." I clear my throat and take her hand, then kiss the back of it. "Do me a favor, beautiful?"

She takes a step closer to me and breathes in my face.

"For you? I'll think about it…" she says, angling her chin up at me and lowering her eyelids to half mast. *Crite…I don't have time for this.*

I lean in and whisper close to her mouth. "If you see a blonde Cloudy wandering around here looking as lost as…well, a Cloudy in Tinkerer Square…" I let my bottom lip brush hers, and her eyelids close the rest of the way. "Take her to Azeris for me, all right?

I take a step back from Farah and kiss her hand again. She opens her eyes, then smiles, and for a second, I'm not sure if she's going to tear what's left of my clothes off, or just beat my brains out with her wrench. I feel the itch of sparks crackling in my hands, then race up the back of my neck, so I suck in a deep breath to cool them out. Lighting up *now* would be a bad idea.

"Where you heading in such a hurry?" she asks in a low voice and takes a few steps toward me, her wrench in hand.

"Told you, I need to find your brother. It's important," I say. "Can you do that favor for me, beautiful?"

"So long as you promise you'll be around to make it worth my while. Wrangling a Cloudy girl ain't exactly on my to-do list for the evening, wise?"

"Have I ever let you down?" I say, grinning. Farah opens her mouth instantly in what I know will be no end of examples, so I close the distance between us and kiss her to stop the flow before it starts. She presses her wrench against the back of my neck and pulls on either end, crushing my mouth against hers. Pins and needles start in the palms of my hands, and I ball them into fists against her hips to stop the feeling, then push back from her. She laughs at me.

"More where that came from if you make it back before I change my mind," Farah says. I cock an eyebrow at her and start to ask her if she remembers what I asked her to do, but she cuts me off. "And yes, I'll leash your Cloudy for you, crite...get then. I'll tell my brother you asked after him."

"Thanks, Farah. I owe you one."

"More like ten," she says with another snort, then blows me a kiss off her grease-streaked hand.

"No doubt," I add, then watch her walk back to the dark pod of bays in the makeshift scrap metal shelter.

I get about ten steps in the opposite direction, then hear my last name shouted behind me.

"Wright! Hang back!" I turn around expecting someone far away, but Finn Winter, Farah's brother, has already closed the distance between us.

His black hair is combed straight back from his forehead, which makes his thick dark brows and round, brown eyes stand out.

"Finn! Man, I was looking for you."

"Where ya been? A lot's gone down since you whiffed," he says, looking over his shoulder at his sister. He grabs my elbow and starts walking with me.

"Finn! I'm not trying to take your shift!" Farah calls after us.

"I won't be long! I'll cover you later!" Finn yells back to her, but it's lost in a litany of swear words coming from their bay. He turns back to me and laughs. "She's gonna kill me."

"Well tell me what's been going down before she does. I need to find Grisham."

"That's the last place you want to go," Finn says, looking at me like my hair is on fire. I push my hand through it without thinking just to make sure.

"Why? I need his help to find a friend, and I need to do it before dawn."

Finn shakes his head. "Tarriff took over his game. Grisham's in exile now."

"On the Southside, I heard. What's *the hole in the sky*?"

"Who told you that?" Finn asks, giving me a side eye as we walk past more crumbling brick buildings and people puffing on Extract, which makes the air noxious with the smell of spoiled oranges every several feet.

"Crite, is everyone lighting up now?" I cough and pull the collar of my wrecked dive suit over my nose and mouth."

"Since Tarriff took over, yeah, pretty much. Who told you about the hole in the sky?"

"Eddie, why?"

"Ears..." Finn spins his finger in the air close to his chest, trying to hide the gesture. "Follow me."

CHAPTER 26
Blackwater
Jazz

Arco's wall of ice goes up again, but there's nothing I can do about it. Not here, and not now. He doesn't believe it's not my fault that I'm connected to Liddick. He doesn't believe it's nothing personal...but I also know the only reason he doesn't believe any of that is because at this point, if I'm honest, maybe I don't even know myself. *Could Liddick really be the one tapping into my channel? Who was the man with the eyepatch?*

It's going to get heavier, more confusing, the deeper you go into the Grid, Lyden thinks, but I don't answer him as we make our way back to the circle of consoles around the virtuo-cine chairs and the column of colored Grid layers. The Platform layer at the bottom looks like a dark, churning sea that is so real I half expect it to splash over the edge of the base. Strips of color shoot upward, then bleed into a thick blend of bands that range from black to purple to yellow to white, and everything in between.

"Pirate ships, baby!" Avis says, vibrating with excitement as we move past the white consoles and take our seats again around the undulating color column.

"We tweaked their codes in the med bay—two-second delay for adrenaline and cortisol. That should prevent the freeze in pulling them out next time," Liam says. Eco nods, but he's not happy about something.

"What's the problem?" Arco asks him abruptly, and I stare for a second wondering if his latency Empath receiver ability is getting stronger. Eco looks at him like a machine, expressionless as the white lights over his cheekbones start to flash red and blue every few seconds like flames that are trying to catch.

"The code evolved again while you were all getting your diapers changed," he says. Jax puts his forearm in Arco's chest to keep him in place.

"You're welcome to load all these patches into the Glyphs yourself," Arco says through his teeth.

"Happy to. We'd be done by now and wouldn't have to worry about World War Four breaking out against the three organizations that just *happen* to sustain life as we know it right now," Eco says, looking away like he's bored.

"Enough," Tark sighs, then turns to Arco. "You're the only ones who can see the incarnation of the original message Jack embedded, which happens to have The Seam's message on the flipside. It's designed to reach Empaths, not Alpha Channel testers," he adds, glancing back at Eco in admonishment.

"Let's just get this over with. One down, right? Three to go?" Arco asks, walking through Jax's arm and climbing into his virtuo-cine uplink chair.

Calyx nods. "Jazz, if you hear or see anything... *internally* again, just try not to panic. We'll be monitoring, and the best thing you can do is wait for it to pass, all right?"

"Why is it even happening?" I ask. "Why now? Just because I swallowed the biochip, so it's working like the NET?"

"That's the only explanation that makes sense...and if you're getting messages that clearly, it must mean that whoever is on the other end of them is getting closer."

I nod, reenergized. My dad, Liddick, everyone... maybe they really are getting closer. I look over at Arco expecting to see the same enthusiasm, but he's studying the ceiling, the muscles flexing in his jaw with all the words he's not saying. Immediately, the excitement of a second ago crashes into the hard concrete floor. Does he actually think I have any choice in this with hearing Liddick? That I can just announce *hey, anyone who's coming into my head without my permission, you can stop now, I'm good!*

He doesn't understand. He knows how he feels, but he doesn't know why...he doesn't like that you're connected to Liddick, but he knows it's not your fault, Lyden thinks... speaking of people coming into my head without permission.

I don't care. I can't control what Arco thinks. I can't even control what I think lately.

Yes, you can. It's not going to be easy, but you're not alone. I'll try to run interference in there if Liddick taps into your channel again.

I nod as Calyx starts counting down. "All right, we're dropping you about a third of the way through the storyline. That's where the algorithm predicted it would be most likely to encounter the Glyph. Ready for upload in five...four...three...two...."

I don't hear the last number over the rush of the ocean and something creaking close by. Everything is blindingly white at first, but then I start to make out dark shapes—long lines and blocks that come into focus. Voices emerge over the sound of the sea, but I can't understand the words they're saying for several more seconds. I feel a hand grip my arm, and that's when everything snaps into focus.

"Are you all right?" Arco says, holding onto me a little too hard. I twist to loosen his grip.

"I'm OK; are you?"

"Yeah, stay close to me, all right?" he says as the wooden ground under our feet shifts upward, causing me to stumble into him. He catches me and reaches for the railing at our side to steady us both, and his eyes go wide, flickering in the sun. "For once you listen to me," he says around a smile, which makes heat rush into my cheeks even with the cool sea spray misting everything.

"Arco, I—" I don't even know what I planned to say… something like *it's not my fault,* or *you have the wrong idea about this connection I have to Liddick,* but none of those words come out. He stares at me, waiting, and I have no choice but to shake my head, dismissing everything. His face slips from warm and anticipatory to neutral again, distant, safe behind his wall, and I take a deep breath to fill the empty space spreading in my chest now.

"No! Let go!" Myra suddenly yells from somewhere. Arco spins around, but neither of us see her right away. A tall man with a long white shirt and a black scarf tied around his head is trying to drag her away from the railing, but she won't release it.

"Hey!" Arco yells across the deck, and Lyden is already running toward them.

"Put her down!" Arco yells again, then takes off running too, but he doesn't reach them before Vox rushes over to the man and kicks his kneecap as hard as she can. The man lets go of Myra immediately and collapses to the floor.

"You're everywhere there's trouble, aren't you?" Lyden laughs, gathering Myra into his arms while Fraya rushes over.

Vox shrugs. "It's what I do."

"Is everyone all right," I ask, running over to them and looking specifically at Myra until she nods. "OK, so we're on a pirate ship now?"

I scan the horizon in every direction, but there's no land to be found, just endless, churning black water.

"Stowaways!" the man who grabbed Myra yells, which summons about ten other men toward us. Two finish climbing down from the ropes dangling from the enormous sails, then the others make their way to us from different sides of the deck. They're all dressed in the same loose, lightly colored shirts and tight, dark pants, some of which are tied off around the shins while others are just ripped and tattered on the edges. "Brazen as daylight too, just standing starboard!"

"We're not stowaways!" Myra's voice cracks at the man with the scarf.

"Then what are ye?" another man asks, this one short and tanned with no hair at all, I notice, when he pushes his scarf back from his forehead to wipe off the sweat, then pulls the whole thing down around his neck.

"We're…" Lyden starts, but then seems to freeze. He pushes both hands through his dark hair and pulls in a deep breath. Why is he suddenly so afraid? His anxiety grows and spreads to the point that my own chest starts to tighten with it.

What's wrong? Breathe. This is a cine, remember? I think toward him, and my chest relaxes a little.

*It's all the water…*he finally thinks. *It was just a flashback; I felt the itch starting—the itch that means the gills they put in me are opening.*

I don't know what to say for several seconds. What advice or comfort could I *possibly* give him to help him relax. I have no idea what it must be like to have actual genetically modified gills, let alone all the trauma of nearly drowning as they tested them out over and over again. I stop trying to think of what to say and instead, start trying to feel…to imagine. I'm terrified.

It's all right, you're not alone, I think because it's the first thing that comes to mind, but also, because I think I'm halfway saying it to myself.

Lyden nods, then takes in another deep breath and blows it out like he's getting ready to run a race.

"Listen, we'll work for our passage, all right? We didn't mean to stowaway; we just…got lost," he says, but the angry looking men don't seem appeased.

"Are any of you sick!?" Fraya shouts above all the grumbling of the men gathering more and more closely around us. They stop advancing and look around for her. She steps forward from the rail where Arco and I were just standing, stumbling to keep her footing for a second as the boards under our feet angle upward, then level out again with the rolling sea. "I'm a doctor—if any of you are sick, I can help you," Fraya says again, lifting a black bag at her side. *Where did she get that?*

"Bring her to Royce! Make a hole!" a man in the distance yells.

"Make a hole for the cap'n!"

Another man, this one very dark skinned and thin walks quietly up to Fraya and grips her arm. He doesn't seem hostile at all, but I see the wince on Fraya's face when his fingers close just above her elbow.

"I'm going with her!" I say, taking several steps toward them both. Arco moves quickly in my wake, but before I can tell him to stop, two other men grip his arms and hold him in place. He struggles against them, which only makes them more irate.

"It's OK! Stay here and keep *watch*," I say, thinking of the Glyph that has to be here somewhere, and wishing for once that Arco could hear my thoughts like Liddick, Vox, and Lyden can.

"Royce is your captain?" Fraya asks, shifting the loop handles of the black bag around her forearm and tying off her long, auburn hair in a knot at the nape of her neck as we walk. I look back at Arco one more time and nod. *He understood what I meant about keeping watch…good.*

The tall, skinny man still holding Fraya's arm looks down at me and suddenly grabs mine, too. Instinctively I pull back, but his bony fingers are like a vice.

I close my eyes for a second and make myself take a breath—*stop tweaking…it's just a cine…*I think, grateful that Arco didn't see the miniature struggle.

I look up at the man, whose irises are actually nearly black. I nod once, and he pulls us toward a narrow doorway. Once we get close enough, it opens on its own, but nothing is on the other side except endless dark and the sloshing of water, which seems magnified now.

"Scale de rope," the man says with a thick accent I don't recognize. He motions to the right side of the door opening with his hand like he wants us to get out of the way. When we cross, he rolls his eyes, making the black irises disappear completely so all I see are his bulging white eyeballs against his nearly black skin. "De rope! It's right dare!" he says again, pointing to the upper right corner of the doorway.

"What does he want us to do with the rope?" Fraya whispers to me.

"Take it! *Scale* de rope!"

"He wants us to get the rope, I think. It must be hanging just inside the door..." I say, then close the distance between the door and where I'm standing.

On the inside of the frame, I feel the sharp fibers of the thick rope as I pull it out.

"This?" I ask, holding it up.

"Yes. Dat. Scale now," the man says, and the breath I've just taken stops hard and cold in my throat. I cough until I restore my composure.

"Sorry, what?"

"Scale! *Descend.* Now!" the man answers.

"You want us to lower ourselves *literally,* on this rope? Into...the water down there? How is there even water down there?" I ask, feeling myself start to stammer, so I bite my inner lip.

"*Descend,*" the man says through his teeth this time. "De cap'n down dare."

CHAPTER 27
Southside
Liddick

Finn's dark eyes narrow just enough that I know not to ask questions—not here. I nod, and we walk on in silence until we get to the edge of Tinkerer Square. The dark pavement with the occasional sand bleed showing through gives way to *mostly* sand with a few patches of dark pavement. The Southside is the most decrepit part of the Badlands. The faded spray paint on the cement block buildings is crumbled away in places, leaving incomplete art and writing. It looks like someone splashed gray paint over the graffiti, and any second another splash will come to wash away the rest of the tagging. The street lamps spill daylight into the darkened alleys, but I know better than to look down any of them. The last thing I need right now is to be followed by some tweaker.

"All right—we're past the noise now," Finn says, letting out a heavy breath.

"What happened to this place?"

"Tarriff, man. He drove Grisham out about a month ago. Wired everything from Tinkerer Square to the edge of the Southside to keep heat on the street. Eyes. Ears…"

"But why? We were starting to fix this place," I say, looking over my shoulder to make sure we're not being followed by anyone in the alleys we've just passed.

"Power. Tarriff came into some credits recently. Got himself some new GE teeth just like the Cloudies, and suddenly, Extract is all over the street. Grisham thinks someone is supplying him, and he's funneling the coin somewhere, after his kickback, of course. Nobody can process milkweed at the rate he's putting it out there."

"Is Grisham trying to fix this?"

"He's locked down, man, but at least he's got people out there reporting back," Finn answers after a long pause.

"And you're one of them, aren't you?"

Finn shrugs. "You caught that sub to Gaia just in time, Wright. Though, I gotta say I'm glad to see you. Would be nice to get back to work putting things right around here again."

"What about the old crew?"

"Still here, but since Grisham was cut loose from his contacts, they've gone dark."

I shake my head. "We'll put all this right. What did Grisham do anyway?"

"Double dipped, man. He was working on a hack for The Seam, but then threaded his own port-network through it. They cut him off after that…something about him putting them at risk."

"Well yeah. Not like him to be so sloppy. What was he thinking?"

"Power, man," Finn shrugs. "It got to him I guess."

I blow out a breath. Nothing is how I left it here. "I need his help to find a friend. She had to wander out this way from…Skyboard."

Finn shoots me a wide look. "You let a *Cloudy* out of your sight around here? And a *girl* Cloudy?"

"Don't hotwire me, man, I know," I say, watching the dirt blow across what's left of the pavement in the distance. "That's why I need Grisham's grids, all right? I need to find her before morning."

He narrows his eyes at me this time, but I shake my head so he doesn't ask me anything else.

"Well, I don't know if he can help you. Tarriff took most of Grisham's gear and reprogrammed it. Nobody cares about spying on the sky anymore."

"That's the one place they should be watching," I say under my breath as we pass more decrepit buildings, then shake my head to deflect any of Finn's questions. "So, where are we going?"

The occasional patch of dark pavement has been replaced by puddles of water in the sand, so I slow down and start watching my step.

"Yeah, man, you have to eyeball for swallows like that in the sand out here," Finn says, noticing me shift. "They're worse during high tide. So, like, right now," he adds, then cocks his smudge of an eyebrow at me and chuckles. "This is basically the worst time we could be going to the hole in the sky."

I look up and see nothing but the gray haze that always covers the sky—always except for that night I climbed the dune with Jazz and saw the stars for the first time in I don't even know how long. I should have said something about them instead of telling her about my stupid scar…instead of that whole stupid situation with Liam. Maybe she wouldn't be in this mess if I had.

I step in a puddle and feel the earth inside it wrap around my foot, then my ankle, trying to pull me into it. I jump before I think about it, seeing a tunnel shark gripping my leg in my mind instead of just wet sand being displaced.

"Whoa! It ain't gonna eat you, Wright," Finn laughs, gripping my forearm to steady me as I kick my leg free. *If you only knew, man. If you only knew,* I think.

"Yeah...I'm just pressed. I need to find my friend," I say, finally pulling free from the quicksand hole. We round the corner before Finn can say anything else.

The alley is narrow, and there's nothing at the end of it except a shadow between the buildings, about halfway up. I squint, and realize it's actually a building, *what*? I stop walking.

"The hole in the sky," Finn says, nodding at me. "The base is glass. At night it looks like a hole in the sky because the dark part of the build—"

"I get it, I get it..." I say, waving off the rest of his obvious explanation. "Grisham is up there?"

"That's about the only place he can go anymore. Eyes and ears everywhere else just waiting for him to breathe the wrong way."

"How do we get up there?"

"We don't. Someone will come in a minute—they're watching too."

On cue, two men come out of the shadows and make their way to us, both of them with their hands wrapped around the same kind of white baton the guards in the Phase Two Gaia facility had. My adrenaline spikes with the memory, and the palms of my hands start to prickle and itch. *No…no…no….I can't flame out up here.* I ball my hands into fists and clear my throat.

"Finn," one of the men says. I can't see more than his dirty face in the shadow of his dark hooded shirt. His hand is shoved inside the zipper over his chest, but he takes it out and lets it fall to his side. "Who's this?"

"Man, *Liddick Wright*," Finn says.

"The Cred-Fed?" the other man asks, pushing his hood down. His hair is dark and greasy, pulled away from his face in a pony tail like Finn's. I glare at him.

"Just tell Grisham I'm here. I need his help," I say.

"Thought you caught a golden sub and went off to be a demigod like your brothers," the first man says, pushing his hood back now too. He's older, maybe as old as Azeris, and significantly less greasy than his partner, though his huge nose looks like it's been broken a few times, and his teeth are chipped and brown…the ones that are left, anyway. But still, there's something about his eyes …he looks familiar. Then it hits me.

"*Grisham?*" I ask, and the corner of the man's mouth pulls to a smirk.

"Follow us," he says, putting his hood back up as he and his skinny sidekick lead us back into the shadows. We stop right in the middle of one of the buildings, about twenty feet from the glass tower holding up what looks like a single room. I look over at Finn for answers, and he nods at me.

"It's all right. Just keep going," he says, then takes a few steps forward after the two men, who walk directly through the concrete blocks. *Just like the walls of Phase*

*Two…*I think, wondering why I didn't feel the buzz of the energy field like I did there.

On the other side of the wall is a set of stairs, then another. At the top is another solid concrete wall, which we also walk through. On the other side of this is a half destroyed room with several floating grid screens, some with scrolling blue text, and what looks like the beginnings of a few different kinds of transfer hubs with various parts strewn around. Lights hover in the air a few feet below the ceiling, and there are no windows.

"Good to see you," the older man says, pushing his hood down again and then waving his hand over his face. The nose I saw a second ago shrinks and straightens, the mouth widens, and the destroyed teeth morph into a solid white bar just like Dez's.

"Grisham! It is you. Why the charade down there?" I ask.

"A lot has changed around here," Grisham says as the other man throws off his hood and falls into a wrecked couch behind the half built hubs just a few feet from us.

"I told him about Tarriff…about the Extract," Finn says like a confession, but Grisham waves him off with a nod.

"Of course, of course," Grisham says, walking behind one of the floating green grid screens and tapping something into it. "Last I heard, you were living the dream on the ocean floor," he adds, then looks up at me.

"More like a nightmare. I need your help, Grisham— Azeris is here with me. He's on his way to his hab, but I have a Cloudy friend who is lost somewhere out here. I need to find her before the sun comes up."

Grisham narrows his eyes and laughs out loud, shakes his head at me, then goes back to examining the screen. He taps a few more things, then moves to the screen next to it and reads the sudden deluge of scrolling text.

"*Now* this makes sense," he says as the text starts rolling so fast I can't see the individual lines anymore. "About an hour…that's how long you've been topside?"

"Yeah, how did you know that?"

"Time stamps…clocked you and four others crawling out of the swallow field," he says, gesturing to text that comes and goes, then looks at me. "You crawled up through those from the *ocean floor*?"

"Grisham, that's a long story that I'm happy to tell you, but I need your help finding one of the people who came up with me first—she's…from *Skyboard*," I say, catching the word *Cloudy* before it comes out of my mouth as I see Grisham's bar wedge of teeth scraping his bottom lip like he always does when he's thinking.

"All right, all right. But if it's so urgent, why didn't you just go to Azeris's hab? Why come find me here in this…paradise?" Grisham laughs, pushing his graying curls out of his eyes. For a second I can imagine him in his prime, when he worked with Azeris in the virtuo-cine spec-check facility at Skyboard North—before they moved the whole operation to Admin City about twenty years ago. Now, though, he's a tech scavenger like the rest of the Tinkerers in the Badlands, those slick manners and genetically engineered teeth are all that's left of his high society days.

"You're the only one who can help me, Grisham. I need to find her before daylight and get her back to Azeris's hab," I say, knowing Azeris and Jack need to figure out how to reverse our Vishan treatments, not to mention how to rig a port-carnate link to Admin City. Grisham levels his icy gray eyes at me and smiles.

"And why is that?" he asks slowly, and I get the feeling he already knows the answer. "Matter of life and death, is it?"

I shrug. "It usually is if I ask for your help, isn't it?" I say, but he just keeps staring at me with that stupid grin on his face—the kind that says he loves holding all the cards, no doubt because he hasn't held any since Tarriff took over the port-carnate game around here. "Come on, Grisham. She's from Skyboard—blonde with day-glow blue eyes, man. *Here,* in the Badlands," I say, hoping this will remind him that the world doesn't revolve around him. He takes a seat in a steel chair, then props his feet up on the pile of spare parts.

"OK, Liddick Wright," he says. "For old time's sake, I'll help you find her…and then you'll help me," he adds. I glance at Finn, who seems as clueless as I am.

"Help you do what?" I ask.

"Tarriff has something that belongs to me. I want you and Azeris to get it back."

CHAPTER 28
Blackwater: Part Two
Jazz

I'm the first one to grab the rope, holding onto the knots I now notice. I can hear the splashing of the water below and have no idea if there is a platform or something I'm supposed to lower myself to, or if I'll find the water first. *Why* is there no light?

"You can't expect us to help the captain with no light," I say, stopping on the rope. "We need to see what the problem is, don't we?"

The dark-skinned man with the thick accent narrows his eyes at me and exhales through his nose. He raises his chin to one of the crew in the gathering crowd behind Fraya, then turns his unblinking stare back on me.

After another minute, the crewman returns with a lantern that looks *ancient* with its thin iron handle and oil wick flame. He shoves it at Fraya, then pushes her shoulder in my direction.

"Now you have light. *Descend*," the dark-skinned man says, his voice booming on the last word. I continue lowering myself down the rope as Fraya walks toward me and starts doing the same, hooking the lantern on her belt. The light falls over a square platform about 15 feet down above the water, and I sigh in relief.

"There's a platform above the water! I don't see anything else, though," I say to Fraya, who is still about only halfway down the rope when I get to the end of it. The dark water all around us splashes and laps against the wooden walls of the boat, which makes the lashed boxes and oars and everything else that's tied to the walls float out, then crash back in with a series of random thuds. Fraya drops to my side from the rope just as a huge splash sounds from the other side of the room. She holds up the light after we both jerk our attention toward the sound.

"Hello!" Fraya calls.

"We're here to help you! Captain Royce?" I shout.

"I don't see him," Fraya says, then looks back up through the hole in the ceiling. "Hey! There's no one down here!" she calls upward, then lets out a high-pitched scream.

"What! What's wrong!?" I turn to her, then see the hand wrapped around her ankle. I grab Fraya's arm to keep her from being pulled into the water, but the hand isn't trying to do that—it's just holding on perfectly still.

"I can't...push it...away!" she says, trying to wrench her foot out of the hand's grip, then starts to rear back her other foot to kick it."

"No! Wait," I say, not knowing why kicking the hand seems like a bad idea, but it does—especially when all the fear seems to settle and I almost feel...*comfortable*? "It—he...won't hurt us," I add, straining my focus like I'm trying to hear something far away.

"How do you know?" Fraya asks, her voice steady, but clipped.

"I don't know; it's just a feeling," I answer just as a *head* starts to surface in the water...dark roots at the base of long, blond strands, which give way to dark eyebrows —the left one slashed by a white scar near the outer edge. My heart starts to hammer in my chest. *It can't be…*

But it is. Liddick's blue eyes surface, then stare straight into me.

"Liddick?" I whisper, but when he tries to respond, water just pours from his mouth.

"What?" Fraya says, "Jazz…"

"No more water…" Liddick finally says, and I immediately reach down to him. Fraya grabs my wrist.

"Jazz!"

"It's Liddick! Fraya, help me!"

"That's *not* Liddick, Jazz!"

Immediately, Liddick lets go of Fraya's ankle, then dives back into the water. I fall onto my knees and grip the edge of the platform.

"Liddick! Come back!" I shout to the twenty feet of water spreading out before us. "I'm going after him," I add, then start to get to my feet so I can dive in.

"Stop! You're seeing things—Jazz, that wasn't Liddick! That person was…I don't know, but it wasn't Liddick. Listen to me!" Fraya says, squaring my shoulders and forcing me to look at her.

"I *saw* him, Fraya. I *heard* him. He said, 'no more water…'"

"That's not what I saw or heard. I think whoever it was, Captain Royce, I guess…was dead, and from the look of the sores on his bloated body, he's been dead awhile."

"*What?*" I say, shaking my head at her.

"He floated to our platform, Jazz. Rammed into it with the shifting water…those sores were like what Pitt had from the spores before he died. You were looking *right* at the body."

"No, you answered me when I said he wouldn't hurt us…when he grabbed your ankle…you asked me how I knew," I say.

"Nothing grabbed my ankle. And I asked you that because those sores…that infection is highly contagious. I just tweaked before I remembered that this was only a virtuo-cine."

"No. *No,* I saw him and heard him…we have to help him. That's Liddick, and he's alive, Fraya!"

"If that's what you saw, that dead body must be the glyph. Isn't *no more water* what Liddick said to you back at Gaia after his port-carnate stunt? When you helped him reset his nanites? It's in your mind, Jazz. It's the code talking to you."

I take a deep breath and press the heels of my hands into my eyes. *Stop tweaking…stop tweaking…* I tell myself. *She's right. That had to be the glyph.*

"What's happening!? Are you all right?" Arco calls down to us.

"We're fine!" Fraya answers. "But we need a plank and more rope, or a barrel.

"A *barrel*?" Arco shouts back through the opening in the upper deck just as a splash of water soaks Fraya and me.

"Wha—?" Fraya's eyes go wide as water drips from her face. "What was that…?"

Another splash temporarily blinds us, but then I see a man's bare back surfacing with three flexing gills slamming closed before going back under the water.

"There! You saw that! You saw Liddick's back!" I turn to Fraya, gripping her arms and nearly shaking her off the platform before I shout up through the first deck latch. "What did you do to him!?"

"No! Jazz, listen to me. That was a *shark*! They put us down here with a *shark*!"

"Pull them up!" I hear Arco screaming at someone above deck. "Now!"

"Dey must treat de cap'n!"

"He's already dead! Pull us up!" Fraya shouts, grabbing onto the rope, but it's ripped from her hands. "We *can't* help him!"

"Bring them up!" Arco shouts, but his voice is lost in a sudden crash of other voices and the sounds of struggle. I look around the dark, flooded lower deck for another way out, but none of the stray ropes are long enough to reach the hatch above us.

*We need to get out of here…*I think, then see the back of Liddick's head and shoulders pushing through the water toward us….his gills flexing—gasping in the air.

Jazwyn, stay away from him. It's not Liddick…it's not even the right glyph. Don't let it touch you, Lyden says in my head, which stops my frantic scanning and pulls my attention to the hatch in the ceiling.

What? But it— I start to answer.

Listen, I just got a breakthrough message in my channel from Calyx—just trust me for right now. She wouldn't risk doing that unless it was urgent, he adds just as a rope ladder tumbles down through the hatch. *Climb up—now!*

"Fraya, come on!" I call, and she immediately starts climbing up the rope. I start to follow her, then hear another big splash behind me. Liddick is pushing himself up onto the platform after us, his wet, blond hair falling into his eyes. His teeth are clenched as he closes his hands into fists against the platform and lifts himself out of the water.

"No more water…no more water…" he says through his teeth, the three gills that run the length of each of his sides flaring open, then snapping closed as his chest expands and collapses.

"Liddick! Stop!" I shout down to him as Fraya and I continue scrambling up the rope ladder. He just looks up at me with his brows drawn together like he's in pain.

"There will be no more water-based, nor core-depth risk of suffocation to mankind with this breakthrough," I hear a monotone voice say, but I don't know where it's coming from. Then Liddick's expression twists, like he hears it too. He clenches his teeth again and grabs the ladder rope, shaking it as hard as he can. I lose my grip and feel myself falling, but then am jerked abruptly to a halt.

"Jazz!" Fraya calls down to me. "Hold still, I'm coming! Don't move!" she says, and I notice I'm hanging by my left leg, which is tangled in the rope ladder. I try to sit up as fast as I can, reaching for the ladder, but the pain in my head is suddenly so intense it freezes me in place.

It hurts! I think, shutting my eyes. *Lyden, what's happening!?*

Calyx must be trying to block your neural channel so the code can't track you—stay calm, they're working on it!

Liddick's voice gets louder and louder in my ears, and a pressure starts to build behind my eyes. I squint, and the image of Liddick flickers, then blurs.

"Jazz! I've got you!" Fraya yells, and I feel a hand close over my wrist just before it positions my fingers around one of the rope rungs.

"I can't open my eyes," I say, my eyelids now feeling like they're nailed in place.

"OK, here! Take the rope. Can you pull yourself up?"

"I think so," I answer, feeling for the rope with my other hand too. I find it, then start climbing again.

"We're almost there! Keep climbing!"

Liddick's voice begins to fade as the pain in my head grows, like an icepick drilling into the center of each eye. I squeeze my eyes shut even more tightly, then feel hands close around both of my wrists as they yank upward, hard.

"What's wrong? What happened!?" Arco's voice is close, and I feel hands move over my face. "What's wrong with your eyes? Can you see?"

All I can do is nearly scream in reply with the intensity of the high pitched buzzing now flooding my head.

I hear something faintly over the debilitating sound and force my eyes open. Arco's mouth is moving, but I can't hear his words. He looks at Lyden and says something, then starts talking silently to me. I shake my head and have to close my eyes again.

Liddick! I shout in my mind, but hear only the paralyzing buzz as everything fades to a blinding white.

***

"I tried, but it's getting faster," Calyx says in the distance. I can't open my eyes against the bright light, and when I try to turn my head, nothing happens.

"It's targeting her—we can't send her back in."

"That's exactly why she needs to go back in. Do you want to patch this code or not?"

"It's too risky, Eco. She is not an Alpha Channel tester."

"What…happened?" I manage to say, the words in my throat feeling like they've been rolled in sand.

"Jazz!" Arwyn says as a warm hand folds over mine and a cold circle forms in the center of my forehead. "This won't hurt, just stay still for me for a second, all right?" Arwyn adds.

"There's no breech. I told you she was tough enough…" Mr. Tark says from somewhere.

"What's…" I start to ask, but Arwyn hushes me.

"Shh, don't try to talk yet. It causes too much neural activity, and right now we're trying to keep you off the radar, OK? Just try to relax. We'll explain everything when you wake up," she says, her voice getting quieter and quieter against the distant sound of water lapping against a barrier, and the almost imperceptible whispered echo of *no more water.*

CHAPTER 29
Quid Pro Quo
Liddick

Grisham scrubs his hand over his patchy stubble, then pushes his long gray hair to the side.

"Why does *Azeris* have to help me get what you want from Tarriff?" I ask.

"Because I can't imagine you just shoved my virtuo-cine equipment under your bed at mommy and daddy's before you left for Gaia. That means Azeris has it," Grisham smiles and widens his eyes, waiting for me to contradict him.

"What does Tarriff have that belongs to you in the *virtuo-cines*?"

"My port network—all the neural loading points for the commercial infobits, the subliminal ad ports, all the input sources I've mapped on the Grid," he answers, then pushes over a small metal cylinder with his foot. It falls down the pile of scrap tech equipment, then rolls across the room. "I'm locked out of direct access, so the only way in is through the back door I built in the virtuo-cine network.

"So you've been building another uplink hub to The State's Grid...with *scrap* tech?" I ask, watching the cylinder clang into the far wall. Grisham shrugs and half smiles proudly.

"Can't get equipment through normal channels anymore," Finn says. "And I can't exactly go picking it through underground channels for him with eyes and ears everywhere these days," he adds, which snaps me back to the problem at hand. Dez has no idea the danger she's in, or the danger she will probably bring down on us if I don't find her.

"Grisham, my friend won't know to keep her mouth shut about Azeris and our plans to use his port-carnate hub if Tarriff picks her up."

Grisham's face sobers. He glances up at his assistant and nods. "And why would you be using a port-carnate hub? Crow, bring the speakers," he says. The skinny man slips through a crack in the far wall.

"Because I need to catch up with the rest of my friends in Admin City. We escaped from Gaia…everything we thought they were doing is true. They're experimenting on people, Grisham. Please…"

"Admin City, huh? All right—I'll help you find your friend, but listen to me. The longer Tarriff has my network ports, the more control The State has over everyone else, understand? We have less than a hundred and fifty years topside before this air becomes unbreathable—think they care about us? *Pshhh*," Grisham says.

"We're still on the same side. I know *Gaia* is corrupt, but replacing State propaganda with Seam propaganda didn't work before," I say. "They still took my brothers even when *you* were filtering the feeds. They put *gills* in Lyden, Grisham. We need to hit them with something harder than public service announcements."

He stands and crosses his arms over his chest. "Mr. Wright, I've come to understand your conviction," he says, then starts talking to the ceiling. "These days I'm in favor of a more…direct approach. Let's just say The Seam and I are on the outs; call it a difference of philosophy, but we do still agree that the port-cloud needs to come down. The only way that's going to happen without turning society upside down is if port-carnate becomes mainstream first, but they're taking their sweet time on that agenda," he says, shaking his head. I bite the inside of my cheek to keep from rolling my eyes.

"I don't have time to debate logistics with you right now, but I'm still on board to help you, all right? First, I need you to find my friend before Tarriff does."

Grisham's skinny assistant slinks back through the door with two flat, metal circles, holding them up and tilting them back and forth like he's trying to get them to dry or something.

"Got the speakers," he says, bouncing his eyebrows, then sets the disks on the floor in front of Grisham.

"Load everything from the swallow field to the North sector. Draw coordinates for every GE female under age twenty with a Skyboard bioprint," Grisham says, walking toward the flat disks with his arms still crossed over his chest. Crow, his assistant, sits crosslegged in front of the disks, then starts typing into a hovering green holographic keypad. The second he stops typing, images of different girls walking around, sleeping, or talking with other people start populating the small projected grid field, but then all the images disappear except one—Dez. She's walking past the far edge of Tinkerer Square, past the crumbling outer warehouse buildings toward Skyboard North.

"What's the timestamp on this?" I ask. "She's walking toward *Skyboard*."

"This is live—you'll never catch her, even if you leave right now," Crow says just as the image of Dez disintegrates. "See? She's already out of range."

I pinch the bridge of my nose trying to hold back the pressure building in my head, but it doesn't work.

"She said she's from Sundial City…that has to be where she's going now," I say to the floor, then look up at Grisham. "I need to find her."

"You won't make it. She's been walking at least a few hours, and will be a few hours ahead of you the whole way. You said you'll need to be back to Azeris's hub by daylight?"

"I'll find a quick way to him once I get to Skyboard North. I still know some people there."

Grisham looks at me for a long time, then sighs.

"Crow, bring the rattle trap, would you?"

Crow's face blanches. "But I'm not done building it."

"It's done enough to get him there," Grisham says. "Just going to be a bumpy ride."

He motions for Crow to pass him the holographic keypad, which Crow pushes toward him. Grisham starts typing, and Crow shrugs at me before heading back through the door.

"Well, Mr. Wright…I may have a solution to your problem, but it won't be without hazard," Grisham says as he finishes typing, then nods at his keypad. Crow returns with a flat, circular hub that he can barely reach around and sets it down next to the two disks he used to scan for Dez.

"I don't have the buffers in, and the field isn't stabilized yet," Crow says. Grisham waves him off.

"Like I said, it won't be without hazard."

"Is that a port-carnate hub?" I ask, half hoping it is and half hoping it's not. I haven't seen a hack job like that since the first public service announcements against port-carnate tech came out when I was a kid.

"Almost," Crow says, snorting.

"I need you to enter the Grid and deactivate the firewall around my port-network, then freeze Tarriff's access for about ten minutes. I just need a small window —a little hole in the sky," Grisham says. His eyes flash like the blue in a fresh match, and I can feel his hope ignite in my stomach. *He thinks he can get everything back...that everything can be made right again.* "So, I'll get you to the edge of the hill—do you still have your Skyboard biochip?"

"As far as I know," I say. "Azeris masked it before I went to Gaia so it wouldn't come up as contraband if they scanned us."

"Then I'll get you to the dome checkpoint. Once you're at Skyboard, though, you're on your own. You find your friend and get back to Azeris by whatever means you may still be able to charm for yourself up there, and then you link up with me to download the instructions to restore my port-network. If I don't hear from you in the next 48 hours, I'm putting you wide—your picture, your bioprint, your port-carnate logs...The State will pick you up in a minute and ship you down to Lima. Agreed?" Grisham looks down his long nose at me.

"Agreed. I know what to do once I get to Skyboard—people will help me there. I just need to get there before Dez."

"Are you sure she'll even make it there?" Finn asks. "It's a hike from the perimeter to the edge of the dome. Not to mention the sand traps and strangle bushes."

"Can you help me with that?" I ask. "I'll pay for trackers. You know I'm good for it."

"*Tonight*?" Finn sighs. "I'd have to leave now to stir them up."

"How many can you get?"

"Well, the old crew will come just because you're asking. The new ones, though? The five of them will probably want at least a hundred credits. *Each.*"

"Done. Just get me their networks; I'll get it all transferred."

Finn nods. "All right. I'll send those to Azeris; I'll let him know you lost the Cloudy, too," he smirks, then shoves me.

"Get out of here." I force a laugh, but my stomach twists at the thought of Dez in the Badlands, let alone outside the perimeter. The Fringe are the ones who make those sand traps—the people *Vox* calls Fringe.

Finn smiles, then slaps me on the shoulder. "Stop looking so worried. Let's get back to work."

I nod at him. *We're going to do this. We're going to start fixing everything around here again…if I survive this hacked port-carnate hub,* I think. "Take care of yourself. If you find her, take her to Azeris, all right?" *And thank you.*

Finn nods, then raises two fingers to his forehead and brushes them toward me before disappearing through the door.

"What's that bracelet?" Crow asks, jerking his chin at my wrist cuff. "Can't have any metal in this thing."

"I don't know what it's made of. They put them on us to go to Gaia. It's supposed to have my records on it, but there's more. It's fused to me—I tried to get it off; it just gets tighter."

Grisham crosses to me and grabs my wrist, then taps my bracelet cuff with a wrench. The sound is hollow and lasts a few seconds like the timber of a bell.

"Parmide," he nods. "Can't get this off without a neural disconnect. I can't help you with that—at least not until I get my port-network back and can reinstate my trade channels. Just consider it more incentive to deliver, Mr. Wright.

"I'll deliver. Just make sure you get those instructions ready for download. I'm not going to have a lot of time to wait around once I get to Skyboard."

"Well, you can't go to Skyboard wearing...*that*," he says, eyeing my ripped dive suit. "Crowie, give him that coat."

"But I just printed it!"

"Print another one."

Crow rolls his eyes and throws his long black coat at me, too hard for how close he's standing, and the sleeve whips me in the face. I narrow my eyes at him and press my teeth together to keep what I want to say in my mouth.

"Thanks," I manage, then put on the coat. "So this thing will send me to the Skyboard checkpoint? There's a hub there now?"

"Not *exactly* to the checkpoint. There's a trader post about a quarter-mile from the dome. It's beyond the swallow fields, but you may have a few strangle bushes to negotiate."

I wave him off. "Who's at the post?"

"Ensign," Grisham answers, and the second I hear the name my eyes close in a long blink. I let out all the breath in my lungs.

"Ensign…" I say, shaking my head. "Grisham, he's a complete troglodyte."

"He can collect my credits, and if anyone gets wise, he can keep them quiet. For good. That's all I need out there," Grisham says, grabbing my bracelet again and needling it with a long silver pin. It immediately shrinks around my wrist, hard.

"Ow, crite!" I say, instinctively making a fist, like that will stop the contraction. Surprisingly, it does. "*Whoa…*"

Grisham nods, satisfied with himself. "Definitely parmide," he says. "Don't let anyone from the hill poke around with that. It's government grade; people there will know that, and then you'll have shadows everywhere you go."

"Thanks, let's just get this over with," I say, then step into the center of the ridiculous homemade port-carnate hub, which I see is rusted on the inside. *Great…watch me get blood poisoning,* I think, then remember my nanites. "Wait!" I shout, but it's too late. The white light floods the hub, and the room full of scrap metal fades away.

CHAPTER 30
No More Water
Jazz

Sand dollar, wake up, Vox says in my head. Her voice is loud and clear, like all other sounds have somehow been vacuumed out of existence. I try to open my eyes, but I can't.

What's wrong with me. What's happening?

They unjacked us all for now. Something about the code trying to defend itself. It knows we're trying to stop it.

I try to think of a reply to this, but the words won't come. More than that, it's like I don't even have words at my disposal. I try to shake my head.

"Jazz? Are you awake?" Arwyn asks, taking my hand. I open my mouth to talk, but still can't seem to make sound come out. "It's OK, we had to put in several neural blocks, so some may not have worn off yet."

"Wh…?" I manage.

"It's a lot to explain. The code is changing. When you patched the first Glyph, it triggered a self-defense mechanism in the code that we didn't know about," she says just as Eco takes a step toward me.

"We thought when you saw Liddick in the cine, it was a form of NET connection, but now it's more than that—the code knows we're trying to stop it from spreading the news about Biotech and the others suppressing port-carnate technology," he adds.

"Tell her everything. You said it was *hunting* her," Arco snarls.

"Because it *was* hunting her," Eco fires back. "That's why things went south in the last cine. Once it registered her neural signature, it started pulling what it needed to draw her out of the plotline she was in."

"Why her? They all have Empath traits," Jax adds. "Vox and Lyden are even both *Readers*."

"She was the strongest Empath that close to the Glyph, so her signal was more apparent. She's also the one who patched the last Glyph," Lyden answers from his virtuo-cine chair across from me.

"Why did she see things I couldn't see, though? I was *right* there with her, and I didn't see Liddick," Fraya says, sitting up in her chair.

"All right, everyone just take a breath," Calyx says, walking into the circle of us. She stops in front of the cylinder of spectrum colors that are spinning so fast it almost looks like a long, gradient rainbow cloud floating in the air.

"Jazz isn't going back in there," Jax says. "Not if these Glyphs are going to be hunting her now."

"Is someone going to tell me what's going on?" I finally ask as I push myself to sit up, and my head immediately starts spinning. I close my eyes again.

"Try not to move too quickly. The neural blocks take a while to completely wear off, so you might feel a little disoriented for the next few hours," Arwyn says.

"Why did you give me neural blocks? And…Liddick. He was—" I start to explain, but Liam holds up a hand to stop me.

"That wasn't Liddick. The code found memory scraps in your mind, Jazwyn...the way Liddick looks, sounds, things he's said."

"Why?"

"Because the code is fighting back. It's trying to change the game on us," Tark says, walking into our chair circle after Calyx. He scrubs his big hands over his now visible black and gray stubble. "Your father is one hell of an Omnicoder."

"What are you talking about?" I say, shaking my head.

"Dad built a failsafe into the code," Jax explains. "When he and Liam built the warning for us on the front end, he left the back end open for when The Seam was ready to add the last few lines and expose Gaia and the others," Jax says.

"We already know that...it doesn't answer why they had to give me neural blocks."

"Unfinished code is a weak point because if the last lines of code are unwritten, someone could just as easily write in a change or abort the code all together. That's why Dad built in the firewalls...a defense protocol in case Gaia or Biotech Global, or any of them got wise and tried to stop The Seam's messages from going out."

"So it's hijacking memories to *distract* us from finding the right Glyphs to patch?" I ask, turning to Calyx, then feel anxiety from Vox's direction.

A river of tingles runs down my spine when I think of the code trying to reach into our memories to distract us, and especially Vox's memories...all the experiences she must have had on her boundary scouting journeys—the strangle bushes, falling into traps the people *her* people call Fringe had set for passersby.

"What a stupid idea," Vox says out loud, then shoots me a glare. *I don't need your pity, sand dollar,* she thinks, obviously eavesdropping in my thoughts.

"It's brilliant, actually," Jax answers, glaring at Vox. "Why design a single firewall when you can design one that customizes to your own personal emotions. Fear, especially. This code learns *you* in order to keep *you* out."

"All right…so it's going to try to play mind games with us to distract us from the real Glyphs? That's what you're saying?" I ask. Jax nods. "OK, but Calyx broke in to that last cine and told Lyden that what I saw wasn't the real Glyph. Why can't she just keep doing that if the code starts fighting back again?"

"It's too dangerous," Lyden answers as he gets out of his chair and stretches his neck. "Fastest way to have a psychotic break is to entertain multiple realities at once. When we're jacked into the virtuo-cine network, our reality here has to be suppressed, or pretty soon we'd just lose all sense of what's real and what's just virtuo-cine."

"Fine, but Fraya couldn't see what I saw. Can't we just use that as an indicator of what's a real Glyph and what's a decoy? We all saw the bartender in the other cine, right?" I ask, but as I look around the room, I get the sinking feeling that they really aren't going to let me go back in.

"Jazz, this code is specifically tuned into you now, and not in a good way anymore," Arco says, swinging his long legs out of his chair, then leaning on his forearms.

"Good. So I'll attract the decoys. It will make identifying the real Glyphs that much easier."

"Jazz, it's just too—"

"Arco, it's not up to you, OK? I'm *going* back in there. I know what's happening now, and I won't get sucked in by a decoy again."

Arco closes his eyes in a long blink and clenches his teeth, obviously frustrated.

"I don't like it either," Jax says, crossing his arms over his chest. Ellis grips his shoulder.

"Look around here at how many people are monitoring her. She'll be all right," he says.

"Why are you letting this continue?" Eco turns to Tark behind one of the console stations. "You know she has to go back in. That code is only evolving faster, and we only have one Glyph patched. We have to plant at least *three* more if we want to stop them from giving pro-Gaia messages to every random Nascent Empath who walks into a virtuo-cine."

"We never found the right Glyph on the pirate ship…" Myra startles, suddenly covering her mouth. "Does that mean we're going back into *that* cine?"

"No. The code in that one has already mapped Ms. Ripley, so it will lock onto her right away," Tark says. "We have a few other new releases we can use, but they're not slotted to be as popular as the ones we've already selected."

"Maybe we can return to *Blackwater* for the last patch…after the cine has refreshed several million times. The code may forget Jazwyn's configuration by then," Calyx says.

"In the meantime, everyone should just rest for a few hours, at least until Jazwyn's neural blocks wear off completely. Are any of you hungry?" Arwyn asks.

"It's not the commons area from Gaia, but what we have is hot," Lyden says. "We still have the matter boards, right?" he asks Calyx. She nods, then looks at Tark.

"All right, take a break. Ms. Hart, keep her levels on screen," Tark says with a quick nod at Arwyn, then at me.

"I will," Arywn says, taking a few steps toward Lyden before addressing everyone. "Just follow us."

***

Arco slips into position next to me as we make our way down the long, white corridor after Lyden and Arwyn. Liam is arguing with Eco just behind them, and I suddenly feel a sense of urgency to find my father and Liddick. I turn around and search for Calyx, but she's not behind us.

"What's wrong?" Arco asks. "Is it your head?"

"No, I need to ask Calyx and Tark about my dad. They promised they would scan for him and—"

"For Liddick," Arco finishes my sentence, and something in me snaps at the tone of his voice—smug, assuming.

"If you have something to say, just say it, Arco. This hot and cold from you has to end." I stop walking and stare at him, watching the muscles under his cheekbones flex as he presses his teeth together. A wall of anger blasts into my chest from him, and I'm confused all over again. "Arco, *why* are you so—?"

"Because even when he's *not* here, he's in your head, Jazz, all right!?"

His eyes flash, then all at once soften. He closes them, then locks his teeth together again as he puts his hands on his hips. "I'm sorry," he says after a few breaths. "This is stupid, especially here and now." He shakes his head and gestures to the corridor, then turns away from me to follow the others.

"Arco, stop. It's not stupid if it's bothering you," I say, but he doesn't slow down. "Arco!" He finally stops, but doesn't turn around to face me. "Hey…" I add, catching up to him.

"You don't have to say anything, all right? I'll handle it. I never should have brought it up back there—you have those neural block things to deal with."

"Will you just *stop* already?" I say, reaching for his arm as he tries to move past me. "I don't know what's happening, OK? Whatever they were saying about this mind mapping thing I did to Liddick, I don't know what that means. Now, I'm hearing and seeing Liddick even though he's not here, and I don't know what *that* means, but neither of these things affect how I feel about you. *You* don't have anything to do with it, all right?" I add, but he still doesn't say anything, or even look up at me from studying the ground.

"It's fine."

"Arco, stop trying to act like nothing is wrong when something *is* wrong. You know I can tell when things are off with you. The mixed messages confuse me."

"It's just not a big deal, Jazz…"

"It's a big enough deal that it keeps hijacking your mood. That's the thing about problems. Just because you ignore them doesn't mean they disappear. If this is going to work with us, we have to talk."

"Fine," he says to the floor. "Are you afraid you're going to lose him?"

"Of course. I'm afraid of losing my dad, Zoe, Dell, and all the Vishan too. I don't know how any of this is going to work out now, if we'll ever see any of them again. It's *terrifying*."

The sharpness in his face softens at this. He takes in a long breath.

"I'm sorry. I just don't like looking stupid, and I don't like random thoughts pushing me off course. Not being able to keep Liddick off my sonar even with everything going on now does both those things," he sighs.

"It's because they're not thoughts you're having, they're feelings…and they don't make you look stupid, Arco."

He looks up at me, then seems to resolve something for himself as he takes a step closer.

"I'll try to—" he starts, but is cut off when Jax bounds back into the corridor.

"Hey, come on, I'm hungry!" he says. I jump, and Arco starts to laugh, abandoning whatever he was going to say as he takes my hand.

CHAPTER 31
Jumper
Liddick

The light is more intense now than it was in the port-carnate hub I rigged at Gaia Sur. The flash hits me before I have a chance to close my eyes, and then it's too late. The cold jets through to the back of my skull and freezes everything, like my head is filling with ice water until I can't feel anything.

Just as quickly as it started, it stops, and I hear the sound of wind blowing hard outside. I can't see anything around me, and suddenly everything is hot. *Crite, here it comes...*

It starts with nausea, which spreads just like the ice water behind my eyes a minute ago.

"Well, what have we here?" a pinched voice says. *Ensign.* The heat in my stomach spikes. "Oh...ope...ope, hold the boat. Liddick Wright? Do you believe that's what the transmission right here says? I'd show you, but you're bat-blind at the moment," he says, chuckling like a snorting horse. I force my eyes open, then try to stop the room from spinning. *I'm going to die this time...I think. Ensign is a mollusk, and nobody except a biodesigner can reset my nanites here...*

"Skyboard..." I manage to croak. "Biodesign...get Spaulding."

"Spaulding?" Ensign's idiot laugh explodes in the little room—the force of the sound wave hitting me in the chest. "*Lief* Spaulding? Well, let me just send a buoy hop right on up to the good doctor. I'm sure he'll take you right now! Right ahead of Sera Lim and Dice McClain!" He laughs until he coughs, then wheezes, and I'm almost glad I can't see his bloated face yet.

"*Ensign!*" I spit through my teeth, then blink my eyes hard to clear my vision. "Tell him…to come. His brother and sister are in…trouble…"

I don't hear anything for another minute, but then Ensign starts moving around in the room. I need to get out of here before whatever corruption has started in my neural channel gets too strong.

"And how do *you* know his brother and sister? They catch that golden sub too?"

"*Yes,*" I hiss at him. "Ensign, listen…I'm sick. The transfer corrupted the nanites they gave us at Gaia. Patch him my bioprint—here, take it," I say, extending my hand. "Take it!" I say, louder this time, which makes my head spin, but Ensign shuffles around again. My heart hammers in my chest at the prospect of him actually getting the transmitter.

He's just as big and ugly as ever when my vision starts to clear. He's turned away from me, and his stringy ponytail is gone, shaved clean, revealing a stack of fat rolls at the back of his neck. *How does someone only have fat rolls at the back of their neck?* The thought floats through my mind, which seems to make me even dizzier and more nauseous.

The outpost shack is smaller than I thought, cluttered with more scrap parts and no windows. It's dark except for a few floating halogen spheres over the console area where Ensign is sitting. I get to my hands and knees, then manage to push to my feet, bracing against the shack wall. Ensign spins around and looks at me.

"Did you say nanites?" he asks. If I had even a handful of reserve strength, I'd use it to strangle him. "You really do look like scud," he says, widening his eyes and chuffing a laugh again.

"Where's the transmitter?" I ask, scanning until I see it wedged between piles of scrap tech on the console station behind him. I brace one hand against the wall as I stagger over to it. Ensign stands up and takes a step toward me.

"Lief Spaulding ain't gonna make a hop over here from Skyboard," he says, gripping my arms and squaring my shoulders. He kicks the chair he's just vacated to the wall, then pushes me into it. "Collapse right there, will ya? I'll get someone."

Ensign picks up the silver disk transmitter, which is about as big as a plate, and flattens his palm over it. A green holographic grid appears about a foot above it, along with a keypad. I try to stand up, but then fall off the edge of the earth into a sea of black.

***

"Cred-Fed, wake up."

"Crite, it's only been ten minutes, En. Got a date or something?"

The woman's voice is familiar, but I can't sort it out from the rest of the noise whirring in my head. A low hum, no, a buzzing.

"Heyyy," Ensign drags out the word. "I got *important* things to do."

"Yeah, dry up!" the woman laughs, and I hear someone shuffling toward me. Cold fingers touch my cheek. "I mean, it's not gonna last, wise? But it'll get him vertical for a few hours at least."

"As long as he's out of here before the Grid scan. Last thing I need is a fugitive Cred-Fed showing up here," Ensign answers. I force my eyes open and try to lift my head, expecting the room to nosedive, but it doesn't.

"Well, good morning, sunshine!" a woman with short, spikes of black hair and a little heart tattoo on her cheek says. She takes the toothpick out from the corner of her mouth and taps her teeth with it. "So, you've got about two, three hours tops before my coagulant wears off. Made it myself," she says, winking at me and smiling.

"What did…you do…to me?" I ask, feeling like I'm pulling up the slow, heavy words from a tar pit somewhere in my chest. The smile falls off the corners of the woman's mouth.

"Saved your life; you're welcome," she says with a huff.

"Sorry," I say. "I mean…how…?"

"Just laced a biocard with my secret formula. Enny here says you scrambled up those fancy nanites from Gaia on account of you being a chutz and didn't program your hub for 'em," she says, nodding at Ensign, who beams.

"Why…can't I talk…move?" I ask, starting to feel the panic set in.

"Oh, yeah. You're gonna feel backed up for a while, wise? Muscle responsiveness, speech, thinking even. Sorry, low grade oil, but at least you're not dyin'. At least not yet."

"*Oil!?*" I ask, trying to push up from the chair to my feet.

"Yeah, same viscosity as blood. Don't worry, I purified it. 'Sides, I only used a thimble full. Little grease never killed anyone."

"Crite…" I shake my head, then press the heels of my palms into my eyes and take a deep breath.

"Grisham had me forward your digits to one of his biodesign contacts on the Mountain when your code bounced back to him like Swiss cheese. I already loaded the coordinates into your channel," Ensign says, tapping the side of his head.

"What?" I ask, trying to process what he's saying.

"Yeah, ain't just Skyboard that's got fancies. Activate the map by thinking *Corva Clay*. That's her name, wise? Grisham said she'll untangled the rest of your innards and help you with your *project*, whatever that means." Ensign slaps his thighs and gets to his feet. "Now, if you don't mind, I need to get your stink out of here before the State scan comes through. Delia here is gonna help me, aint'cha, Delia?" he adds, winking at her. Delia giggles, and I'm positive the wave of nausea that hits me isn't just because of my hacked nanites. I get to my feet and try to walk toward the little shack door.

"Thank you," I say over my shoulder to Delia, who is already under Ensign's tree trunk arm, twirling her finger in one of the holes in his tank top. I swallow hard to keep from roarfing.

"Sure, thing, minnow. You start feeling cold, though, and you've got about a handful of minutes until you're chum, wise? Best get on, then," she says, waving me out the door with the back of her hand. Ensign makes a clicking sound with his mouth, and I push my feet out the door.

The air is thick and heavy with sea salt and sulphur, and the sky is hazy as I make my way out of the sand and to the gate that surrounds the base of the Skyboard mountain. My biochip should still work, unless Delia fried it with whatever she injected into me. *Only one way to find out,* I think, trying to stand up as straight as I can when I see the chrome archway of the checkpoint.

The metal droid inside the wall just before the arch sits behind a plexiglass window, then turns to me as I approach. His face is silver and expressionless. *Why don't they just put hair and flesh tone on these things,* I think, creeped out when its mouth begins moving a fraction of a second out of sync with the overly enthusiastic voice. Green laser dots flicker on in its eyes.

"Good evening. Please remain still while I verify citizenship," it says. I hold my breath and watch the shimmering barrier grid inside the archway to my right. The same grid that extends up for miles and surrounds the mountain in a dome. "Welcome, Mr. Wright," it says after a second, then extends a chrome plated hand toward the grid, which quickly dissipates.

"Tell the Council to make you a face," I say, walking through the archway, which crackles behind me as the barrier grid reforms. Floating halogen spheres begin glowing along the paved road in front of me—smooth and silver like the droid at the checkpoint gate. *Corva Clay,* I think, skeptical that Ensign's ham-hands were able to program anything into my neural channel. But then an arrow like the one at Gaia Sur appears to my right.

I'm sorry, Mr. Wright. It is after business hours for Cobra Cape, Oxygen Bar and Holistic Health, the female arrow voice says in my head. I roll my eyes. *Ensign, you mollusk,* I think, then squeeze my eyes shut tightly to refresh this hack job neural map.

COR-VA CLAY, I think, enunciating the words in my head.

Corva Clay, Biodesigner, is expecting you, the arrow voice says, then flattens into the polished silver street and starts moving forward. I follow it.

How long is this trip? I think.

Corva Clay, Biodesigner, is located at 17 Vista Del Mar, Crescent City. Estimated arrival, 17 minutes by heliocar. Please approach landing pad.

I groan out loud, then look around for other people within earshot, but the street is deserted.

Occupancy? I think.

Two other passengers will share your heliocar, Mr. Wright.

*Cancel car, I'll just—crite…*I think, just as I see the silver, cylindrical heliocar appear over the treetops several feet in front of me. It shoots a beam of light onto the street corner and follows it down.

Trip engaged. Please board the heliocar, Mr. Wright, the arrow voice says in my head as the side door hatch slides open. Two Skyboard girls are already inside, one with straight, pink hair, and the other blonde like Dez. They both look up at me with iridescent purple eyes, then smile their bar wedge smile. I step into the car, into the light, and their smiles disappear.

"*What* is all over your face? Is that...*dirt*? One of the girls asks, her face contorting in disgust.

"*Milled* grade, ladies. Only the finest from Admin City," I say, hoping they stow it now.

"*You're* from Admin City?"

"Where else would I get milled grade soil? The *Badlands*?" I force a laugh, but I don't even care if they don't buy the story. "If you'll excuse me, I'm going to nap this hop," I add, then close my eyes and let my head fall back against the seat. "It's been a long day."

CHAPTER 32
Into the Fire
Jazz

We follow Arwyn and Lyden into a lounge area with a long counter against the back wall and a coffee table in the center of a circle of connected black couches. Lyden goes to the counter and pulls several mugs and plates from the cabinet. Arwyn sits down on one of the couches next to Liam, and Eco sits on the far other side of them both. No one talks.

"Soooo," Vox finally breaks the silence, kicking her feet up on the coffee table and leaning back on the couch next to Liam, spreading her arms behind her. "What aren't you all telling us?"

Eco's eyes snap to Vox, and Liam turns to face her.

"You know everything we do," Arwyn says.

"We know everything *you* do, right. But not them," Vox answers, jerking a thumb at Liam and another at Eco. I can feel the anxiety in both of them rising, besides the lights in Eco's cheekbones suddenly starting to flash red and white being a dead giveaway.

"What's happening?" Arwyn asks, then turns to Lyden, whose back is to us. He flattens his palms on the counter and lowers his head. "Lyden..."

He blows out a breath and starts passing out mugs of coffee.

"I programmed grilled cheese," Lyden says, then blows out a resigned breath. "Jax, take over?"

"On it," Jax says, making a B-line to the matter board. Lyden takes a seat next to Arwyn and leans over on his forearms.

"What's going on? Did Calyx scan for my dad and Liddick?" I ask. Lyden meets my eyes, and my stomach drops.

"There was a port-carnate transfer logged about two hours ago. The atom configuration matched Liddick's bio print."

"So they made it! They transferred!" I say, but Lyden's expression doesn't change.

"That's good news, isn't it?" Fraya asks, helping Jax plate the grilled cheese from the matter board.

"The entry and exit hubs aren't from the Phase Two facility or Gaia Sur, which is good news," Lyden answers, taking a plate from Fraya. "Thanks."

"That means whatever hub he did use isn't government grade. Azeris's hub is the only non G-grade hub that is strong enough, not to mention the only one that knows how to reach our coordinates. If it were his, we'd have received a transfer request," Liam says, taking a mug from Jax.

"What's the problem? He's topside, right? You have an intake and an arrival?" Arywn asks, narrowing her eyes at Lyden.

"I didn't want to say anything until we knew more," he says. "Jazwyn was already starting to pick up something off with me, and she had enough to handle in there."

"Lyden, what is happening? *Where* are my dad and Liddick?" I ask.

"The arrival report registers topside, but the hub is what we call a *ghost* because the coordinates are shuffled every second," Eco interjects. "It's untraceable—a homemade hack port."

"OK, well he has friends everywhere. He must have met up with some of his connections. Maybe even one of Azeris's friends..." I trail off as it dawns on me that if Liddick were with Azeris, he wouldn't need to use a homemade hacked port from anywhere else. I look at Lyden, who nods at me.

"We don't know where he is, only that his reconfiguration came back incomplete," he says, carefully.

"What does that mean?" I ask, feeling the hairs on the back of my neck prickle. "What does that *mean, Lyden*?"

Arco puts his arm around me and pulls me toward him.

"He didn't have his nanites neutralized like we did before we transferred," Myra says to herself, then looks up at me, her eyes wide with realization. "Oh, Jazz..."

"What? You're saying what, Lyden?" I press.

"Some of him...may not have reassembled at his destination. We don't know how much."

"But that could be the result of inferior logging tech; it could mean *anything*," Arwyn says, defensively.

"I know, that's why we didn't say anything," Lyden answers quietly, gesturing to Liam and Eco.

"Right now we don't know anything except Liddick is —*was*—topside as of two hours ago," Eco says. "You'll just have to let us work on this. Navigating the Platform of the virtuous-cine network is taxing enough without having your focus diverted by worrying. In fact, that worry is probably what caused a weak point for the code to exploit in you, Jazwyn."

"You're *blaming* her for worrying?" Arco asks, glaring at Eco.

"I'm not blaming anyone for anything. She just needs to focus, or this is all going to be for nothing."

"Where are Calyx and Tark?" Avis asks around a mouthful of grilled cheese. "They should be giving us status reports or something."

"That's a good idea," Fraya says. "Can we ask them for that?"

"We're doing everything we can, trust me," Liam answers. "We want to find everyone as much as you do, but right now, all we can do is wait for more input."

"He knows what happens if he transfers with nanites; he wouldn't have done it again without a plan," I say, shaking my head. "He made it somewhere safely, I would know if he—" I start, but can't finish the sentence.

"*All* of this is why we didn't say anything. It's too soon to know what's happening, so everyone just refocus on the job at hand, all right?" Eco says, taking a bite of his grilled cheese, his cheekbone lights flashing blue and white as he chews.

"Try to eat something," Arco says, gripping my shoulder. I take a bite of my sandwich and look at the white floor.

I know you're all right. I know you wouldn't leave my dad in that place...you all made it out, you had to make it out...I think, trying to picture Liddick's face. I close my eyes and lean on Arco's shoulder.

"Tired, yeah?" he whispers into my hair.

"Yeah. It's been a long day."

***

"Jazz…" Arco whispers. "Time to go back in."

I open my eyes to find everyone getting up from the couches to follow Calyx and Tark, who must have come for us.

"OK," I say. My voice sounds rough in my ears as I get to my feet. Arwyn crosses to me.

"The neural blocks should be worn off by now," she says, looking into my eyes. "Your pupils look like they're back to normal. How do you feel?"

I shrug. "Normal, I think."

"She slept about an hour," Arco answers as we make our way back to the circle of virtuo-cine chairs, where Calyx and Tark are leaning over a console and gesturing wildly at whatever is on the display.

"That can't be good," Arco says.

"What happened?" Lyden asks, pushing his way toward the spinning colored cylinder in the middle of the circle of console stations. "Where's the queue? The Platform is black."

"That's what happened," Calyx says. "We're trying to get back online now—it went dark about an hour ago."

"That's our only access to the Grid," Eco says with panic rising in his voice. He runs into Arco's shoulder and knocks him into me as he rushes toward Calyx. Lyden moves behind one of the empty consoles.

"It's here! We're still connected; we're just…blind."

"Where's the queue?" Liam asks, crossing to look over his brother's shoulder at the floating screen.

"It's been wiped. I'm trying to pull the last load from the cache."

"We already tried that," Calyx says to Lyden. "It's been dumped."

"Who dumped it?" Liam asks. "We're the only ones with access."

"Apparently not," Lyden says, frantically typing. "Somebody else is using the back door we created…the temporary disconnect was just a ripple effect. They're not targeting us."

"Are you sure?" Tark asks, crossing over to Lyden's console.

"I'm sure, see?" Lyden points to a section of the scrolling green code, then touches it with his finger. A band of flames appears about three inches to the left, which melts a blackening hole in the code three inches to the right. "This is the access point from an hour ago. It opened up next to that firewall."

"Find out where that signature is coming from," Tark says, turning to Calyx.

"Well, whoever this is used *our* hack to get in. The firewall identified our signature and is blocking our access everywhere on the Grid now," Lyden explains.

"Change our mask, then," Eco says.

"Working on it." Lyden pulls his hand back from the code, and it returns to lines of scrolling green numbers and symbols.

"What's happening?" Myra asks.

"It looks like we have company…in there," Arco answers, angling his chin at the rotating tornado of gradient colors in the middle of the console circle.

"Look!" Avis shouts, pointing to the bottom layer of color, which flickers from black to…*flying starships*?

"It's working! We're back in!" Ellis says. "Is that *Xenotrope 6*?"

"No," Tark answers, backing away from his console. "*Cannibal Planet.*"

No one says anything for several seconds, but the temperature in the room seems to drop several degrees.

"What does that mean?" Myra asks in a small voice. "Jazz, what are they saying?"

I swallow hard.

"It means we have to find the Glyph before the other Glyphs eat us," Vox says, rolling her snake eyes. I catch her glance at me then and feel panic harden in my stomach like a ball of ice.

"It's just a virtuo-cine," I say, reminding myself as much as everyone else. "It's not real. If we were topside, we'd be paying twenty credits to get into this storyline, right?"

A little color returns to Myra's blanched cheeks. "But I've never wanted to go into the horror cines," she says, and Fraya puts her arm around her.

"It'll be OK. You won't be alone," Fraya says.

"That's right. We're all going to stick together, Myra, OK? We'll find the Glyph and get out," I add.

"Cannibals? *That's* the cine you had queued for us?" Arco asks, looking at Tark.

"We didn't pick the cines, Mr. Hart, your fellow youth did that. Those Glyphs are set to generate in the most popular cines because of the algorithm Jack wrote," Tark answers, shaking his head.

"I hate this," Myra starts losing her composure again. "I don't want to do this anymore."

"We'll be all right," Fraya repeats, squeezing her shoulder.

The Platform level at the bottom of the swirling cylinder of colors stops flickering, and a campsite with tents appears along a river.

"That doesn't look so bad," I say, angling my head toward the 3-D hologram.

"Maybe the cannibals come when it's dark. That's what I would do," Vox says, sticking out her bottom lip like she's just made the decision for herself.

"Vox!" I hiss at her.

"What? It's not like you can just walk up to someone who's *wide awake* and start gnawing on them. Element of surprise, you know?"

Myra starts crying. I narrow my eyes at Vox, who just shrugs.

"Just come on," I say, moving toward my virtuo-cine chair. Everyone follows, and chills run down my spine when I see the campsite from a minute ago darken on the Platform—the sun is going down.

CHAPTER 33
The Mountain
Liddick

Arrived: Corva Clay, Biodesigner, the arrow voice says in my head as the heliocar lands. The Skyboard girls have already gone. *I must have been out cold*, I think as the door slides open and the illuminated arrow appears on the ground. I've never been to this part of Skyboard North… *Crescent City, is that what the arrow voice said*? I look around for something familiar, but even the buildings are different than the lower settlements here on this mountain. They're short and wide instead of tall and narrow. *Must have to do with the way the wind hits the buildings this high up,* I think as the short, stout buildings flank the narrow street, which curves around clockwise. *How much farther is this place*? I ask the arrow map in my mind.

Estimated time of arrival is three minutes. Please proceed two blocks, and the destination is on your right. Corva Clay, Biodesigner. 17 Vista Del Mar, Crescent City; Skyboard North, American Preserve.

The next two blocks are either uphill, or the nanite hack Ensign's friend gave me is starting to wear off. My lungs start burning with every breath, and I feel beads of sweat collect on my upper lip.

No way I'm this out of shape…not after crossing the Rush one-and-a-half times, then crawling up six miles of dirt tunnels without even half of this exhaustion, I think, but then am interrupted by the sudden arrow voice.

Corval Clay, Biodesigner. Arrived.

The building to my right isn't anything special. It's white with two pillar columns like most of the other buildings on this mountain, the only difference being the terracotta roof and canopy of ridiculous terraform palm trees. The floating halogen spheres go out the rest of the way up the street as I approach the building, like someone has flipped a switch. In the same instant I feel like something has been switched off inside me too…the burning in my lungs moves to my legs, which I don't understand since I'm not heading up the incline of the road anymore.

Just get to the door, Wright, I think, fighting to push aside the fatigue and returning nausea.

The double doors are made of thick, frosted glass, and don't budge when I try to open them. I lean my forehead against the cool surface and close my eyes, then almost immediately fall on my face when the door suddenly opens.

"Oh!" a tall, dark-haired woman startles. "You must be Liddick—here, let me help you," she says, putting my arm over her shoulder. "Ash, the gurney," she says to a tall, Mediterranean looking man who makes me do a double take for how much he resembles Pitt, Dez's oldest brother.

*No, he's dead. He died before we ever left Gaia…the spores…*I think as everything starts to spin.

"I'm Corva Clay. Grisham said you would be coming. This is my assistant, Ash, so please don't struggle. We're going to help you," the woman says as her assistant lifts me onto the gurney. I can't even keep my head up, let alone try to fight him, even if I wanted to.

"It's the Gaia nanites…from the port-carnate transfer," I manage to say as we move through the white -walled lobby, then into a wide, also white corridor with several rooms along each side.

"I know—Grisham uploaded your transfer receipt. Try not to talk," she says as a bright light hits me in the eyes. "You're going to feel a lot better in about five seconds—the neural freeze will stop your nausea and vertigo, but unfortunately, we won't be able to give you a full block. You're going to be awake for this procedure, Mr. Wright…bear with us."

Cold settles in behind the fading heat in my chest and legs, and I press my teeth together to keep them from chattering.

"C-cold…" I manage to say.

"Quite normal—just take shallow breaths," Corva says as the sound of hydraulics starts next to my ears, then stops as quickly as it starts. "As I suspected from your transfer receipt, you have stage four corruption of the S-class nanites you received at Gaia Sur. It's too far gone for me to reset them, so I need to purge them, all right? This isn't going to hurt, but you'll experience an itching sensation under your eyelids for about thirty seconds. Just squeeze them closed as tightly as you can, and it will be over before you know it. Ready? One…two—*what*?"

"What's wr—wrong?" I ask through my chattering teeth.

"You also have…a DNA mutation? Ash, scan please," Corva says, glued to her screen. "I've never seen anything like this," she says, following the scrolling green hologram of text the machine in front of her is projecting.

Crite, the Vishan treatment…I think, then close my eyes.

"Have you been exposed to any toxins? Anything… radioactive recently?" Corva asks.

"No, it's…DNA…binding," I answer the best I can. It seems to be enough of the missing piece she needs because she raises a thin, dark eyebrow at me and types something into her holographic keypad.

"But where—? Never mind. All right, hold still—I need to strip that first, then I can remove the corrosive nanites," Corva says just before a high-pitched sound needles through my eardrums. I try to raise my hands to cover my ears, but they've somehow been strapped in restraints.

"Hey!" I yell through my teeth.

"It's for your own safety, Mr. Wright. Please be still."

After another second, the high-pitched sound softens, but only a little, and I'd gladly take it back if it meant I wouldn't have to feel the itch of ten thousand ants under my eyelids. I squeeze my eyes shut as hard as I can to stop it, but the feeling only drills deeper into my skull, into my nostrils, my mouth, down my throat.

"Clear," Ash says from somewhere far away.

"All right, there we go," Corva says, and the crawling feeling finally stops. I try to suck in a breath and open my eyes, but the effort sends me into a dizzy spiral of nausea all over again. A fog settles in my head, and my arms and legs start feeling heavy.

"What's…happening?" I ask, wanting to say more, but I just can't make the words come out.

"I'm sorry I couldn't put you under for the procedure; the neural block would have interfered with the nanite purge. You can sleep now, though, Mr. Wright. I've just given you a sedative.

"No…I have to…" I trail off. *I have to find Dez before morning…*

***

I can't open my eyes beyond a squint with the bright sunlight pouring through the window. This isn't the same triage room I was in last night. Instead, it looks like a little guest bedroom with bright yellow walls and a normal sized bed in the middle of the room. There's a sink in the corner, so I get up and splash some water on my face.

The long black coat Grisham's man gave me hangs on a coat rack next to the door, and the remains of my dive suit have been replaced by a white pair of pants and a plain white shirt. My boots are wedged under the bed with a new pair of socks next to them, so I pull them both on and open the door.

More bright sunlight hits me in the face as I walk into the corridor. I turn the corner straight into an office where Corva Clay is sitting at a clear desk typing on a green holographic keyboard.

She turns to face me. "Good morning, Mr. Wright! I hope you slept well."

"What time is it?" I ask, looking around to figure out where I am.

"Just past eight a.m. Please help yourself to the matter board in the kitchenette if you're hungry. Coffee?"

"No, thank you. I need to get to Sundial City—" *Crite…Azeriz and Jack…they'll think the sun got me,* I think.

"Sundial City? Is this to do with the friend Grisham said you were looking for?" Corva asks, moving away from the clear desk. She pushes her viewer from her eyes onto her head, which shifts dark hair off her face. *She's not as old as I thought she was…maybe my brother, Lyden's age.*

"Did he find her? Did he find Dez?"

"No, but Grisham said to tell you that someone named *Finn* did."

As soon as I hear his name, my chest constricts and my stomach sinks. If Finn found her, she never made it to Skyboard North.

"Where did he find her?" I ask, hesitant to say the words because if I don't say them, I can't know for sure. If I can't know for sure, it's possible she's not dead…that she didn't die alone, disintegrated by the sun all because of me.

"I don't know, that's all he said. The message just came about an hour ago," Corva says, gesturing to the viewer on the top of her head. She sets it on the clear desktop and stands, then takes a few steps toward me. "All right, you look like you're ready. Listen, I told Grisham that I was out now. This is the last time I patch up his crew. Tell him not to send anyone else here," Corva whispers as she walks me to the door on the other side of the little office. "Tell him I have a legitimate practice now, OK? I don't want any affiliations with The State or The Seam. We're even."

"All right..." I say, but I have no idea what she's talking about. She opens the door. "Take this with you," she adds, handing me a small, clear bottle with a blue pill inside. "It will help with exhaustion by stabilizing your red blood cell count. Several were purged with the nanites. You need to rest, but I suspect you won't do that in the near future."

"No, I need to get moving," I nod. "Thank you for helping me. You saved my life."

Corva shrugs and attempts a smile, but it doesn't stick.

"That's all I ever wanted to do. That's why I became a Biodesigner. Remind Grisham of *that* too," she says, then shuts the door.

I stand there for a second trying to process who she thinks I am, but it takes too much energy. I turn toward the street, but then look back at the building, which is not the same one from last night. *How did I get here*? I think just as a heliocar lands across the street, and the door slides open. A man with sunglasses leans toward me from inside.

"Mr. Wright?" he asks.

"Yeah?"

"Get in."

CHAPTER 34
Cannibal Planet
Jazz

They're not sending us in at night… I think, not taking my eyes off the Platform level at the bottom of the swirling cylinder of colors.

"This is not the beginning of the cine. We're sending you in about halfway through because that's where the algorithms are predicting you'll have the most luck finding the correct Glyphs," Tark says. "Remember, if you see or hear things that are familiar, but uncomfortable, that's the code's firewall at work. It knows you're trying to put it to bed, so be careful not to lose your focus in there," he adds, then nods to me. "Ms. Ripley, since you have already been identified, it would be wise to stick with a partner at all times."

"I don't want to go in. I don't like horror cines," Myra whimpers in the chair next to Fraya. Her eyes are squeezed shut as she slowly shakes her head from side to side.

"Can't she sit this one out? You were going to pull me out," I say to Calyx.

"You all need to patch a Glyph, and we can't predict which of you will spot it in each cine. The one in *Cannibal Planet* may be the one that speaks to Myra," Eco says without missing a beat.

"It's OK," Fraya says from the chair next to Myra. "We'll stick together, all right? You won't have to be alone in there."

Myra nods and wipes her face, trying to pull herself together. If Liddick were here, he'd know exactly what to say to help her. *Why can't I think of anything to help her? Maybe because **I** don't have any answers!?*

"Wait—" I say. "Before we go in, you're going to keep working on finding my dad, Liddick, and the others, right? When we come out, you'll be able to tell us something?"

"We'll do our best, Jazwyn," Calyx says. "Your dad has our ports; if he's able to contact us, he will. And even if something happened, we're sweeping the Grid every few minutes for unauthorized access attempts. If any of them are trying to get to Admin City, we'll see them."

I nod, then take a deep breath as Calyx leans over the shoulder of a woman at the console closest to her.

"Queue cine, advanced to second act," she says.

"Yes, ma'am," the woman seated at the console replies, and everything starts fading to white.

***

It's dark when the bright light fades, so dark I can't make out anything for a few seconds as my eyes adjust. The ground under my hands is covered in smooth fabric…I'm sitting down, and the sound of the river current crashing and lapping helps ground me here in this cine—*and it is a cine. I'm in a virtuo-cine,* I think, trying to make the mental switch.

"Jazz!" Arco whispers from somewhere close by.

"I'm here," I answer, a few seconds later hearing the buzz of a zipper opening. *I'm in a tent...*

"OK, good. I'm going to find the others," he says, then closes the zipper to my tent again.

"Hey!" I call after him as I make my way out. Fraya and Myra are already walking toward the campfire where a few other people are sitting. "Have you talked to those two yet?" I whisper, catching up to Arco. He shakes his head.

"No, I woke up lying on the ground right there and came over to your tent when I heard your voice."

"There's Lyden," I say, nodding to the edge of the riverbank.

"Where's Vox?" Arco asks, scanning in every direction."

"I don't see her. She has to be here somewhere. They sent us in all together, so we should all wake up in the same place, right?" I ask, but Arco just shakes his head, having just as much virtuo-cine experience as I do.

"Lyden will know, come on," he says, heading toward the river.

"Stay in the light," the woman sitting on the far side of the campfire says. She pushes her long, tangled hair behind her ears, and I see the dirt smeared all over her face.

"What *happened*?" Arco asks, but the woman just keeps looking into the fire.

"There were twelve of us this morning," the man next to her answers. He puts his arm around the woman and pulls her closer. They're about the same age as we are now that I can see them in the light.

Fraya and Myra take a seat on one of the logs closest to the fire.

"What do you mean? Where did they go?" Myra asks in a pressed voice.

"They didn't leave," the girl says without looking away from the fire, but then looks directly at me. "They were taken."

Myra threads her arm around Fraya's and presses her lips into a tight line. The fire pops, shooting sparks into the air, and I jump.

"Taken by *what*?" Lyden asks, now climbing over one of the log benches, then taking a seat next to Myra.

"They separate you from the group, then chase you down," the girl says. "They're too fast."

"*Who*?" Arco insists, turning his back to the fire and scanning the woods around us again.

"We don't know. We never saw them coming. They chased us into the woods; we managed to get away, but our friends…" the boy trails off. He scrubs a hand over his face and takes in a breath, then shakes his head at us.

"I want to get out of here. Tell them to pull us out," Myra pleads with Fraya, then turns to Lyden. "Call Calyx. Tell her I want to go back."

"Myra, it's *all right*," Lyden says, gripping her hand. "Just stay focused."

She starts to argue, but then a crash in the woods cuts her off.

Vox, I think. "We have a friend out here somewhere," I say. "We need to find her."

"Don't go in the woods. They'll come back. You have to stay here by the fire," the girl says, panic rising in her voice as she struggles to her feet.

"Ava, stop," the boy says in a quiet voice. "It's OK… don't—"

"No, I'm not going through that again. I'm not…" The girl collapses into sobs on his shoulder, and Myra goes ghost white, the fear rising in her like flood water that is about to drown us all.

*This is a virtuo-cine…this is a virtuo-cine…it's not real… it's not real…*I think. *Vox, where **are** you?*

"We need to stay focused. We'll go together. You said they isolate first, then attack, right? We won't let that happen," Lyden says.

"No!" Myra shouts.

"OK, OK…Fraya, you and Myra stay here with…Ava? And…?" Arco asks.

"Rand," the boy says.

"Lyden and I will go look for Vox. Jazz, you should—"

Arco starts, but stops abruptly when he meets my eyes, resigned that whatever ideas he had about me staying behind just aren't going to happen. He blows out a breath, then turns to Myra and the rest of the small group. "We'll be right back. Whatever happens, just sit tight. Don't run off alone," he adds, looking straight at Myra.

"We'll be all right," Fraya nods, pulling Myra in closer. Lyden gets to his feet, and the three of us make our way toward the crash we just heard.

The air gets colder as we get farther from the firelight, and I wish we still had the Vishan ability to generate our own flames...especially if there really are cannibals in these woods.

"Why would she not wake up with us?" I ask Lyden. "Why would Vox regenerate in here apart from us? We were all sent in together."

"I don't know—it shouldn't have worked that way," he answers, then stops in his tracks as little sparks start jumping at the base of the tree line just a few feet in front of us.

"That looks like static," Arco says, taking another step toward it.

"No, stop," I say, feeling something heavy settle over my chest. "Something doesn't feel right in there."

"Vox can't be anywhere else, Jazz. It's just water over there and the clearing behind us. Everything else here is woods," Arco says just as we here another crash. The sparks along the tree line flash again a few seconds later. "That *is* static," Arco decides, then scans the sky. Thousands of stars speckle the dark with the exception of one spot where it's entirely black.

"Look at that," I say, pointing. "It's like...a hole in the sky." *A hole in the sky*? I think, feeling like the phrase isn't really mine somehow, like I've borrowed the words.

"It's not a hole," Arco says, finding a rock on the ground, then hurling it at the empty blackness. Seconds later, a hollow metallic clang sounds, then the thud of the rock hitting the ground. "Something is up there."

"I saw starships flying around a planet in the Platform before we came in here," I say. "What if we're not on earth here...what if—?"

"No!!" Myra screams, and we all start running back to the campsite to find out why.

Fraya is swinging a partially charred log at Rand and Ava while Myra throws whatever she can find at them. Spotlights from the sky start flooding the ground all around us, but there doesn't seem to be any reason for the chaos.

"What happened? What's going on?" Arco shouts as Rand tries to shield Ava from Fraya's wild swinging and Myra's rock throwing. "Stop! What's going on!?"

"It's them! They're the cannibals!" Myra shouts.

"We're not cannibals! You're split!" Rand yells in reply. "She just started screaming all of a sudden and scrambling backward. We were just sitting here!"

"Stop! Fraya stop swinging! What happened?" Lyden says, putting himself between the burning log and Rand.

"I left for two minutes to see if there were any supplies in that tent, then Myra started saying they had pointed teeth. They got up, and I just thought...I thought they were trying to attack her," she explains, lowering the smoking log when she sees how terrified Rand and Ava are. "I'm...sorry..."

Myra shakes her head and wrings her hands. "No, I saw them. I saw his teeth. She said we shouldn't try to come here. We should leave before they take us too, but then I saw *his teeth*," Myra says, even louder now than before. She picks up another rock and throws it at Rand.

"I don't have pointed teeth!" he shouts, then shows them. Myra screams and throws another rock.

"He's a cannibal! He's a cannibal!"

"No! Myra, stop...it's the code! This must be your cine..." Lyden says, looking at Ava. "She told you they would *take us too*, those were her words?"

Myra nods furiously. Lyden looks at me and nods. *That's the part of the code about Gaia. That's the Glyph,* he thinks.

Myra has to transfer the code...she won't go near them like this.

"Ava, would you step away from Rand for a second. Just cross over to us?" Lyden says, but Ava violently protests.

"No, no...I'm not leaving him. She's split. We didn't do anything."

"Just for a second, please," I say taking a step toward her.

"Stay away from us! You're probably the cannibals!" Ava yells, clinging to Rand, but then he screams and starts thrashing. When Ava moves away from Rand, I see *Vox biting his shoulder* in the firelight!

"Vox! What are you doing!?" I scream. Arco's eyes are wide, and Lyden looks just as shocked as he does. Vox wraps her arms around Rand and pushes him as hard as she can toward Myra, who starts hysterically screaming. Fraya freezes, then remembers her log and starts hitting Vox with it, embers scattering to the ground with each blow.

"Let him go! Vox! What are you doing!?" I shout again.

Vox growls, her yellow eyes flashing in the firelight, which also shows that her teeth are bloody...and *pointed.*

I gasp, frozen where I stand. *How can this be happening? Is everyone seeing this?*

Ava shrieks at the sight of Rand's blood in Vox's teeth, but Vox just bites him again and runs him straight into Myra, shouldering Fraya and her log to the ground in the process. Rand falls next to Myra, and Vox straddles his back.

"Give me your hand!" Vox shouts at Myra, wrestling her wrist away from her body and pressing it against Rand's neck.

"Stop! I don't want to die! No!" Rand yells.

"You *are* a cannibal! I knew you were a cannibal! You're all cannibals!" Myra sobs, just as the bright light from the spaceship hovering above us washes the whole thing away.

CHAPTER 35
Friends in High Places
Liddick

I look at the man in the heliocar for a second, then look up and down the metallic street. The engineered palm trees stretch out in each direction, but they're the only other company I have out here. I have a bad feeling about this.

"Who are you?" I call over to the car. The man lowers his sunglasses to reveal a white patch over his left eye. "*Eddie*?" I ask, squinting in disbelief. His greasy dark ponytail is gone, and his white tunic is not only clean, it actually looks new.

"I clean up all right, yeah?" he says with the same Badlands accent. "C'mon, already."

I make my way to the heliocar and get in. A keypad and two large screens wrap around the front of the rounded, white console, which flashes as a whole once the door slides closed behind me.

"Why are you here?" I ask as Eddie pushes a few buttons.

"Siam's," Eddie says to the car's console, which flashes again as we lift off. I press my teeth together and take a deep breath…I *hate* heliocars.

"Eddie, what the—" I start, but he interrupts me with a hard slap to my back.

"I don't know how ya did it, but Grisham is back in action. He's back in the game."

"What? Eddie, where are we going?" I say, forcing my teeth apart.

"Grisham sent me. Said you have a package to secure."

"What does that have to do with you?" I ask, making the mistake of looking at the tops of the palm trees swaying underneath us. My head starts spinning, and I quickly look away.

"Grisham said you might need some assistance. I'm here to take you to the assistance. He's in a hurry for you to deliver that package, wise?"

"I can't deliver anything until I find my friend. She was heading to Sundial City—that Biodesigner back there told me Finn found her," I say. "Are you taking me to Finn?"

"No, man. I said I'm taking you to some assistance," Eddie says, pushing up his sunglasses.

"Get Grisham on the comms—I'm not doing anything for him until I find my friend. That was the deal."

"You think Grisham is gonna put himself in the air like that? He just now surfaced—sit tight. Your assistance is in Sundial City."

Eddie tells me every conceivable detail about this heliocar for the rest of the trip, but at least he doesn't reek of spoiling oranges anymore. *How did Grisham managed to dry him out in 24 hours?* I think. *Eddie must have run straight to him once he came down enough to put one foot in front of the other.*

He sets the car down in front of an oxygen bar with a line of Cloudies winding out the door and around the limestone building. The word *Siam's* hovers in neon blue letters over the storefront, and the windows on each side of the door stretch from the ground to the top of the roof. Each of them project 3-D holograms of Cloudies getting various treatments like blue light skin peels and pheromone sea salt scrubs. An interactive pink, female coded hologram even walks up to us and starts laying out her spiel.

"You look like you could use an *Insta-Z*, Liddick and…Anonymous Channel—free five minute sample; guaranteed REM cycle, or your credits back! I'll book you with Brexta, inside now…" she says, tapping into her hovering pink palm display.

"No," Eddie says, holding up a hand. I narrow my eyes at him…*Anonymous? How did he get an opt-out neural channel?* "No thanks, doll. Maybe another time," he says as we walk through the hologram girl and under the chrome plated archway of the door. Inside, every oxygen bed is occupied, each enclosed by a carbon hologram wrap. Some still look like giant black eggs, but others have surreal coral reefs turned on, and some show a sweeping pan of miniature snow-covered mountain ranges. On the other side of the bar, three plank tables are set up with a line that winds around all the way back to the door. The technicians are painting *dirt streaks* on the customers' faces…*what the?*

"Eddie, where are we go—?" I start, but am interrupted when we walk under another chrome archway into a back room. A tall, blonde woman with lavender eyes and long red nails turns to us and smiles. Her bar wedge teeth are so white they almost glow, and her pressed white suit looks like it's probably too tight for her to sit down.

"Eduardo! Your milled grade soil is a smash! You must extend my thanks to Griswald. I appreciate his shipping direct from Admin City so we could be the first boutique to offer servicing. And this must be…Ludwig?"

"Lidd—"

"Yes, this is Ludwig, Charisse. Griswald says to extend his thanks for your…*cooperation*. His hub is currently being serviced, and we need our best man back in the storyboarding room as soon as possible," Eddie adds, nodding at me. I give him a sideways look, but he just keeps smiling like an idiot.

"Of course, of course…right this way," Charisse says, waving a hand over a section of the wall that falls away just like the one at the Phase Two Gaia facility. "And here we are. I'll just be out front if you need assistance with this old model…I'm sure yours are the latest upgrade."

"Well, yes, but we appreciate your hospitality all the same. Griswald will be in touch about lunch on the observation deck soon," Eddie says, winking obnoxiously. Charisse blushes, and her whole suit turns the same shade of pink.

"Whoa…" I whisper before I can catch myself.

"Do you love it?" she asks, running her hands over her hips. "It's *called sentient silk*…anger makes it turn black, happiness, white, sadness blue…"

"So, then pink must be…desire?" Eddie almost slurs, and I cringe for him when she wrinkles her nose just enough that it registers. He's such a skod. Charisse laughs, and her suit fades to yellow, then returns to white.

"Well, I'll just be up front. Nice to meet you, Ludwig. Do come back and see us on your next research trip," she says, her suit warming to pink again when I kiss her hand.

"I couldn't resist if I tried," I say, finally putting some of these pieces together. She puckers a kiss at me, and her pink suit deepens to red as she makes her way back through the chrome arch. I turn to Eddie once she's out of earshot. "All right, what was all that? *Ludwig*? Really?"

"Stow it and swallow this," he says, handing me a little silver square from his pocket."

"A biochip? I already have one of those. How do you think I got through the Skyboard checkpoint?"

"This one is a temporary override. Grisham's been monitoring you since you left, man, just to make sure you didn't have any tails. But now you do. You can't go through this port-carnate hub as Liddick Wright. Gaia just put out a net for you and the rest of your group—if your bio signature shows up in a port-carnate log, a virtuo-cine connection, or anywhere else on the grid, and they'll grab you. Grisham already sent Finn with a mask for Azeris to install over his hub, so you should get to Admin City without too much fanfare. You're lucky they haven't clipped you yet," Eddie says.

"Was a girl with Finn? Did he bring her to Azeris?"

"Grisham didn't say anything about a girl. Swallow that already, will ya?"

I swallow the stupid silver biochip, then grab Eddie's shoulders.

"Look, I need you to tell Grisham that I'm not doing anything for him in Admin City until I get word that my friend is all right. Do you understand?"

"Yeah, man, yeah."

"And I need you to find Finn. Tell him to stay at Azeris's hab, all right?"

"*Yeah*, man! C'mon, get in the hub. I got ten more minutes before I have to jet, and I mean to get one of those pheromone scrubs, ya feel?"

I roll my eyes at Eddie, then climb onto the silver disc of the port-carnate hub. It lights up, and a clear barrier closes over me like a dome. Eddie waves and blows me a kiss. I roll my eyes again.

"Tell Finn!" I shout, but I know he can't hear me now. I can barely hear myself over the loud whirring that starts as the light cranks up and my hands start going cold.

***

I don't remember closing my eyes, but they won't open when the light fades. After a few seconds, the crackling sound also stops, and I hear Azeris.

"Thank you, Krishna," he says, then blows out a breath straight into the audio capture. I try to wince, but my face is still frozen. "All your parts are in one piece, chief."

"You're a lucky frog," Zoe laughs, but the urge to do the same feels like an icepick in my chest.

"Liddick, you're going to feel some pins and needles like the first time you transferred, that's normal. When Corva stripped your DNA, she had to strip all your port-carnate imprinting too. Just try to breathe," Jack says. All at once it feels like fire ants start biting my fingers, then arms and legs until the sensation runs up my neck and over my face. I try to swallow as hard as I can to push the feeling out of my ears, but it doesn't work.

"Aaannnd….that should do it," Azeris says. A whoosh of air hits me in the face, and I can move again. I feel myself falling, but someone on either side catches me. I open my eyes, and finally, the prickling fire ant feeling passes.

"Thanks," I cough to Jack and Finn, who are on either side of me. "Dez…did you bring her?" I ask, barely able to put air behind the words as I turn to Finn. He looks at Jack, then back to me. "What? Where is she?" I cough again, forcing out the words.

"I brought her back, but she told Grisham she didn't want to go to Admin City. I gave Azeris the infobit Grisham sent to explain everything."

"Where *is* she?" I almost shout, gripping his shirt the best I can.

"He sent her home, man…to Sundial City."

"*That* was not our deal!"

"I told him you'd be stung about it, but he said he couldn't help you until her dad helped him. He said Azeris could keep his virtuo-cine tech on account of you're not gonna need it now."

"What!?" I say through my teeth, but that's all I can get out before my throat locks up.

"I don't know, man. He quick got her talking about who she was, who her family was, did some tear wiping, then started tapping away at his screens. Next thing I knew, he was having me go fish up Eddie. When I got back, there was a suit and a heliocar out back, but your Cloudy girl was gone," Finn explains. I push my hands through my hair.

All right…calm down, I think…take a breath. Dez is safe, right? She's with her dad. Grisham must have made a deal—trading her for her dad's help…for getting the temporary biochip and for getting Grisham reconnected with some equipment, with some contacts…

"Are you all right?" Zoe asks, crossing to me.

"Let me see your eyes," Jack asks.

"I'm fine!" I say too loudly, still trying to sort through this mess in my head.

"We don't have a lot of time, son. Grisham's info bit card said there's a flag on our bioprints. It can only be from Gaia. We need to get to Admin City before the temporary overrides he sent wear off. We have to go now," Jack insists.

"Then it's true," I say, trying to keep the panic in my gut from rising. "Grisham wouldn't have been able to find the flags on us on his own—he didn't have that kind of access to the Grid," I say. "It was all he could do to send out a local scan for Dez."

"I don't know, man," Finn answers after a second. "After I got back with Eddie, Grisham just shoved an infobit card, a hub mask, and three biochips at me and told me to give them to Azeris. He's been monitoring *you* since the minute you left the hole in the sky, and he probably still is."

"I haven't been anywhere or seen anyone who could have helped him like that. It had to be Dez's father, and men like him don't just trust people. He wouldn't have dealt with Grisham at all without proof that Dez was really there…he must have scanned for her on the Grid and saw that she wasn't on the Gaia mainframe anymore," I think out loud. "That must be how he saw we were flagged."

"Why does this matter, man? You need to get out of here," Finn says.

"Because! It matters because we need to know what we're walking into now *before* we walk into it!" I shout. "I have to figure out if Spaulding is on our side or not, and I can't *think* with this stupid reconfiguration fog!"

"He's just trying to help, wise?" Zoe says, flipping a tangle of copper hair out of her eyes.

"I'm sorry," I say, blowing out a breath. "Look…the first thing Dez's dad is going to do will be to get her a medical scan. He'll find out about her Vishan treatment, that Tieg is missing, and that Pitt is…dead. He's going to want to hold someone accountable for all this," I say, unsure where these thoughts are so urgent all of a sudden, or why I'm feeling so tense. Then I realize the tension isn't coming from the thoughts at all…it's coming from Jack.

"The code…" he says, reading something on the console in front of him. "We need to get to Admin City. Now."

CHAPTER 36
Marked
Jazz

"We have a problem," Calyx says before I can open my eyes.

"Why? The second patch is populating," Tark answers.

"It's not that; look…"

"When did you pull this?"

"I didn't. Jack sent it about an hour ago. We just broke the encryption," Calyx says.

"My dad…?" I whisper, trying as hard as I can to push out of my virtuo-cine chair. I force my eyes open. "You heard from my dad?" I ask, pinning Calyx to the wall with the question.

"Yes, he's safe. He'll be here shortly, Jazwyn."

"What about the others?" I ask. Calyx nods, and the next breath I take feels like the first one I've ever taken. *They're all safe.*

"There has been a complication, though…" Calyx adds. "The Skyboarders are not with the rest of their group."

"What happened?" Arco asks, sitting up in his chair.

"We don't have all the details, but Jack's message said the girl is topside somewhere, likely in Skyboard North. She ran away from the group after her brother disappeared underground, and…she's not well."

"*Dez* is sick? What's wrong with her? What happened to Tieg?" Fraya asks, panic rising in her voice.

"Like I said, we don't know all the details. We also can't send you back into the Grid, at least not yet," Calyx adds, and everyone starts talking at once.

"You've been temporarily compromised," Tark says, raising his hands to quiet us down. "There is a flag on each of your bioprints now. We pulled you off the Grid as soon as we got the message from Jack."

"What does that mean?" Myra says in a small voice.

"So far, it looks like no one was tracked, but we're keeping you offline until we can find out more information about the flags…*our* tech should have picked them up," Tark takes in a deep breath, then blows it out. "But we can talk about this after you decompress. Congratulations on patching the second Glyph, Ms. Toll."

"I didn't do it. Vox did…" Myra says, looking warily at Vox, who bites the air several times at her. Myra's face turns white.

"Vox!" I hiss, but she just laughs as Arco gets to his feet.

"Who put flags on our bioprints? Gaia?"

"That would be my guess, Mr. Hart," Tark answers.

"Then even if they did track us to the Grid, wouldn't they just think we made it topside and went into a cinehouse there?"

"No," Eco answers without looking up from his console. "You can only get on the Platform level here in Admin City."

"Does Gaia know we're here now?" Myra's voice pitches.

"No, not yet," Tark answers, glaring at Eco.

"But they *could* if we went into another virtuo-cine?" Fraya asks. Tark pulls in another deep breath.

"All we know is that your flags aren't warrant level. You've just been flagged with locators."

"So they want to find us, but they don't want anyone to know about it," Ellis crosses his arms over his chest. "That means they want to get rid of us."

"You've known that since your Leviathan imploded, Mr. Raj," Tark says, raising an eyebrow.

Arco presses his teeth together, making the muscles in his jaw jump.

"If *we* have flags now, so will the others right? Gaia is going to track them here," I say, the words sticking in my throat.

"No, they used temporary identity override biochips. I just put the mask in place to match the receipt requests that Jack sent, see?" Eco answers, nodding to his console. "An adult male cosmetics chemist named *Rizzo Trench,* his assistant, and a teenager just came out of encryption as Azeris Frank, Jack Ripley, and a *deceased* girl named Zoe Frank…"

"What? Zoe is *dead*?" Myra's voice cracks.

"*No…*" Fraya says, crossing to Myra. "She's been gone for six years, remember? They just reclassified her bioprint."

"And this trajectory log is Liddick's: *Ludwig Sprague, storyboarder technician*—"

"*Ludwig*!?" Vox snorts, interrupting.

"Where would they get identity override chips?" I ask, looking up at Arco. He shrugs.

"Liddick is mixed up with a lot of people…"

"Wait…*where* are you going?" Eco scrolls furiously over his hovering console screen, shaking his head again.

"What's the problem?" Liam asks.

"Your brother's trajectory. He's being rerouted to another hub…"

"Another hub? Where?" Lyden asks, standing and crossing to Eco's console.

"I don't know; the ping comes back different every time I send it—whoa, this just got encrypted above our pay grade." Eco blows out a breath, and the lights embedded in his cheekbones flash red and white.

"Nothing is above our pay grade," Tark says, pushing toward Eco's console and waving Calyx over.

"Well, someone is scrambling it. All I can see is that the destination hub is here in Admin City." Eco points to his screen. "See? The coordinates jump with every ping, but they're all Admin City Z-codes."

"What does all this *mean*? Are they following us? Is Gaia coming here?" Ellis asks too loudly. Eco shoots a glare at him, the lights from his temples flashing only red now.

"No! Calm down. No one is scoping anything here. Someone just rerouted *Liddick's* port-carnate destination. Someone who can only see *Ludwig Sprague*."

"Are you sure that's Liddick?" I ask. "Why wouldn't Teig and Dez be with him? Maybe it's a mistake."

"We'll have to wait until they arrive to find out if they used a different hub because that's the only other launch from the same location as your dad and the others, and at roughly the same time. It can't be anyone else, especially not a storyboarder technician porting from the *Badlands*," Eco continues.

"But that makes no sense. If they all left from the same hub, they should have been able to enter their destination coordinates," Lyden says. "How did Liddick's get rerouted?"

"His trajectory was adjusted remotely; see the entry point?" Eco points to the screen again. "Someone doesn't want anyone to see where *Ludwig Sprague* is really going."

"All right," Tark says when we all start talking at once again. "When are the others arriving?"

"17 minutes," Eco answers, and Calyx's eyes dart to him.

"Have team two clear the bridge—tell them we're in route," she says. Tark nods, and Eco stands to leave with Calyx.

"I'm going too!" I shout after them.

"You would only be a danger to both yourself and them, Ms. Ripley," Tark says. I try to protest again, but Vox cuts me off.

"We have *flags*, sand dollar, remember?" she almost sings between biting her nails, then fashions her hand into a pretend gun and shoots it at me. "We're *outlaws*."

"That's correct, Ms. Dyer. Ms. Ripley, your location would blip at the first Plank station, and you would be terminated at the next by people you'd never see coming," Tark answers. "Whoever planted these flags wants you to feel like you can go about your business, which is exactly why you have to lay low for now."

"I am *not* just going to sit here," I say, pushing out of my chair. "We need to *do* something…my dad and the others are on their way, right? Then we need to find out who is controlling Liddick's hub," I add, lacing my fingers behind my neck as I start pacing.

"Ms. Ripley, we can't risk—"

"Just *finish* the game," Vox sighs, resting her ankle on her raised knee as she lies back in her chair. Everyone turns to look at her.

"Didn't you hear them? No one can go back in. We're all marked, Vox. Gaia will lock onto you if you go back in," Jax says. Vox starts humming, then pauses.

"How many Biodesigners and Omnicoders does it take to make a temporary bioprint chip?" She asks her chewed fingernail, then starts chewing it again. "I mean crite, imagine what could be done with *two* Biodesigners and Omnicoders…" she adds, forcing her yellow eyes to open wide in mock surprise at her nail.

"Wait…" Arwyn says to the floor, then to everyone else. "Of course. We can do this. They can go back in and finish patching the Glyphs."

Vox sighs again, then swings up to a sitting position and grips the edge of her virtuo-cine chair.

"Arco's slightly less annoying sister…they need you to tell them more words," she says, then starts swinging her feet back and forth like a kid sitting on a swing. "Here, I'll help. It rhymes with: *you will give a shi*—"

"*Chip!*" Arwyn cuts her off. "We'll give you all a new, temporary bioprint chip. Then you can go back into the cines without flags."

"We won't be able to find the Glyphs if we have a masked bioprint, though," Arco says. "Didn't you tell us the Glyphs are designed to seek out the Empath neural structure?"

"Liam and I can embed that into the new signatures. Then when Jazz's dad gets here, he can just update the rest of the evolving code," Arwyn answers, but Tark shakes his head.

"We've been down this road…"

"Skull, she's right. The code is spreading the wrong message to more people by the second. It also knows we're trying to alter it," Liam says. "Jack won't be here and up to spec for hours—what if the code learns how to create a firewall that won't even let him in by then?"

"I'm getting a read on *Ludwig Sprague.* He's entered the Grid," one of the technicians says, staring into her console, then types something. A green holographic screen appears in the air a few seconds later, then zooms in on a series of coded lines.

"*Liddick* is going into the cines?" I ask.

"He's already been preloaded onto the Platform, sir… with an embedded *storyboarder* credential," the technician says, then raises her eyebrows at Tark. "Sir, he's accessing our cine queue…"

"Crite…" Tark sighs, then turns to Arwyn and shifts his hands to his hips.

"It's not his fault…" she says, shaking her head.

"He's clearly the hack on our side door into the Grid. He can change the virtuo-cine plots with that credential. Do you know what that means, Ms. Hart?" Tark asks.

"He's not the hack. Someone has an agenda—it has to be whoever hijacked his port trajectory," Liam adds, stepping out from behind his console. "He's not stupid, Skull, and even if Jack did tell him about The Seam's plan for the sleeper message, he wouldn't try to stop it. He's not a traitor."

"If anything, he'd be thinking *Gaia* was trying to stop the code from evolving to reach everyone out there. If he's going into the Grid, he must have a valid reason," Lyden adds. "He's been with Azeris and Jack all this time, Skull. There's no reason to think he's not on our side."

Tark shakes his head again and presses his lips into a tight line.

"Then why would he be going into the cines under our hack? No, we can't risk—"

"Let Arwyn and Liam make the bioprint chips so we can find the other Glyphs. I'll find out why Liddick is on the Grid instead of on his way here with everyone else," I say. Tark stares into me with his gold panther eyes the same way he did when Vox, Liddick, and I came out of the practice virtuo-cine in his class.

"All right," he says, turning back to Arwyn after a long minute. "Make the chips. But make back up replacements; the only tech on hand right now is C-grade."

Arwyn nods, then gestures to Liam.

C-grade? I think.

It's old tech, but that's OK, Lyden thinks. *It will work.*

"C-grade tech is glitchy," Arco says, as if on queue. "Do you have a plan for when it shorts, and we're on the Grid with a giant red bow on our backs for Gaia?"

"My instincts are to agree with you, Mr. Hart," Tark says, and I'm afraid the next thing out of his mouth will be to reconsider his decision to let us go back onto the virtuo-cine Platform.

"That's the risk we have to take," I blurt before Tark can say anything, then turn to Arco. "We can't worry about how far down it is when we know we have to take the leap regardless, right?" I nod to him, but he just tilts his head like he's about to tell me something he knows I don't want to hear. "Arco, if we don't go back in there now, that code could evolve to the point that not even my dad can fix it or stop it. Everyone will think Gaia, Carboderm, and Biotech Global are actually trying to *save* people instead of just using them to save *themselves*. And if Liddick is somehow a part of that at all..." I trail off, unable to even consider the possibility. "We just can't let him."

Arco looks at me like he doesn't believe what I'm saying. I almost don't believe what I'm saying, but I know Liddick wouldn't betray us. I also know if I'm wrong, I'm the only one who can stop him.

CHAPTER 37
Playing with Fire
Liddick

Before the bright light of the port-carnate hub totally clears, I'm already sitting in a…virtuo-cine chair? I squint, trying to make out where I am.

"What is this?" I finally say out loud. My throat is raw, and I hear my voice cracking in and out of a whisper like when I transferred to Azeris's hub.

"Try not to move or talk yet, Mr. Wright. Dr. Cole stripped your DNA, remember?" a passing shadow says.

"He's connected," another man's voice says. "The cine queue is tapped as well; he can drop any time."

"Let's give him a minute to get his bearings."

"*Cine* queue? Where am I?" I say, trying to blink to clear my vision.

"You are in a storyboarding facility in Admin City, Mr. Wright; that's all you need to know," the first shadow says. I blink again and see that he's a tall, thin man with unnaturally blue eyes…*a Cloudy.*

"Where are my friends? We ported at the same time," I say, trying to sit up, but my muscles won't engage.

"I imagine they are wherever they were intending to go," he says with a shrug. "Mr. Grisham said you would be the only one entering the Grid with us today. Are you ready for your instructions regarding Mr. Tarriff's firewall?"

"Yes, but—"

"Good. We've secured your connection through the virtuo-cine network. I understand you were once quite an aficionado," the thin man says.

"Listen, I need confirmation that Dez is all right—tell Grisham this isn't what we agreed!" I try to shout, but my voice hollows on the last words. The thin man tries to hide his smirk, which makes me want to kill him.

"Mr. Wright, your DNA callous layer is *gone* now. You'll need to be patient with your reconfiguration."

"There's no way you work for Grisham. Spaulding arranged for this clearance level, didn't he?" I cough. "Grisham didn't even have a port-carnate hub with tech from this *decade*—he couldn't have brokered Grid access like this," I say, trying to lift my arms to reference the small, white room that looks like it came straight from a spaceship.

The thin man narrows his small, iridescent blue eyes at me, then smiles a bar wedge smile.

"I'm afraid I'm not at liberty to discuss my employer, Mr. Wright," he says, then turns his back to me to walk behind a pedestal style console. After a second, the back wall lights up with projected 3-D virtuo-cine images. One is of horse-drawn wagons and dirt roads, another shows an old pirate ship on a choppy sea. These and the rest of the cines immediately flatten, then peel off the wall like giant posters and stack on top of each other horizontally. After a few seconds, thick bands of light-to-dark colors start forming between the layers, spreading them apart until the whole thing looks like a giant spinning rainbow cylinder from floor to ceiling.

"You seem to have recuperated your strength, Mr. Wright. Are you ready to log into *Transcendence*?" the tall man asks, looking up from his console at me.

The bottom layer becomes 3-D again, forming into a star field with two planets in the distance. The one closest has land masses and water, but also three broad rings around it.

"What is that?" I ask.

"The planets *Evion Eight* and *Halcyon*, Mr. Wright. They're part of the virtuo-cines *Infinitum* and *Transcendence*, which take place on these planets respectively. You're bioprint has been embedded with the clearance you will need to temporarily reboot the virtuo-cine network portion of the Grid from within *Transcendence*. The refresh will seem like it happens immediately, but Mr. Grisham will be able to get behind Mr. Tarriff's firewall before it has time to completely regenerate."

"That's all I have to do? I don't have to take down the firewall myself?"

"Not with the storyboarder clearance you've been given. Just find the login and upload the reboot command to the network; you'll be able to see the actual code behind the cine graphics with your storyboarder credential."

"How do I upload the command? How do I find the login?" I ask.

"The same way you initiate *all* biocode, Mr. Wright. You touch the source," he says, looking up from his console and raising a pencil thin dark eyebrow like I'm the stupidest person in the world. I stare at him, and he sighs. "If you aren't *sure,* simply manifest a *reset register* graphics display," the thin man says, now looking down his obviously engineered needle nose at me. He closes his eyes in a long blink before looking back down at whatever he's typing into his console. "Just think of the words, Mr. Wright. They'll appear over the graphic you need to touch to enter your credential and launch the reboot," he says on a long exhale.

"Fine, so I reset the virtuo-cine network server, and I'm out? You'll pull me out then and put me back on the original port trajectory I had before you rerouted me here?"

"Yes, your job is to get in, reboot the virtuo-cine network, and get out. Please note that Mr. Grisham will continue monitoring your progress topside. If you compromise the mission by revealing your purpose in any way, your locator flag *and* those of your friends will be changed to warrant flags. I hear Lima is incredibly hot this time of year…" he smiles without looking at me. I try to sit up, but the chair has already started strapping me in.

"You didn't answer if Grisham would be putting me back on my trajectory after this."

"Please sit back and relax, Mr. Wright. You'll be dropping in five…four…"

"Wait, I need to know how I get back to my friends after all this is done!"

"…three…two…"

"Hey!!"

"…one."

***

Sheets of blue code scroll in front of my eyes for a second before dark military boots materialize in front of me. They're running fast, and it's only after I notice this that I realize I am running too. The ground is burnt orange with no vegetation as far as I can see, and the only person in any direction is the one filling those boots just up ahead. It's a girl.

"Hey!" I yell up to her, but she doesn't slow down. "What are we running from!?"

"Folger, you're not funny! Hurry up!"

Guess I'm Folger, I think, picking up my pace. I catch up to her, but I can't see her face through the glare on her helmet. I squint up at the purple sky and see two bright objects, a big red disc, which must be the sun, and a smaller dark gray one, plus three horizontal streaks that jut halfway into the sky.

"Hey! So really, why are we—" I start, but the deafening cracks of sound and light stop everything when something knocks the wind out of me. Dirt suddenly pushes through my teeth; I cough and spit, but can only see a white and gray haze and hear a high-pitched buzzing. It feels like it's trying to push its way out of my eardrums, harder until it gets sharp. I cover them with my hands, and then feel the wet, sticky blood running down my neck. *Crite...*I think, spitting again. The ringing starts to subside, and the pain shifts from sharp to deep before settling into my teeth.

"Folger!" The word sounds yelled through a wall. I look around, and see her outline getting closer, trying to crawl to me.

"Are you OK?" I shout, but my voice sounds far away.

"My leg!" I look down at her, but don't see anything that looks like it could be an injury. "We need to get back to the boundary before they catch up!"

"Who?" I shout again, putting her arm over my shoulder. I still can't see her face through her helmet, especially not with the layer of dust lacing the rounded glass.

"Folger, crite! The Transcendents!" the girl says just as the haze clears enough to see a circle of lights in the ground just ahead. "There it is!" she says, pointing to the circle.

We stumble into it, and the haze, smoke, and noise clear all around us.

"We've got her, Captain!" a man in a silver shirt says, and another man lifts the girl with me onto a gurney. I stand up and press the heels of my hands into my eyes until someone grabs my wrists and pulls them away.

"Let's have a look then," a woman says. "Bixby, I want the log from the Captain's suit—triangulate the helmet malfunction and send it to Kryder in C-deck for debugging."

A light hits my eyes before I can even try to open them. I squeeze them shut, and more blue code scrolls upward, faster and faster until I open my eyes again.

"Aye, ma'am," a man says.

"Hey...*hey!*" I hold my hands out to create some space.

"Sir, I need to examine for debris," the woman's voice says, sternly this time.

"I'm good," I say, holding my arms out to keep everyone at bay as I blink away the code enough to see the floor come into focus. It's dark and smooth, and I can see my reflection in the nearby silver console...*wait, that's not me...*

I jump, watching my hands, which aren't my hands, fly up and touch the face in the reflection. I feel them touch my face, but I'm not this *old*. I don't have dark hair or a pointed beak of a nose like this. *It has to be the bioprint mask,* I think, then stumble backward. Instantly, two more men are on either side of me gripping my arms.

"Sir, we need to get you to the med bay," one of the men says just as we turn into a large, white room with hologram grids, columns of text, and the blue, internal outline of a 3-D body from head to foot...all the organs, veins, and bones displayed. The men lift me onto the flat table in the middle of the room, and the 3-D body hologram lowers over me.

"Be still, please, sir," the woman who insisted on seeing my eyes a minute ago says. I finally get a look at her. The red hair...the dragon lady nails, the pointed bird-like face. *Rheen!* I think, then nearly jump off the table when half her face is replaced for a second by scrolling blue code.

"Folger! What's wrong with him?" another woman's voice asks. I turn toward it, but she's just a sheet of code too. I take a deep breath...*Focus, Wright,* I think...trying to calm down. After a second, her long, brown hair is sticking to her face, but not so much that I can't see her features. *Jazz?* I think...she has the same golden brown eyes, the same long, thin nose and thick, dark eyebrows, but she's *older*, maybe twenty-five?

"Ri—" I start, then catch myself. *This is a cine. I'm in a cine...the firewall. All right...just find the login and upload the reboot command. Stop tweaking...*"Rid—iculous," I stumble, hoping something else will come to me when the two men who hauled me in here, along with the Rheen double and older Jazz stop and stare at me.

"What's ridiculous, sir?" the Rheen double asks.

"That...you're all fussing like this," I say, as surprised as everyone else seems to be at the words coming out of my mouth. "I'm fine; just get me out of this heap," I add for good measure, gesturing to the tattered launch suit I'm still wearing. One of the men pushes a button on the side of my collar, and the suit starts deconstructing... folding down over itself in panels until it falls into a perfect square on the ground.

"Recycle it," Rheen's twin says to one of the men.

"Yes, ma'am."

"Will you at least let us scan you for internal injuries?" she asks, raising a thin red eyebrow at me.

"Greene," I say, not realizing I'm reading the small nameplate on her silver shirt out loud until I hear it come out of my mouth. She raises her other eyebrow at me.

"Well, your eyes are fine. Now let's talk about your internal—"

"I'm *fine*," I interrupt. *Didn't someone call me Captain a minute ago? And everyone is calling me sir...I'm in charge here,* I think.

"It's my job to make sure you're healthy, sir," Rheen's twin insists. "I just have your best interest in mind."

I turn back to her because something isn't right...*why is she working so hard to make sure I know she's trying to help me?*

"Folger, we can't risk going back in. We almost lost another deployment crew down there!" older Jazz says, wincing as another woman in a silver jumpsuit scans her upper leg with a wand, then moves her fingers over the floating blue hologram projection of a broken femur bone. It starts to knit back together. Greene takes a step over to older Jazz and taps something into the side of the leg hologram. She immediately settles.

"Just a sedative, Lieutenant Ridley. You need to rest."

CHAPTER 38
Infinitum
Jazz

Arco sighs, but I see a smile fighting at the corner of his mouth.

"Are you and I actually on the same side for once about Liddick?" he asks. I shrug and return his almost smile.

"I just want to do the right thing," I say. "We need to make sure we're all still in this together, and if he's been talked into doing something against The Seam, I want to help him."

Arco nods, but the spark of his smile fades until it goes out completely.

"So what's next, then?" he asks, turning to Tark.

"Next, you swallow these," Arwyn answers, making her way back through the corridor to the circle of virtuo-cine chairs with Liam at her side. She holds up a fistful of test tubes.

"Are those the chips?" Ellis asks, scrambling out from behind a console along with Avis.

"Does it matter which one they take?" Avis asks, reaching for the tubes, but then pulls his hand back when Liam glares at him.

"They're color coded; we customized each one," Arwyn answers. "Jazz..." she adds, handing me a tube with a flat blue square about the size of my thumbnail. She passes each of the tubes to the other Empaths.

"We just swallow these?" Arco asks, eyeing the red chip at the bottom of his tube.

"One bite, and then they'll dissolve. The tech isn't new, so they might take a few bites to initiate," Arwyn answers.

"Who's in this?" Vox asks, holding her yellow chip up to the light.

"You're all listed as demographics testers with Empath neural structures, so the virtuo-cine Glyphs have two reasons to interact with you. We're hoping career coding you all as testers will reverse the firewall evolution. With any luck, instead of trying to scare you away, the Glyphs will try to positively engage you now," Arwyn explains. Vox gives her a deadpan look.

"But who's in this square?" she asks. "What faces are we wearing in there?"

Arwyn winces a little, but tries to cover it with a laugh.

"We didn't name them…" she says with an awkward smile. "With the tech we have, I could only build a level one mask onto your DNA baselines, but that will be enough to filter your neural signatures and general appearance on the Grid. That way, you won't *look* like yourself to the Glyphs…facial recognition won't be transmitted. These chips won't last long, though, so you may need to dose again after this cine."

"All right, let's get this over with. What's this cine?" Arco asks.

"It's called *Infinitum*—Action/Adventure genre that takes place in the same universe as the final virtuo-cine in our queue, *Transcendence*. We can't tell which of the cines Liddick is in now because his signature keeps jumping between them, but he's in one of them," Tark says.

"Will we be able to see him even though he's masked as that Ludwig person?" Vox asks.

"You won't be able to see him because he'll appear as whatever character he's embodying, but you may be able to sense him," Arwyn answers.

Some of us more than others, Lyden says in my head. I look over at him in time to see the last of his smile fall away.

"You'll be entering at the climax of *Infinitum*, which is where the algorithms are reporting the Glyph will likely be," Tark says. "Bottoms up, then," he adds, nodding to the test tubes.

We all tip them up and bite down on the chips. Mine fizzes against my cheek, making prickles run down my spine. I flinch.

"It will feel like your hands and feet are falling asleep for a second, but that's just the DNA mask overlaying your cells," Liam says. "You can get back into your chairs once the chip has dissolved."

"Feel any different?" I look up at Arco as we make our way to our chairs.

"Not really," he answers, but the tension in the air around him suggests otherwise.

"Are you sure? What's wrong?"

"Nothing..." he starts, and I clear my throat. "All right, I don't like the idea of hitting the ground in the middle of a tense situation. Tark said we were landing at the climax, which means there will be no time to prepare or to think…just to act," he says.

"You're good at that, though, Arco. You knew exactly what to do when the Leviathan was about to self-destruct, and you didn't exactly have a bunch of warning about that," I say.

"That was different. I was in my element."

"Which you didn't know until you got there."

He looks over at me as I climb into my chair, then smiles and nods just a little as his seat conforms to him. The neural link rods hover over his temples, and I watch the lights running across the front of his shoulders blink blue and white until everything washes out.

***

Strips of color appear in the whitewash background until I see red, smokeless torchlight in the corners, wooden beams, then concrete blocks making up the windowless walls around us. Wooden beams run across the low ceiling too, and the floor is made of concrete. *Is this some kind of bunker*? I think.

A tall, white-haired man is gripping Arco's shoulders and talking seriously, looking him right in the eyes, while Lyden and Vox stand on either side of him. Fraya and Myra are standing behind me as a very tall, very thin woman suddenly grips my shoulders.

"Rinna, you know he won't stop until they listen to him, but you must make *him* listen," the woman says.

Her eyes are so light blue they're almost translucent, and her pale skin shimmers in the red light.

"Wha—I mean, who has to—?" I start to ask, then suck in a breath when I see the gill flap open and close on her neck.

"Kray," the woman says, looking over her shoulder at Arco, who is now wearing a black cloak. The tall, thin man standing in front of him lifts the hood over Arco's head, then passes one to both Vox and Lyden. "He will listen to you," the woman adds, pulling my attention back to her.

"What am I supposed to make him listen to?" I ask, panicking when several other abnormally tall, thin people pull open doors the size of the wall itself. Several of their children pick up torch bases, then pull red flames up in their hands just like Arwyn and the Vishan. I nearly swallow my tongue.

"Rinna? Are you listening?" The tall woman asks, snapping my attention back to her.

"Yes, sorry…what?" I stammer.

"He must convince the others of our gifts, not engage in hostility. We are on the same side as the Council, and he must promote peace among the unprotected." The woman swings a dark cloak like Arco's over my shoulders, then covers my head with the hood just before pushing me toward the blinding light of the open door.

"Wait, now? We're talking to people now?" I ask, turning to Fraya and Myra, both of their eyes wide.

"Yes, child. It is the Gathering time."

"*Gathering* time? I repeat, remembering the Vishan's Gathering when they burned the tribal scars onto Liv and Rav.

"They will *not* listen to me on this, I'm telling you," Arco says to the tall, pale man escorting him, Vox, and Lyden to the doors. "I don't believe in this. I don't believe the Council!" Arco raises his voice, and everyone in the bunker stops talking, moving, and maybe even breathing.

"Kray, we've discussed your responsibility to your people as their chosen representative," the pale man finally says. "You must quell this uprising."

The color fades from Arco's face, and I feel my chest freeze in the wake of his reaction. He tries to say something, but the words won't come out.

"Go to him, Rinna. He must address the untreated," the tall woman pushes me into the growing circle around Arco, which snaps his attention to me. Loud chants start in the dark outside the open doors, which makes several people rush to close them.

"No!" the pale man shouts. "Let the untreated come to Kray if he will not go to them. Let them come for all the Transcendents if he will not protect us."

"I'm *not* authorizing anything!" Arco shouts.

Authorizing? I think, "Arco—I mean, Kray, look at me," I say, but Arco is completely absorbed in a conversation that only he seems to be having. *He's seeing something,* I think.

One of them has to be the Glyph, Lyden says in my head. I look around for him, but don't see him anywhere in the crowd.

"Tell them how the Council gave us light in the dark," someone behind Arco says.

"The breath in our lungs!" another says.

Arco shakes his head when a few more of the tall, pale people behind him shout instructions. "You must choose!" Kray, they will only listen to you!"

"Tell them to accept Transcendence! Save them from themselves!"

The crowd outside the bunker closes in on us, pushing us through the door into the darkness just as the crowd from outside approaches us. I scan for Vox and the others, but they've been swallowed into the group too.

"Jazz!" Arco shouts, his eyes wide and wild as he scans for me. A few seconds later, someone grabs my shoulders and pulls me onto a rolling platform.

"Kill the mutants!" someone yells once we're several feet from the bunker.

"Resist the Transcendence!"

Two tall, pale girls are hauled onto the platform with us, along with Fraya, Myra, and a very young boy.

"Stop!" Arco shouts just as a sheet of red fire flies up from his shoulders. The crowd quiets down, but several short, tanned men jump up on our platform and hold us all in place.

"Let Kray speak!" someone yells.

"He's Transcendent! He's not one of us anymore!"

"I *am* one of you!" Arco yells over the crowd as the sheet of red fire shrinks to a glow. Lyden and Vox move in behind him. "We can't keep fighting each other like this!" he says, meeting my eyes. I nod at him. "We are not the enemy…"

"He's right! It's the Council! They're the ones stealing our humanity!"

"They're trying to save humanity!" a pale, thin man a few feet from Arco shouts. "What will happen in a hundred years when the lands completely flood and the seas boil? Will you condemn your grandchildren?"

"At least we will die out as human beings!" someone else shouts from within the crowd of short, tanned people.

The crowd mumbles again, and Arco raises his arms to completely quiet everyone. "Is that what you're calling yourselves now, dragging people off in the night, ready to kill them out of fear?" he yells, pointing to our platform.

"They cannot choose our fate!" someone in the crowd replies.

"I'm not authorizing *any* termination!" Arco shouts in answer, then pushes the heels of his hands into his eyes.

His interview...I think. Rheen told him to 'authorize the termination of those he did not choose'. It's the Glyph trying to scare him off...

"Promise him, Kray!" I shout above everyone. "*Shake his hand and promise you will not...authorize their termination.*" Arco looks up at me, his brows slowly relaxing until I think he understands...*find that man... that's the Glyph,* I think, wishing he could hear my thoughts. He takes a deep breath and straightens.

"Who was brave enough to speak up? Who said 'they cannot choose our fate?'" Lyden shouts, scanning the crowd, but no one comes forward.

"I will give you my word in front of everyone here that no one will choose your fate!" Arco levels his voice.

"And what good is your word?" the same man yells from somewhere in the crowd.

Arco's fire completely disappears as he steps away from Lyden, Vox, and the tall, pale others behind him.

A tanned, hairy man steps toward Arco now too, and those around him clear a path. Arco extends his hand to the man, who doesn't move to receive it.

"If my word isn't good enough for you here, then take me with you to the Council. I'll tell them myself—just let the others go," Arco says, making the crowd both cheer and protest. After a few minutes of conferring with several people around him, the man speaks up again.

"Take him! Release the Transcendents," he says. Two men grab Arco as others shoo us off the rolling platform.

"Under one condition!" Arco shouts over the growing chaos. "*You* take me yourself. Choose one of these others if you have to, but have the courage to act as well as talk," he adds, throwing off his dark cloak, his arms bared in the long, belted tunic he's wearing.

The man's eyes narrow as he raises his chin at Arco and nods. He waves off the man on the left and grabs Arco's arm himself.

"Arco!" Myra shouts. Arco looks up at me mouthing the words, *One...two...*as he's hauled past us. "Jazz, we have to do something!" Myra shakes my shoulder, and a few seconds later, everything fades to white.

CHAPTER 39
Ghosts in the Queue
Liddick

The technician snaps closed the hologram of older Jazz's leg, and I'm still not sure if I heard Rheen's lookalike right... Did she call her *Ridley*? I scan for the lieutenant's nameplate, but the glare from the med bay ceiling light makes it impossible to read.

"Don't put any weight on that for twenty-four hours, Lieutenant," the technician says, fixing a band in place just above *Ridley's* knee. When she touches the ends together, the band starts to glow blue. "This will help repair the surrounding area."

"Get some rest, Lieutenant," Rheen's doppelgänger says, then crosses to a white pedestal-style console and begins typing. A hover chair appears from under the lieutenant's table, and the technician helps her into it. When the light shifts, I can finally make out her nameplate: it is *Ridley.* I try to swallow, but my throat has already started closing up. *What's going on in this cine?*

"Don't let her...talk you into sending...anyone else down there, Folger," Ridley manages under her breath, fading out as the chair carries her past me and through the med bay doors. The technician follows her, and I blink hard to stabilize the images that flicker in and out of rows of scrolling code the farther away they get.

"She's dangerous to the cause, Folger," Greene says after a second, jerking my attention back to her.

"Who? Ridley?"

"She doesn't understand that this is everyone's fight. It's only a matter of time before they lose their minds and start killing each other down there. The Transcendents *want* our help to save their people," Greene says, relaying all this like she's being recorded. "What do they have left down there now? Seventy, eighty years before Evion Eight and Halcyon are both completely uninhabitable?" Greene continues as she waves a white baton over my chest. I flinch, instantly seeing her as Rheen with that neural baton at the Phase Two facility. Her eyes widen at me as I get to my feet. "Folger? What's wrong? Lie back down so I can check your—"

"I'm *all right*," I say too abruptly, then nod to her as she finishes tapping into the hologram at the side of my head. "I just need some sleep."

She half smiles, which surprises me since I'm used to the sneer on Rheen's face.

"Your eardrum is repaired—you're lucky it didn't rupture. Just try not to sneeze for the rest of the night," she adds with a wink that seems ...out of character, except I wouldn't know *anything* about this character yet since I was just dropped into this cine. *Do I feel like I know more about her because of the storyboarder clearance?* I wonder. "Cathcart forwarded the latest brief to your room, but if you're not feeling up to meeting with the representatives tomorrow, I don't mind going in your place," she adds as I make my way to the door.

"I'm sure I'll be fine," I say, then wave off the beginning of what I somehow know will be more protesting. *I need to find the older Jazz...I mean, Ridley,* I think, heading down the narrow white corridor, where a floating holographic map appears in front of my face. "Widgets, excellent," I say under my breath, happy to see this storyboarder credential comes with *something* useful. I start pushing the map widget around with two fingers to see where the hell I am on this ship.

"Gaia is trying to lead a global initiative," a man behind me says.

I turn to face him, but apparently too quickly because I just see another wall of scrolling blue code. I narrow my eyes and try to focus on pulling out the images.

"What was that?" I ask.

"I said I haven't heard that term since I was a kid..." the man says, coming into focus now. He's a little taller than I am with a professor's goatee and short, brownish hair, which is gray at the temples.

"That's not what you—" I start, then feel cold water run down my spine. *Is that supposed to be Hart?* I look at him harder—it *is* him, but older, just like Ridley.

"You OK, Captain?"

"Yeah," I say, somehow out of breath. "I mean...what term? You said you haven't heard that term since you were a kid," I ask.

"Widgets," he tries to laugh, then looks me up and down. "You did just come from the med bay, right?"

I nod, still trying to put the pieces together. I need to get somewhere to think.

"Right, there was a little explosion down on...um..." *What was the name of that stupid planet again?*

"Halcyon?" he asks after a minute, dipping his chin and raising an eyebrow at me like I'm the biggest tweaker he's ever met.

"Right...Halcyon," I repeat. He narrows his eyes at me, then nods and blows out a breath just as I notice the lieutenant rank on his collar and his nameplate: *Cathcart. What is this? Rheen—Greene, Ripley—Ridley...Hart—Cathcart...I think. Am I...generating these characters?*

"Should I get Dr. Greene?" Cathcart asks. I shake my head.

"No, I'm all right. I just need to get somewhere to think," I say. "Greene said something about a brief you forwarded to me?"

"Uh, yes, sir. It's just...it's about the latest atmospheric readings from Halcyon. The radiation sickness is progressing faster than we thought down there," he says, holding up the tablet in his hand. "We're going to run out of time before we can reach the rest of the colony..."

"And you've no doubt discussed this with Lieutenant Ridley already, Lieutenant Cathcart?" Greene says, walking up behind him. She shoots me a know-it-all look.

"Yes, ma'am, but—"

"That will be all, Lieutenant. The Captain needs to rest." Cathcart thins his lips and nods, then nods to me before heading back the way he came. She watches him go, then turns back to me. "Folger, you're too casual with these new officers. It sends the wrong message. I'll walk you to your quarters so I know you'll *actually* get there this time," Greene says, extending her hand to the corridor in front of us, then starts walking.

"He said the radiation sickness is progressing faster than we thought. Shouldn't you know something about that if you're the *doctor* here?" I say, too harshly. *Relax, Wright,* I think. *That's not really Rheen. None of this is real… no matter how real it seems.*

"I was going to discuss that with you after you had a night's sleep, but yes. At this rate, we have about a week before the sickness begins interfering with their ability to articulate language."

"*A week?*"

"It's a slippery slope once the radiation reaches the prefrontal cortex. They've already lost much of their rational thought processes because we've delayed in approving more teams…" Greene says, then looks at me like she's waiting for a reaction. I don't give her one. "Folger, it won't be long before the only language they know is violence. We need to send more crews to the surface. There are *children* in those colonies," she adds.

I open my mouth to reply, but the words are stopped in my throat when a mob cine flashes in front of my eyes…people fighting, slashing, *biting* each other, and then it's gone. A split second of chaos, and my first thought is to wonder if I even really saw it at all.

"What's—" I start to ask her what's happening, what's wrong with this cine, but then I realize no one here can tell me. I'm in this alone.

"In partnership with the Carboderm Corporation and Biotech Global, port-cloud resources have safely funded

Gaia's students for decades," Greene says, *clearly*. My eyes snap to hers.

"Repeat exactly what you just said to me," I say, letting my focus on the image of her fall away so I can see the code behind it.

Greene's expression is confused until it gives way to lines of blue code, which flickers in places when she repeats herself. Only, she *doesn't* repeat herself.

"I just said the partnership between the Transcendent Council and Global Cloud Fleet has been strong for decades. We can't abandon them now..." Greene says narrowing her eyes at me. "I think I should take you back to the med bay for another scan, Folger." Her image fleshes out again as she slips her bony fingers with the red dragon lady nails around my arm. I rip it away from her.

"No, I'm fine. Just edgy and tired. I'll see you tomorrow, Dr. Greene."

She closes her mouth, which had fallen open, then nods and presses her lips into a thin red line before walking away. I make my way through the door to my quarters, finally able to stop for five seconds and think.

The room isn't elaborate—small, with a white moulded table and a holographic screen that is already generated.

"Halcyon atmosphere report is in queue, Captain," a female voice says, which can only be the room's computer like in the *Xenotrope* trilogy.

"Later," I say, walking toward the star portal window. I lean my forehead against it and flatten my hands over the cold glass composite. I close my eyes and see nothing but code again, so I open them fast. *Wait...*I think, then slowly close my eyes one more time. "Reveal subliminal text," I say out loud, then watch the symbol patterns behind my eyelids flicker from blue to red in places again. "Latin alphabet. No encryption," I say, hoping there's something to this storyboarder credential. After a second, the red characters actually change to words, and I laugh, letting out the breath I've apparently been holding.

|<access_known; process character interaction? yes; execute most viable? yes; encryption level 4|

*I **am** generating these characters...*I think, then read more of the code:

|<insert_rider><Gaia is trying to lead a||global initiative></insert_rider>|

|<insert_rider><In partnership with the Carboderm Corporation and Biotech Global, safe||port-cloud||resources have funded Gaia's||students for decades></insert_rider>|

"What is this? Propaganda?" I say to myself. "You think pulling people out of my head and putting your words in their mouths will make me believe them? Is that what your idiot programmers think?" I almost shout now, but then take a breath.

"Captain, we have a situation," a woman's voice rushes through my head and obliterates the code; I open my eyes. The white walls of the room around me appear slowly in patches until everything is back to normal again.

"What is it?" I say through my teeth, looking around to see where the voice is coming from, then realize there's an intercom in my wrist cuff.

"It's Halcyon, sir. The Council representatives insist on speaking with you before tomorrow."

"I'll be right there," I say. "Captain out."

"Aye, sir."

I push the heals of my palms against my eyes, bringing back the encrypted code. *This cine is laced...I think. Just like Liam laced the other virtuo-cines with messages. How do they know he did it...did he show them how?* The thoughts come like a crashing wave and pull me under. *I have to stop this...Gaia wouldn't lace messages like this for me; they don't even know I'm in the network. They must have laced this for everyone...I could rewrite it...I could* —"Stop!" I shout out loud to myself and take a deep breath. *Zone, Wright...one thing at a time. Get in, reset the server, get out...that's what Grisham said to do.* "Reveal Reset Register," I say out loud, then open my eyes and look around the room again. There's nothing but the same moulded white desk, white military style bed, the chrome finish kitchen like the galley on the sub to Gaia Sur...nothing that looks even remotely like a reset button, or lever, or whatever. "Crite..." I swallow hard and close my eyes, letting the scrolling code babble swallow me again.

"Sir," the same female voice comes through my sleeve cuff intercom. "I'm sorry, sir, the Transcendent Council leader is insisting on projecting aboard right now to speak with you in person. Authorize?"

I wait before answering, listening to the faint, high-pitched hum of the open frequency.

"Authorize."

CHAPTER 40
Never Saw It Coming
Jazz

The white light seems to fade faster coming out of this virtuo-cine, but maybe I'm just getting used to the process. After a second, the metal balls at the end of rods near my temples retract, and I sit up.

"That's three; we've patched three of the Glyphs now, right?" Myra asks.

"That's right, Ms. Toll. Clever maneuver getting the Glyph to escort you out, Mr. Hart," Tark says with an approving nod, but Arco doesn't look like he's just been praised.

"I thought you said these Glyphs weren't going to try to fight us anymore? That they were going to be drawn to us. That's not what happened in there," he says.

"It tried to use your interview for Gaia against you, didn't it?" I ask. He looks at me hard like he's been looking at Tark, but then his eyes soften.

"It tried. I might have been pulled in more if you hadn't reminded me it was the Glyph," Arco says with a small smile.

"The bioprint masks are showing as functional, so your neural signatures *are* concealed on the Grid. No one knows you're in the cines," Tark says.

"But the tech is old, so the Glyphs might still be able to access your personal memories to build the custom firewalls. At least now we know those are only as strong as you'll let them be, though," Arwyn adds.

"And I personally saw you trying to tackle an alligator bigger than ten of you. Firewall ain't got nothin'," Zoe says, wearing a white jumpsuit like ours as she leans on the doorframe at the far end of the room.

"Zoe!" Myra shouts, bolting out of her virtuo-cine chair. She throws her arms around Zoe's neck, making her tumble back against the wall. She laughs, and so do the rest of us.

"My dad..." I whisper when Azeris walks in behind Zoe. I almost don't recognize him in his white jumpsuit. His dark, curly hair is pulled away from his face in a ponytail, and he looks like a totally different person without the scruff on his face. My chest tightens when I don't see my dad following him in. I lock eyes with Jax, and we both head for the door.

"Wait!" a technician calls after us, but we don't slow down. We're halfway to Zoe, Myra, and Azeris when Calyx and Eco come through the door...with my father.

"Dad!" Jax yells.

"Finally...*finally*..." he says, and we both run into his arms.

"I knew you'd make it. We all came too far for you not to make it," I hear my voice saying, suddenly feeling outside myself somehow. My dad pulls me in tighter, and everyone behind us starts clapping.

When we pull back from my father his black, curly hair is all out of place. He pushes his hands through it and takes a deep breath.

"Good to finally meet you, Mr. Ripley," Tark says from several feet behind us. "Welcome to the Boneyard."

"I appreciate the ride. This is Azeris Frank and his daughter Zoe. They were both invaluable in getting out of Phase Two."

"We're all in your debt," Tark says.

"Skull, we need to borrow Jax, Liam and Arwyn. There was…an *issue* in the transport," Calyx says, putting an arm around Zoe, but it's not out of affection. *She's holding her up*, I think.

"We know—Mr. Wright has…" Tark starts, then notices Zoe's fatigue.

"What happened? What's wrong with her?" I ask, stepping over and grabbing her hand. It's ice cold like Liddick's was after his port-carnate disaster back at Gaia. Liam and Arwyn rush up behind me.

"They couldn't strip the Vishan treatment," Zoe answers with a smirk and a quiet voice. All over again I feel my chest constrict. "You see the sparkles in that one's face?" she tries to smile as she gestures to Eco.

"She needs another dose of Vishan DNA, right?" I ask, spinning around to face my dad. "They said you used it to stabilize Lyden's DNA to make the neural thread for Liddick's virtuo-cines. Can you—"

"We already did that," Eco says. "Splicing the parent DNA from our archive database stabilized her through the port-carnate transfer, but something else is out of sync now," he rolls his eyes, and I want to punch him in the mouth.

"She insisted on seeing you before we took her to the med bay to figure out what it was," Calyx says.

"I'm *fine*," Zoe insists. "Just feels like I've been scrapping a little. Nothing some sleep won't fix..." she trails off, then slides into Azeris and laughs again. He lifts her up and fixes Calyx to the wall with his dark eyes. "Where's the med bay?"

Calyx leads him out of the room with Jax, Arwyn, and Liam, but before my dad can follow, Tark calls over to him.

"Ripley! We have a situation here too."

***

My dad moves behind Tark's console and starts reading the display. He scrubs his hands over his face, then folds his arms over his chest.

"How long has the sleeper code been active?"

"Best guess, four, maybe five months from the echoes we've picked up. That corresponds with the trigger we suspect: Gaia activating the parmide bracelets," Tark answers, nodding in my direction, then to Vox and Arco.

"You heard the messages as soon as they put the bracelet on you?" my dad asks, raising his eyebrows.

"We didn't know it at first, but yes. Vox and I heard what Liddick heard at the port-festival," I answer. "And then Arco started to hear part of the message later. Now, those of us with any kind of Empath tendency can hear it too."

My dad nods. "The bracelets were the catalyst then. Your sudden, heightened reception, for lack of a better word, must have worked like a remote control for the sleeper code."

"That's the best conclusion we came to as well," Tark says. "We couldn't stop it, but we've been trying to patch it until you got here so at least the complete message hits the public."

My dad blows out a breath. "I should have fully disclosed the nuances of that code to you before I handed it over. I just assumed I'd be the one launching it, so there was nothing to disclose."

"Not your fault, Ripley," Tark nods to my dad. "Let's just get the last missing piece of the code updated. The message has only reached Nascent Empaths of varying abilities so far, but it's manifesting as *pro*-Gaia propaganda. We've managed to patch three of the holes so far."

"You've patched them internally? How? With biochips?" my dad asks. Tark nods, but my dad just closes his eyes in a long blink.

"That's a problem?" Arco asks, taking a step forward.

"If the defense sequence has activated, yes." My dad moves behind a console and starts scrolling for something he doesn't seem to be finding.

"The Glyph firewalls have been getting progressively more disturbing," Tark adds, raising an eyebrow.

"Then at least something worked right," my dad answers, typing faster than I've ever seen anyone type into the console. After a second, his brows draw together, and he types even faster. "*Crite...*" he says, pulling back from the console. "The propagation is too far gone...it's embedded itself into the narrative fabric of the virtuo-cine network."

Tark turns his back to the console and puts his hands on his hips as he studies the floor. He walks a few steps, then turns back to the console.

"What does that mean?" Avis asks. "You can't fill in the message?"

"Can you mask it from the outside?" Tark asks, and my dad shakes his head.

"No, it will just attack your system with randomly generated viruses if I try. I built that failsafe in case Gaia or any of their affiliates got wind of the message and tried to erase it from the network. This is all painfully ironic."

"But we can still patch it by accessing the code like we have been, right?" I ask.

"Theoretically, yes. The Glyphs will sense that we're trying to alter the code they're housing, but the only thing they can do is try to scare you off by accessing fragments from your neural threads. They can't infect people with viruses."

"Then this means we just finish what we started," Tark decides. "Oriah, Get Plume on the line and tell her to alert the neighbors."

"Yes, sir," a technician in white replies. My eyes flash to Arco's.

"He said *Plume;* she's in The Seam, Arco."

"I knew she didn't belong with Styx and Rheen at our interviews. There must be other teachers from Gaia too… maybe Reynolt or Stryker."

"What's happening?" Myra whispers, but not quietly enough.

"They're starting a war," Ellis says, almost to himself, but then looks up at Tark. "The *neighbors* are actually your contacts, aren't they? You're going to run the whole campaign right now?"

"We don't have much of a choice, Mr. Raj. The code launched prematurely, and now it's evolving to reach everyone with or without our input. Our original plans will just need to be expedited once we make the message it delivers accurate," Tark answers.

Everyone is silent, and I'm not sure why. What did we think we were doing in these virtuo-cines so far? We've been patching the code so the truth goes out instead of the chopped up version that makes Gaia look *good*. We've been part of making this happen...but I guess we haven't thought about what comes afterward. *What will happen if the port-cloud really does come down*? I think.

"I guess we always thought the coded message could be stopped when you got here, Mr. Ripley," Fraya says, holding Jax's hand, and it's the truest thing anyone could say.

"It's really going to happen..." Avis adds.

"I'm sorry," my dad says. "It shouldn't have happened *this* way. When we launched the code, we wanted to have an infrastructure in place that would help people adjust to living without a port-cloud. Public service announcements advocating the safety and ease of port-carnate tech, free demo hub stations and a new uplink to the Grid that would give real time reports on the air quality improvements...we were going to do so much more than just pull the curtain back."

"Are you sure we can't stop it? Can't we just—" Myra starts to say, but Vox cuts her off.

"What a bunch of *jellies*…" she says, hopping into her virtuo-cine chair. Everyone turns to her.

"What?" Avis asks, narrowing his eyes at her.

"I said you're a bunch of jellies! What do you think we've been doing all this time?" she asks, widening her eyes at Lyden. "Liddick's brother, do you have gills or not?" He looks at her like she's suddenly just screamed at the top of her lungs.

"Uh, I…well, yes, but I—"

"OK," Vox holds up her hand, then fixes her cat eyes on mine and angles her head like she's just given me my queue…and maybe she has.

"She's right," I say as it all finally starts to make sense to me. "We didn't know we would need to escape from Gaia until we got there, right? And we never saw the Vishan coming when we were chasing that message through the tunnels. We never would have guessed a place like the Rush even existed, let alone that we'd have to go through it…but we made it because we stuck together. We figured out what to do. Now we're here, and even though we never saw it coming that we'd be part of directly fixing the world, that's *exactly* what we're doing now. We have to go in and patch the last Glyph, and whatever comes next, we'll figure that out too."

The Council
Liddick

I pull up the map widget again by thinking about where the bridge of this ship might be, and bam, there it is, just like that. *At least something about this storyboarder clearance makes sense.*

I make my way down the corridor and onto the main deck thinking about how much this ship looks like a Leviathan with the wide console stations and metal finish everything. The window at the front of the bridge bows out, but all I see is a black star field.

"Captain on deck!" someone shouts, and everyone snaps to attention. *Crite, I'm already exhausted by this make believe.*

"Sir, the Transcendent Council leader is on standby—privacy field will be activated on your mark," a woman near the front of the bridge says as she taps something into her console.

"Oh, I imagine there are no secrets here. Open the channel," I say, scanning for anything that might look like it could be a reset switch. *Reset Register,* I think, but nothing suddenly stands out. "Crite."

"What is *Crite*?" a tall, lanky man—who may actually be the palest person I've ever seen in my life—says, suddenly standing in front of me.

"Sorry," I say, straightening. "Just an expression. What can I do for you, Councilman?" I add, noticing that his image is actually warping around the edges. *Port-call tech…and bad reception port-call tech at that.*

"Our outer wall was breached by explosives just several hours ago," the tall, thin man says, flattening his hands over his long white tunic. "I know you have already provided many of your crews to guard my people, Captain Folger, but the threat continues. We are not able to hold back the untreated on our own."

"I wasn't aware the explosion compromised your outer wall. I was on the ground with one of my crews when the explosions went off," I say just as Greene walks onto the bridge and takes a seat at one of the consoles to my left. She clears her throat.

"Captain…we know it is much to ask of you, but we simply have no other choice. Please, will you send more crews to help safeguard our city from the untreated. The situation is urgent," the man says, staring like he's trying to look through me with icy eyes just like the Vishan's.

"Let me work on it…" I say, just as it occurs to me I need to get off this stupid ship if I'm going to find that reset button. "We'll get you the help you need somehow even if I have to go back down there myself, Councilman."

He exhales, and for a second, I think he might collapse. Greene inhales sharply like she just caught whatever was about to fly out of her mouth.

"We can't thank you and The Global Cloud Fleet enough, Captain Folger. When…if I may be so bold…do you think you might be able to send help?" the man asks as the images behind him begin to flicker in and out of blue scrolling code.

What is this...I focus on trying to see it, and it appears; I forget all about it, and it appears...how do I control anything in here? Where's the damn reset register!? I yell in my head, and half-a-second later an entire *wall* of blurred widgets appears in the upper left corner of my vision. "What...?"

"I said, if I may be so bold as to ask, when might—"

"No, sorry. I didn't mean to ask that...I, um, let me start working on it now. Give me an hour," I say, trying not to run down the list of blinking, blurring icons floating to the left of the Councilman's head from where I'm standing. He presses his palms together like a closed book, then moves one of his flattened palms toward him until his thumb touches his chest. He bows toward me, and then I see it behind him...the box on the wall with the words *Reset Register* glowing above it.

"Our deepest gratitude, Captain. I will inform my fellow Council leaders, and then will hail again in an hour."

"Where are you now, Councilman?" I say abruptly to the last of his head and shoulders, the only remaining images in the sheets of blue scrolling code in front of me now. "I mean...to guarantee your safety," I add. His image reappears.

"Inside the Hidden City, of course...where the Cloud Fleet has relocated the Transcendents," he says, raising a wispy white eyebrow at me like I should know this.

"Right...of course, I must still be a little foggy from the explosion down there earlier."

The man nods, then repositions his hands like a book and bows to me again before he fades out completely this time, and the black star field appears. I blow out a breath. *That's it. I need to go to the Hidden City and find that box.*

"Folger, you're making the right choice," Greene says from behind me, but I'm only half paying attention as I try to focus on all the blinking widgets for this storyboarder clearance, but the only ones I can bring into focus are a circular button that says **Maps**, a rectangular one that says **Grid Display**, and a square one that says **Graphics Display.**

"Come on!"

"Folger?" Greene jumps out of her seat and rushes over to me. "What is it? Your head? Lieutenant, escort the Captain back to the med bay."

"No! I'm fine. I need to go down to the Hidden City."

"Sir, you're still injured…the explosion. You should rest. We can assemble a team."

"I need to go myself. Put a team together and have them meet me on the transport deck."

"But sir—"

"Am I the captain of this ship or not, Dr. Greene?" I glare at her. She presses her thin red lips into a line, and I see Rheen in her face more than ever. She takes a step back and nods.

"Yes, sir."

"Then do as I ask."

Greene nods again, then gestures to the Lieutenant she had ordered to take me to the med bay. *Now, where is the transport deck?* I think, and the **Maps** widget appears again.

***

I don't remember coming through this part of the ship when Ridley and I first came back from the surface of Halcyon, but I chalk it up to not knowing anything about anything that was happening just then. This deck looks just like the other one, only in place of the huge window that showed the star field, this one has a wide space with four large, circular disks that look like port-carnate hubs. In fact, they look exactly like port-carnate hubs. I look around for the technicians, but only see another long stretch of metallic consoles. *Where the hell is everyone?*

The widgets appear again in the left corner of my view, and this time, I see a new one: a triangular **Glyphs** button. *The characters…perfect,* I think, hesitant to push it, but I have to get off this ship, and doing something is better than doing nothing. I reach out to push the button, and instantly the floor is populated with technicians behind the consoles. *Huh…storyboarders must have control of when things start, which also means they must have control over when they stop,* I think, wanting to test my theory, but the button has disappeared. *Glyph,* I think, but it still doesn't come back. *Whatever. Just get to the Hidden City and get out of this circus,* I think again, shaking my head.

I start walking over to one of the technicians to get the process started when Greene walks through the door with seven others, four women and two men I don't know, and Cathcart. They're all about Ridley's age, maybe 25, and the age of my new face for that matter. I'm disappointed when I don't see Ridley among them, but she wasn't exactly the biggest proponent of going back to the surface.

"How's Lieutenant Ridley?" I ask Greene, whose proud expression immediately falls flat.

"She's still in recovery for another twenty-four hours, then her mission card will be reinstated. She can go out with the next crew, if you'd like to assign her now?" Greene says, almost excited about the prospect of putting Ridley in a position she obviously doesn't want to be in… *I really have generated another incarnation of Rheen.*

"One crew at a time. Let's see what we can do with this one," I say, looking them over, and something in my chest relaxes…*relief? From what?* I think, suddenly feeling like I know this crew, but none of them look even remotely familiar. I shake my head, the relief quickly turning to frustration. *Crite, I need to get the hell out of here already.*

"Sir!" one of the women steps forward, nervous, but almost…compelled to say whatever she's planning to say. I notice the bars on her dark uniform, and her nameplate: *Waverly.*

"Yes, Lieutenant Waverly?" I say just as my heart suddenly starts pounding in my chest. *What is going on?*

"Uh…what are our orders?" she finally says after staring at me for several seconds. I take a few more to try to remember why I called for them again.

"There have been some explosions near the Transcendents' protective city. We need to fortify the inner wall while other crews are dispatched to make repairs, and still others continue to negotiate with the untreated population," I answer, but the words aren't mine. It's like they were just...there. *Storyboarder clearance*? *Was that the baseline script*? I wonder, and two more widgets blip into the upper left corner of my view: an oval one that says **Script** and another oval that says **Improv.** *Huh...*

"Yes, sir," Lieutenant Waverly says, pushing her blonde hair behind her ear, and for just that second I want to pick her up and kiss her. Blood pounds in my ears, and my chest feels like it's cracking down the middle. **What** *the hell is this*? I turn away from her and step onto one of the circular hubs.

"Let's go—initiate port-carnate transfer," I say to the technicians, who all look at me for a second, then at each other, confused. "What's the problem?" I ask.

"Sir, port-carnate is black market tech...the misalignments...it's not sanctioned," one of the technicians finally speaks up. I sigh, having forgotten about the propaganda narrative in this stupid cine.

"Right, of course. Then by all means initiate your...?" I trail off.

"*Cloud transfer*, sir?" Cathcart says. I close my eyes so I don't roll them. *Why* did I generate that mollusk?

"Cloud transfer, of course," I say, *just get to the Hidden City...*

"Initiating, sir. If the team will take their positions."

Lieutenant Waverly moves quickly next to me, and one of the men moves next to her, glaring at me. I have the overwhelming urge to shove him and ask him what his problem is, but the other man moves into position on the other side of me, and the feeling instantly passes. *All of this is split*, I think. *Where's the widget that tells me where these impulses are coming from*? I stop, anticipating the bar of floating icons to reappear, but nothing happens.

"Initializing cloud transfer to M17, grid seven, Hidden City walls. Seven in tow. Surface climate is hostile, sir. Please be advised."

"Noted, thank you," I say, wondering what the hell I'm supposed to use as a weapon. *Why didn't I think of this? I'm losing my touch.* Just then another widget button appears in the left corner of my vision: a square one that says **Self-Defense.** I reach to push it, and seconds later new body armor appears on my arms and chest, along with different batons holstered in a utility belt around my hips. I look up and see that everyone in the team is now also outfitted like this. The woman a few hubs down from me smirks, then nudges the woman next to her and whispers nonsense.

"I'm turning *something* into a dragon this time."

CHAPTER 42
Transcendence
Jazz

After the speech I had no intention of giving, everyone looks at me blankly for a second, then Arco finally nods.

"All right. We'll figure out what happens next after we patch this last Glyph. What are we going into this time?"

This cine is called *Transcendence*—interplanetary action adventure genre. You'll be dropping at about the thirty-minute mark. That's a little earlier than the algorithms predict you'll find the final Glyph, but we're hoping you can interact with as many characters as possible to find Mr. Wright," Tark says. "We'll be monitoring, so if you do find him, hold onto him like you would if your were patching a Glyph. But hold on as long as you can so we can copy his origination code. It takes longer than just uploading a patch."

"What happens then?" I ask.

"Then we'll be able to find out where he is here in Admin City. He couldn't have accessed our virtuo-cine network hack to the Grid from anywhere else. He's here somewhere," Tark says. "Once we find out where he is, we'll send people to bring him to us."

"And they won't hurt him, right?" I ask, but Tark is already shaking his head.

"No. He won't be hurt. That's not how we operate." I let out a breath, then take in another just as Calyx, Liam, and Eco come back through the door.

"Is Zoe all right?" Myra immediately asks.

"She will be; right now she's resting. Azeris is with her, and so is Arwyn," Calyx says, smiling so big the silver ring in her bottom lip glints in the light.

"So you reversed the Vishan treatment?" I ask.

"No, we tried, but we can't reverse that. It's been grafted into her DNA too long, but we did get the cellular breakdown to stop…that's why she was so weak," Liam says. "The infrared light from the port-carnate hub triggered the degeneration…just like the sun would have done."

"How did you get the breakdown to stop?" Fraya asks.

"We doubled up the parent DNA graft from the archive…*gave her another dose*, as you put it," Liam says, then sends me a wink. "Thanks for the idea."

I smile at him as everything in my chest starts to expand, but only because I wouldn't even have thought to give her another dose if it weren't for Liddick's port-carnate debacle, and if Liam didn't look so much like him at that moment.

"So she can be topside? Is that what you're saying?" Myra asks, her eyes wide with hope. Liam smiles.

"That's right," he nods, and the explosion of happiness in the room is almost too much. My vision blurs with tears that come out of nowhere, and I squeeze my eyes shut to focus them again. I turn to Arco when I feel his hand on my shoulder.

"She can stay with us..." I say through another deluge of tears. He nods and pulls me close.

"See, you were right...everything is going to work out."

***

"Last stop, ladies and gentlemen. Patch this Glyph, and your mission will be complete," Tark says as the cylinder of floor-to-ceiling gradient color starts spinning in the center of the virtuo-cine chair circle. The Platform layer looks like it's turning into a star field with a bright orange planet in the foreground, surrounded by three huge rings, and another, smaller planet in the distance.

"Which planet were we on in the last cine?" I ask.

"*Infinitum* takes place on Evion Eight...that's the smaller one in the distance. You'll be going to the planet with the rings...Halcyon in *Transcendence*," Tark says.

"Do you know which one of these cines Liddick is in yet?"

"No, his signature keeps jumping...it's part of his encryption," Eco says. "Don't worry. I'll find him," he adds, narrowing his eyes.

I better find him first, I think. Lyden nods at me.

We'll find him. Don't worry. Eco can't do anything to him ...not with the storyboarder clearance Liddick has.

I take a deep breath as the silver rods lower to my temples, then glance at Arco. He winks at me and smiles.

"You ready to save the world?" he asks. I laugh, and feel a lot of the tension I didn't know I had slip away.

"Ready as I'll ever be," I answer.

"All right, like I said before, you're dropping about twenty minutes into the cine to maximize your chances of finding Mr. Wright. He won't look like himself because of his bioprint mask, which is top of the line storyboarder grade. Do not try to engage him for answers, just make physical contact for as long as you can when you are sure it must be him. We'll do the rest," Tark explains.

"The Glyphs seem to congregate around tension, so it's most likely you'll find it near the climax of the cine," Calyx adds.

"All uplinks are online, ma'am," a technician says. "Dropping in five…four…three…two…one."

I hear voices before I can see anything this time. I turn toward the sound, which is just mumbling at first, but after a second, I hear a name and can also see images starting to materialize.

"Lieutenant Waverly, is your team completely assembled?" a tall, reddish haired woman asks me. She's wearing a white jumpsuit with a glinting name plate just under her collarbone. I try to focus on it…*is it Greene*? I think. "Lieutenant?"

"Uh, yes?" I say, looking around as the bright light starts to fade more and images of a man I don't recognize, but I also see Arco, Vox, and the others appearing around me. They're all wearing the same white uniform as the tall woman, and when I look down at myself, I'm wearing one too. "Yes, we're the team," I say, having no idea what I'm talking about yet.

"Good. For the next 24 hours, under no circumstances are you to leave the Captain, is that understood? He's still recovering from the last ground assault," she adds, then glances over to a tall man standing by some circular discs on the floor.

"Yes, ma'am," I say, following her eyes. The man who must be the captain turns around, and the hairs on the back of my neck stand up. He's a little older, maybe Lyden's age, and has black, wavy hair that reminds me of Pitt. His sharp, pointed nose seems sharper and longer when he narrows his eyes at me, which are a bright, unnatural blue like Tieg's. *Maybe subordinates aren't supposed to make eye contact...*I think, and look away as quickly as I can.

"How's Lieutenant Ridley?" he asks the woman who was just talking to me. She turns to face him, and for a second, she looks exactly like Ms. Rheen from Gaia. They talk for a few more seconds until the captain suddenly looks directly at me again. Panic swells in my chest, but it's not mine. I feel the urge to leave, *now*...I just want to get out of here, but I'm not sure where the urgency is coming from.

Something isn't right in here, Vox says in my head, but I can't turn to look at her while the captain is trying to stare a hole through me.

We've been here exactly eight seconds, I think in reply.

Long enough for him to start drilling eyes into you, like stupid Tark all over again from that stupid barbarians cine back in Gaia.

I don't answer her, but see her heading toward the captain out of the corner of my eye.

What are you doing? I think, my heart crashing into my ribs.

Watch this, she laughs, and I know immediately that whatever she's about to do won't end well.

Vox, no! Stop whatever you're going to do! I think, but she doesn't stop, and I suddenly hear myself shouting at the captain. "Sir!" I say. He turns to me looking as startled as I feel.

"Yes, Lieutenant Waverly?" the captain says. My heart is pounding so hard in my ears now that I almost can't hear anything else. I look up at him, and now, can't seem to look away.

"Uh…our orders…what are we doing here?" I finally ask, immediately feeling stupid, but at least Vox has stopped her approach. The captain clears his throat.

"There have been some explosions near the Transcendents' protective city," he answers, then jumbles something about needing to go down there, wherever *there* is, but something about the way he's talking makes me not believe him. He's…*distracted* somehow.

"Yes…sir," I say, then push away the hair that falls into my face. I should feel relieved, but everything seems *more* panicked now. *What is happening to me?*

"Let's go—initiate port-carnate transfer," the captain turns abruptly to the technicians, who all look at him like he's split.

Vox nudges me forward, and the captain starts watching me again, so I feel obligated to stand next to him when he stands in one of the circles near the back of the room. Arco moves into the circle next to me, then leans in.

"I don't trust him; what are you picking up about him?" he asks. I shake my head, not sure how I feel…

relief and panic all at once? That doesn't make any sense. The tall, reddish haired woman almost seems to be standing guard over the console stations, and I feel a sense of relief that she's not coming with us…wherever it is we're going.

"I don't trust *her*," I whisper to Arco. He nods back at me, and then the countdown starts.

"Initializing cloud transfer to M17, grid seven, Hidden City walls. The surface climate is hostile," the technician adds.

Does that mean the weather or the people down there? I think toward Vox.

Do I look like I speak spaceship lingo, sand dollar?

Body armor suddenly appears out of nowhere on my arms and chest, as well as everyone else's.

"Whoa," I say under my breath, then feel the panic rise up all over again. *Where are we going that makes it necessary to wear this…?* I swallow the lump that forms in my throat.

Finally, we're going, Vox thinks in reply, eavesdropping like she tends to do, then elbows Myra. "Last round. I'm turning *something* into a dragon this time," she says out loud. I feel a laugh bubbling in my stomach and a smile pulling at the side of my mouth, but then I stop feeling anything as a white light washes out everything again.

CHAPTER 43
The Hidden City
Liddick

For a minute I think there must be a loading error when I see three white bands reaching up from the horizon, fading out about halfway up the sky, and then I remember there are rings around this planet. Surreal. In all the virtuo-cines I've been in, I can't believe I've never been on a planet with rings.

I turn around to see the team that Greene rounded up, but I need to shake them so I can find the server reset box I saw in the background of the Councilman's transmission from the Hidden City…wherever that is.

"Where are we?" one of the women says in a cracking voice over the helmet comms system. I squint to see her nameplate in the bright light. *Carver.*

"We're on…." *Crite…what's the name of this planet?* I think, and seconds later the word *Halcyon* appears in the lower corner of my vision just like if I were reading it on a screen. "We're on *Halcyon*, Carver, and we need to get to the Hidden City before the sun sets," I add, looking up at the huge red mass, which is about three times the size of our sun. I have no idea what happens after sunset here, but in my experience it's better to be behind walls at night than without them.

"Do we have an envoy?" the same man who stood in the transfer hub next to me says. His nameplate reads

Porter. I almost say it out loud, then catch myself staring, trying to figure out what is so familiar about him. I clear my throat.

"No, the Transcendent's can't risk going beyond their walls now," Cathcart answers just before I can get a word out, which makes me want to punch him. "Sir, if we have to be down here, may I suggest getting behind—*what?*" he stops talking just as a light appears behind us. When it fades, Lieutenant Ridley is standing there. "Cass?" Cathcart says. "But your medical clearance?"

"Greene said I was on a 24-hour medical suspension when I asked what exactly you were both doing down here without me. But then all of a sudden there was a Captain's override on my suspension, so here I am," Ridley says over the comms. Everyone looks at me.

I didn't authorize—wait…when I was disappointed she wasn't with the team… I start to think. *That must have been all it took to change the narrative with this storyboarder clearance…crite.* "Uh…yes, well, we needed some veterans on this one," I improvise, but Ridley just scowls at me.

"The brief said we're supposed to move into the Hidden City to guard the new wall, and more teams are coming in behind us to *manage* the untreated natives. You know what that means, don't you Folger?" Ridley asks, but doesn't give me time to answer before jerking a thumb at the other team members. "It means new transfers like them are going to get killed down here. This planet is done…the radiation goes two miles into the ground," she adds.

"So we should just let people here die?" Lieutenant Waverly shouts. Ridley rounds on her.

"Listen, transfer. Do you have any idea how many teams we've lost down here? And all we have to show for it is a gated city of about a hundred people that Greene and her team genetically modified to withstand the radiation. We can't get to everyone."

"Genetically *modified* one of the men asks over the comms—the same one who glared at me when we first transferred, and is now glaring at me again.

Stellar, I think, squinting to see that his nameplate says *Richards. Is he trying to get me to advertise the genetic engineering? What a chum propaganda storyline; nice try, programmers. Where's the stupid reset switch so I can get out of here?*

"It's a lost cause. There's no way to modify the rest of the colony…they don't even *want* to be modified," Ridley starts to answer, but I'm tired of everyone's yapping.

"Look, you can have a nice back and forth about ethics and logistics and anything else you think is outer ring later. Right now, we need to get to the Hidden City and neutralize the threat there. Those are my orders, do we all understand?" I ask. Ridley narrows her eyes, but Lieutenant Waverly starts *smiling* at me. Blood hammers in my ears again, and I don't understand…*what is it with that Glyph?* I shake it off, then look at the huge orange wall in the distance.

"Sir, we're about two miles outside the Hostile Zone. That's a mile closer than your team was yesterday when it dropped at our current coordinates. The untreated are *moving,*" Cathcart says, looking at a tablet. I look out on the orange, hazy horizon in the direction he's facing, but only see a heat mirage blurring everything.

They're coming to us, I think. The words just float into my head, along with the idea that the untreated people apparently need these genetic modifications for their own good...they need to be sedated so we can help them. As soon as I think this, the **Script** icon appears in the upper corner of my vision again. This time, I reach up and press it. The words **Script Approval** appear in place of the icon almost immediately, and Greene's voice floods the comms.

"Sir, we've just confirmed that the Hostile Zone is closing in on the Hidden City. They've moved a mile more, and surveillance suggests they are beyond diplomatic talks now. We've reached last resort measures...if we embed sleeper gas pockets at your current coordinates, we can neutralize the violence and treat them before anyone else gets hurt. Permission to proceed?"

I just approved that narrative, didn't I? I think. *Is that what this clearance does...floats suggested script ideas for approval?*

"Sir!" Ridley shouts over the comms. "This is *not* our problem!"

"Authorize, Dr. Greene. Give us an hour to get clear, " I say, then shoot a glare at Ridley. *I don't care if she looks like her ten years from now, Jazz would never be this selfish—mollusk programmers. You should have put Grisham in that role,* I think.

"You're going to *authorize* genetic modifications?" Lieutenant Porter asks, which brings me back into the moment. I blow out a breath.

"Listen, these two are bent out of shape because we keep losing people to the violence down here," I say, gesturing to Ridley and Cathcart. "Knocking out the untreated will take care of that problem. They're beyond reasoning now, understand? After they're out, we can treat them, and the radiation sickness will stop making them violent, got it?" I say in a hurry to get moving. All the Glyphs gape at me as Porter storms off, but I don't care. *We need vehicles…*I think, and the **Script** button appears a second later. *Excellent, I'm getting the hang of this storyboarder clearance.* I push it, then hear Greene over the comms again.

"Sir, the sleeper gas pockets are ready for laser insertion on your mark, and crews will then deploy. Your hovercraft are 93% transferred; please stand by," she says.

"Wait, if the ship is going to knock these people out, what are the crews coming for then?" Carver asks in the same cracking voice as before.

"Those would be *surgeon* crews," Cathcart says, as helpful as ever just as air-bikes materialize behind the group.

***

The wall of the Hidden City actually isn't a wall so much as it's a shoulder high circle of sand around exactly nothing.

"Well, it is called the Hidden City," Richards says, laughing at his own joke. I can't decide if he or Cathcart annoys me more.

Reveal Register, I think, then scan the air over the top of the encircling sand. Blue, scrolling code flickers into the image for a second, and then…nothing again. *What? I saw the box in the Councilman's projection. I know it's here!* I think. *Enter! Materialize! Reveal Hidden City!* I yell in my head again, but nothing happens. *Getting in here is the whole reason I have this stupid storyboarder clearance, isn't it?*

"How do we get in there?" Carver asks in her crackling voice, and I almost round on her this time.

"Cathcart, I'm sure you're dying to enlighten Lieutenant Carver…" I say, taking a deep breath to pull myself together. He raises a bushy eyebrow at me, which makes him look even more like a know-it-all professor.

"Sir, you just…"

"Of course *I* know…by all means, *you* explain how we get into the Hidden City to Lieutenant Carver," I add, trying to look as indignant as possible.

"Well…we just have to let them know we're here. The gate can only be opened from the inside," he says to Carver.

"Exactly!" I say, then push the comms button in my collar, which is the same, now that I think about it, as the one from my Gaia dive suit. "Dr. Greene. Please hail the Council chair and let him know we're at the gate."

"Yes, sir," she replies. A few seconds later, the ground begins shaking, and one of the other women in the crew starts screaming.

"Not again! No…No!"

"What's happening!?" Carver shouts.

Their fear hits me in the chest, sharp at first, then heavy…it's *actual* fear, but Glyphs don't project fear. Glyphs don't project anything.

"Relax! It's just the gate opening!" Cathcart yells over her screams. Ridley tries to restrain the other woman, who is trying to pull off her helmet.

"Get off! Get off!!" the woman yells, then takes a swing at Ridley.

"Whoa! Are you split!? Dr. Greene, medical emergency for Lieutenant Brisbane, please extract… now!"

"Locked on, extracting," Greene says over the comms in reply as Brisbane slaps at her legs. *What the hell is happening*? I think. *Glyph malfunction?*

"It's all right! Listen to me, it's gone, OK? It's miles and miles away!" Lieutenant Waverly tries to get Brisbane to focus, but winds up thrown to the ground. Something in me snaps, and I run over to her just as Brisbane disappears, and everything is quiet again.

I kneel next to her and feel ice flood my veins when she doesn't move. *Wake up…wake up…*I think. *Rip, wake up!*

In that second, Waverly's eyes open. She stares at me through the helmet glass as blood trickles from her eyebrow. Richards rushes in front of me and helps her up, and I stumble backward, out of the way. *What just happened…*I think, trying to slow everything down.

"Are you all right? Hey, hey, look at me," Richards says, studying her eyes, which are fixed on me. I can't look away from her until anger rushes over me when I realize Ridley is shaking my shoulder.

"Hey?" she says.

"Sir? Do you need medical?" Cathcart asks.

I don't have time to answer either of them before Greene's voice floods the comms again.

"We've sedated Lieutenant Brisbane; she won't be returning to the surface. Your liaison should be there any minute, Captain."

"Dr. Greene, Waverly may also need—" Ridley says over the comms.

"I'm fine," Waverly interrupts, turning out of Richards's hold to face me again. "I'm not going anywhere except inside that city."

CHAPTER 44
Transcendence: Part Two
Jazz

"Where are we?" Myra asks. Her voice sounds like it's coming from inside my head until I realize I'm wearing a helmet. I turn to her and see she's wearing one too.

"We're on...." the captain's voice comes over the comms system, and Myra and I both turn to him. "We're on *Halcyon*, Carver, and we need to get to the Hidden City before the sun sets."

Myra raises her eyebrows at me and mouths the words *I'm Carver*, then tries to stifle a laugh.

"Do we have an envoy?" Lyden asks, taking a few steps toward the captain just as a bright circle of light appears a few feet away. A dark haired woman steps out wearing the same white uniform and helmet as we are, and she's not happy.

"Cass? Your medical clearance?" one of the crew asks, surprised.

She tells him the captain cleared her, but says it with narrowed eyes and a raised chin like she's daring him to contradict her.

Guess someone didn't want to get out of bed, Vox thinks.

"Apparently we're supposed to guard this new wall from yet more hostiles. Care to tell this lot what that means, Folger?" she asks, but before the captain can say anything, she immediately gestures *to me* and says we're all going to be killed. She almost shouts that the planet is doomed anyway, insinuating we should all just leave everyone on it to their fate. I can't even believe what I'm hearing.

"So we should just let people here *die*?" I ask. I can't help it; it comes out before I can remind myself that this is just a cine. I roll my eyes at myself when it all catches up with me. *None of this matters. None of it's real,* I remind myself. She gives me the same dirty look she was giving the captain, obviously thinking I was rolling my eyes at her…*great.*

"Do you have any idea how many teams we've lost down here?" she narrows her eyes at me, walking up quickly like she's going to grab me. I feel prickles of heat run down my neck like the Vishan fire starting to light… but I know that's long gone now. "Greene and her team could only genetically modify a hundred people to withstand the radiation down here. We can't save everyone," she adds, then knocks my shoulder back with hers as she passes me.

"Genetically *modified*?" Arco asks.

"We can't get to the rest of the colony, and even if we could, they don't *want* to be modified," the woman fires back, but the captain cuts her off and says we need to get on with the mission. She looks like she's going to crawl out of her skin, and I smile at him.

"Sir, we're about two miles outside the Hostile Zone. It's moved a mile closer since yesterday. The untreated are *moving*," the same crewman—Cathcart, according to his nameplate—says. *Are the untreated the same people that were in the last cine? The tanned people who hauled off Arco so he could talk to the Council?* A barrage of words pours over the comms, but I don't have time to process everything before I hear Lyden in my head.

You see what this is all about, right?

What are you talking about?

*The untreated are the ones **without** genetic alterations... They've just fictionalized everything in this cine,* he adds, and a second later someone is screaming into the comms.

"This isn't our problem!" the dark-haired woman who was just in my face yells, then rounds on the captain.

"Authorize, Dr. Greene. Give us an hour to get clear," he answers, then turns to the woman like he's going to grab her.

"You're going to *authorize* genetic modifications?" Lyden asks, stopping him in his tracks. The captain says something to him, but I can't hear what it is over the comms. Whatever it is, it makes Lyden walk away from him looking like his hair is on fire. *They're going to perform the genetic alterations when these people are **unconscious**,* he thinks, then takes a deep breath and blows it out slowly. *This storyline is starting to feel like propaganda to me...we're both getting pulled in. Just think about finding the Glyph,* he thinks, and I know he's telling himself this as much as he's telling me.

More instructions about crews deploying come over the comms then, and nauseating panic hits my stomach.

"Wait, if *the ship* is going to knock these people out, what are the crews coming for then?" Myra asks. When I turn to her, the nausea gets worse.

It's just a cine, I mouth to her, but I can't tell if this is what helps, or if it's just the sight of hover bikes suddenly appearing next to us that erases her anxiety.

It's not a dragon, but I'll take it, Vox thinks, then raises an eyebrow at me and walks to a bike.

***

We aren't riding long before we stop at a big circle of orange sand that seems to be at least a quarter mile around, but there's nothing inside it.

"Well, it *is* called the Hidden City," Arco says through a muffled laugh when he rides up next to me.

"How do we get in there?" Myra asks, and the captain suddenly whips around to face us.

"Cathcart, explain how we get into the Hidden City to Lieutenant Carver," he says, but something is wrong with him…I can feel his nerves scratching inside my chest like an itch I can't reach.

What is wrong with him? I think toward Lyden.

I'm picking up the same…mania? Or maybe it's anxiety? But Glyphs aren't supposed to project emotion.

Could it be…Liddick? I almost don't let myself think it.

"Dr. Greene," the captain says over the comms. "Tell the Council chair we're at the gate."

"Yes, sir," she replies, and a minute later the ground under our feet starts shaking like it did in the Rush when the tunnel sharks attacked us. When I look over at Fraya , I realize this must be her feeling. She immediately starts screaming.

"No! Not again!"

"What's happening!?" Myra shouts.

I'm standing between them, not sure which is my fear and which is theirs, but I am sure that it's all compounding like a weight on my chest. I have to stop this.

I grab Fraya's shoulders to make her look at me, but she just starts screaming again, this time swinging her arms everywhere like something is attacking her.

"Get off! Get off!!" Fraya slaps at her legs like something is crawling all over them. *It's the tunnel shark…she must be seeing the tunnel shark wrapping around her all over again.* I think.

"Fraya! Listen to me, it's gone! It's miles and miles away!" I shout, trying to grab her shoulders again so she'll look at me. She does for just a second, and her eyes are like a trapped, wild animal's. She pushes me as hard as she can, and I see her swatting at her legs again just before everything goes black.

***

There's noise somewhere far in the distance, muffled, but then it gets louder and clearer until it sounds like shouting in my head.

Wake up…wake up…Rip, wake up!

I open my eyes and see Liddick leaning over me, but he's blurry. I blink hard to make my eyes focus, then see the captain's unnaturally blue eyes looking down at me. His dark brows are are drawn together as I try to sit up, and my head starts pounding. Arco is next to me in seconds helping me up, but I can't tear my eyes away from the captain, who now looks just as shocked as I feel.

"Are you all right? Hey, hey, look at me," Arco asks, moving in front of my face.

I nod absently, then swallow hard trying to figure out what just happened. *It must have been a flashback…Fraya had a flashback from when the tunnel shark attacked, and that must be what happened to me too just now…when Liddick was kneeling next to me after I fell. That has to be what happened, I think.*

"Lieutenant Brisbane is sedated. Your liaison should be there any minute, Captain." Dr. Greene's voice is loud in my helmet.

"Dr. Greene, Waverly may also need—"

"I'm fine," I say the second I hear the dark-haired woman's voice trying to get rid of me. I don't know why I can't stand her, but I suddenly realize that's exactly how I feel about her…she just feels like a lie. Everything she says, everything she does, it's like she's purposely here to sabotage me, even though that doesn't make any sense. Arco's hands are gripping my shoulders, but anger has made me feel steady on my own two feet again. I nod at him, then turn to the captain, ready to find this last Glyph.

"The only place I'm going is inside that city," I say just as the last of the rumbling stops under my feet.

CHAPTER 45
The Hidden City: Part Two
Liddick

The ground stops shaking right after Waverly's declaration that she's not going back to the ship for medical attention, despite the blood that's still trickling from her eyebrow. I want to go to her, but she's just a Glyph…watching her getting thrown during that little earthquake was just too close to what happened in the Rush with the tunnel shark…when Jazz fell on the tanglebush branch and I thought she was gone. I squeeze my eyes shut to push a way the thought. I need to push all thoughts of her out of my head before these cine programmers find a way to use them too for the obvious propaganda they're designing with this cine. I'm damn sure not going to help them.

After another few seconds, another tall, thin, very pale man appears in front of the orange dirt wall, but the edges of him are warping just like the Councilman's in the port-call projection back on the ship. *This must be another one*, I think, turning to the man.

"We cannot thank you and your teams enough for coming, Captain Folger. Please follow me," he says, waving his hand over a section of the dirt wall, which doesn't do anything. He turns back to me when I don't follow. "It's all right, you will pass through now," he adds.

We pass through it just like we did through the wall in the Phase Two Gaia facility. On the other side, tall, thin, pale people with long white hair and light blue eyes like the Vishan's are everywhere. They're all wearing the same kind of long, tan tunics, and when I look more closely at whatever is moving on their necks, I see that they're *gills. How did I not notice this in the Councilman's projection?* I wonder, then realize I wasn't looking at him...I was trying to find the reset switch, which is exactly what I need to do now. *Reset Register,* I think, and see exactly *nothing* change. I blow out a breath and press my teeth together.

"Where did the Councilman call from?" I finally ask the guide. He doesn't turn around to answer me.

"This is a call to action in partnership with the Carboderm Corporation and Biotech Global..." he says, the propaganda sending a stab of anger through me. I move to grab his shoulder, which sinks under the pressure of my hand, then moves through my fingers. I pull my hand back.

"What just happened!?" I blurt, almost jumping out of my skin.

"Apologies...the port-call smart atoms cannot fully mesh," the guide says as his shoulder reforms. "Our access to the port-cloud is not fully functioning because of the protective ion dome over the city. We will be able to take it down once all those in the Hostile Zone are treated." A shiver runs down my spine, and I try to shake it loose. "Again, to answer your question, thank you for answering our call to action. We value our partnership with your crew, and the entire Global Cloud Fleet..." he starts, but is interrupted when one of the new women in my crew tries to tackle him. He stumbles, but then straightens as she falls *right through* him. She hits the ground face first, then springs back up, now dripping with pieces of his port-cloud projection.

"What are you doing!?" Ridley yells, shoving the new woman as the smart-atoms float back to the guide, reconfiguring once they reach the holes she made.

"I'm going to be sick!" Lieutenant Carver yells, then covers her mouth and turns away.

"What the actual hell was all that about?" I say, still in disbelief.

"Why are you liquid?" the woman asks, flipping her black hair out of her eyes.

"He's not liquid!" Ridley scolds again, then finds the woman's nameplate. "Sergeant Diaz, is this your first day out of flight school?"

"*I'm* just a sergeant? What skod decided that?" Diaz says, mumbling something else as she makes her way back to the others. Ridley looks at me like she's just seen aliens land, and I'm starting to wonder if maybe they have. *Where is that stupid reset button?*

"Please accept our apologies, Farrow," Cathcart says to the guide. "We have some new crew members who are not familiar with port-call technology."

"I know about—!" Diaz starts to say until Lieutenant Waverly elbows her hard in the ribs, making her cough. I smile...*that's exactly what Jazz would have done,* I think, then feel blood pounding in my head again.

"It's perfectly fine...I didn't feel anything at all. I suppose there are some benefits to our port-cloud connection not fully functioning. I will take you to the reconstruction site now so you can assess the damage from the explosives," Farrow says.

"I thought you were going to take us to the Councilman?" I say, probably too abruptly.

"Yes, tonight. We have a feast planned to thank you for helping us," he adds.

I press my teeth together again so I don't scream at the top of my lungs at this hologram with skin.

He leads us through orange dirt streets with what seem to be printed houses like the ones back in Skyboard North, only much smaller. They're all the same square shape, the same white color, with the same two front windows and oversized door.

"How did you build these?" Waverly asks, like she's reading my mind.

"We did not build them. They were sent here by the Global Cloud Fleet as temporary facilities during our time of transition," Farrow says, then nods to me. "Your generosity is appreciated."

"No problem," I say, nodding back to him just as Ridley catches up to me.

"We really need all these people to patch a hole in their wall, Folger?" she asks.

"Apparently Greene thought so," I answer, looking back at Cathcart talking up a storm to the new crew. "What's that about?"

"They don't know *anything*—it's like they've never been off Earth before. He's bringing them up to speed on our involvement with the Halcyon Council," she says as the ground starts vibrating again.

"What's happening? We're already inside the gate!" Carver yells.

"Relax, it's just the lasers for the sleeper pockets," Cathcart says.

"Those people back there are being gassed right now?" Richards asks, glaring at me *again*. I'm not taking this from a stupid Glyph.

"What's your *general* problem, Lieutenant?" I say, turning to him. "You've had a bad attitude since you walked onto my transfer deck."

"I just find it interesting that instead of trying to deal with the radiation problem, you think it's a better idea to genetically engineer people to tolerate it."

"You see that big red ball in the sky up there, Richards?" Ridley answers before I can think of anything to say that makes sense, then points to the oversized sun. "That's got about another hundred years before the radiation is so strong it will force everyone into the core of the planet. Got any ideas how to stop that?"

"*Actually—*" Richards starts to answer her, but Lieutenant Waverly grips his shoulder and says something I can't hear. Whatever it is makes him stop talking all together, but it doesn't get rid of his attitude. I'm about to say something to him when we all stop walking. Farrow gestures to patches of orange desert right in the middle of the road several feet away. The street looks torn, like a painting with the desert showing through the ripped out piece.

"This city is as visible through that hole as the desert beyond is to us now," Farrow says. "It is only a matter of time before the untreated discover it and destroy us."

"Where did they get carbon bombs?" Cathcart asks. "That's the only thing that could blow a hole in the parmide wall."

Parmide? I think...*like the Gaia bracelets*? I'm compelled to look at Ridley, who instantly looks guilty.

"Cass, did you...? No...I can't believe it."

"Stow it, Mark."

"That explosion *broke* your leg..."

"What explosion?" Diaz asks, breaking the accusatory silence. The explosion...when I first dropped into this cine, we were running away from the Transcendents.

"Did you set off that bomb?" I ask, and she laughs in my face.

"Folger, you're really a piece of work, you know that? So I'm going to take the fall for this one, huh?"

I shake my head at her trying to put all the pieces together, but something tells me to drop it, fast.

"We'll discuss this later," I say, clearing my throat as Farrow looks from Ridley to me with his mouth falling open. "For now, we need to get this hole repaired. Dr. Greene, we're going to need some parmide down here," I say over the comms.

"I'm tracing your location," Greene says. "I've also found the breech. This will take time to repair, sir."

"How long?"

"A few hours at least."

"Make it happen. Ridley and I are going to find the Councilman while the rest of the team stands watch."

Lieutenant Ridley scowls at me again, but she presses her lips together to keep whatever she has to say to herself.

"We'll get started with the parmide remote repair now," Greene says.

"Thank you," I say, then turn to Farrow. "Repairs will begin immediately, and my team will stand guard here to make sure your people remain secure in the meantime. Now, if you'll take me to the Councilman, we have an important matter to discuss," I add, gripping Ridley's upper arm and giving Farrow a knowing smile.

"What—? Folger, what are you—?" Ridley starts.

"I wouldn't say another word, Lieutenant," I say, then give *her* a knowing look. She scans my face for an answer she doesn't seem to find. *Trust me, he needs to think I'm turning you in,* I think, wishing she could hear my thoughts like Jazz. Maybe she does because her face relaxes.

"Cass…" Cathcart says, shaking his head. "I never thought you would go this far."

"Let's go," I say before she has a chance to reply. "After you, Farrow. Cathcart, you're in charge of the team while I deal with this."

"Yes sir," he says, and we walk on.

"Vox, wait!" Waverly hisses after a second; I *swear* that's what she says when I turn around and see Sergeant Diaz running toward me.

"Hold right there!" I shout, surprised to see she's already so close. She looks straight at me and cocks her eyebrow, but doesn't say anything until I hear her voice in my head.

You're in there, aren't you? she asks.

What? I think in reply, but her expression doesn't change. *Can you hear me?* I ask, but she just looks at me sideways as she turns and walks back to Lieutenant Waverly.

"What was that all about?" Ridley asks. I shake my head.

"Nothing…"

"I will take you to the Councilman now," Farrow says, and we start moving again. I look over my shoulder and see Waverly staring at me, and for just a second, the images flicker in and out, flashing blue code. Just before they reset, Waverly looks exactly like Jazz standing there with a pleading look on her face as she grips Diaz's arm. *Crite*, I think, turning around to follow Farrow. *I need to find that reset button before I can't tell the difference between this stupid cine and reality anymore.*

CHAPTER 46
Transcendence: Part Three
Jazz

The ground finally stops vibrating, and I know the other teams are descending from the ship now to perform the genetic alterations on the sleeping hostiles. I don't agree with it, but if their sickness is making them so violent, I also don't see another way. Lyden is right, though, we're getting too pulled into this storyline. We need to move forward into the Hidden City so we can find the Glyph.

After a second, a pale, tall man with long white hair and an off-white tunic that's belted around the waist appears in front of the huge circular wall of orange dirt. He starts talking to the captain as I look around for Fraya.

Where did she go? I think toward Lyden.

She had a break…Calyx pulled her out. She's in the med-bay now with Arwyn.

Is she all right? I ask. He nods, then points toward the captain who is walking through the dirt…actually walking *through* it like we walked through the wall at Eco's hab. We follow him.

More tall, pale people who are also dressed in tunics are walking around, some of them heading into white, square houses that all look the same…like little boxes with oblong doors and a perfectly square window on each side.

"Thank you for answering our call to action. We value our partnership with your crew, and the entire Global Cloud Fleet" he answers, but suddenly, the captain *lunges* at him, grabbing his arm. He leaps back just as suddenly and studies his hand, shocked.

"What?"

"Apologies...the port-call smart atoms cannot fully mesh," the tall, pale man answers, but I don't know what he's talking about.

Why is he telling us that? I think, then glance at Vox. Her snake eyes are wild when she looks back at me. *Whoa...what's wrong?*

"Again, to answer your question, thank you for answering our call to action. We value our partnership with your crew, and the entire Global Cloud Fleet..." the pale man says again, but then *Vox* runs toward him as fast as she can. She tries to jump on him too, but just winds up falling *through* him, somehow ripping a hole through the middle of him. *Vox!* I think, as she jumps back up with pieces of him...*dripping* off of her.

The dark-haired woman with the captain yells. She pushes Vox as the pieces of the pale man drift back together like the blue goo from the bat in the Vishan cave. I shudder at the memory.

"What happened? Why are you liquid?" Vox asks, staring at the pale man.

"*What*? He's not liquid!" the dark-haired woman narrows her eyes, then takes a few steps toward Vox. "Sergeant Diaz, is this your first day out of flight school?"

"*I'm* just a sergeant? What skod decided that?" Vox says, then heads right for Arco and me. "That's the

Glyph, she whispers. I heard it. I heard part of a message."

"Please accept our apologies, Farrow," Lieutenant Cathcart says to the pale man, then gives Vox a sideways look. "We have some new crew members who are not familiar with port-call technology."

"Uh, I know about—" Vox starts to retort, but I elbow her as hard as I can so she shuts her vent. They're going to send us back to the ship if she keeps this up, and then we'll never get to the Glyph.

"It's perfectly fine…I didn't feel anything at all," the pale man says, then says something else to the captain as I glare at Vox.

What did you hear? How do you know that's the Glyph? I think toward Vox.

He was telling that captain that this was a 'call to action in partnership with the Carboderm Corporation and Biotech Global.' Why would a line like that be in this cine? It has to be one of those subliminal pieces of the message.

I nod at her, then notice Lieutenant Ridley glaring at us. I clear my throat and start looking around.

We pass more white box houses, and I actually do wonder where they all came from with no sign of buildings or even trees anywhere.

"How did you build these?" I finally ask the pale man. Lieutenant Ridley gives me another sneer and then finally turns away as the guide answers me, but I'm too busy wondering what Ridley's problem is to pay attention to what he has to say.

Lieutenant Cathcart falls back, eyeing Vox up and down before crossing to walk on the other side of me.

Now that I see him up close, he really looks like he could be Arco's older brother.

"You're all obviously new to our mission…" he starts, shooting another glance at Vox. "I don't know what anyone has told you, but the Transcendents are not our enemies. The people in the Hostile Zone aren't even our enemies. We are just tired of losing crews when it seems like a doomed cause. They're just too far gone. Lieutenant Ridley up there is pretty adamant about that, but she's seen a lot of people die," he adds as the ground starts shaking again.

"What's happening? We're inside the gate!" Myra's voice is shrill over the comms.

"Relax, it's just the lasers for the sleeper pockets…" Cathcart says, turning to her and holding up a hand.

"Those people back there are being gassed right now?" Arco almost shouts.

"What's your *general* problem, Lieutenant?" the captain fires at him over his shoulder before I can remind Arco not to get pulled in.

"I just find it *interesting* that you think it's a better idea to genetically engineer people instead of dealing with the radiation problem," Arco fires right back, taking a step toward the captain, but he's met by Lieutenant Ridley.

"You see that up there in the sky, Richards?" she asks, pointing to the huge red sun. "In a hundred years, the radiation will force everyone into the core of the planet. This place is doomed. You think you can reverse that?"

"*Actually*—" Arco starts, but I have to stop him before he gets us sent back onto the ship too. I pull his shoulder down to me and mouth *it's just a cine*. He sighs, but finally nods.

The pale man clears his throat, which pulls our attention back to him. He waves his hand toward a giant hole that's somehow in the middle of the dirt road, but there's another image inside the hole...it looks like the orange desert we just came from.

"Where did they get carbon bombs?" Lieutenant Cathcart asks, rounding on Lieutenant Ridley. "That's the only thing that could blow a hole in the parmide wall. Cass, did you...?" he stumbles, then shakes his head. "You wouldn't..."

"Stow it, Mark," Ridley says through her teeth, and there's something about the pinched, arrogant look on her face that actually makes me want to punch her.

Cathcart whispers something to her, and there's awkward silence for several seconds until Vox's voice breaks it like a rock through a window.

"What explosion?"

"*You* set off that bomb?" the captain asks, startling Lieutenant Ridley. She turns to him and *actually* laughs.

"Are you kidding me, Folger? You think I'm going to take the fall for this one?"

They think she blew the hole in the Transcendents' wall? Why would she do that? She's with the crew that's helping them, isn't she? I think, finding Lyden.

It looks like they're setting her up as the traitor, Lyden answers. *The people on the ship are the good guys, genetically modifying people for their own good. I think they're positioning her as the antagonist to the mission.*

"Cass..." Cathcart says, shaking his head. "I never thought you would take it this far."

Lyden nods at me, confirming his suspicion. *And he's apparently trying to distance himself now that she's exposed.*

"Let's go," the captain says, but the way he looks at Lieutenant Ridley is off somehow...familiar somehow, the way Liddick looked at me on the beach after the marlin spoke to us, and Arco was heading our way with Jax.

My heart starts hammering in my chest...*Liddick?* I think.

"Cathcart, you're in charge of the team while I deal with this."

"Yes sir," Cathcart says, too enthusiastically. He turns back to us, but Vox takes off running again toward the captain, and I'm afraid she's going to try to tackle the pale man again, or maybe...*Liddick?*

"Vox, wait!" I call after her, but the captain has already held out a hand to her.

"Stop right there!" he yells, but they just stare at each other in a standoff.

What are you doing? I shout at her in my head. But she doesn't answer me.

She's trying to read him, Lyden thinks, taking a step toward them. Vox finally turns around and starts walking back toward me.

That's your boyfriend, she thinks, her yellow eyes drilling into me. *You saw it. That's why I saw it.*

You think that's Liddick? Are you sure?

*I don't have to be sure. **You're** sure,* she thinks again.

*I'm **not** sure!*

He heard me. I asked him if he was in there, and he heard me.

The captain—Liddick?—takes Lieutenant Ridley's elbow and starts walking back toward the pale man again, then stops and looks back at us…at me. *Is it you?* I think, and I feel him, but just for a second. He heard me. In that second, I know Vox is right. I *know* he heard me.

***

The bright light comes out of nowhere, and I can't see anything until the blurry steel beams of the Boneyard come into view. I hear the hydraulics of the metal rods moving past my ears, and I blink until everything finally comes into focus.

I sit up and see Eco and Calyx bent in front of a console while Tark seems to be arguing with my dad and Liam about something.

"*Transcendence* is unlinked," a technician in white says. I scan for Fraya, but she's not in her uplink chair. Jax is nowhere to be found either.

"What's happening?" I say, getting to my feet. Arwyn makes her way over to me, waving Arco to us.

"It's Liddick…Tark is convinced he's working against us because of the propaganda he's writing with his storyboarder credential. Liam and your dad are trying to get Tark to see reason."

"He's *writing* that stuff?" Arco asks.

"No…I mean I don't think so," Arwyn says, wrinkling her forehead when she meets my eyes again. "It just doesn't look good. We have entry points where he's added script. He seems to know what he's doing in there."

"He's the captain, isn't he? He's Folger?" I ask, but I already know the answer. Arwyn nods. "Does he know it's us in there? Can he see through our bioprint masks?"

"Yours glitched right before we pulled you out. He should have been able to see you then, but he's still making a B-line to the center of the Hidden City, so it doesn't look like whatever his agenda is has changed," Arwyn says, then looks at me long and hard. "Jazwyn, did you notice a striking resemblance between yourself and Lieutenant Ridley?"

"No, I just got the impression she was trying to sabotage us or something. What are you trying to say?" I ask what Arco already seems to know from the way his brows draw together.

"Are you all right?" Ellis interrupts, joining our little circle. He seems out of breath. There's also sweat on his upper lip as a wave of anxiety hits me.

"Are *you* all right?" I ask, studying him. He nods, then shakes his head.

"I don't believe it. He's my best friend," Ellis says.

"Will someone tell us what's happening?" Myra asks, struggling to keep her voice steady.

"Liddick is the captain, and that ghost hologram person is the last Glyph," Vox says *way* too casually.

"You completely ate it with that swan dive," Avis says, starting to laugh until Vox pins him to the wall with her snake eye stare. His face immediately resets to neutral as his eyes hit the floor.

"Everyone just calm down." Tark raises his voice above the commotion. Liam and my dad look like they want to kill someone, but Tark's face is expressionless as he takes a deep breath. "There is evidence enough to suggest that Mr. Wright has been compromised…I don't want to believe it any more than you do, but there's no other explanation for the script he changed with his storyboarder credential, or the characters he created," Tark says.

"What characters?" Myra asks.

"We reverse engineered the structure of Lieutenants Ridley and Cathcart, and also Dr. Greene—their origin codes are memory based, like the firewall codes in the Glyphs."

"So, they're…*personalized*?" Myra asks, confused.

"They think that since Liddick has the storyboarder credential, he created those characters to turn people against Jazwyn and Arco in case they were to become a threat in the future. Rheen is painted like the doting mother, so they think she's the one who recruited him," Liam says, crossing his arms over his chest, almost like he's trying to hold himself back from tackling Tark himself. Arwyn puts a hand on his shoulder, evidently getting the same impression.

Ellis shakes his head. "He would never do that, especially not to Jazz."

"We don't know what his circumstances are now, Mr. Raj. People are capable of almost anything under the right conditions," Tark says. "Regardless, we need to find the last Glyph before he destroys it. If that happens, everything we've done here over the last few days will have been for nothing."

"And what about Liddick? How do we get him out of there?" I ask, still not believing that he'd betray us like Tark thinks he has, but he just shakes his head at me. *Oh, no way,* I think. *Is he saying we're going to abandon him?* "You can't just leave him in there…" I say. "Calyx, tell him!"

She looks up from her console at me sympathetically, pulling her eyebrows together and biting the silver ring in her bottom lip.

"Jazwyn, we've run every scenario…he has no motivation to write the script he's written about genetically modifying that culture."

"He did *not* want to hurt people," I insist, remembering how surprised he was when he found out about the explosion Lieutenant Ridley caused.

"We don't have his side of the story—we can't assume anything yet," Lyden says, moving behind the console with Calyx and Eco to study the code projection.

"Dad, *say* something." I take a step toward him, and he looks up at me from whatever he was watching on the floor.

"We can only see if he tries to go after the last Glyph," he finally answers. "Yes, he entered the network through our hack. Yes, he accessed our cine queue and seems to be writing some questionable things, but as I've said, Skull, I don't believe he's trying to sabotage The Seam's mission. It's what my gut is telling me, even though I don't have evidence to support it."

"I'm sorry…we just can't risk—"

"Take off my bioprint mask. Let me go in as me," I interrupt. "Give me the last biochip. I'll explain to him what's happening out here...I'll ask him to hand over the Glyph. Then you'll see he's not a traitor."

"Jazz, you can't go in there unmasked. Gaia is looking for us...we're flagged, remember? They'll know you're on the Grid and they'll—" Arco stops abruptly like he's deciding something, then shakes his head. "No, it's just too risky."

"It's not your decision, Arco. It's mine," I say, trying not to sound too clipped because I know he just wants to protect me, but this is the only way to get to the truth. I turn back to Tark. "Send me in at the climax of the cine... at the highest point of tension. You said that's where the Glyph would most likely be, right? Send me in, then pull me out. I won't need a lot of time if Liddick can see me as *me*."

"I've known that boy for six years," Azeris says, coming through the ring of consoles with his arm around Zoe. "He gave me a reason again after I thought I lost everything," he adds, looking down at her. "Never met anybody more loyal...and he loves that girl. Ain't no way he'd be the cause of any harm to her." Azeris nods to me, and heat explodes into sharp prickles down my back and up my throat. My heart starts pounding so hard I think it will crash through my ribs, so I take a deep breath and blow it out.

"Let me try to bring him back. *Me...*" I finally manage to say, looking Tark in the eyes just like I did when he tried to stare me down after the barbarian virtuo-cine in his class back at Gaia. *I'm not backing down...I won't be intimidated.*

"I'm going with her," Arco says, taking my hand, then leaning over to whisper into my hair. "I can't just watch you risk everything... I can't just stand by and do nothing. At least let me go with you."

I turn to face him. He's raising his eyebrows, genuinely *asking* me for this. I sigh, and he smiles, letting out the breath he was apparently holding.

"I still haven't turned anything into a dragon," Vox says. "Are you going to show me how to do that or what?" she adds, raising her chin at Eco. He laughs under his breath, the lights in his cheekbones flashing blue and white.

I laugh, too, feeling all the words I want to say get stuck in my tightening throat as Fraya passes the circle of consoles with Jax, then climbs into her chair as Myra and Lyden climb back into theirs, too.

"We're going back in with her," Fraya says. Tark shakes his head, but finally shrugs.

"Queue it back up," he says to the tech as he walks behind another console.

I turn back to Arco, speechless. He moves his hands over my face and looks at me hard, his hazel eyes lighting.

"Ready to go save the world?" he whispers. I swallow and nod again in reply. He leans in and kisses me this time, then strokes my cheek. "Then let's go save the world."

CHAPTER 47
Reset Register
Liddick

I can't get the image of Jazz out of my head, standing there just watching me. She called out to *Vox*…not Diaz, *Vox*. And I know I heard what I heard: *You're in there, aren't you*? It was Vox's voice. Could the programmers get her *voice* from my memories? What would be the point of it? She said, *You're in there, aren't you*? That has nothing to do with the propaganda in this stupid cine. It has nothing to do with the storyline at all. There's no agenda whatsoever to that…

"What's raking your coals?" Ridley asks as we follow Farrow deeper into the Hidden City, where the streets are darker and all the little white house structures have disappeared.

"Just a lot on my mind," I say.

"Like selling me out?"

I look straight into her eyes and decide that no, she's nothing like Jazz. How else does Ridley think we're going to get to talk to the Council Leader? This is win-win…she gets to sabotage this mission, and I get to flip the reset switch. Why is this hard? I can't say any of this with Farrow right in front of us, though, so she's just going to have to think I'm betraying her. I don't care…she doesn't even exist…*why am I even thinking about this*?

"You're taking us to the port-call room, right?" I ask Farrow, who is just a few steps ahead of us. He turns and looks down his long nose at me, then glances at Ridley, but doesn't answer. Something is wrong. "What's the status of the parmide repairs?" I say quickly over the comms, loud enough so Farrow can hear me.

"About fifty precent complete, sir," Dr. Greene says.

"Hold right there. Resume on my command."

"Sir?"

"You heard me. Stop reconstruction of that wall. Resume on my command."

"Uh, yes sir."

I stop walking. Farrow turns to face me, and I look up, studying his long, thin, chalky face. His wild, icy eyes are narrowed under his white brows like he knows something I don't, but he doesn't have any cards. I'm the one with something he wants, and I'm done playing games. I want out of this cine. I want to find Jazz.

"So, are we going to that port-call room, or what?"

"What is of such interest to you there?" Farrow asks, and Ridley nods.

"Yeah, what are you so bent about in that room?"

"Be quiet," I tell her. "And that's between the Councilman and me, Farrow. So you can take me there right now and deliver *her* to your superiors—she's the one responsible for blowing the hole in your wall in the first place..."

"Folger!" Ridley interrupts, trying to pull out of my grip, but I hold on tighter.

"*Or*...I can just let that hole stay open. The Hostile Zone is closing in; you knew that, right, Farrow? They should be only about a mile out by now."

Farrow's eyes go wide, almost as wide as Ridley's. I look away from her because she really does look like Jazz, but she's *not* Jazz. She's not even real.

"Folger, we were together on this," Ridley says, almost whispering, which feels like a spike right through the middle of my chest. I freeze for a second.

Don't tweak...she's just a character in a cine. Find the switch and get this over with, I think, pressing my teeth together.

"That wasn't me," I say, and it's true. My first memory of Ridley is nearly getting blown up with her. If Folger was her co-conspirator in betraying these people like she was insinuating back there with the crew, that happened before my boots were hitting the ground. *There's nothing to feel guilty about here. Press on,* I think.

Farrow studies my face again, and I try to keep my expression neutral. I'm the one with the power; he doesn't have a choice.

"All right," he finally says, then wraps his long, bony fingers around Ridley's arm. She winces, then tries to jerk out of his grip. I bite down harder to keep from reacting.

"Folger! You can't do this! Why!?"

I don't look at her because I know if I do, it will be all over. Farrow will see me crack and the power will shift again. I have to look like I don't care...*and I **don't,** damn it. This is a cine. I don't care about this woman; she's not even real!*

"So, what's it going to be, Farrow? You going to be a hero for your people, or are you going to let them get torn apart by savages?" I say, knowing he has no idea those savages are already unconscious and being treated by the surgeon crews from the ship.

"There's no one coming!" Ridley yells, and I close my eyes in a long blink, kicking myself for even thinking this ...it must have made it part of the script—stupid storyboarder credential!

"Ridley, stow it! That's an order!" I yell, but it doesn't do any good.

"The surgeon crews are already deployed. The Hostile Zone is neutralized...they're already under treatment!" she follows, still struggling to get free of Farrow's grip.

His eyes dart to mine, and I know I have to talk fast: "She still blew the hole in your wall. Who do you think authorized the surgeon crews, Farrow? That was me. And all I have to do is make one call to stop them—one call to reverse the process...to reverse *your* treatment, and that of the entire protected population. Are you hearing me, Farrow? Take me to that port-call room!" I yell at him. I yell through him, and in a second, the map icon appears in the corner of my vision with a glowing arrow path in front of me.

I blink, and in that blink, Ridley finally manages to pull out of Farrow's grip. She starts running directly along the arrow path...*how can she see that*? **Can** *she see that*? I think? I take off after her as fast as I can, but it all seems like slow motion with Farrow just a few footsteps behind me.

Different holographic room layouts flash into my vision, and I swipe them away so I can keep my eyes on the glowing arrow path. Ridley *must* be able to see it because she follows it even when we come to a fork in the path, which has turned into a tunnel at some point. We veer left, and I feel Farrow's sharp fingers digging into my arm. I pick up my pace, and it falls away just as I nearly trip across the threshold at the end of the glowing arrow path. The Councilman is sitting behind a desk, wearing the same tan tunic he wore in the port-cloud call. Farrow moves to stand next to him in the hub.

"Liddick!" I hear, then see *Jazz and Vox* rush over the threshold with Hart, Fraya, and Myra in their wake.

"Stop!" I shout, pointing to them as I move toward the real Farrow, who's standing in the port-call hub not far from the desk. I pull out the neural baton that appears in my belt, and everything in my head that was racing a million miles an hour stops abruptly and crashes inside my skull. I raise the neural baton to the real Farrow, then catch my breath. "Where is it?" I say…but he just shakes his gaunt, oblong face at me. I kick the port-call hub, and the projection of him next to the Councilman disappears.

"Where is *what*?" the Councilman hisses. "You said you were here to help us."

"I'm here to help *me*," I shout at him, trying to keep everything straight. *That's not Jazz. That's not any of them. But she just said my name…was that real?*

"Folger, just do it! End this whole thing already so we can go home!" Ridley yells.

"Stop acting like you know me! You don't know me!" I yell back, looking from her to Jazz, not sure how they're both standing there or why And why am I generating *Hart* and the others? Ridley's eyes widen, and she shakes her head.

"What's wrong with you, Folger?" she asks, quietly this time.

"Captain, what's happening down there? Should we resume construction of the parmide wall?" Greene says over the comms. I don't answer her. This is all coming apart...I shut my eyes tight to make everything stop for a second.

"Liddick! Listen to me!" I hear Jazz's voice again, and a line of ice runs down my back. The programmers are getting desperate...*I must be close. I am close...Reset Register,* I think, then scan the dark walls in this hole in the ground. The reset box begins glowing on the wall just a few feet away, and my breath catches *Finally...finally...I* think, then throw the cover open.

Liddick! Stop! my brother says in my head...*my brother? He's a Reader?* Lyden comes from nowhere and pushes past the others. He holds out both hands to me like I'm about to jump off a bridge or something.

"Get out of my head!" I shout, reaching for the lever inside the box. I look at him hard, but I can't control my focus, which goes in and out, changing from images of him to blue code. Lines of red text scroll, then disappear again. I can't hold my eyes still long enough to read it, but I know that red means the code has been encrypted... *That's not Lyden. None of them are real.* I reach for the lever again. "Go away! Get out of my head!" I shout at them again, but hear Jazz one more time.

Liddick, I know you're in there! *I know it's you*! She thinks. I turn to see her running into my arms, throwing hers around my neck and holding on tight. *It's her…it's really her.*

"Rip?" I say into her hair, hearing my voice crack. She nods, then pulls back, smiling with tears running down her face.

I want to believe it. It's the only thing I want to believe, but it's all a lie. I know it's a lie when Vox rushes toward the lever suddenly riding some kind of enormous green lizard with *wings*. I can only shake my head because it's too ridiculous even for her. No, they're *all* Glyphs. The programmers have already hijacked my thoughts, and now they must know I'm about to shut this propaganda split show down. *I'm an idiot. I'm an idiot for believing you*! I shout in my head to all these Glyphs, then grip the lever as hard as I can and pull.

CHAPTER 48
To Save the World
Jazz

I climb into my virtuo-cine chair last, then immediately sit up.

"Wait! What about the biochip to patch the last Glyph?" I ask.

"Since the Glyph revealed itself to Ms. Dyer, her chip will have the best chance of grafting. Just get her close, Ms. Ripley," Tark says.

"Jazwyn...thank you," Liam says. The blond tips of his hair fall into his eyes when he nods to me, making the dark roots visible. He pushes them back, just like Liddick does.

"He'd do the same for me...for any of us," I say. Liam presses his lips into a line that is on its way to a smile until he presses it harder into place.

"What happens if this doesn't work?" Fraya asks. "I mean, what happens to Liddick?"

"We won't have any way to trace him unless we get that origin lock...but that will require physical contact for more than five seconds. twenty, at least. Even then, that only gives us his launch point. When he disconnects from the Grid, he'll be a ghost again," Calyx answers.

"We'll find a way to track him Jazwyn. I promise you that," Liam says. "Just find him and let me do the rest."

"Let *us* do the rest." My dad grips Liam's shoulder as Azeris moves to his other side.

"Patch that Glyph first and foremost, do you understand? Without that, we're back at square one," Tark adds, sobering everyone to the task at hand.

"All right, you're going to be dropping at the climax of *Transcendence*, so be ready. Things may be abrupt," Calyx says just before a man's voice starts counting down.

"Ready for drop in three…two…"

I close my eyes, but instead of seeing dark, I see bright light that disappears as quickly as it comes. Lieutenant Cathcart is standing next to the now halfway repaired hole in the street with the desert on the other side. He looks totally bewildered.

"Where did the captain go?" I ask, already out of breath somehow.

"He's with Ridley…they were both following Farrow down that corridor," Cathcart says, then starts talking over the comms to the ship. "All right, please confirm, you have stopped parmide wall repair on the *captain's* order?"

"This way!" I shout, running in the direction Cathcart pointed.

"Hey!" he shouts after us, but we just keep running.

"This looks just like the Vishan tunnels!" Arco says, and he's right. The walls look like they're carved out of a mountain, black, jagged, shiny slabs of glass-like rock mixed in with dull brown…years and years of sand layers flowing like rivers through the sea of black. A light at the end of the tunnel is bright enough for us to see where we are, but I still feel like I'm going to crash into something at any second.

Liddick! I shout in my mind, hoping we're close enough that he'll hear me, but I don't get a response.

I hear voices up ahead, but I can't make out what they're saying. "Liddick!" I yell out loud this time, but still don't hear anything.

The light is getting brighter. We have to be close! Vox yells in my mind as she runs up alongside me. We cross into a big, dark room with torches on the walls like in the Vishan tunnels and see Lieutenant Ridley. She's standing behind an older, pale man who's sitting behind a huge stone desk. The captain—*Liddick*—is standing in the far corner of the room with the pale guide, except…there are now *two* pale guides.

"Stop!" Liddick yells, pointing at us, then pulls a neural baton like the ones from the Phase Two Gaia facility from his belt and holds it to the throat of the pale guide closest to him. "Where is it!?" he shouts again, then kicks the circular stand the guide is standing on. Instantly the other pale guide disappears.

"Where is *what*?" the man behind the desk barks. "You said you were here to help us."

"I'm here to help *me*," Liddick says through his teeth, and I try to reach for him.

Liddick…can you hear me? Can you see me? I think, but he just looks at me like I'm split.

"Folger, just do it! End this whole thing already so we can go home!" Lieutenant Ridley shouts.

"Stop acting like you know me! You don't know me!" Liddick shouts back, pushing the neural baton harder against the pale guide's throat.

"Listen to me!" I yell so Liddick can hear me, but he just looks at me again like I'm a ghost.

*Finally…finally…*I hear him say in my mind.

*I found you…*I think.

"Get out of my head!" Liddick yells as he reaches for something on the wall, but there's nothing there. "Go away! Get out of my head!" he shouts again.

Liddick, I know you're in there! I know it's you! I think as hard as I can. He stops grasping at the wall, and I run to him before I realize what I'm doing. I wrap my arms around him as hard as I can. *I know it's you…I know it's you…listen to me!* I think.

"Rip?" he whispers, and it's all I can do not to choke. I pull back from him, and he moves his hand to my face as he looks in my eyes like he's trying to find something there…like he's trying to find *me* there. I laugh and nod as my eyes start burning and my vision blurs with tears. But then he jerks his eyes to something behind me, then shoves me away, shaking his head. *I'm an idiot! I'm an idiot for believing you!* he thinks, reaching for the wall again, and everything flashes to white.

***

When I open my eyes again, everyone is yelling. I blink hard to focus my vision, and sit up too fast.

"You're not disconnected!" a technician yells. The room spins for a second, but then resets itself.

"I am now," I say, sitting up.

"What happened?" Arco asks, jumping out of his chair, then he grips his knees as the room no doubt starts spinning for him too.

"It's gone! I don't know, it's just gone!" Eco says, frantically typing.

"Look out," Calyx says, nearly pushing him out of the way as she takes over typing. "It's wiped...everything. All the patches..." she says as the blood drains from her face.

"What *happened*!?" Arco shouts this time.

Calyx straightens as Eco starts typing again, shaking his head the whole time as the lights in his cheekbones stream a solid line of red. My dad crosses to me and puts his hands on my face.

"Are you all right?" he asks. Jax is at his side in a minute. I nod to him, and he wraps his arms around Fraya. My dad does the same with me, but I push back from him.

"What happened? Why is everyone tweaking?"

Tark stands like a statue covering his mouth with a fist as he stares at a console screen, and my stomach sinks with dread. I look over at Liam, who's biting down so hard I can see the striations of muscles jumping in his jaw. He just keeps shaking his head.

"It's not true...it's not true..." he says over and over again to himself.

Lyden scrubs his hands over his face, then pushes them through his dark hair. He blows out a long breath, somehow already behind a console when he looks up at us.

"The patches have been purged..." he says in a quiet, slow voice. "Somehow, Liddick reset the whole virtuo-cine network. Everything we did is erased," he says.

"Why would he do that? He was acting like he was seeing things in there...something must have happened," I say, still not quite sure I understand what's going on.

Eco shakes his head and stops typing. "He's gone...no more *Ludwig Sprague* anywhere on the Grid. We got a lock on his uplink origin, though; it's a Mainframe office in Admin City, the East side, which is locked down tighter than The State. He couldn't have gotten in there without help," he says.

"So, someone put him in there; that's possible," I say, refusing to believe Liddick would betray any of us.

"He still used the storyboarder credential to find the Reset Register. That's where he was heading the whole time. Here are his plot points." Eco projects a green, holographic grid in front of the now motionless, gray virtuo-cine layer column. Red dots move in a fluid, clear vertical path in the code, which I can't read from where I'm sitting.

"What are you saying? What are you saying *exactly*?" I ask, but my stomach drops under the weight of the answer I know he already believes.

"He wasn't randomly finding his way through that cine. His target was to reset the server. He betrayed us—there's no reason he would have accessed our hack or our cine queue unless he found out about the sleeper code and wanted to stop our patch efforts. He's working for the other side," Tark says like he's just stating facts, and without looking away from that same console screen he's been staring at.

"He wouldn't do that," Azeris says. "Not in a million years."

"Well, it's done," Eco adds. "The patches we put in place are gone…it was all or nothing. The pro-Gaia, Carboderm, Biotech Global propaganda is going wide, but that's not the worst of it. It somehow leaked into the subliminal feeds too just before everything came back online. Gaia saw us coming."

Everything in me goes numb. I don't know what to think, and I don't know what I feel. It's everything and nothing all at once. *It can't be true. I felt him,* I think. *He knew it was me. He wouldn't do this.*

He said he was there to help himself…something happened to him. That's not Liddick anymore, Vox says in my head, but I can't even pull words together to respond. I look at Lyden, who seems lost and hollow.

"It doesn't make any sense," he says, shaking his head, but he's looking right through me. "There has to be something we're missing…" he moves back to the console and starts typing like a doctor resuming CPR pulses over a dead patient. I feel all the hope drain out of the room as if it were spiraling down a hole in the floor. I feel it run out of me, too, from the bottom of my chest straight through the center of the earth and into outer space on the other side.

My legs stop working, and I move to the cold floor, resting my face against the steel base of one of the virtuo-cine chairs. I close my eyes.

"What happened to you..." I whisper. "Liddick, what happened to you..."

Arco sits beside me and runs his hand over my hair, then moves his arms around me, pulling me to him. I feel like I don't have any bones anymore, and if it weren't for my skin, I'd spill in a thousand directions like water. He rests his chin on the top of my head and holds me like I'm going to disappear if he breathes...like he knows I'm made of water too.

"What does this mean?" Myra asks from somewhere very far away, and there's silence for a few seconds until Calyx answers her.

"It's over. Our hack is gone...vanished in the reset," she says. "I've been trying to get it back, but there's already a new firewall in place around the whole virtuo-cine network. We're back at square one."

"That means there's only one way to stop them..." my dad says. "That message will reach *everyone* on the Grid within days if it's already leaked into the subliminal feeds. We have to take down the port-cloud ourselves before the message gains political traction."

"But what does that *mean*?" Myra's voice cracks under the weight of the answer we all know, but are afraid to say out loud.

Tark pulls in a breath, then blows it out as slowly as he can, buying us a few more seconds in the world we know before his gold eyes finally look up from the console.

I know in that moment I have to say the word so he doesn't have to. I have to say it because I know he's spent his entire career trying to find a way to avoid it...trying to find a better way. I have to say it to make it real, to make it begin because the sooner it begins, the sooner it will end…one way or another, once and for all.

I open my mouth and am suddenly terrified, suddenly hoping the word will just voluntarily come out, but it won't. It sits on my tongue like a planet, and I have to imagine that I am an exploding sun just to force it out. When I hear it, it's barely there, barely even a word like the last echo in a canyon…

"War."

EPILOGUE
Liddick

The first thing I see when I open my eyes is my fist, still gripping the Reset lever that isn't there anymore. My knuckles are white, and the strap around my wrist is biting into my skin. It releases all at once, and I nearly hit myself in the face.

"Well done, Mr. Wright! Well done!" I hear the same shadow voice as before...*I'm back in the virtuo-cine chair. I'm done. I did it*...I think.

"I reset your stupid server. Now send me back to my friends," I say just as a man comes out of the shadows.

He's tall with slick, black hair and bright green eyes, just like Pitt's. He looks down his long, narrow nose at me and cocks his head.

"So, you're Liddick Wright," he says. "Dezzie has told me so much about you."

I nearly swallow my tongue. "Mr. *Spaulding*?"

"Call me Van," he says, trying to bend his lips into a smile, but it's not working. I feel panic closing down my lungs, so I try to take controlled breaths.

"I tried to help her. I went after her..." I say, sure that he's probably going to kill me.

"I know you did. I know, and it's because of you that she's here right now. What would she want with that biodesigner practice I had waiting for her here in Admin City anyway, right?"

"What?" I ask, shaking my head and getting to my feet as fast as I can. *Where's the door...*I think. *How is there no door in here?*

"My children were on a track to complete their career training at Gaia Sur before you came along," Van Spaulding says, leaning back against the wall and studying his nails.

"Gaia took both my brothers. They made one of them put gills in the other one!" I shout, but Van Spaulding barely looks up at me.

"A choice they made when they refused to use their obvious talents for the greater good," he says, then goes back to studying his nails. "But I digress. Dezzie isn't well, you see. She's been through quite a lot of unnecessary hardship with the loss of her brother, Pitt, to those spores, then having to leave Tieg in those tunnels with some *creature*?" he asks, looking up at me. "Is this true, Liddick?"

"I *tried* to help her! If she'd have gone back in that tunnel, something would have taken her too. I went looking for her when she ran off!"

"Well, despite all the trouble and heartache you've caused her with this, not to mention with Jack Ripley's daughter, Dezzie still seems to want you around. That means I have to find a use for you. She's been through enough, don't you agree?"

"I need to get back to my friends," I say, but as the words are coming out of my mouth, I know it's pointless.

"I don't think you still have friends, Liddick Wright," Spaulding smiles, then nods to the shadow man. I can see his hands tap something into his console, and a few seconds later, the last part of the virtuo-cine I was just in starts replaying in the middle of the room...with Jazz, Vox, my brother, Lyden, and the others. Everything in me locks up in disbelief.

"It really *was* them? They were really there?" I ask, feeling all the breath leave my lungs.

"Oh, yes. They were masked by archaic level one bioprints because of the flag on their neural signatures, but The Seam's technology is unreliable. Ancient, really," Spaulding says, but I can't process it all as I watch the rest of the cine play out...the Reset lever I was reaching for wasn't even there, at least not from their perspective. None of what I saw or heard registered to them at all...I look completely *split*.

"I didn't know what was real in that cine—I thought the programmers just pulled memories of them out of my head so I'd go along with the propaganda...I thought that's what the cine was programmed to do for anyone who went into it, " I say, but not to him, or to anyone except myself. I just feel like I have to say it out loud.

"Well, lucky for us *they* didn't know that," Spaulding laughs, breaking my self-contained bubble, and I feel myself crash back into reality. Blood starts pounding in my ears, and I glare at him.

"You did all this. *Why*? Why did you set me up?"

"I didn't do a thing. You wrote that propaganda and sabotaged their efforts to patch their pathetic code message all by yourself. You are brilliantly intuitive, I might add."

"I didn't write any propaganda!" I protest, but then feel sick...*the storyboarder credential...*I think. *I didn't care* *about the plot. I just wanted to get to the Reset lever.* Spaulding must see the realization dawn on my face because he just smiles that bent smile again and nods at me.

"And *bonus* kudos for leading us straight to The Seam's message with whatever psychic connection you seem to have to the Ripley girl. We never would have known about the embedded sleeper without the neural bridge access you provided," he laughs.

"What embedded sleeper?" I ask, my mind racing almost as fast as the blood hammering in my head. *Those random thoughts about the Platform…the counting…it really was Jazz…is that what he's saying?*

Spaulding laughs even harder. "You really have no idea, do you?" he manages to ask between guffaws. He moves behind the console and starts typing something, and Grisham's stupid face appears.

"Grisham! What the hell is happening? None of this was our deal!" I shout.

Spaulding is laughing so hard now he can't even put a sentence together. I look around for something to throw at him, to throw in general, but there's *nothing* in this stupid room.

"Cred-Fed, listen to me…things have changed," Grisham says. "This is all for the better now. We're going to *the top*."

"What are you *talking* about? You used to want to help other people. We were making things better topside!"

"And a lot of good it did. But then you brought me Van Spaulding's daughter, half out of her head. How could I not leverage that and make things easier? I thought you were a smart kid...come on...how do you think you got all those breaks? Like I've got heliocars on standby? I couldn't even check my voice messages with Tarriff locking down my tech."

"We had a deal! I reset that server for you...you were supposed to help me get my friend back. I trusted you, Grisham!"

"I helped her get to a safe place. I delivered; you delivered," he shrugs. "I'm not leaving you hanging here. You'll work with me now."

"No! Are you split? I need to find my friends!"

"Friends? You really think you still have friends Cred-Fed? *You're* the one writing that propaganda in the cine. Hell, they think you sabotaged their patchwork efforts. Eco probably electrocuted himself reacting to that!" Grisham laughs, then coughs. "Serves that arrogant little skod right."

"I didn't know how that storyboarder credential worked! I didn't try to sabotage anything!"

"Doesn't matter. The only thing that matters is what *seems* to have happened. You've seen too much to join your so-called friends with The Seam. You're dead to all those people, anyway, kid. Time to start over."

*There has to be a way out of this...*I think. *All right, calm down. Try to play their game...* "Start over with what?" I ask, trying to slow down my breathing.

Spaulding claps his hands in front of him and steps out from behind the console. "Glad you asked. The first thing I'm going to need you to do is lead a team back into those tunnels and find Tieg," he says. Then we'll discuss your new career field, storyboarding, with strict monitoring, of course. You've shown quite a bit of promise," he says with a half smile that turns my blood to acid.

"I'm never going to work for you…I'm not going to help you lie to everyone about Carboderm and Biotech Global, least of all about Gaia!"

"But you already *have* helped me…" he laughs again. "More than I ever could have hoped. You're a natural."

I start to protest, but Grisham starts talking again before I can get a word in.

"Cred-Fed, don't be stupid. You have nothing to go back to now, don't you see that? Your parents think you're tucked away becoming some kind of diplomat—Spaulding already arranged for the long term clone, just like the ones for your brothers. You're an outcast now, just like me, but we'll get back at them all."

I shake my head. "Jazz wouldn't believe any of that. She knows me better. I just need to see her and explain."

"That won't be possible, I'm afraid," Spaulding says. "And I have other plans for your time."

"You can't do this!" I shout, but it doesn't make any difference.

"I'd love to stay and continue catching up, but business calls. Take a few days and let it sink in, Wright. I'll be in touch," Grisham says through a bar wedge smile just before his projection disappears.

"I really should be getting back too." Spaulding nods to his shadow man, who waves his hand over the wall behind him. It dissipates into a doorway, where another person is standing in the shadows. "Get him cleaned up and deliver him to his new habitat," Spaulding says.

"And be sure he understands the...*dangers* of running off." He laughs, then goes through the door with the original shadow man.

The other one steps into the light wearing a white knit hat that matches his seamless shirt and pants, which look just like the ones *Eddie* wore when he picked me up in the heliocar.

I shake my head at him. At myself.

I should have seen it coming.

"Just tell me one thing, Finn," I say with the last of my energy. "Were you working for Spaulding the whole time you were pretending to help me find Grisham?"

He pulls off his hat, and his black hair falls loose around his shoulders instead of in the ponytail I'm used to seeing him wear. He walks toward me, expressionless, then looks over his shoulder. When he turns back to me, he's smiling.

"Stop looking so worried, man," Finn whispers. "Let's get back to work."

Don't forget to join the Tracy Korn's VIP Reader
Group below for exclusive bonuses and news:

www.bit.ly.com/ElementsReaders

Visit The Elements Series on social media!

https//www.facebook.com/TheElementsBookSeries

http://twitter.com/ElementsSeries

http://elementsseries.tumblr.com

http://instagram.com/elementsseries

Acknowledgments

Of the three books in The Elements series so far, AER was the hardest to write because it was the last push toward the peak of the series. Like all last pushes, it required the most energy when there was the least, but as the saying goes (and as I told myself often throughout the writing), I did not come this far to only come this far. As a result, the characters stretched—against their will, which is usually the case, isn't it? Some of them discovered they had internal pillars of strength while others found their ceilings crashing down on them. It became clear as their narratives unfolded that, along with any of us in such situations, they would either do what needed to be done to overcome their obstacles, or they wouldn't. One thing I wanted them to learn along the way is that if we don't transcend our environments, there is no one to blame but ourselves, and if we do, there are usually countless people to thank. As the pages of AER progressed, the book became about fear and the fallout of selfishness it causes for some, as well as the bravery and depth of character it can bring out in others. I found myself wanting to write about how sometimes when we are the surest, we can be the most lost, and when we feel the most lost, we have only to look inside for our true North. For me, this book examines the dichotomy of illusion and reality down that path and all the fascinating places in between. We made it, guys, and I would like to thank the following people for their help in that endeavor: my fantastic beta readers, Katie Casavan, Ron and Deb Commons, Emily Gangloff, Abby Gray, Sami Hensely, Margarita McClain, Xavier Moss, Chris Nance, Dominic Porter, Lorelei Porter, Tracy Siri, and the irreplaceable Anna "Iron Chef" Swenson. As always, Jim Emmons and the University Park Barnes & Noble staff, with Liza, James, and Jon at the Carmel, Indiana Barnes & Noble, thank you for your ongoing support, encouragement, and for being awesome friends in storytelling. I'm going to make characters of you all yet. My former students involved with this project, especially Arianna, Devlin, Derek, Josh, Liam, Olivia, Timmy, Will, and Zoe, thank you for inspiring the souls of these characters. To me, you will always be real life superheroes. My great friend and writing partner for well over a decade now, Ryan Bachtel, thank you once again for your objectivity and honesty. Your friendship and candor are priceless to me. Mom, thank you for your unwavering support and faith in whatever path I choose. My belief in myself came from your belief in me; I remember the day you told me you knew I could horse whistle if I just kept working at it…I wouldn't be who I am today without you (and I definitely wouldn't be able to horse whistle). My kids, who are almost not kids anymore, thank you for inspiring me daily with your bravery, tenacity, kindness, and for being genuinely loving, happy, thoughtful people. You have made my life the greatest story of all. Finally, my husband, James, of nearly 25 years, thank you for weathering the best and the worst with me, and for being a constant refuge. As we navigate through this wild life, I may be the gale, but you are the eye of the storm.

And readers…thank you for sharing this undersea, out of this world adventure with me, if only for a little while.

About the Author

Tracy Korn's years of teaching high school English have convinced her that young people superheroes. Their resiliency, drive, and passion in making the world a better place inspired her character driven, high action and adventure YA fiction. When she's not writing/reading/teaching, she coaches FTC robotics and tries to learn everything she can about filmmaking and virtual reality game design.

Tracy holds Master's degrees from Indiana University in Secondary Education, in Language, Culture, and Literacy Education, and in English. She lives in Indiana with her husband and their two very own superheroes. Stay in touch at **www.TracyKorn.com.**

Facebook: **http://www.facebook.com/AuthorTracyKorn**
Twitter: **http://twitter.com/Tracybonics**
Instagram: **http://instagram.com/tracy_korn**

9 781946 202727